Praise for Anne Randall:

'Randall has grown in confidence since her debut, and this is as **assured and clever** a novel of "tartan noir" as you could hope to find' – *Daily Mail*

'A **well-paced and gripping** crime fiction debut' – *Choice Magazine*

'An **outstanding debut**' – *Daily Record*

'**For fans of Stuart MacBride,** this is a delight to read. A J McCreanor is a welcome addition to the Scottish crime scene. Glasgow is in very dangerous hands' – *Crimesquad*

'A super story with a breath-taking ending that leaves you wondering whether the truth is better left unsaid at times. I loved this story and am keen to read more by this author in the future. She is definitely **a name to watch!** Highly **recommended**' – *Eurocrime*

'**Fast paced, exciting and gritty** crime debut . . . fans of Ian Rankin and Val McDermid will be delighted to add a new author to their must-read list' – *Candis Magazine*

'**Brilliant**' – *The Sun*

Deceived

Anne Randall

CONSTABLE

CONSTABLE

First published in Great Britain in 2018 by Constable

A CIP catalogue record for this book
is available from the British Library.

ISBN: 978-1-47212-279-7

Typeset in Palatino by SX Composing DTP, Rayleigh, Essex
Printed and bound in Great Britain by CPI Mackays

Papers used by Constable are from well-managed forests
and other responsible sources.

MIX
Paper from
responsible sources
FSC
www.fsc.org   FSC® C104740

Constable
An imprint of
Little, Brown Book Group
Carmelite House
50 Victoria Embankment
London EC4Y 0DZ

An Hachette UK Company
www.hachette.co.uk

www.littlebrown.co.uk

For Don

Chapter 1

He often wondered about people like himself. Killers.
He knew that they did sometimes give themselves away.
It could be that they developed a nervous tic, or that
beads of perspiration formed quietly but conspicuously
on a top lip. They may have glanced around apprehen-
sively, or perhaps stared straight ahead, laser-focused on
their mission? Any of these could potentially have
alerted others to their intent. It was only on rare occasions
that a killer radiated a sinister, noxious aura, a hint of the
violent act that they were about to commit. Perhaps evil
may have oozed through their pores; its toxicity palpable?
When this happened, when an innocent encountered a
killer, he or she intuitively moved away. They did
not want to linger in the same train carriage or share a
bus seat with evil. Instinctively, wordlessly, they were
repelled and quickly moved off, out of the evil orbit.
To safety. They hoped.

But he knew that he was not like them, for he was Mr Average. Capital M, capital A. He could walk directly in front of you and you wouldn't notice him. He could assure you of that. He was unmemorable, unremarkable. And therefore deadly. The assailant was casual in his approach. He strolled on through Mount Vernon, towards Hamilton Road. He believed that the quiet residential area was a fine place to live. Knew also that as a successful killer, an *intelligent* killer, that he should blend in with his surroundings, become merely part of the background noise to the intended crime and not immediately identifiable as its principal player. Voila! he thought. Let the drama begin.

It would soon be winter solstice. The warmth and predictable glare of the sun was at its weakest in the year. In fact, for killing, it was the most perfect of conditions. He breathed in the cold air. The earlier promise of snow had been delivered and a soft covering of white shrouded the landscape as he walked the deserted road. He knew that families would be packed into their homes, colleagues at their work places. All safe. All sound. Perhaps, some looking up at the darkening sky and refusing to venture out? Stay home. Stay in the office. Stay safe. Most of the Christmas shoppers had gone into the city centre to browse tinsel-draped department stores in search of yet more rhinestone baubles. The killer welcomed the white pavements and roads, secure in the knowledge that the fresh snow would obliterate his footsteps. Better for him to move ghost-like through the neighbourhood, then be gone, without a trace. How helpful, he thought, of the Christmas season and of the universe to favour him. He had risen at dawn and had driven his car to the area and parked up. He had prepared.

Quietly, he approached the elegant, detached, sandstone villa, noted that the name on the plaque read 'St Guinoch', the name of a saint. Perhaps the occupier believed that St Guinoch might protect him? He offered a silent hope that he didn't. That would be too superstitious, too religious. Frankly, just plain fucking wrong. He walked up the path. He wondered briefly about his intended victim. Could he have done anything differently, which may, potentially, have changed the course of today? Or had his destiny been written in the annals of time? Eternity, he thought to himself, was littered with these dates. He knew that the question would never be asked. There simply wouldn't be the opportunity. The time was now, he had been chosen. The killer believed that everyone had a prescribed time, when they would be released from their physical body and catapulted into the next world. Whatever that would entail. If it were the Christian tradition – and why not, since it was after all Christmas – was it to be heaven or hell or some halfway house of perpetual suffering? Purgatory? Which was more real, the pagan solstice, Yuletide, Christianity or Father Christmas? Which was most relevant? He stopped himself. As for conversations concerning what he was about to do, who on earth would be listening? God? The Devil? He chuckled, he was such a sentimentalist at times. He approached the front door. He bent over and quickly pulled on the dog mask, straightened up, reached forward. At least he had granted his victim a carefree lunch. He was all heart, really. He rang the bell. Leaned on it a second time just for effect. Just because he could. Beneath the mask, he smiled.

2.30 p.m.

Inside

Michael O'Donnell was thirty-nine years old and of Irish–Italian origin. He had dark hair, brown eyes and had inherited his Italian mother's smooth olive skin. He had a strong nose, high cheekbones and full lips.

He was just under five foot nine and knew that he was considered handsome.

It was just after their lunch and the smell of freshly baking soda bread permeated the air. Michael stood in the kitchen of his villa, carefully washing his dead mother's good china bowl. It had been from a dinner set she'd been given on her wedding day and had been her favourite. It had been hand-painted, the figs, grapes and lemons around the rim both colourful and strong. He had loved that pattern when he had been growing up. Now there was just the one piece left from the whole set and it was an object he treasured. It was a link from his mother, through him, to his daughter, Paula. He took it out of the soapy water and rinsed it under the tap. Grabbed a tea towel and began drying it. The reassuring hum of the dishwasher told him that the rest of the dishes would be taken care of without his intervention. He thought of his mother and his father; he had been close to them both. He missed them very much and wished that they were still alive to be part of Paula's life. She had never met her grandparents and that troubled him.

He heard the doorbell ring. Twice.

Michael cursed softly under his breath, hoped that the bell wouldn't wake Paula. She needed to take a short nap every day after lunch, as her energy levels plummeted.

He made his way through to the hallway, almost tripping over Paula's rucksack, which had been dumped on the floor. He realised that he was still carrying the bowl. He retraced his steps and placed it carefully on the kitchen work-surface before making his way to the front door. If it was another double glazing/conservatory bore, he'd make a formal complaint. There had been three of them in the area recently, ringing bells and annoying folk with their 'special offers' or stuffing unsolicited brochures through letterboxes. He'd thrown the brochures straight into the recycling bucket. If, as he believed, the Mount Vernon area was being targeted, he would be bringing it up at the next meeting of the Residents' Association. He wasn't going to put up with this kind of bloody nonsense. As if he didn't have enough to contend with at present. As if life wasn't complex enough.

The textured glass on the door meant that he couldn't see the person on the other side. He hated that glass. Depending on the angle of the sun, he either only managed to get a hazy idea of the height of the person, or, more likely, the light was split into hundreds of tiny prisms which meant that he had no idea who was on the other side. Paula's mother, Jayla, had chosen the dark glass, and Paula wouldn't let him change it. He peered at the door, through the fractured light, and all he could make out was a distorted figure in various shades of dark. And why did this person have to ring twice? He frowned as he opened the door.

It was the speed with which it happened. The flash of a blade before he could properly assess or process what was in front of him. The dog's sinister grinning face. Michael felt one, two, three, rapid slashes, deep enough and angry enough that it seemed only a split second had passed between him looking down to touch his shirt before staring at his bloodstained hands in astonishment. He felt panic as all 176 lbs of him staggered backwards before crashing onto the floor. There was no time to call out to Paula, no time to warn her. No time to tell her to call the police. Just. No. Time.

The assailant was inside quickly and stood over Michael, checked for a pulse, but it was over. The job had been done well, an excellent kill. Efficient. He dragged Michael into the living room as fresh blood haemorrhaged silently, persistently, across a cream rug. The killer deftly skirted the body but tramped in a pool of blood before he ran into the hallway. He paused in front of a display cabinet which held a series of upturned crucifixes. He removed his mask, smiled at the grotesque figures and their exquisite dying throes. Such sweet inspiration. Then he made for the stairs.

The killer began to climb, stealthily, carefully.

He had one more job to do. And he had to get it right.

Chapter 2

4.30 p.m.

Sarah Price

The wintery sun had almost gone, as forty-one-year-old Sarah Price stood in the bedroom of her semi-detached house in Tollcross. She felt her hands shake as she quickly mixed the second extra-strong gin and tonic. Bloody hell, she thought. You're not eighteen. Get a grip. She sipped the G and T, knowing that, unlike wine, he wouldn't smell the alcohol on her breath and it didn't make her feel sleepy. A perfect antidote to her nerves.

She smoothed down the black, mid-range designer dress. The store assistant had assured her that it 'exuded glamour'. It was black crepe and mercifully had sleeves to cover the flabby area at the top of her arms, her bingo wings. She hated her upper arms. The store assistant had told her that wearing the designer dress would make her feel 'empowered'. Sarah sighed. Maybe if she were still a size twelve? What had her old friend, Maria told her? 'Fake it till you make it.' It was a shame that they had fallen out, but Maria had detested her last choice of partner. A 'friends with benefits' arrangement, which Maria had told her was

7

useless. 'He doesn't respect you. It's gone on too long. He's selfish. You give in to his every demand. The things you do just to keep him. It's ridiculous. You wouldn't even tell me his bloody name.' They'd had an argument and hadn't spoken since. Sarah tugged at the hem of the dress. It wasn't that short, but because she lived in trousers and practical shoes, wearing a new dress and boots felt odd. As if she were younger somehow. She checked her make-up. Thought of her date. She had a good feeling about this one.

This was a real face-to-face date. She'd researched some of the dating apps again and, frankly, they'd made her nervous. Online, all she seemed to find were men who just wanted sex, a 'hook-up' or a 'let's just see what happens' scenario. She was fed up with them. In her last relationship, a long-term arrangement she felt was going somewhere, she'd given it her all, but, by the end, she'd felt cheap and used. Despite the huge effort she had made to support him and his beliefs, her absolute unconditional love and a desire to help him in every possible way, however challenging, for many years, he still refused to commit. Finally, she'd left him. Then he had admitted that he'd taken other lovers. It was over. A week later a random leaflet had come through the letterbox, a flyer wedged in between the adverts for double glazing and hedge cutting. After pursuing their website, and having read lots of positive testimonials, she'd joined Looking4Love. They were expensive, but she wanted to cut to the chase and find a man who wanted a relationship. Plus, you could do a search based on geography, she didn't want to find someone too far away. There had been six matches in a reasonable area. She sipped her drink, told herself to slow down. This evening was all about connectedness. Her gut instinct told her that Rob Carter was the real deal. She glanced at her laptop, at his profile picture. He had an open face and a lovely smile. He was tall, slim and tanned. He was wearing a smart black jacket over an open-necked white shirt.

Looking4Love
Profile picture of CJ200
Unclaimed treasure

Home: The wonderful Drymen and also St Andrews, Scotland. (Although the above picture was taken while I was on holiday in Rethymnon, Crete. Hence the tan. I am now somewhat paler.)

About me: Height 6' 2" (187 cm).

Hair: dark/ going on for salt and pepper.

Eyes: Blue.

Body type: Muscle -ish (200 lbs).

Past Relationship? Ended amicably when she accepted a (long overdue, in my opinion) promotion to New York.

What am I looking for? To find the love of my life. I'm a hopeless romantic!

Children? No, but I don't mind if you have any. (Or how many.)

Religion: Not sure about the whole God thing but I'm open to discussing it, if it's your thing.

Star sign: Pisces. Romantic. Bit dreamy.

Occupation: I own my own computing business.

Looking for: A lovely, kind soul. Height, weight, no issue. I just want to meet a warm, compassionate lady who I can treat to a lovely meal. (OK, to be brutally honest, I would like someone who has an appetite, no evangelical dieters, please. I love to cook and eat out a lot and hope that you can join me!) A perfect storm of imperfection. (Congruence is important.) Be real, please don't try to be perfect. Airbrushed perfection doesn't interest me. An animal lover would be good as I have a couple of rescues – an elderly cat and a whippet. They're not going back! Plus, I've been adopted by a feral cat who has trained me to feed him daily. I live in a four-bedroom house on the outskirts of the Queen Elizabeth Forest Park. It's a very beautiful place. The scenery is incredible.

Age: I'm forty-four, so anyone between thirty-four and fifty-four?

Describe yourself: I am kind (so I'm told). An animal lover (obviously). A foodie. I read a lot and am a member of the Goodreads community. I love to laugh. I have a holiday cottage overlooking the harbour at St Andrews. It's great to take off for some downtime. I love art, particular favourites are: Picasso, Matisse and Braque. I like long walks with the dog and pub lunches. The venison at my local restaurant is wonderful.

Sarah loved venison. Rob seemed warm and kind, unlike the men she usually met. She recalled that her deceased mother had delighted in goading her: 'You're short and round but more importantly you're stupid around men.'

This latter insult had been added when Sarah had married Ian Price because she'd been fourteen weeks pregnant. When she'd told Ian about her pregnancy, he had pressurised her to have an abortion, but Sarah had ignored him and eventually he had agreed to the wedding. Ian Price had turned out to be a violent and abusive husband. Sarah had been eight months pregnant when she'd discovered him in their bed with a barmaid from their local pub. She left him and managed to find a flat she could afford, and then her son, Nick, had arrived. The birth had been traumatic, but she'd recovered and had held her sweet, soft and beautiful child. She had cradled him in her arms and touched his tiny fingers and knew that she had been right to carry on alone.

'You spoil him,' her friend Maria had said.

'Nick will never respect you. He's ruined,' Ian had complained. 'It was a mistake to ever have him and then split up our family. You are so fucking selfish. He'll never bond with you. Ever.'

And Nick had, until recently, never truly bonded with her. Not in the way she had wanted him to. Not until the last six months. Years ago, when he had started primary school, a teacher had mentioned attachment disorder and she had laughed. She had known that her son would come round. Given time. And the last six months had been great, they'd barely argued. The rage seemed to have disappeared. She understood that boys sometimes took after their father, and what a mistake that had been. But Nick had never been a mistake. Unlike Ian. She wouldn't let her ex interfere now. Or think about the bloody shambles that he'd made of his life. She opened her make-up bag and took out a compact, double-checked her make-up. Patted some powder over her nose. She was early, that was good.

She glanced at her watch, 4.55. Excellent, because five was her lucky number. And had been since childhood. Astra, her best friend's mum, had been a hippy who was into numerology. Astra had told her that the numbers of her birthday and birth year added up to five. Five would always be her lucky number. 'Trust it,' Astra had told her. 'Think of it as the five points of a star.'

When Sarah had divorced Ian, she'd announced it on 5 May at 5 p.m., but Ian still hadn't taken it well. Her lucky number hadn't worked at all that time. She put Ian out of her mind. She wondered if she should text Nick. He was meeting friends at a gig at King Tut's, some band called the Rubes, she'd never heard of them. And then was maybe staying with his dad for part of the weekend. Best to leave them to it. Nick didn't need to know that she was going on a date. Ian would snarl at her as being 'mutton dressed as lamb'; he was still jealous of her, still angry about the break-up, even after all these years. Somehow in his addled mind she was still his wife and therefore 'his property'. Neither Ian nor Nick needed to know that she wasn't going to meet Maria for a girls' night out. She hadn't even let Nick know she was dating. She wouldn't put him in that position again. Once she had confided in him about her having a date, but Ian had interrogated him, forced it out of him. Ian had turned up at the restaurant and made an ugly scene. 'You're my wife, till death do us part.' He'd managed to punch her date before security had heaved him out. It looked like a broken nose. She'd never seen her date again. He'd looked terrified but hadn't gone to the police. Who could blame him? You didn't want to go up against Ian Price. So, any other dates she'd had over the years had been conducted in secrecy. She'd even waited until her son had gone out before changing from her Christmas jumper into the dress.

Of course, she'd cyber-stalked Rob, his Facebook page, Twitter, Instagram, LinkedIn. All to the good. Even his Goodreads page was practically identical to hers, they liked many of the same books, thrillers mostly. She favoured Tess Gerritsen, while he loved Harlan Coben. And Rob had been the fifth person to contact her on the dating site. There was absolutely no way that he could have known that was her lucky number, but she saw it as a good omen.

'Come to Drymen,' he'd said. 'If you get the train to Balloch, I can pick you up from the station. We can go for a walk and then find a nice restaurant for dinner, there are great places to eat. There are great bars. Fantastic food. You'll love it. I'll have you safely back home in Glasgow by midnight,' he'd reassured her. Her son knew the area well, he was a walker. Another good omen, she thought.

6 p.m.

Queen Street Station, Low Level

Carol singers collecting for a homeless charity: 'Away in a Manger', 'The First Noel', 'Hark! The Herald Angels Sing'. Sarah dropped a two-pound coin in their collection tin.

When the train arrived, Sarah took a seat beside the window. She took off her coat and folded it carefully. Placed it on the seat beside her. The train wasn't particularly busy. There were several free single and double seats. A man got on and walked down the train. He was around thirty-five, with a shaved head and a thick neck. He wore camouflage fatigue trousers and a matching jacket. Worn trainers. She thought of the new trainers Nick had asked for, designer trainers. Dolce & Gabbana Portofino trainers would leave her £5 change from £530. She'd bought them anyway. She hoped that they'd bloody last. She was just relieved that he hadn't asked for the appliqué version which would have set her back another £300. Sarah thought

13

of her overdraft, which sat at £1,900. Of her credit card, which hovered on the £4,000 mark. She knew that she had three personal loans, amounting to over £13,000, but she didn't even want to go there. Her job as a supply teacher at various primary schools paid reasonably well but as any one-parent family knows, the money doesn't go far enough. And she worried about Nick in his beat-up third-hand little red Fiesta. She wished to God Ian would buy him a newer car. He really was a selfish prick.

'Is this seat taken?' The man smiled at her. Nicotine-stained teeth, a missing incisor.

Instinctively, she glanced at the empty seats around her. Manners got the better of her. She moved her bag and coat onto her lap. 'No, it's not taken.'

'Only I like a bit of a chat.' He paused. 'My work can be so isolating.'

She glanced out of the window.

'I expect you'd like to know what it is I do?'

Oh God, Sarah thought, one of those types. 'Of course,' she said. Again, the manners.

'I'm a song writer. You know the band the Rubes? Well, their biggest hit, "Enchanted", is my song, it was written by me. They ripped me off. That fucking Madison De La Fontaine is a liar. I told her that she was a thief too and I told her that I'm taking it to the police.'

'Right,' said Sarah quietly.

'You don't believe me?' He was on his feet, glaring at her.

Sarah felt uncomfortable. How long to her stop? She looked at the passenger across the aisle from her, deep into her Kindle. The sound of the train, rhythmic and steady. She felt herself begin to sweat. Wondered if she should move carriages.

'I've a brand-new silver S60 Volvo sports saloon parked at home. It's a fabulous car but I don't always use it for short journeys. Plus, I'm afraid it will get keyed. People can be mean.'

Sarah took out her mobile phone, 'Sorry, I just need to send a text.' Wondered to herself why she was apologising.

'Go right ahead. I'm only being companionable.' He paused. 'That's the word for it. Isn't it? companionable?'

She ignored him. Quickly texted Rob. Waited for a second, hoped for a quick reply. Nothing.

'Is that an iPhone?' he said peering at her phone. 'Can I have a look?'

She stuffed her phone back into her handbag. 'It's an old one.'

'My name's Frankie.' He offered a hand. 'Frankie Fermin. Remember that name 'cause I'm going to be big one day. When I get the royalties I deserve from bands like the Rubes. They fucking owe me.'

Spittle escaped from his mouth and fell on her new dress.

'And you, what's your name, pretty lady?' Fermin sat down again.

'Sarah.'

'Sarah what?' Again, more saliva.

'Sarah Price.'

'Well, Sarah Price, since we're sharing this little part of our journey together, why don't you tell me about yourself?'

She stared out of the window. Saw her own reflection. Knew that the journey was less than an hour to Balloch. Knew that she would be OK. The train stopped and the Kindle-reading woman and the others got off. She and Fermin were in the carriage alone together.

'You're not very chatty, Sarah.' Fermin scowled at her.

'I hope that you aren't one of those stuck-up women who think that they are too good to talk to me?'

She wondered if she should run to the next carriage. Would he pursue her? And how would she get past him? She could smell alcohol on his breath. He stank of it.

'Are you going somewhere nice, Sarah?'

'I'm meeting someone.' She heard the anxiety in her voice.

'Your boyfriend?'

'Yes,' she lied.

Finally, they arrived at Balloch station. Rob had explained that there was no train to Drymen. 'And the bus takes for ever. I'll pop over and pick you up at Balloch.'

Fermin glanced around the empty platform. 'Where is he then? This boyfriend of yours?'

'He must be outside.'

'I'll wait with you, Sarah,' said Fermin. 'I'm a gentleman like that.'

'There's really no need.'

'You can't be too careful, Sarah. I should know that, given that I'm a man of the world. You'll be safe with me.'

She felt her heartbeat race. 'I'd really rather you didn't.'

'But I insist, Sarah. You can't be alone here on a night like this. Look at the snow, you'll freeze. And all you have on under your coat is that rather lovely dress. I do like your dress, Sarah. Is that all right for me to say that?'

She said nothing, hurried towards the exit.

'And your lovely shiny boots.' He walked beside her. 'They look new. Are they?'

She kept walking.

Fermin kept pace. 'Only you can't be too careful nowadays what with the whole ugly feminist movement.

What was once simply flattery can now be misconstrued as abuse. Us guys have a hard time with you ladies.' He let out a little high-pitched laugh. 'Ball-breakers that you all are now. Aren't you?'

Outside there was one car waiting. A green Nissan, but Rob drove a VW Golf. She waited. The driver flashed the lights. She approached the car.

The man was around her age, with salt and pepper hair and a tight smile.

'I was waiting for my daughter, she didn't get off the train. Probably missed it, she's always late. Are you OK, only you look anxious?'

'I was supposed to be meeting someone. He's not here. He's driving from Drymen. He lives out by Queen Elizabeth Forest Park.' She knew she was nervous and talking too much. She glanced behind her. Fermin was waiting.

'Is he bothering you?' asked the man.

'I'm fine,' said Sarah. 'He chatted to me on the train. A bit overbearing. Guy called Frankie Fermin.'

'You need a lift someplace? You're all alone here in the station.'

'I'm waiting for my boyfriend. He'll be along in a minute, I expect.' She heard a certainty in her tone that she didn't feel.

'Right, I'll be off then. I need to pick up some nutmeg. The wife's run out and what with Christmas coming...'

She glanced across the station. Fermin walked away.

'You sure you don't want me to wait, in case he comes back?'

She swallowed. 'Positive.'

'I'm Bernie, by the way. Bernie Morrison.'

'Sarah Price.'

'Good luck, Sarah. Hope your guy gets here soon. He's probably been held up on the road. This weather!'

But twenty minutes later she was still waiting when Bernie passed by again. 'You still here? My daughter's now not coming until tomorrow. My wife's going mad, she's made her favourite dinner, and my daughter's turned vegan, mind. Now we'll bloody have to eat it. Kids!' He paused. 'You look cold, you sure you don't want dropped somewhere, Sarah? My wife would be happy for you to come back to ours and have coffee. Or a bloody vegan snack. The next train back into Glasgow isn't due for another hour.'

Sarah hesitated. 'I can't get a signal.'

'Join the club. Honestly, we had a mast out of town but . . . Listen, I'm sorry, I need to go. The wife will be wondering where I've got to. First the daughter drops out, best I don't too. Your friend will no doubt come along. Maybe held up on the A811. There was an accident about two miles up the road, a two-car collision. Ambulance and fire service are there already. Looked nasty. I just kept on driving. No point in rubbernecking, it doesn't do anyone any good, does it? But there was a tailback on that side of the road. Maybe your friend got snarled up in it?'

She watched him start the car.

'You sure I can't drop you somewhere?' he asked.

She thought about it. 'No, I'll just wait for the train home.' Suddenly freezing cold, a chill wind cutting across the snow. She was horrified by the idea that Rob may have been in an accident.

'My wife has the fire burning all day. She'll soon have you heated up. You look pale. I hope I didn't upset you taking about the accident. I'm sure it'll all be fine. You can call him on our landline, if you have his number? Maybe he has his times or dates wrong?'

'I only have his mobile.'

'That's the way of it now though, isn't it? Our daughter doesn't even have a landline.' He paused. 'Do you live in Glasgow?'

'I'm a teacher there,' said Sarah.

'Primary or secondary?' he asked.

'Primary.'

'Which school?' he asked.

'I do supply teaching,' said Sarah. 'Why so many questions?'

'I'm sorry, I can be too direct. Drives the wife and daughter mad. It's just that I'm interested in people.' He smiled. 'The daughter was lecturing me the other week. Told me that I'm old-fashioned. Also told me that she now identifies as non-binary. I wonder if she's going to bring home a man, a woman or someone who identifies as non-binary too. I can't keep up.'

'It's their choice how or if they want to be labelled. Or not,' said Sarah. 'It's not our choice to impose our labels on them.'

'Yes, I know. I just don't want to say the wrong thing. It's a minefield for folk my age. Not to put our foot in it. I'm not even sure what some of the terminology she uses, means. LGBT, for example.'

'It stands for lesbian, gay, bisexual, transgender.'

'The wife was brought up religious. She's not at all comfortable with it. Are you OK with it?'

'Of course. I work with kids, I don't want them to be labelled.'

'You have kids?'

'I have a son. He's gone to his dad's for the weekend. I just need a bit of a break.' She'd gone in too soon, as usual. Defending herself. As if leaving Nick wasn't OK. 'Honestly, I'll be fine.'

'I'll be off then.'

Ten minutes later and Sarah checked her watch for the umpteenth time. She was anxious that Fermin would return. The small station was deserted. She quickly made another call. It was finally answered.

She ran back outside as a car pulled up. She got in. She heard the relief in her voice as she turned to the driver. 'Thank goodness you're here. There was this—'

But she didn't have a chance to finish her sentence.

The sharp prick in her neck was a syringe. She grabbed at it, but her hand was punched away.

The car drove off into the still, snowy night.

Chapter 3

9 p.m.

Ian Price

City Centre

The Golden Key Casino was quiet. Three middle-aged men in jeans and fleeces stood facing the betting terminals – casino, roulette and fixed odds. Each man figured himself to be a competitor. They were all addicts. There were a few lone people at the bar, staring into their drinks. Ian Price ordered a pint of lager before taking his place at one of the machines. Roulette was his favourite, but he gave them all a twirl. Price was five foot seven and proud of his tight, sinewy body whose muscles had been defined by cage fighting over the last decade. But now, the beginnings of a soft paunch played across his stomach. A diet of burgers and chips coupled with copious amounts of lager meant that his body, if not his personality, was softening. He had red hair and the only remarkable thing about him was the size of his hands. They belonged to another man. Someone much bigger.

The casino, open twenty-four hours a day, seven days a

week had been Price's second home for several years. They served the kind of food he appreciated – all-day breakfasts and pie and chips. Of course, they had a fine dining restaurant where couples on first dates or anniversaries splashed out on prime rib steak or lobster, but for him, food was fuel to keep him going, usually through the night. When he'd had just enough alcohol and was sufficiently sleep deprived, when his eyes ached from the flashing lights, he could lie to himself about his life, about how he'd make it big and would play the casinos in Las Vegas. One day, he thought, one day his ship would come in. He was pretty sure that it was close. He could feel it, could practically taste it. True, he'd had a few duff deals, but this new job was a sure thing. He pressed PLAY! Watched the lights flash and waited with an addict's adrenaline coursing through him. Nothing. No payout, no flashing lights. No congrats. Sweet fuck all, in fact.

His mobile chirped a text. *The usual.*

He texted back, hands trembling, sweating. *Got it.*

Sure, he'd been in prison, served his time in Barlinnie with some hard bastards, but just the thought of Manus Shore and Big Eddie Wallace made him nauseous.

Price wiped his forehead with a damp hand. He needed to hold his nerve. He was now a recognised keeper. He was holding guns for two of the most well-respected gangsters in Glasgow. No professional outfit held their own guns nowadays, the smart thing to do was to employ someone non-related, someone the police wouldn't link to the organisation. It was a win-win situation, he held them in his lock-up, out by Balmaha and when they were needed the guys took them from him, used them and returned them to him. All completely under the radar of the police. Or it would have been if bloody Mackenzie Willmore had kept up his end in Stranraer. All Willmore had been told to do was convert the replica weapons into some semblance of working guns and hold them. But he'd fucked up and the police were alerted when he went AWOL. Everyone thought he was lying low until he could get away, instead he was found with a bullet through the back of his head. A professional execution. That wasn't going to happen to him, thought Ian. He had no intention of messing up. He thought again of Manus and Big Eddie. They had already called him earlier in the morning, an emergency had arisen. Two Glock 9 mm pistols had been ordered.

Now Price had the guns safely back in his lock-up. Nothing had been fired. It had only been an extortion deal at a mini-market in Shettleston. The owner had refused to pay for protection, but with the production of the pistols, a deal had been swiftly agreed.

Price thought of his ex-wife, Sarah. 'Till death do us part, bitch,' he muttered under his breath as he pressed PLAY! Marriage should mean a lifetime of commitment, at least for her, and if he couldn't have her, well he'd make damn sure no one else could. He rubbed the knuckle of his right hand, smiled at the memory of the last loser she'd tried to date. Their son Nick had let it slip that Sarah had been on a date and he had gone to the restaurant. Two minutes inside and the date guy had a broken face. Job done.

The man to his left, who was missing an ear glanced at him. 'You look like you've just run a marathon.'

'How's that then, Mono?' asked Price.

'Sweaty, a bit flustered,' said Mono. 'What's the problem?'

Price ignored him. Stood in front of another machine.

He felt his heart race, he dug the nail of his thumb into the palm of his hand as he pressed PLAY! Again, nothing.

'Are you pulling an all-nighter?' asked Mono.

'Nah. Not tonight, I've got my son staying over.'

'How old's Nick now? Seventeen? Eighteen?' said Mono.

'Eighteen.'

'How's he doing?'

'He's at the King Tut's with his pals at some gig.'

'Who's playing?' asked Mono.

Price sipped his drink, 'Some band called the Rubes. Never heard of them. I don't recognise any of the music Nick's into.'

'Getting on, are you?'

Price ignored him. 'He was whining on about me picking him up after the gig.'

Mono sipped his drink. 'And I'm guessing you said no?'

'I told him I'm having a decent drink. It's the weekend for fuckssake. I deserve it. I'm not standing here having an orange juice. Plus, it's not like he's useless. It's his mother that's made him so bloody dependent.'

'Better than you having to pick him up at the campsite at Balmaha,' said Mono. 'Remember that malarkey, when was it?'

'Last June, some friend of Nick's had her eighteenth birthday party,' said Price. 'The bloody midge bites had me scratching for a fortnight. I don't know how anyone can camp in this country. And who wants to walk the West Highland Way at his age?'

'You just went up there to spy on your ex-wife,' said Mono.

'Shut it you.'

'Nick got a job yet?' asked Mono. 'I think he needs to be out earning a living.'

'He's still farting about at college.'

'Which one?'

'The College of Visual Arts. Despite being ace at computing, he still thinks that his future lies in Art. He's going on to art college in Brighton.'

'You reckon he'll be the next big thing?' laughed Mono.

'Mibbe.'

'Doesn't take after his old man then,' said Mono. 'Right I'm off. I've got a date with a woman. Tinder.'

'Enjoy.'

'You seeing anyone?' asked Mono.

'A couple. On and off,' said Price. 'One of them is bloody demanding.'

'Later,' said Price. 'By the way. You know anything about that recent murder over by Springburn? The guy got done with a sawn-off shotgun?'

'Why would I?' Price stared at Mono.

'Looks like someone's keeping the guns. Then the gangsters use them and return them. Like a book borrowing situation at the library.' Mono stared at Price. 'I hear that they are called "keepers".'

Price turned away, hit the machine again, 'No comprehendo, Mono. I've no idea what the hell you are on about. I did my time in the Bar-L. I'm completely clean now.'

'Yeah,' said Mono making for the door. 'Yeah, right. Sure, you are. Squeaky clean.'

Chapter 4

10 p.m.

Nick Price

King Tut's Wah Wah Hut was a Glasgow institution. Every-one, from Oasis, Radiohead, Florence and the Machine, and Paolo Nutini had played there. Three hundred fans crammed into the intimate venue. Nick was around five foot eleven and would perhaps fill out in time, but for now he still had the rangy limbs of a young animal. A clean-shaven young animal with a mass of curls and a lopsided smile.

It was an eighteen-plus place and Nick had been asked to show his ID when ordering a drink. Once inside, a drunk girl had lurched in front of him and swayed to the music, she'd shifted to the right, missed her footing. Instinctively, Nick reached for her, steadied her. 'Take it easy, there.'

'Get your fucking greasy hands off her.' The guy was beside Nick in an instant, holding a plastic cup of lager.

Nick recognised one of the Roach twins, Brock, who was a five foot eight, peroxide blond model who attended the CoVA.

Brock grabbed the girl roughly. 'You stay with me, don't start going off alone.' Brock stared hard at Nick. 'There are perverts around here. Complete fuckwits.'

Nick ignored him, took out his phone. A text from his friend Hudson:

I'm close to the exit, where u?

But it was useless trying to move, they were packed in like sardines. Nick watched the band until a quieter song began and the crowd relaxed, and he had a chance to move. Finally, he made it through the heaving crowd, spoke to Hudson. 'You're later than expected. You've missed most of the set.'

'Mum went on and on with the talking, especially about Dad and that despite what he did he really loved us all. The bloody dinner went on for ever. She knew I had a ticket for this gig and it was agreed I'd go to the meal then duck out after the main, but you know what she's like, she gets obsessed with family and bloody tradition. Especially at Christmas. It's way fucking worse since Dad killed himself.'

Nick did indeed know what his friend's mother was like. 'I'm sorry, Hud. Maybe she just needs to process her grief?'

'Yeah, don't we all though?' Hudson glanced at Nick's drink. 'Another lager?'

'No, you're all right. I'm off to Dad's. I need to drive,' said Nick. 'He wouldn't take a night off the booze, so I'm only having the one.'

'He's a shit, your dad,' said Hudson.

'Can't contradict you there.' Nick paused. 'Did you at least get a decent view of Madison De La Fontaine?'

'Yep. She gave it her all. I read a recent interview with her. Apparently, she's dating some pathologist. Yuk. She's a hell of a rock star.'

'Yeah.'

'I reckon she must be mid-twenties, it said in the paper she's bisexual. A fucking perfect storm of a woman,' said Hudson.

'Thought you wanted to be with Tala De Luca?' said Nick.

'I do but in real life.'

'And the Madison De La Fontaine woman?' laughed Nick.

'Just in fantasy life,' said Hudson, morosely staring into his lager.

'So, ask Tala out for God's sake,' said Nick.

'Tala fancies you. I see the way she looks at you in class.'

'I don't feel the same way about her, Hudson. You like Tala then go for it.' Nick took out his mobile, scrolled through his contacts list. 'Here's her number.'

'You're kidding me?' said Hudson. 'I couldn't call her, I wouldn't know what the hell to say to her.'

'Take it,' said Nick. 'You never know, you might find a reason.'

Hudson dutifully punched the number into his contacts list. 'I won't ever use it.'

'You might,' said Nick. 'You were at her party up in Balmaha.'

'Yeah, me being your friend was the only reason I even got invited to her eighteenth.'

'Yep, and you got the midge bites to prove it.'

'Shame Tala did too. I think she was allergic to the buggers.' Hudson opened a packet of cheese and onion crisps. 'You still doing bits of the West Highland Way?'

'Yeah, I did a thirteen-miler the other week,' said Nick.

'I don't fancy all that walking in the middle of nowhere.'

'It helps me plan my studies,' said Nick, making his way to the exit.

'I don't make fabulous art.'

'Some of the tutors think that you do,' said Nick. 'They reckon that you're the best.'

'No chance. Plus, I don't do bloody long walks. I don't think I've ever done anything memorable,' said Hudson.

'I doubt that you ever will,' laughed Nick.

'Where's your mum, by the way?' asked Hudson.

'She's off out with Auntie Maria.'

'I hope she bloody relaxes. That woman is on my case way too much. She thinks I'm a bloody mass murderer.'

'Well, Hud. There are several missing women in the Glasgow area. And some from our college. And you are a bit of a psycho,' said Nick.

'How's that?' said Hudson.

'You're obsessed with Tala and then there's the genes.'

'You've got a cheek to mention my genes.' Hudson finished the crisps.

'My dad wasn't banged up for stalking and imprisoning young women. And then he hanged himself. Maybe it's hereditary? Like father like son.'

'Shut it you.' Hudson threw the balled-up crisp packet at Nick. 'You can talk about fathers!'

Nick dodged it. 'Just saying, Hud, just saying.'

They made their way to the exit.

Chapter 5

Geneva

Marc

Marc De Luca was standing at the window in his luxury hotel room in Geneva. The room had floor-length windows from which he could view Lake Geneva, resplendent in the moonlight. He watched the people below exit the hotel, small as ants, scurrying to their chauffer-driven limousines. Wealthy and well dressed, they could influence many things but, unfortunately for them, not the weather. Marc watched the rain, small drops but many, incessant. Stay out in it too long, he thought, and you would be drenched, it would perniciously cover the body, at first a fine mist settling on hair, on overcoats, then through the fabric, washing down faces, flattening expensive hairstyles, dripping down wealthy necks.

The conference had been interesting, talks about expansion, management, ongoing structure and strategy. He flipped open his laptop, crossed to the minibar and poured himself a large brandy, he deserved it. His dinner at the

Lake View restaurant had been fantastic. The foie gras was exceptional, but he was developing a bit of a pot belly. He needed to cut back. Soon, he lied to himself. He crossed back to the desk, sipped his drink. Very nice. He had just been awarded a substantial pay rise after persuasively arguing that to keep him, his employers had to offer him a better package. He was well paid, but he brought in millions for them. His salary had to be commensurate with that. They didn't need to know about his gambling debts.

He watched the computer screen blink into action and run the program he was proud to have created, which allowed him to watch his young wife Autumn, without her knowing it. Moderating from afar. He felt God-like watching her. This was his world, a world he had created. Perhaps he was a god? But God was vengeful, surely? He'd read the Old Testament as a child. Remembered Leviticus 20:10 – 'And the man that committeth adultery with another man's wife, even he that committeth adultery with his neighbour's wife, the adulterer and the adulteress shall surely be put to death.'

He had watched her having drinks and dinner with several people over the last year. And so, Autumn, his Autumn, was on dicey ground. When they'd first met she had been so grateful to leave her tiny flat and move in with him. Now, he wondered, did she think she could do better? With her expensively highlighted hair, her manicured nails and expertly whitened teeth, all of which he had financed. He watched his young wife. Studied her.

IT. It was his first love. It helped that he was intrinsically good at it and happy to keep up to date. This helped in all manner of ways. He could access his wife's computer. Autumn wasn't aware of it but the little camera on her laptop could be remotely switched on. He finished his brandy, topped up his glass. Earlier, he had watched her in her bedroom, changing to go out for the evening. Heard a YouTube performance from her favourite singer in the background. Autumn dancing. He'd frozen the image. It was a lovely shot. He would have rung and told her how great her hot little body looked, had she not already told him that she was in bed with a migraine. Poor girl. Unlike his parents, Ruby and Enzo, Marc wasn't at all religious, but if he had been, he could believe that Autumn had made nothing short of a miraculous recovery. The mother of his little boy, Tomas. The Madonna? Or was she the whore? Marc had watched Autumn slip into sexy underwear. The little minx. She'd danced out into the hallway and into her walk-in dressing room. Away from the computer's tiny all-seeing eye. No worries, he pressed another key. Picked her up in the dressing room, where she had selected a dress. One he had bought her on their last anniversary. Expensive, short and sassy and meant to be just for him.

He had stopped short of spying on his daughter, Tala. His mother Ruby had rung again earlier. He'd let it go through to voicemail. She was concerned about Tala. He knew that Tala was unhappy but what teenager wasn't? Anyway, he hoped that she would win the bloody prize at CoVA and that would put a smile on her grumpy little face.

Marc went back to his seat. He had a list of the men Autumn had brought home to their bedroom. In recent weeks they'd included a salesman from a local double-glazing company who were targeting the area. A headmaster from a local school. But by far the worst was Michael O'Donnell, a governor at the college Tala attended.

'How tacky.' Marc spoke to the monitor. 'How can you bring him into our home, our bedroom, Autumn? How can you sail in with someone whose daughter goes to the same college as mine? Have you no shame?'

Marc answered himself, 'No, Autumn, you haven't. None whatsoever.'

Chapter 6

The Moderator pressed send.

DEADdOGdEADdOGdEADdOG**YOUAREDOINGWELL**
TALAdEADdOGdEADdOGdEADdOGdEADdOGdEAD
dOGdEADdOGdEADdOGdEADdOGdEADdOGdEADdOG
dEADdOGdEADdOGdEADdOGdEADdOGdEADdOGdEAD
dOGdEADdOGdEADdOGdEADdOGdEADdOGdEADdO
G T A L A W E L L D O N E d E A D d O G d E A D d O G d E A D
d O G d E A D d O G d E A D d O G d E A D d O G d E A D d O G
d E A D d O G d E A D d O G d E A D d O G d E A D d O G d E A D d O G
d E A D d O G d E A D d O G d E A D d O G d E A D d O G d E A D
d O G d E A D d O G d E A D d O G d E A D d O G**TALA**dEADdOG
dEADdOGdEADdOGdEADdOGdEADdOGdEADdOG
dEADdOGdEADdOGdEADdOGdEADdOGdEADdOG
dEADdOG**CONTINUETOGETSTRONGTALA**dEADdOG
dEADdOGdEADdOGdEADdOGdEADdOGdEADdOG
dEADdOGdEADdOGdEADdOGdEADdOGdEADdOG
TALAdEADdOGdEADdOGdEADdOGdEADdOGdEADdOG
dEADdOGdEADdOGdEADdOGdEADdOGdEADdOGdEAD
dOGdEADdOGdEADdOGdEADdOGdEADdOGdEAD
dOGdEADdOGdEADdOGdEADdOGdEADdOGdEADdOG
TALAdEADdOGdEADdOGdEADdOGdEADdOGdEADdOG

dEADdOGdEADdOGdEADdOGdEADdOGdEADdOGdEAD
dOGdEADdOGdEADdOGdEADdOGdEADdOGdEdEAD
dOGdEADdOGdEADdOGdEADdOGdEADdOG**TALA**dEAD
dOGdEADdOGdEADdOGdEADdOGdEADdOGdEAD
dOGdEADdOGdEADdOGdEADdOGdEADdOGdEADdOG
dEADdOGdEADdOGdEADdOGdEADdOGdEADdOGdEAD
dOGdEADdOGdEADdOGdEADdOGdEADdOG**TALAIS**
STRONGINHERNEWFAMILYdEADdOGdEADdOGdEAD
dOGdEADdOGdEADdOGdEADdOGdEADdOGdEADdOG
dEADdOGdEADdOGdEADdOGdEADdOGdEADdOGdEAD
dOGdEADdOGdEADdOGdEADdOGdEADdOGdEADdOG
dEADdOG**TALA**dEADdOGdEADdOGdEADdOGdEADdOG
dEADdOGdEADdOGdEADdOGdEADdOGdEADdOGdEAD
dOGdEADdOGdEADdOG**TALA**dEADdOGdEADdOGdEAD
dOGdEADdOGdEADdOGdEADdOGADdOGdEADdOG
dEADdOGdEADdOGdEADdOG**TALAYOUAREPARTOF**
OURFAMILYdEADdOGdEADdOGdEADdOGdEADdOG
dEADdOGdEADdOGdEADdOGdEADdOGdEADdOGdEAD
dOGdEADdOGdEADdOG**TALA**dEADdOGdEADdOGdEAD
dOGdEADdOGdEADdOGdEADdOGdEADdOGdEADdOG
dEADdOGdEADdOGdEADdOG**TALA**dEADdOGdEADdOG
dEADdOGdEADdOGdEADdOGdEADdOGdEADdOGdEAD
dOGdEADdOGdEADdOGdEADdOGdEADdOGdEADdOG
dEADdOGdEADdOGdEADdOGdEADdOGdEADdOGdEAD
dOGdEADdOGdEADdOG**STRONG**dEADdOGdEADdOG
dEADdOGdEADdOGdEADdOGdEADdOGdEADdOGdEAD
dOGdEADdOGdEADdOGdEADdOGdEADdOGdEADdOG
dEADdOGdEADdOGdEADdOGdEADdOGdEADdOGdEAD
dOGdEADdOG**SUPPORT**dEADdOGdEADdOGdEADdOG
dEADdOGdEADdOGdEADdOGdEADdOGdEADdOGdEAD
dOGdEADdOGdEADdOGdEADdOG**TALA**dEADdOGdEAD
dOGdEADdOGdEADdOGdEADdOGdEADdOGdEADdOG

dEADdOGdEADdOGdEADdOGdEADdOG**TALA**dEADdOG
dEADdOGdEADdOGdEADdOGdEADdOGdEADdOGdEAD
dOGdEADdOGdEADdOGdEADdOGdEADdOGdEADdOG
dEADdOGdEADdOGdEADdOGdEADdOGdEADdOGdEAD
dOGdEADdOGdEADdOGdEADdOG**ONEOFUS**dEADdOG
dEADdOGdEADdOGdEADdOGdEADdOGdEADdOGdEAD
dOGdEADdOGdEADdOGdEADdOGdEADdOGdEADdOG
dEADdOGdEADdOGdEADdOGdEADdOGdEADdOGdEAD
dOGdEADdOGdEADdOG**TALA**dEADdOGdEADdOGdEAD
dOGdEADdOGdEADdOGdEADdOGdEADdOGdEADdOG
dEADdOGdEADdOGdEADdOGdEADdOG**TALA**dEADdOG
dEADdOGdEADdOGdEADdOGdEADdOGdEADdOGdEAD
dOGdEADdOGdEADdOGdEADdOGdEADdOG**TALA**dEAD
d O G d E A D d O G d E A D d O G d E A D d O G d E A D d O G d E

Chapter 7

Heaven

Hell

Purgatory

She couldn't tell if she was in heaven or hell or somewhere in between. She was as light as air and had no sensation of her body, no awareness of time. She was floating high above her life and its conversant routines, far above the clouds, looking down. There was no pain. No fear.

But, in time, she returned to herself, settled into the familiar sense of who she was. She occupied her space. It was then that it hit her. Reality. She knew enough to realise that whatever had been familiar, whatever had represented *home and safety* had now gone. She knew that she had to let go of the longing for it. The desire to return. Let it go. It was done, it was over. Her abductors were going to kill her. She closed her eyes. Heard one of them enter the room, she felt the rough handling of the intravenous cannula. Felt the twist of the tourniquet, tight. Tighter. Knew that she was getting another dose of the medication. Prayed that it might kill her. Whispered an incantation, 'I want to die.'

'Not yet. It's not over.'

The prick of a needle, the rush of consciousness, the pain flooded her senses. Her heart heavy with the fatigue of having been restarted. She felt it hammer through her chest, resistant and resentful.

The figure bent close to her face, she saw spittle fly from behind the dog mask. 'Try to remember what got you here. Can you?'

She tried to unscramble the memories, to the 'before' when she had been snatched. And now the 'after', when all she wanted to do was to go back to the place before the pain. She tried to look at her hands. She felt her fingers sticky with what felt like mucus. Traced her thumb over one, found it was a stump. What were they doing to her? The medication hit again and she was instantly transported back to the demons.

Her mind raced through the images, saw the upturned crucifixes litter the room. She wondered about a God and if He felt love. Then why wasn't God here? Was this His punishment for her not believing? For not righting the crucifixes?

Images of people flashed across her mind, ghoul-like, tall and foreboding, grey eyes judgemental, bony fingers pointing. The figures came and went, leering, staring and pointing. One accused her of causing her own death and when he turned his face to her, his face was the face of a devil, who smiled at her stupidity. 'God's love? Is this what it is?' he'd sneered. 'Then let the mockery begin!'

'I want to live!'

But the whispered response in the room interrupted her. 'Don't you know? This is how evil people die?'

She stared up at the snarling dog mask. Felt herself sink

back into her body. She looked at the laptop beside her. Felt every part of her quiver.

tHE dEADdOG mANIfEStO

Some of the tasks required by tHE mODErAtOR
In nO particular oRdEr

As mEMbERS of the dEADdOG community yOU will be required to complete aLL tASkS before pROGrESsING

bRANdING (The skin will be branded in some way with the image of a dead dog) dEADdOG

sHArING to dEADdOG (Sharing your personal history as a means of renouncing the unbelievers)

dArING for the dEADdOG community (Daring to stand up and to stand out)

dOInG for the dEADdOG community (Displaying a commitment to the group)

rEINFOrCING the unity of the group through Sacred Sacrifice. (We are aLL oNE)

sACRIFIcIAL Lamb to Slaughter (aN oFFErING)

tHE uLTImATE gIfT (Your own uNIqUE pERsONAL oFfErING)

Chapter 8

Tala

She closed her eyes. She had done something awful. Eighteen-year-old Natala De Luca, or Tala as she preferred, was supposed to be at home looking after her four-year-old stepbrother Tomas but she wasn't, she was standing in an empty train station, close to the track. Waiting for a train that wouldn't stop. That was the point. She'd been given the task. She knew what she had to do. She had been told.

She wore her favourite green Doc Martens boots. Ignored the pain of her most recent tattoo. She had ten minutes to wait. She used it by thinking about them. Her tribe. She'd been invited to become a member of the group after her eighteenth birthday. There were a series of tasks to complete. Before 'The One'. dEADdOG was an online community of teenagers like her. Melancholic and disassociated with their parents. Not at one with a world they believed didn't rate them. She knew the world didn't value them, they didn't fit in. She had been delighted when they had invited her to join the closed group. Long before then she had tried to talk to her father. He had informed her, from his luxury hotel, that teenagers had always been drawn to outsiders. A band of people like themselves, their tribe. Like that had helped. He would never have understood that the Moderator allowed her and the others a platform where they shared experiences and bonded with each other. No matter that Leroy was in Chicago, Bernarda in Paris, Gisilberhta in Berlin. It was no barrier in the global village which is the World Wide Web. Tala felt closer to Leroy than to anyone in the world. Leroy was nineteen, lived in Chicago and wanted to be an artist. He desired it as much as she did. His parents were insistent that he become an accountant. Tala understood the struggle to be real, to be congruent and how hard it could be. As did Gisilberhta and the others in the group. Tala was closer to them than she was to her own father. The group really 'got' her and her frustration with not being a great artist. She thought of an art tutor at the CoVA, Ms Barnes Olsen, who was encouraging, but Tala knew that she would never be a great artist, not like Frida Kahlo or Georgia O'Keeffe. Tala had read everything about Kahlo, that there was some belief (although others disputed this) that she had overdosed. She had taken her ending into her own hands. Tala thought that was the bravest thing she had ever read. Especially about someone as immensely talented as Kahlo. Tala thought that, at best, she was a mediocre artist and that thought haunted her and almost ate her alive. Sure, her work had garnered comments that it was remarkable, but also from some, that it was derivative. Only Assistant Principal Kirkpatrick had given her any real helpful critique. And she knew what that was all about. And if she couldn't be a great artist then what was the point of life? Plus, there was this guy that she liked at college, well she was invisible to him. She'd even invited him and his stupid, dorky friend to her eighteenth birthday party weekend. Her father had sprung for a cottage in Balmaha for her and some friends. Some had camped. One had been carefully ferried to and from the party, by her father, a precious cargo. But that was six months ago. It had been a disaster.

Tala leaned in towards the track. Balanced on her tiptoes. Felt the snow on her face. Thought of Leroy. Then other images forced their way into her mind, her stepmother, Autumn, who hated her. Autumn was obsessed with work and socialising. Tala felt that she was invisible both at home and with some at college. Autumn favoured Tomas. Her father was working away for months at a time for an arms company. Right now, she knew that he was holed up in another luxury hotel in Geneva, no doubt drinking expensive brandy. He told people that he was in 'Defence', and had told her to do the same. 'There are nuts out there who would react badly, if they knew, Tala.' But he had no time for her. The last time he'd been home they'd argued. 'Oh, grow up, Tala. Can't you help Autumn out a bit more? You have a really cushy life here. I could tell you some horror stories about the countries I've been in and the poverty and suffering of the children there.'

'Yeah,' she'd replied, 'the ones you saw from the window of your five-star hotel? It must have been a nightmare for you, Dad. All that expensive brandy and foie gras.'

The slap had stung but she'd refused to cry in front of him, instead she did as she always did and left the room. Dad was only interested in what made him happy: money and Autumn. He never talked about Tala's mum any more. Or visited her grave. It was like she had never existed. Like she was an inconvenience in his past. Tala missed her mother so much. She wanted to be with her.

Tala had locked the door of her bedroom and had sat on the bed crying, had opened her page for comfort, as Gisilberhta had recommended. She'd read it again.

dEADdOGdEADdOGdEADdOGdEADdOGd
EADdOG**WELCOMETALA**dEADdOGdEADdOG
dEADdOGdEADdOGdEADdOGdEADdOGdEADdOGdEA
DdOGdEADdOGdEADdOGdEADdOGdEADdOGdEA
DdOGdEADdOGdEADdOGdEADdOGdEADdOGdEAD
dOGdEADdOGdEADdOGdEADdOG**TALAWEL**
COMEdEADdOGdEADdOGdEADdOGdEADdOG
dEADdOGdEADdOGdEADdOGdEADdOGdEADdO
GdEADdOGdEADdOGdEADdOGdEADdOGdEADdOG
dEADdOGdEADdOGdEADdOGdEADdOGdEADdOGdEAD
dOG**TALA**dEADdOGdEADdOGdEADdOGdEADdOGdEAD
dOGdEADdOGdEADdOGdEADdOGdEADdOGdEADdOG
dEADdOGdEADdOG**WELCOMETALA**dEADdOGdEAD
dOGdEADdOGdEADdOGdEADdOGdEADdOGdEADdOG
dEADdOGdEADdOGdEADdOGdEADdOGdEADdOGdEAD
dOG**TALA**dEADdOGdEADdOGdEADdOGdEADdOG
dEADdOGdEADdOGdEADdOGdEADdOGdEADdOG
dEADdOGdEADdOGdEADdOGdEADdOGdEADdOG
dEADdOGdEADdOGdEADdOGdEADdOGdEAD dOGdEAD
dOGdEADdOG**TALA**dEADdOGdEADdOGdEADdOGdEAD
dOGdEADdOGdEADdOGdEADdOGdEADdOGdEADdOG
dEADdOGdEADdOGdADdOGdEADdOGdEAD
dOGdEADdOGdEdEADdOGdEADdOGdEADdOG
dEADdOGdEADdOG**TALAWELCOME**dEADdOG
dEADdOGdEADdOGdEADdOGdEADdOGdEADdOG
dEADdOGdEADdOGdEADdOGdEADdOGdEADdOG
dEADdOGdEADdOGdEADdOGdEADdOGdEADdOG

dEADdOGdEADdOGdEADdOGdEADdOGdEADdOG
TALAdEADdOGdEADdOGdEADdOGdEAD
dOGdEADdOGdEADdOGdEADdOGdEADdOGdEAD
dOGdEADdOGdEADdOGdEADdOGdEADdOGdEAD
dOGdEADdOGdEADdOGdEADdOGdEADdOGdEAD
dOGdEADdOG**WELCOMETALA**dEADdOGdEADdOG
dEADdOGdEADdOGdEADdOGdEADdOGdEADdOG
dEADdOGdEADdOGdEADdOGdEADdOGdEADdOG
TALAdEADdOGdEADdOGdEADdOGdEADdOG
dEADdOGdEADdOGADdOGdEADdOGdEADdOG
dEADdOGdEADdOG**TALAYOUAREPARTOFOUR**
FAMILYdEADdOGdEADdOGdEADdOGdEADdOGdEAD
dOGdEADdOGdEADdOGdEADdOGdEADdOGdEADdOG
dE**OURSISTERTALA**dEADdOGdEADdOGdEADdOG
dEADdOGdEADd

With Gisilberhta, Tala felt that she had a sister. She'd sent a message. *This world is full of fakes, people who are stupid and vacuous and full of materialistic shit. Even the other girls at my college are fake. Fake nails, fake eyelashes, fake smile. But you are real, Gisilberhta.*

Gisilberhta had responded with heartfelt agreement.

Tala now took out her mobile, held the phone out to the track, panned across the deserted station, held it up to take in the heavy snow-filled clouds dispensing their Christmas offering. Posted it to the group. She heard the distant rumble of the train. She read the comments coming in, scrolling down the side of the screen.

You and I are at one. To our shared journey. Leroy.

OMG that looks spooky! Roberto

Прощай (goodbye)

You going to jump? If so, congrats on it being your big day. Simmy2

Yeah, better to leave this place on your own terms! JanUSA3

Hasta siempre (until for ever) Emilio

She heard the train grow closer, braced herself for the backdraught. Leroy had tried to explain it to her using terms she didn't understand, including references to Bernoulli's Theorem. All she knew was that when a train rushed through a station, she felt the air around her conspire with the universe and destiny to pull her under. She felt the diamanté wolf ring her mother had bought her dig into her palm. Tala, she had told her, in some cultures, meant 'wolf'. Her mother had told her this to keep her strong. Tala felt that it suited her, she had to be strong for the challenges. She'd researched it and found out that, genetically, dogs were 99 per cent wolves. She kissed the ring. Whispered, 'I.A.N, I.A.N.'

She heard the thunder of the train as it passed her, so close she could have reached out and touched it. She felt her body unsteady, the immediate, seductive pull towards the track. But Tala had held herself back. This wasn't the time or the place to die. No, of course not. That had already been decided for her, a time and date set. She turned towards the exit. A few seconds later, she sent another link to the group. Her eighth step.

Soon, she had her response.

MODERATOR: 'wELL dONE. wELL dONE tALA. bE pROuD oF yOURsELf, oF yOUr sTRengTH.

45

Chapter 9

Sunday 13 December, 7.30 a.m.

Detective Inspector Kat Wheeler, Police Scotland's Major Investigations Team (MIT) #1

It was just before dawn when Wheeler ran through the almost empty city streets. She was glad that the previous evening at the White Hart Inn, she'd stopped at her third glass of Chardonnay. Now she was up for her usual five-mile run. She ran most days, was ex-army and proud of it. Snowflakes landed on her lashes and cheeks and she flicked them away with impatience. Her short blonde hair was already soaked. Despite the impact of the weather on her morning run, she loved this time of the year. Winter, especially the time just before Christmas, was her favourite. This early in the morning she almost had the streets to herself. Her long legs covered the distance comfortably as she headed back to her flat in the Merchant City.

She made her way up to her landing, taking the stairs two at a time. She could smell turpentine from the flat opposite hers. As she passed, the door opened.

'Good morning,' a voice said. 'Are we neighbours?'

The man was around her age, six foot three and maybe 200 pounds. Muscular. Short dark hair and a wide-open smile. The resemblance to some film star was there, Wheeler couldn't think which one. She held out her hand. 'Kat Wheeler.'

'Sebastian Hawk.' His handshake was firm, and she noticed his deep brown eyes. How interesting to have a new neighbour. And he seemed pretty cool.

'I'm just off out for breakfast. I'm taking my cousin Aubree out as a treat to say thank you. I hear that the new place, Labyrinth, over on Byres Road is good, if pricey, and it opens at seven, which must surely be a good thing for us early birds?'

'I heard it's great, I haven't been yet,' said Wheeler. She suddenly felt self-conscious. She was soaked to the skin and knew that she must look a mess. Fleetingly wondered why it bothered her.

'Why don't you come in for a quick coffee? Another day when you have time? Let's get to know one another.'

Wheeler smiled. 'Sure. Right now, I'm running late.'

'I understand, work is always waiting. See you around.'

Wheeler kept moving.

In her flat, she slipped into a warm shower.

(Acting) Detective Inspector Steven Ross, MIT # 2

Across town, DI Steven Ross lay in bed in a high-ceilinged room in Great Western Road. The flat was sparsely decorated. Its occupant, Aubree Rutherford, a mature student at Strathclyde University doing a Masters in Criminology Research Methods, was low on funds. The flat was also cold. Ross thought of his own warm and cosy place. He needed to get back to it. He lay on his stomach, his head turned purposely to the left. He swallowed hard, ran a parched tongue over dry lips. His head throbbed in a particularly painful way that a hangover had of warning him he wasn't young enough to keep drinking the way he had been used to doing. At least not without accepting the consequences. One of which was the fact that Aubree was lying fast asleep beside him, her long red hair spread out across her pillow. She was working part-time at the White Hart Inn, but then he'd known that already. Wasn't that why he had suggested it as a venue? She stirred in her sleep. Last night had been a mistake. Aubree was beautiful, and her body language had told him she still thought he was attractive, but they had history together and it hadn't worked out before, so why had he even gone there again? Why had they both decided to give it another try? He already knew the answer, at least on his part. Alcohol.

The previous night, once in bed, Aubree had told him that she'd felt a little dizzy. He had reacted quickly, there was absolutely no way he was having sex with a woman when she was not crystal clear that she wanted him to be there. So, he had lain naked next to her, holding her until she had drifted off to sleep. And just before she did she had told him the one thing he didn't want to hear. 'I'm in love with you, Ross. I have been since pretty soon after we first met.'

And he'd told himself that she was too drunk to know what she was saying.

But even his drink-addled mind had reminded him that he didn't love her. That wouldn't matter as much if there wasn't someone who he was connected to. But he hadn't gone there. Instead, he'd gotten up and made his way into the kitchen, drank two long glasses of cold water before returning to the bedroom. He'd debated whether to just leave then and there but it had been 3 a.m. and taxis were hard to come by in the run-up to Christmas. Office parties and general festivities meant that he would have to queue for hours or walk home to his flat in Argyle Street. It wasn't far, but he'd been too shattered to walk.

He closed his eyes.

Painful flashbacks to the previous night and the ill-advised drinking game suggested by Detective Constable Alexander Boyd began. 'How to reinterpret some of the new initiatives for effective communication between the departments?'

The landlord of the White Hart had given the team from Carmyle Police Station free hand in the back room. Big mistake. Immediately, shots had been ordered, and Boyd had become the quizmaster for the evening in the 'old speak' versus 'new speak' quiz. The winner would need to down a final round of tequila shots. The unfortunate loser, a round of Tabasco shots. By way of inspiration, both sets of glasses had been helpfully lined up in neat rows.

'So, just for the newly initiated,' Boyd had called out, 'we used to say, when asked to do something we were reluctant to do . . .'

The team chanted, 'No fucking way!'

'Correct! Now what do we say?'

Hands on invisible buzzers, first one off, 'I'm not sure that's a feasible way forward!'

'A point to you, sir!' Boyd had yelled. 'Now. If I were to say in new speak, that at the station we "were a tad dis-organised"? What would that sound like in old speak?'

'This place is fucked,' a female constable, obviously drunk, had offered.

'One point to you, madam!' Boyd had been at his flamboyant best and had slammed the wooden gavel on the table with the authority of an auctioneer in his saleroom.

And so, it had continued. Partly because of an ongoing, corrosive resentment that things were changing, that Police Scotland, including MIT, was changing, terms and conditions were being manipulated and overtime was pretty much being rescinded. Yet the real job, the job that they had all signed up to do, remained the same. Catch the criminals. Make a solid case and watch it go through. Result. But the team, including Detective Sergeant Ian Robertson who Ross knew had previously been completely teetotal, were hammered. All except his partner, Kat Wheeler.

There had only been one person who wouldn't have been welcome. A journalist who was going to be shadowing the team as part of a process leading up to publishing a book on true crime. No one at Carmyle Station knew who the contact had been who had agreed to this guy becoming embedded in their team. On the surface, the team would have to accept him, but Ross knew that resentment simmered.

Ross pushed his foot, gently, tentatively out from under the sheet, probed the cold air. He inched his other foot out. Dragged fourteen stone of gym-honed body out of the bed. Normally, he prided himself on his fitness. He wasn't feeling it right now.

In the bathroom he stared into the mirror. His dark hair was flattened, his pale blue eyes were bloodshot. Christ, he looked a fucking mess.

He glanced at his watch. It was 8.15 a.m. Two minutes and he would be dressed and gone. He quietly returned to the bedroom, collected his crumpled clothing, grabbed his boots and dressed quickly. He exited the room and was tiptoeing through the hallway when he heard a sound he didn't want to hear. A key turned, and the main door opened. A light flashed on. Ross felt nauseous and turned away. He swallowed, turned slowly to face the man. He was his height, six foot three, and muscular. Maybe a few years older than Ross. Short dark hair and a wide smile. Looked a bit like a film star, thought Ross. Clooney, maybe?

'Good morning.'

Ross kept his voice reasonable. 'Morning. I didn't know anyone else lived here?'

'Sorry,' said the man. 'I used to live here.'

'I'm just leaving,' said Ross.

'So, I see, friend.' The man smiled. 'Is Aubree around?'

'She's asleep.'

'By the way, I'm Seb. Sebastian Hawk.'

Ross shook the extended hand; the man's grip was firm.

'You are?'

'Steven Ross.'

'Aubree's my cousin. I was staying with her for a bit, my new flat needed painting before I could move in. I came over to treat her to a decent breakfast. I didn't know she had company, otherwise I'd have left it for another day.' He peered at Ross. 'She didn't mention that she had a date.'

'It was a spur of the moment thing,' said Ross. 'Excuse me.' Now he really did just want to leave. Quickly.

'Sure. It's important that we have our own space.'

Ross tried for a smile. Failed. His mobile rang. 'I need to take this. Work.' He swallowed, his mouth parched. Head throbbing. He stepped out into the landing and half closed the door behind him.

It was Wheeler. 'What the hell kept you? You need to get yourself over to Mount Vernon. Hamilton Road.'

He listened while she filled him in on the details. 'Murder victim. White male. Looks like he was stabbed to death in his home, nasty stuff.'

'I'll be there ASAP.'

'You want me to come over and pick you up?' she offered.

He paused. 'I'm not at home.'

'Ah, I see.'

He said nothing.

'A new romance?' asked Wheeler.

'I'll be there soon.'

'Sorry to cut in on a date.'

He heard the laughter in her voice. He dropped his mobile back in his pocket, felt his stomach turn as acid made its way into his mouth. He lurched back inside. He passed Seb Hawk again, saw him grin.

'You're not looking so good. You should have let your colleagues, whoever they are, deal with that. I'm sure, whatever business you're in, there are other folk at work who could cover.'

If he'd had the energy he'd have told him that he was wrong, that he was an (Acting) Detective Inspector and a member of the Murder Investigation Team and this was his crime scene. As it was Ross just made it to the bathroom, slammed the door behind him, rammed home the lock and retched into the bowl.

A few seconds passed before he flushed and watched as the water foamed around the bowl. He checked his face again in the mirror. Nothing had improved. If anything, the dark circles under his eyes had become more prominent and his skin had taken on a wax-like sheen. Romance, Wheeler had asked. This was turning into a bloody nightmare.

Chapter 10

Like many areas in Glasgow, Hamilton Road was calm, leafy and residential. Today though, the area had been taped off and the presence of uniformed police officers and Scene of Crime Officers' vehicles were broadcasting loudly to neighbours that there had been a major incident.

DI Wheeler parked up and moved past a group of rubberneckers and the press. Heard the call-outs and the comments. Ignored them, walked on towards the house.

'Wait up.'

She heard Ross behind her. She waited for him. He looked hungover, but she reminded herself that Ross, despite his gym habit, still ate rubbish and drank too much. And, if she were being honest, it was beginning to show.

She watched as he half jogged towards her.

'Morning.'

'You look rough.' She smiled.

'Thanks. I feel rough. Plus, I managed to lose my keys last night. I'll need to check with the pub. Had to knock up my neighbour Mary to get a spare set. It's a fortune to get some others cut.'

'Nightmare,' said Wheeler.

'I suppose you're just back from a bloody run?' he asked.

'Yep.'

'Don't be so smug, no one likes a show-off.' Ross tried for a smile. Got about halfway.

'I think I might try for the half-marathon in June. What do you reckon?' said Wheeler. 'Are you up for it? Competition time?'

'The idea of running over thirteen miles makes me feel queasy.'

'Because?' She looked at him.

'Hangover.'

'Thought so. Lightweight,' said Wheeler. 'I've just taken up kick-boxing. It's a brilliant workout.'

'Not to mention a great self-defence,' said Ross.

'Yeah, that too,' said Wheeler. 'You made good time.' She waited.

Ross walked on. 'OK, what do we have?'

'ID has him as Michael O'Donnell, thirty-nine years of age. A Mrs Payne found him this morning. She was his cleaner.'

'Where is she now? '

'In the front room with uniform.'

Wheeler marched past the uniformed officers, towards the officer issuing regulation coverings for the crime scene. Beyond, the SOCOs were carefully combing and photographing the garden and surrounding area.

Ross looked at an inscription carved into the wall. 'St Guinoch?'

'A Scottish saint,' said Wheeler.

'So, our victim was religious?' said Ross. 'Not to mention well off.'

'Guinoch was a medieval saint. I think the name

predates our victim living here. And yes, the house looks to be worth in the region of upwards of half a million.'

'Robbery gone wrong?' asked Ross.

'Unlikely, according to Mrs Payne. Nothing seems to be missing and there was no sign of a struggle.'

'Then he knew his killer?' said Ross. 'He opened the door. No sign of forced entry?'

'The victim's daughter, Paula, is missing,' said Wheeler. 'She's epileptic and is completely medication dependent and some days can't walk far without assistance. She is prone to fitting, even with the medication. Looks like she may have been abducted.'

Inside, the hallway had polished wooden flooring and Wheeler noticed bloody footprints. 'Here's hoping for some clear DNA.' She sniffed. 'What's with the horrible saccharine smell in here? Look at all these scented candles.' She walked through to the living room where a macabre stage had been set. Michael O'Donnell was on the floor and, beneath him, blood had drained into a once-cream rug, staining it crimson. On the floor an Apple iPhone and MacBook had also been contaminated. But it was the smell that made her want to retch. Wheeler recognised the pathologist in attendance, Hannah Scott-Fletcher, who even when at murder scenes wore a flick of eyeliner.

'Hannah, what can you tell us?' asked Wheeler. 'Roughly speaking. Just a ballpark?'

'I'd say he was killed in the last fourteen to eighteen hours.'

Wheeler stared at what was left of Michael O'Donnell. 'He had no chance to defend himself,' she said softly.

'None whatsoever,' agreed Scott-Fletcher. 'He was stabbed. The first wounds were seriously deep, whoever did it was intent on killing as quickly as possible. At least initially. Later, they slashed his body gratuitously. There was no need for it, he would have already been dead, it was merely choice.'

'Looks like it might have been personal,' said Ross. 'Someone had a grudge against our boy.'

'Could be, or maybe the killer just felt safe enough with him being dead to express their anger or rage at the world?' said Wheeler.

She studied the body in front of her. The victim looked about five foot nine and his face in death was peaceful. He had dark hair and eyes, high cheekbones.

'Your victim was a good-looking man,' said Scott-Fletcher. She pulled off her gloves and rolled them into a ball. 'I'll have more for you after the post-mortem, you'll have everything in my report. Until, then—' she glanced at the body '—it's over to you, Wheeler.'

'Cheers.'

'You coming to Madison's gig at The Round next week?'

'Wouldn't miss it,' said Wheeler. 'Unless this case takes over.'

'So, we shouldn't expect you then?' laughed the pathologist.

'Probably not.'

'She played King Tut's last night, a sold-out gig. Plus, she arranged for some of her fans who have disabilities to meet her backstage.'

'Congrats,' said Wheeler. 'It all sounds very feel good.'

'She had extra security on the door.'

'Because?' asked Wheeler.

'Some tosser has been stalking her,' said Scott-Fletcher, 'claiming he wrote the lyrics and the music to "Enchanted".'

'Guess it comes with the territory,' said Wheeler. 'Did she report him?'

'Didn't have to, he'd already reported her to the police. Guy name of Frankie Fermin.'

'Catchy name,' said Wheeler.

'Found the runt in his usual camouflage fatigues skulking in the bushes outside our flat last week.'

'Does he reckon he's in the SAS or something?' asked Wheeler.

'Nuts,' laughed Scott-Fletcher. 'Anyway, he didn't show at her gig.'

'Still, she needs to keep an eye on him,' said Wheeler. 'Get her to call me if she needs to talk.'

Wheeler turned to Ross. 'Uniform are doing the house-to-house interviews and taking statements. Keep me informed the minute they have anything.'

'Meanwhile?' said Ross.

'I want a look around the house,' said Wheeler. 'Such a frenzied attack meant that the killer left here with Michael O'Donnell's blood all over him or her. Plus, there is potentially a daughter missing who doesn't have her medication.' Wheeler glanced at the photographs on a shelf. Michael and Paula. Older pictures with a woman holding a baby. The woman was early twenties, dark-haired and slim. Her deep brown eyes were kohl-rimmed. A bright smile. Paula's tiny face held close to, presumably, her mother, her upturned nose almost touching hers. Wheeler reached for the photograph, turned it over, 'Jayla and Paula' was written on the back.

'This woman in the photograph must be the mother. Find out where she lives. If the girl is anywhere, she may be with her.'

The stairs rose towards a stained-glass window depicting a wildly colourful scene of a beheaded man. 'The head of John the Baptist being presented to Salome,' said Wheeler.

'Charming,' said Ross.

Wheeler glanced up at a heavy, ornate black crystal chandelier.

'Whoever Michael O'Donnell was, he had taste,' said Ross, following her gaze. 'Somewhat gothic but taste nevertheless.'

Wheeler skirted the SOCOs and made her way down the hall. 'Not sure I wholeheartedly agree, Ross. I think there's something very much amiss in this household.' She gestured to another glass display cabinet. Inside were rows of glass domes, all had inverted crucifixes, in some the crucified figure's face was contorted into a grotesque grimace, teeth bared. Others had ragged slash wounds, dark blood and organs spilling out.

'Bloody hell,' said Ross. 'Satanism? Here in Mount Vernon?'

'Black magic?' asked Wheeler.

'I've seen these types of crosses in lots of horror films,' said Ross. 'But never as regular home decoration.'

They passed several more upturned crosses dotted throughout the house, the tortured figures pleading silently for redemption.

Wheeler felt claustrophobic, the house seemed to press in on her. The almost overpowering saccharine smell in the place. 'Let's step outside for a second, Ross. I need to take in some air.'

Outside, she made her way towards DS Robertson. He had always been thin, but recently he'd become skinny. She'd heard on the grapevine that he was living alone. His personal style was, however, still of the highest standard. He wore a smart brown suit, expertly cut, and his dark hair had been cut into a fashionable geometric style. His shoes, even in this weather, had been polished and a familiar lemon scent of aftershave hung in the air.

'Your take on all this?' she asked him.

'House of horrors, Wheeler. I don't know what the hell's going on with the crosses and the candles, but I couldn't breathe in there.'

Wheeler was not superstitious. There was no way she even believed in evil, but the house had a presence that she couldn't identify. And the clear-thinking Robertson had felt it too. She took a deep breath, welcomed the crisp, cold air deep into her lungs, before turning. 'Let's get back inside, Ross.'

Chapter 11

In the front room, the cleaner was perched on the edge of a black velvet sofa, a damp handkerchief clutched in her hand. She was late sixties, slim. Her short hair was neatly parted to one side.

'Michael was such a lovely man. If I'm being honest I had a little bit of a soft spot for him. Although I'm happily married.' Mrs Payne instinctively touched her wedding ring, rotated it agitatedly around her finger. 'I was just saying to my friend Ruby, that Michael needed someone to look after him.'

'Do you know if Michael had any enemies?' asked Wheeler. 'Someone who would want to harm him?'

'Oh, dear no! Michael was an absolute angel. Everyone who knew him would say so. I'm not religious, not by a long shot, but Michael was as close to an angelic human being as is possible.' She sniffed into her handkerchief. 'Honestly, he was lovely, a real sweetheart.' She twisted her ring again.

'Would you like me to call your husband?' Wheeler asked.

'No, that's all right, that smartly dressed colleague of yours, standing outside, has already called him. He's coming to collect me.'

'Did Michael have a partner?' asked Ross.

'No, none that I knew of, but maybe he had someone in the shadows? He may well have been seeing a couple of women on the quiet. We don't always know these things, do we? There were . . .' she paused '. . . certain rumours. Of course, people love to talk, don't they?'

'Rumours?' prompted Wheeler.

'That Michael was a . . . well, the phrase used was that "he was a bit of a player" but on the quiet. That people had seen women come and go after dark. I didn't listen to them. I never listen to gossip. And so what if he had a lady friend?'

Wheeler smiled at the quaint use of the term for lover. 'Can you tell me about the crosses in the glass case?'

Mrs Payne shuddered. 'Oh, I think they are horrible, just terrible looking things. I feel the eyes of Christ, or whichever figure it is, following me when I'm passing them. And from such a hideous position. I hate them.'

'What was their significance?' asked Ross. 'Black magic?'

'I never asked. If I'm being honest, I was afraid to. I liked Michael very much and didn't want to know about—' she put her index fingers in the air, made quotation marks '—darker things. Michael only mentioned them once, on my first day cleaning. He said that they were originally from Paula's mother's collection.'

'Jayla?' asked Wheeler. 'The woman in the picture?'

'Yes.'

Wheeler waited.

'She was an American, you see. From Long Island. I'm not sure whereabout in the US that is, but my husband said there was a movie made about a place where bad things happened . . .' She drifted off.

'Go on,' said Wheeler gently.

'Michael mentioned that she'd been an exchange student at his university when they met. But I never met her. He didn't talk about her, only that one time. And to warn me about the crosses.'

'And the cloying smell?' asked Wheeler.

'I know, it's awful, isn't it? Michael burned scented candles a lot as there was always a smell in the house, I've cleaned everywhere but it remains pungent. Michael even had the drains done twice by a local handyman, but still, the smell persists.'

'Can you tell me about Jayla?'

'The poor child never mentioned her mum and I don't like to bring it up. Paula gets depressed and I think she might be a little suicidal at times.'

'Any idea where Paula's mum is now?'

Mrs Payne shook her head. 'None. Paula's a little frail angel. She looks so like a young Audrey Hepburn. So very beautiful. I love her. We all do. She's not at all well. It wasn't uncommon for me to come to clean and there would be an ambulance sitting outside the house.' Mrs Payne looked about her. 'Where is the child?'

'We don't know at present, we're trying to locate her. Do you have any idea where she might be?'

'Nowhere without Michael.' She paused. 'Oh, my goodness, Paula's missing, isn't she?'

Wheeler said nothing.

'She's missing! Whoever killed Michael has taken little Paula. What kind of a person does that? You must find the monster; this person is sick. Absolutely sick. They need to be locked up before it's too late. Well, of course it's already too late. I'm sorry.' Mrs Payne gave way to the tears that had been threatening.

'Did you see anything untoward recently?' asked Wheeler gently 'Was there anyone unusual hanging about the area?'

Mrs Payne dabbed her eyes, 'There were a few salespeople from the double-glazing companies. I had two gentlemen arrive on my doorstep in the past few weeks.'

'Do you have their contact details?' asked Wheeler.

'No, I threw their leaflets straight into the recycling. I don't believe in that sort of cold-calling.'

'And Michael? Do you know if they contacted him?'

'No idea. All I know is that Michael usually came home to have lunch with Paula, then she would have gone upstairs to have a short nap. That's what they did, they ate together most days. He was so supportive of her. He did use carers for most of the longer stretches when he had to go out. Although Paula was fine on her own for a few hours. The carers were from some agency. The details are on the wall in the kitchen.'

'When did you last see Michael?'

'Last Wednesday. I bumped into him in the street. I was walking my friend Ruby's little dog. Ruby's been in hospital. Her granddaughter, Tala, used to walk the dog but she's dropped off. I think she's depressed, like little Paula. Teenagers get like that sometimes, don't they?'

'Did Michael mention anything in particular?' asked Wheeler.

'No, only that he was excited about how Paula's work at the CoVA was coming along.'

'CoVA?' asked Wheeler. 'The local art college?'

'Yes, the College of Visual Arts. Students go there between sixteen and eighteen, it sets them up for art college. Michael was a governor there and Paula is a student.' Mrs Payne paused. 'Well, on the days she could make it in. She had good days, when she was very strong, and bad days, when she was awfully poorly. That said, she has gained a little weight over the past five or six months, which means that she's a little stronger.'

'Is there anything else you can tell me about Michael?' asked Wheeler gently.

'He lived for little Paula. She's a poor wee soul. She's got all this awful stuff happening to her. She's very fragile. I often used to say to Michael that Paula had gossamer wings. Poor little thing.'

'She sounds very poorly,' said Ross.

'She is so incredibly delicate.' Mrs Payne sniffed.

'What about a boyfriend?' asked Wheeler.

'Oh, dearie me, no. That would be out of the question. She is such a poorly child.'

'What about her friends or Michael's?' said Wheeler. 'Who did they spend time with?'

Mrs Payne stared at her. 'I'm afraid I don't know. We weren't close, I just came in to clean.'

'Do you have any idea where Paula might be?' Wheeler repeated. 'Who she might have gone to?' Wheeler knew the next twenty-four hours would be crucial.

'Friends? I'm not sure. She knew some people at the CoVA, but other than that it was pretty much her and Michael. They were absolute best friends. They lived for each other.'

'Wasn't that unusual?' asked Ross.

'What do you mean? I'm not sure I get you, Inspector Ross? Paula has epilepsy and other medical complications and so is heavily dependent on her father. I viewed that as quite normal.'

'Is there anyone you think might have wanted to harm Michael?' Wheeler persisted.

'No.' Mrs Payne paused. 'Although he did play chess with a handyman, the one who did the drains? I never liked the look of him. Sinister-looking man.'

'Go on,' said Wheeler.

'It's his eyes, yellow-brown in colour like a cheetah, like he was ready to spring,' said Mrs Payne.

'Do you have a name?' asked Wheeler.

'Vlad or something. He wore a big thick crucifix around his neck.'

'Which only means he's Christian?' asked Wheeler.

'It reminded me of the upturned crosses.'

They continued the conversation for another few minutes, Wheeler recognised that the woman was striving hard, as good people do, to try to help, to offer up the golden nugget, the piece of information that would break the case and lead the police to the killer. Wheeler had seen it all before, but her gut told her that Mrs Payne had nothing more to offer. The details of whoever had killed Michael O'Donnell and abducted Paula, weren't going to be supplied by her. A uniformed officer gestured to Wheeler from the doorway. She spoke quietly. 'Your husband has arrived. He'll be outside waiting beyond the police cordon.'

Wheeler stood, gave the woman her card. 'If you think of anything else, please be in touch.'

In the hallway, Wheeler walked back to the display of crucifixes, grabbed her mobile phone and took some shots. The SOCOs would have photographed everything and the pictures would be mounted on the boards back at the station, but Wheeler wanted her own pictures. The figures and their hideous expressions seemed so completely incongruous in a family home.

'Grim, aren't they?' said Ross.

'Certainly, they're not pretty, but are they meaningful?'

'In as much as they are in a house where a man has been murdered and his fragile and medicine-dependent daughter has disappeared. And all that "lived for each other". Sounded awful to me. Having to nurse your kid just to keep her alive.'

'It sounded like he basically devoted his life to keeping Paula well,' said Wheeler.

'That kind of attention is pretty unusual,' said Ross.

'You think it's odd that he cared for his daughter?'

'Unusual to be that close. Sounds a bit claustrophobic if you ask me,' said Ross.

'And you being the expert on familial relationships?' said Wheeler.

'You don't need to tell me about family relationships,' Ross grumbled. 'I could write a bloody book about them.'

'Jeez and we're right back to you again. You *aside*, Ross. If Michael and Paula existed entirely for each other,' said Wheeler, 'then Paula is on a short fuse. Without her father's psychological and emotional support, she will go downhill extremely fast.'

'Fair enough,' said Ross.

'And where is the mother, Jayla? The woman in the photographs? We need to locate her ASAP.' Wheeler strode ahead. 'We need to get everyone on it.'

'Let me give you a heads-up, Wheeler,' said Ross. 'You heard the boss ranting about budget and stats and the precarious position of Carmyle Police Station. He's refusing to pay anything more than a couple of hours' overtime.

I reckon our small team is all this case has. I think his hands are tied because of budgetary constraints.'

Wheeler knew that he was right. Carmyle Police Station, in Glasgow's East End, was slap bang in the centre of the triangle that was Auchenshuggle, Mount Vernon and the South Lanarkshire border. If this case was yet another unsolved murder on the station's log, it would mean the nail in the coffin for them. Police Scotland was under immense pressure to make personnel cutbacks, save money on buildings and, finally, come in somewhere relatively close to budget. She knew that closing Carmyle Station, an old building with strip lighting and dodgy heating, and merging it with one of the others – either Shettleston or London Road – made financial sense. If she was being honest with herself, she should be looking for a way out. Maybe she needed to do just that. There were other opportunities and she was ambitious. She snapped back to the case in hand, reminding herself that she loved the old station, whatever its flaws.

She turned to Ross. 'Right, let's get on. I want a quick tour of this house, then it's back to the station. I'll grab us some breakfast on the way, you look like you could do with something.'

'I feel like death heated up,' said Ross, following her to the door.

'That's what you get for partying so hard.'

'Thanks,' said Ross.

'By the way, since you weren't home last night, can I ask if there's a new romance on the cards?'

'It's complicated,' said Ross.

'It always is with you.' Wheeler smiled.

'Let's go explore the house,' said Ross, moving on.

'I need to get focused. I really don't feel very well. My head feels like it's about to explode.'

Wheeler glanced back at the personnel carrying the victim's lifeless body out to their van. It was concealed in a body bag and the crowd of onlookers outside wouldn't have as much as a glimpse of it. She thought of the victim, of his missing daughter. Of Paula's mother, Jayla, who would soon receive the news about her missing daughter and murdered ex-partner. It was a bloody mess. Like most murders. She turned to Ross. 'Quit whining. All this tragedy happening, a devoted father savagely murdered and his vulnerable daughter missing and you're complaining about a bloody self-inflicted hangover.'

'Thanks for the sympathy, Wheeler.'

'I'll buy you coffee later.'

'And a pastry?'

Wheeler walked through to the kitchen. On one of the work surfaces was a large china bowl; it looked hand-painted, with colourful figs, grapes and lemons around the rim. On the wall, a list of carers and phone numbers. Wheeler took down the name of the agency too.

On a shelf, ring binders. She reached out and took one, opened it. The files were colour coded and meticulously arranged. 'Something called the ketogenic diet is listed under "essential".' She glanced at the information. 'Listen to this, Ross. This is Paula's diet. This kind of a diet,' she read aloud, 'if rigorously followed can be successful in treating epilepsy.' Maybe this was a backup if the medication isn't working? Or maybe this is more esoteric?' She scanned the notes. The word 'ketosis' leapt out at her, she recalled a young female constable who had used the term when she'd joined a meal replacement slimming group. The notes had been annotated, Michael O'Donnell's penmanship was precise, accurate but difficult to read because it was so small. 'Results via research very good: different seizures/syndromes. Epilepsy/spasms.'

'Sounds grim,' said Ross.

Wheeler flicked through the folder, pages of heavily annotated printouts. 'The (MCT) diet. Medium chain triglyceride.'

'Geez,' said Ross. 'A bit of a culinary tightrope.' He picked up a folder. 'There are dozens of photocopied pages describing a high protein/low carb diet and photographs of food. All heavily annotated.'

'LGIT,' said Wheeler. 'Low glycaemic index treatment. I doubt that whoever abducted her will bother with trying to control her condition with diet.'

Ross peered over her shoulder. 'Looks like her father was desperate to help her. But a little obsessive, don't you think?'

'If it were someone in your family you'd do anything to try to help them. Wouldn't you?'

'I guess,' said Ross doubtfully.

Wheeler scanned the remainder of the notes. 'Michael had considered a change to Paula's anti-epileptic drugs, AEDs. Plus, he'd faithfully recorded his daughter's bowel movements.'

'Her bowel movements?' said Ross. 'Yuk.'

'"Constipation is a problem for Paula on this diet. My child has no energy. Paula sounds depressed. I think she may be suicidal." Finally—' Wheeler flicked through the pages '—there's a pile of data from various hospitals, including Great Ormond Street, detailing the link between diet, seizures and AEDs.'

'I think that there's taking an interest and then there's this,' said Ross. 'It's obsessive. Look at these.' He gestured to the laminated menus pinned to the wall. 'Aren't they just a little OTT?'

'Certainly, careful menu planning,' said Wheeler. 'But who wanted him dead? And why? A stay-at-home dad, by all accounts a devoted dad.' She looked in the cupboards. They were full of specialist ingredients. In the centre of the room a broad oak table and two matching benches. There were slate placemats, a vase of pale pink carnations and a deep red poinsettia. Wheeler knew that the ubiquitous poinsettia was popular, but she had counted at least three in the house so far. 'The usual Christmas plant,' she said. 'Flores de Noche Buena.'

'A red plant,' said Ross. 'So?'

'Flowers of the Holy Night,' said Wheeler.

'Because?' said Ross.

'The red was believed to symbolise the blood of Christ,' said Wheeler.

'So, the house is named after a saint, the plants are a reference to Christ's blood and we have inverted crosses upon which figures are crucified upside down and looking like they are screaming in agony. Satanism?'

'Keep an open mind, Ross. Let's just keep digging.'

In a small study Wheeler found more medical journals, thick volumes and various literature about epilepsy including another annotated folder 'Research'. She flicked through more notes. '"The New Way Ahead for Epilepsy", Dr Miriam Studley. "Research on MBPS", D. B.'

'So much stuff,' said Ross.

'More books on Satanic artefacts and beliefs. Some literature around esoteric religions,' said Wheeler. 'Plus, lists of how to treat some of Paula's symptoms, including the side effects of her medication.'

'Michael O'Donnell was also a reader.' Ross slipped one of the books from the shelf. 'Or they both were.'

Wheeler checked the titles. 'The classics, Orwell's *Nineteen Eighty-Four*, Fitzgerald's *The Great Gatsby*, Tolstoy's *Anna Karenina*, Steinbeck's *The Grapes of Wrath*.' She paused. 'And Nabokov's *Lolita*.'

'*Lolita*? I saw the film once. Old guy fancies the daughter of his new partner.'

'Yep,' said Wheeler.

'Art or . . . ?' said Ross.

'I've never seen it.' Wheeler slipped out another book, flicked through it. 'Satanism and its history.'

'Reinforces all the crosses,' said Ross. 'What is all this? He's from Glasgow but this place looks like it belongs in Amityville, New York. Place of the famous killing in the seventies. Associated with devil worship and satanic cults.'

'And you know all this how?' asked Wheeler.

'You never watched the documentary about making the film, *The Amityville Horror*?' said Ross.

'Nope. Never seen it.'

'It's really interesting. You should watch it.'

'Look.' Wheeler walked over to a framed picture of Michael carrying a toddler, a woman standing beside them.

'"The three of us in Amityville",' said Wheeler reading from the hand-written script underneath the photograph. 'His wife, Jayla. She's the same woman in the other photograph.'

'And my reference was spot on,' said Ross. 'Amityville.'

'Yeah, but no one likes a smart arse,' said Wheeler. 'Especially a smug one.'

Ross pointed to a map taped to the wall. Underneath it was written, 'The house in Amityville'.

There was a chess board on a small table. 'Looks like the game was interrupted,' said Wheeler.

Upstairs, the bedrooms.

'Michael was way into taxidermy,' said Wheeler, looking around. There were dozens of examples, large ravens, snarling minks, slinking foxes. 'Your take?'

'Pass,' said Ross. 'I'm feeling nauseous again.'

Accents of taupe and grey in the room were set against the predominant white. Wheeler looked inside the built-in wardrobe. Each article of clothing was hung properly on a hanger. Shoes had their own shoe trees. Above Michael O'Donnell's bed a framed picture of around fifty butterflies, their neatly pinned gossamer wings iridescent under the glass.

Paula's room had a couple of upturned crucifixes and many art prints. There was a purple bedspread, bright pink curtains and a wall of framed prints. 'It's a riot of colour. Matisse, Picasso, Braque and Derain,' said Wheeler. 'Looking at these prints, she has a love of Fauvism.'

'Fauvism?' asked Ross.

'Fauvism was a style used by early twentieth-century artists. *Les fauves* is French for "wild beasts".' She looked at the prints, recognised Kees van Dongen and Henri Matisse amongst others. 'Michael and Paula's rooms are so very different.'

'Isn't that the case with every parent of a teenager?' said Ross.

Wheeler glanced at a plastic pillbox on the table beside

Paula's bed. The duvet had been pulled back and, again, there was no sign of a struggle.

A large bright pink heavy chair sat resplendent beside the bookcase.

'The stand-out piece,' said Ross.

'It's a commode,' said a SOCO walking into the room. 'It's never been used. Perhaps the father feared that one day the daughter might not be able to make it to the loo?'

Wheeler knew the Missing Persons Network would have gone into overdrive and that Paula O'Donnell's photograph would have been circulated to every force and media source. She looked around the room. Was the garish pink of the commode a touching attempt by a father to make what might become a difficult situation for his daughter appear lighter, less depressing? Wheeler peered into the en suite. The wooden door had been heavily marked where something had been dragged through.

'I think those marks were made by her wheelchair. Some days she had little strength, other days she had more energy. By all accounts, looking at her living style, she had good days and bad days,' said the SOCO. 'I know, I have a son with a similar condition. It's very difficult for them. Very frustrating.'

Wheeler and Ross made their way through the house.

'This place is pristine,' said Ross. 'How do you manage to live with a teenager and still have such a pristine house? Even with a cleaner? I think we're looking at OCD. I think Michael or his daughter, Paula, or both, verged on the obsessive.'

Wheeler looked around the room. 'What is this place telling us, Ross?'

A young uniformed officer stood in the doorway.

'A neighbour has just given a statement. A Ms Abigail Hart says she spoke to Michael O'Donnell five days ago. Ms Hart has only just moved into the area and they got chatting in the local mini-mart. Her son is having liver trouble and Michael mentioned that Paula's liver was becoming damaged due to the severity of her medication and said that he'd been willing to offer to donate part of his liver to Paula. That's why he didn't drink alcohol.'

'Good work,' said Wheeler.

'I can't imagine giving anyone part of my liver,' said Ross.

'I'm not sure, given your drinking habits, that it would be much good to anyone,' said Wheeler. 'But if it was your kid?'

'Probably best that I don't have any,' said Ross.

Wheeler paused. 'Let's go back to the beginning. The cleaner discovered the body. She had a key to the house and let herself in. The door hadn't been forced.'

'Ms Hart mentioned that all four houses on this side are rented,' said the officer.

'Except for Michael O'Donnell's?' asked Wheeler.

'Yes. She's renting and wanted to vent about her landlord. Michael told her that his had been rented, some years back. The neighbour told me Michael had concerns regarding ex-tenants. Said something about how he'd always meant to change the lock, but it would mean replacing the door. Something about his kid loving the glass.'

'So maybe leasing agents and presumably former tenants all had keys?' said Wheeler. 'The place could be awash with them. And very difficult if not impossible to trace?'

'But surely former tenants would have had to return them?' asked the officer.

'They could easily have had copies made before handing back the originals,' said Wheeler. 'Let's get that checked.'

'I always made copies of keys when I rented,' said Ross. 'Especially when I was a student.'

'Because?' said Wheeler.

'To make sure I got my full deposit back at the end of the lease, no matter how much damage I'd caused.'

'How so?' asked the uniformed officer.

'If I didn't get my full deposit back, I'd take whatever amount was on offer then go back in and nick stuff and sell it at a car boot to make up the difference,' said Ross. 'Fair dos.'

'Geez. And you're the police,' said Wheeler. 'What hope is there?'

'Fair is fair,' said Ross, walking on. 'Fair is bloody fair.'

Wheeler looked at the young officer, gestured to Ross. 'For God's sake, don't go by his example.'

The officer smiled. 'I hear you, DI Wheeler. I hear you.'

Chapter 12

As they made their way towards the car, a perma-tanned blonde woman in her late twenties called to them. 'What's going on here?' She was holding the hand of a little boy, around four years old. She attempted to walk down the street, past the police cordon.

Wheeler blocked her path. 'There's no access. You can't go any further.'

'Says who?'

Wheeler flashed her ID. 'And you are?'

'Autumn De Luca, I live at number fifty-five. What's going on?'

'Did you know Michael O'Donnell and his daughter Paula?' asked Ross.

'My stepdaughter Tala attends the same college as Paula. The College of Visual Arts.' She glanced behind her. 'I thought Tala was just behind me. Honestly, that girl. Teenagers all have their moods, but this one has only the one. Grumpy.' She raised her voice. 'Bloody hell. Hurry up, Tala, for goodness sake!'

Wheeler watched a teenage girl dressed in black clothes, green Doc Martens boots and a scowl take a sharp left and keep walking. Whatever relationship Autumn De Luca had with her stepdaughter, it wasn't a good one.

'Tala!' shouted Autumn. 'Where the hell do you think you're going?'

Wheeler watched the girl begin to run, her black hair flying, her green boots hitting the snowy pavement. Wheeler noted that Tala didn't look back.

'She's up half the night and gets little to no sleep,' spat Autumn. 'She's on her bloody headphones all the time. She says that she's listening to music. Doesn't even know how a decent human being behaves.'

'Teenagers,' said Ross, trying for sympathy.

'Oh, that one's not just your average teenager. Tala's given me and her dad, Marc, no end of grief. One suicide attempt after another over the years.'

'I'm sorry, she sounds very troubled,' said Wheeler.

'Is she hell?' said Autumn. 'It's all just to do with her being a huge drama queen. Her so-called suicide attempts are all about manipulation. Tala has her dad wrapped around her little finger. Anything Tala wants, Tala gets.'

'Did you see anyone acting suspiciously in the area?' asked Wheeler, changing the subject. 'Anything unusual?'

'A couple of double glazing blokes were going door to door.' Autumn bit her lip, 'That's all. It's a quiet area. Pretty dead really.'

'Did you get the name of the company?' asked Wheeler.

'No, we have traditional sash windows. It wasn't worth my while.' She paused. 'Oh my God, why are you asking all this? Where's Michael? Bloody hell, is he dead? Or Paula? Shit. How . . . I mean, what happened?'

'We're just beginning the investigation. What can you tell me about Michael O'Donnell?'

'As I said, I didn't know him that well, but you know what he looked like. He was very attractive, and I'm married and my husband, Marc, works away.' Autumn faltered. 'And Marc isn't the most relaxed of husbands so for Michael and I to be friends, well, it would have been difficult. People gossip. You know what some folk are like.'

'Is there anything else you could tell us about Michael?' asked Ross.

'From what I know, he was pretty selfless. Michael devoted his life to his sick daughter. He told me that he had helped bring Paula into this world and the child would always have his support throughout his lifetime.'

'That was very noble of him,' said Ross.

'He did everything for her, he was such a devoted dad. Absolutely dedicated to her. He was always talking about her,' said Autumn. 'It got a boring, to be honest. He went on and on.'

'I thought you didn't know Michael O'Donnell well?' said Wheeler. She saw the woman blush.

'Oh no, I didn't know him well at all. But it was the common consensus, at least among the mothers around here, that he was that kind of a dad. Now, Tala's dad is the complete opposite, he insisted that she live with us and we pay everything for her, but he's often out of the country and I'm stuck with Tala. Not that she's grateful at all. I ask you, what kind of a daughter isn't grateful? Anyway, I'm not as soft as my husband, I've been strict with her. I'll sort her out.' She glanced behind her. 'The little rat's done a runner, hasn't she? Well, I'll make sure that she gets her comeuppance later.'

'And Paula?' asked Wheeler.

'I didn't know her well. Fragile girl.'

'Did Tala know her well? Can we have a chat with Tala later? Perhaps at the college, with the other students?'

'They never socialised much as far as I know. That said, Tala rarely even speaks to me.'

'Did you ever visit the O'Donnells at home?' asked Wheeler.

'Oh no, I've never been inside the house.' Autumn looked away. 'I certainly won't ever want to go into that place now.'

Wheeler watched Autumn De Luca's body language. 'Did Michael ever have occasion to come to your home?' she asked. She saw a faint blush. Heard the too quick answer.

'No, of course not. Why would he?' said Autumn. 'Don't be ridiculous, I'm a happily married woman.'

'We have to ask,' said Wheeler. 'I'm sure you understand.'

'Now, I need to go get Tala.' Autumn grasped the hand of the toddler and dragged him in the direction her stepdaughter had gone.

'Whatever the whole truth of the matter is,' said Wheeler turning to Ross, 'Autumn De Luca isn't telling it.'

'You reckon Autumn was one of Michael's "lady friends" that Mrs Payne referred to?'

'I wouldn't say it was a mile off the mark,' said Wheeler.

'Or a spurned lover?' said Ross.

'Uniform will get a statement and find out about her whereabouts when Michael O'Donnell was murdered.'

They walked towards the car.

'Autumn is full of anger and resentment,' said Wheeler.

'Certainly, she's not a natural stepmum for the kid who ran off.'

'Right, let's get back to the station.' Wheeler slammed the car door, heard the familiar sound of Ross whining.

'That bloody journalist is due in today. Why do we need someone shadowing us? I mean, it's pretty unprofessional. I think . . . '

She let him rant, tuned out. Understood that he was hungover and also that he felt protective of their colleagues and the old station. Knew that he sometimes just needed to vent. She thought again of the young girl who had run off. Wheeler thought of the case, wondered if Tala De Luca was somehow involved in it?

Chapter 13

Carmyle Police Station

Wheeler strode towards the doors of the station, sipping a hot drink. She and Ross had hastily grabbed coffees and a couple of pains au chocolate from a café on the way. If she were being honest, she'd stopped off mainly for Ross's sake. He looked pale and wan. Hungover wasn't the word for it. She wondered about his general health. She knew that he didn't cook, so often didn't eat well. Other than going to the gym, he wasn't great at self-care. Nevertheless, she enjoyed the caffeine hitting her system and the sugar rush from the pastry. The remnants of last night's party with the team were completely gone. Her early morning run had set her up and she felt focused and motivated. She glanced at Ross. 'How are you doing?'

'I'm still suffering. But the food is helping.' He finished the last of his pastry, scrunched up the paper bag and stuffed it into his pocket.

'You're not as young as you used to be, Ross.'

'I'll have you know, I'm in my prime, Wheeler.' He glanced at her. 'In case you hadn't noticed?'

She let the door go behind her. Ignored him as she took the stairs and made her way towards the incident room.

The team were gathered.

'First up, DI Wheeler if you could update us?' asked DCI Stewart.

'Boss.' She glanced up as the door opened and a figure stood in the doorway. He had changed and wore a smart fitting suit and tie, but his smile was still as broad.

Stewart spoke, 'Ah, here's Seb Hawk now. As we discussed, Police Scotland are excited to be contributing to a book about being a Police Scotland officer, more specifically being part of MIT and our ongoing changes. After the success of other true crime books, the powers that be agreed to a Scottish venture.

'This isn't professional,' Wheeler heard Ross mutter. 'This guy shouldn't be here.'

'Sour grapes, Ross?' said Boyd quietly. 'I know you probably want to be lead officer on this case, since you reckon you're the most handsome and therefore the most likely to have a part in the television series, should the book be optioned. That aside, the guy certainly does resemble Clooney, don't you think?'

Wheeler glanced at Ross, saw a blush begin at his neck and make its way up over his face.

Ross stared ahead. Said nothing.

Wheeler watched Hawk enter the room, keep his gaze on Ross a fraction too long. She wondered if they knew each other and how? If they had met already, why hadn't Ross mentioned it?

Stewart gestured for her to continue. She glanced at Hawk who was folding his considerable frame into one of the plastic chairs. She took out her notebook and cleared her throat. 'The victim's name is Michael O'Donnell. The body was found by the cleaner, Mrs Adele Payne, at around eight o'clock this morning, the signs point to Mr O'Donnell being dead for approximately fourteen to eighteen hours. The cause of death was knife wounds. The pathologist at the scene, Hannah Scott-Fletcher, thinks our victim was killed around lunchtime Saturday.' She carried on, filling in more details. She saw Hawk quickly taking notes.

'Any known motive?' asked Stewart.

'None, so far, boss. Scott-Fletcher says he was most likely killed quickly. The killer was strong enough to overpower the victim, who was around five foot nine.'

'Was there anyone else in the house at the time. Any witnesses?' asked Stewart.

'We think the daughter, Paula, was in the house. It was customary for her to go for a nap after lunch. She's epileptic with several complications arriving from this and is medication dependent. She is . . .' Wheeler paused '. . . at present missing from her home.'

'Not what we need right now,' said Robertson.

'What do we know about her?' asked Stewart.

'Her mother's name is Jayla, but we don't know her whereabouts or even if she is in the country. Paula attends the College of Visual Arts, the CoVA. As we know, it's a well-respected art college. Michael was a governor there. She is often frail but has good days and bad days. She is dependent on prescription drugs.'

'You think the killer abducted her after her father had been murdered?' said Stewart.

'Looks like it,' said Wheeler.

'Then get the media department onto this. I want an appeal out on the television ASAP.'

'She couldn't walk far on her own, some days. Muscle wastage was suggested by Mrs Payne. And Paula occasionally used a wheelchair.'

'Is it missing?' asked Stewart.

'It's still there,' said Wheeler.

'Could Paula have taken off?' asked Robertson. 'I mean with some help?'

'There are other days when she is more robust,' said Wheeler.

'What kind of a freak abducts a kid like that?' asked a uniformed officer.

'Absolutely,' said Wheeler.

'So, let me get this straight,' asked Hawk. 'Our killer rings the doorbell and when it's answered, kills Michael O'Donnell, then snatches the sleeping daughter, Paula, while completely drenched in blood and no one has seen anything? Is this for real?'

'Welcome to our world,' said Ross.

On the board were photographs of the layout of the murder scene. Michael O'Donnell's body was on the floor, the picture showed blood splatters, a soiled rug.

'Michael O'Donnell possessed a most unusual collection of artefacts, including inverted crucifixes in the house,' said Wheeler. 'There were many books and references to satanism in his home.'

'So, I see,' said Stewart, standing in front of the photographs. 'What the hell is going on here? Can someone please explain this to me?'

'They look like references to the occult or some satanic practice,' said Boyd.

'Michael O'Donnell practised the occult?' Stewart's voice had risen an octave.

'Not necessarily,' said Robertson. 'I think some of them may be references to a religious practice.'

'Go on,' said Wheeler.

'In the Roman Catholic tradition, the upturned cross can be a symbol of unworthiness. When Simon Peter was going to be crucified, he did not want to be killed in the same way as Christ as he felt unworthy.'

'Simon Peter?' asked Ross.

'One of the apostles,' said Robertson. 'He denied Christ.'

'Right,' said Ross.

'He felt that he was unworthy,' repeated Robertson.

'So, they crucified him upside down?' asked Ross.

'Yes,' said Robertson. 'It's referred to as the Petrine cross. Calling for people to reflect that they are unworthy in some way, or of something.'

'Request all CCTV from Hamilton Road and the roads in and out of the area,' said Stewart. 'I want it now.'

'It's already in the system, boss.'

'And there is a map in the house of a residence in Long Island,' said Wheeler.

'Amityville in Long Island,' said Ross.

'Relevance?' asked Stewart.

'I get it,' said Boyd. 'There was a mass killing there in the mid-seventies. Seems it was a haunted house afterwards. There's been quite a few movies made of it, about the whole good versus evil debate.'

'Does evil actually exist?' asked Robertson. 'Do you think?'

The room was silent.

Stewart cleared his throat, handed out the information and closed the briefing. 'We need to find this killer before he or she kills again. And we need to find Paula O'Donnell. Right, team, let's get to it.'

Wheeler stood. The energy in the room was charged. Everyone looked motivated. Only one person sat, head down, scribbling quietly. Seb Hawk.

Chapter 14

Telling herself that she wasn't going to die. Knowing that she was going to. She watched the dog as it worked quickly. Carefully. The syringe slipped in effortlessly. God knows what it was injecting into her. Who was this person and why were they doing this? The radio was on in the background and chattering voices filled the room. Then it cut to music. An old Christmas classic, about having a Very Merry Christmas. Then another one, something about a Marshmallow World. It made her want to cry but her eyes felt dry and itchy. She looked out of the window. Outside, it felt like the woodland was closing in on her. She felt her body limp, pliable. Cuffs on each wrist linked to the bedhead, the same with her ankles and the bottom of the bed. She'd stared at the dog through a fog of medication. She hated it. Why wouldn't it just let her die? She felt herself slip into the fog again, heard herself begin to talk to ghosts from her past, pleading with them. Heard her voice move to childlike when she had called to her mother. Miss Myrtyle, an old teacher at her primary school. She remembered that Miss Myrtyle had organised the nativity play. Sitting on the floor of the classroom, in the dark. Miss Myrtyle shining a light onto the plaster wall of the classroom, a guiding star. They'd then begun to sing 'Silent Night'. She drained her list of comforting memories and beseeched the walls to rid her of the awful puppet shapes dancing across them. Shapes that included her death. Shapes she knew that she could not control. A puppet master out of sync, devoid of meaning. She struggled to control her thoughts as they slid and slipped around her mind, colliding and merging and making no sense at all except to remind her that she was dying.

And that calling out for help was hopeless.

Chapter 15

Nick and Hudson

'Hurry up for God's sake,' said Hudson. 'I'm absolutely freezing. I could catch hypothermia.'

Nick fished in his jeans pocket for the house key. 'I've got it here somewhere, Hud. Quit complaining. You always exaggerate.'

'I don't.'

'You do,' said Nick. 'And by the way, as a satanist, should you be invoking the name of the Lord?'

'Right, be a smart arse then.'

'Besides it's Christmas,' said Nick. 'The weather has to be seasonal.'

'Fuck that.'

'You are such a romantic, Hud.'

'But, honestly, what I said earlier is true. I swear, it's the God's honest truth. I am not a virgin now. I'm telling you.' Hudson tried and failed for gravitas. 'Honest to God, Nick.'

'I don't believe you, Hud.'

'How's that then? Why would I lie, Nick? Tell me?'

'You never could lie effectively, you're hopeless,' said Nick. 'Your face gives it away, plus your tone of voice is so awestruck at the thought of getting with a girl, it's like you're rehearsing a part in a film or a play. Add to that you think that you're a bloody satanist.'

'I fucking am so. I'm a real satanist.'

'Yet you live at home with your mum and a new stepdad? Hardly diabolical.'

'It's too expensive to get a flat.'

'Not if you're in league with the devil, surely?'

'I told Simon Wardyke,' Hudson huffed, 'and he believed me.'

Nick turned the key in the lock. 'Simon Wardyke is an idiot. And a virgin. You two just trade juvenile fantasies.'

'I'm hurt,' said Hudson.

'You'll get over it,' said Nick.

Hudson glanced nervously around the room. 'Is your mum home?'

'No chance, mate, you wouldn't be here otherwise. She's still off having some downtime with Auntie Maria.'

'Didn't know your mum had a sister.'

'She doesn't, Maria's a close pal of Mum's. I've always just called her my auntie.'

'Your mum hates me.' Hudson opened his rucksack, took out a can of beer. Held it up to Nick. 'Cheers.'

'Cheers, Hud, but I can't contradict you there about Mum, except that you have given her cause.' He walked through to the living room.

'She hates that I'm a satanist. That I'm a rebel.' Hudson opened the can, sipped his beer. 'I'm really out there.'

'She doesn't bloody know that you even think all that shit. To her, you're just a wee boy.'

'She hates me. Us outsiders are very put upon. My religion engenders both hate and loathing. I even tried to get a satanist group going at the CoVA but nothing doing. We are doomed to be eternally the outsiders.'

'Shit.' Nick laughed. 'It's fuck all to do with that.'

'Then what?'

'Remember when Mum caught you smoking spliffs in my room while I was in the shower? I mean, come on.'

'It didn't do any harm.' Hudson sniffed. 'Christ, Beelzebub wouldn't have cared.'

'Mum hates all that dope shit,' said Nick. 'And again bringing Christ into it?'

'I can't smoke at home,' complained Hudson.

'You can hardly breathe at home. You should have a wee word in Beelzebub's ear about that. About just how controlling your mum is.'

'It only started after Dad killed himself,' said Hudson.

'I know,' said Nick, 'but your mum has to let you grow up.'

'You're telling me? I bloody live with the nightmare that is my mother and the idiot of a stepfather.'

'Sorry, Hud.' Nick's voice was soft.

'How are you going to afford art school in Brighton?' asked Hudson, changing the subject. 'You said that you were worried about finances?'

'I'll manage, Hud. Student debt like everyone else.'

'OK, mastermind, I'll tell you another way.' Hudson was suddenly animated. 'Maybe you could sell your young and virile body? I was reading on this website about male escorts and the money they rake in. And I thought that maybe I could—'

Nick cut across his friend. 'You're a dreamer, Hud. You'll end up getting a job in our local McDonald's and settling down here. You'll never leave this place.'

'I might do.' Hudson sniffed.

'What did you think of the gig last night?' asked Nick.

'Fucking phenomenal,' said Hudson. 'The Rubes are incredible. What says you?'

'I wanted to be up there on the stage.'

'In a band?' said Hudson. 'Up there with Madison De La Fontaine and the rest of them?'

'No, as an artist. I want to be big, like Damien Hirst or Tracey Emin.'

'You think you can make it? They seem to be at the top of their game. There's not much money in art for the rest of the pile.'

'But some artists do make it and they make a fortune,' said Nick.

'It's true, though, isn't it? I mean, financially, if you made it, you could get the Porsche. How awesome! I'd sell my soul to the devil if it would get me Tala De Luca's attention.'

'You're a dreamer,' said Nick. 'But since you're a satanist, why not just ask Beelzebub for a Porsche? Or exchange your soul for a date with Tala?'

'Tala's gorgeous. Her arse in jeans is a truly lovely thing. That right there is the one and only reason that I know there is a God.'

'Don't you mean Beelzebub?'

'Yeah, whatever.' Hudson sulked.

'You just said you'd been with someone,' said Nick. 'Aren't you loyal to Tala?'

Hudson blushed.

'Liar.'

Hudson's blush deepened.

'What age are you?' laughed Nick.

'Old enough to be in love with Tala De Luca. Badly.'

'No wonder my mum hates you. All these lies.'

'She thinks I'm going to—' Hudson adopted a baby sing-song voice '—corrupt her little baby boy.'

Nick playfully shoved him through to the dining room. 'Fuck you, nutter. We're here to study remember. I need to get a decent grade if I'm to get into Brighton.'

'You only want to go to see the ladies do naked life modelling,' said Hudson.

'Not at art school they don't, perv. What century are you living in?'

'Mr Van Der Berg says you should go into IT. You're shit-hot at it and it's the way forward.'

'You're the IT dude, Hud, you should go for it. You could control us all by your sinister online presence.'

'Who says I'm not doing that already?' laughed Hudson.

'True. But art it is, my boy, for me. The University of Brighton beckons.' Nick strode ahead. 'My future.' He paused. 'And you?'

'I'd go to art school if I could.' Hudson looked at the floor. 'If my stuff was deemed to be good enough.'

'You'd never make it as an artist,' said Nick. 'It takes resilience.'

'OK then, I'll stick with IT and controlling folk via the net.' Hudson opened a packet of salt and vinegar crisps. 'I meant to ask, what did you do with the fox cub you rescued?'

'I called the SSPCA, the animal rescue place over by Cardonald as a start.'

'Is it going to be OK?'

'I think so. They said that they would contact the wild-life section, and someone would be on it. You worried?'

Nick stared at his friend. 'Hudson? Are you coming over all sensitive on me now?'

'Shut it. The psycho Roach twins are going to come after you. You know that, don't you? They put it all on Facebook, they are threatening you with—'

'Forget about the bloody idiot Roach twins. I saw one of them at the Rubes gig last night. He was totally out of his mind. Shit-faced drunk. Besides, they're complete arseholes.'

'I prefer the more accurate definition of psychopath,' said Hudson.

'Let's get started,' said Nick. 'We need to get results.'

'*You* need to get results,' said Hudson. 'Though I reckon you're going to get the bursary award from Francesco Soule, for the most promising student.'

'Yeah, right,' said Nick.

'Your work is pretty outstanding,' said Hudson. 'Although, to be fair . . . '

Nick paused. 'Go on.'

'I think that Tala's is better.'

'You would, muppet.'

'But it is, isn't it?'

'Let's get to work,' said Nick. 'Whoever gets Francesco Soule's bursary is one lucky bastard.'

Two hours later and the art homework had been completed, Nick had amassed copious amounts of notes and Hudson had maybe a page and a half of scrawl that even he couldn't decipher. Nick was well on his way to completing his portfolio, the images required for the selection process and his 250-word statement on artists who had influenced him, the challenges he faced and how to resolve them. Hudson on the other hand had mainly googled football results and had watched his favourite bands on YouTube while finishing multiple packets of crisps. Either way, both believed that they had had a productive couple of hours.

Chapter 16

Carmyle Police Station

Boyd stood in the doorway. 'Anything I can get you, Wheeler?'

She looked up from scanning the statements. 'If you could arrange for DI Ross to get his arse in here that would be great.'

'I'm afraid that's not possible.'

'Because?'

'He's not answering his mobile. I've already left two messages for him.'

'I'd appreciate it if you could find a way to get him here. It is after all his bloody job.'

'In the absence of being able to deliver Ross, what about a coffee?' asked Boyd.

'Black, I need the caffeine hit.' Wheeler turned back to the paperwork. Uniform had amassed a pile of statements from neighbours. The agency had provided them with a list of all carers who had seen Paula over the years.

'Poor little Paula never remembered having the seizures, just that she felt a bit peculiar. It was her dad who watched over her . . . he kept her safe. The poor man was terrified that she'd fall and hit her head during a seizure. He was at his wits' end. He recorded everything about the seizures, the time of day they happened, if there was anything which triggered them. If she said anything or made any noise at all during them. The trouble was, her symptoms would change all the time. Sometimes she would be stiff and her movements jerky . . . at other times she'd be as floppy as a rag doll. Then, at other time, she'd be robust.'

'After the seizure Paula only ever wanted to go to bed and lie down. Sometimes he'd have to carry her up the stairs. I think he felt guilty because he thought that somehow . . . he or his wife had passed on a faulty gene to Paula . . . that she had inherited the condition . . . Michael did everything he could for her . . . even kept her on special diets, think it was the ketogenic diet . . . Ate it with her. The poor man loved food and almost never got to treat himself. She wasn't so happy either. What kid is, not being able to eat what all your friends are eating? Who wouldn't want a McDonald's or a KFC? Some days, Paula looked ready to faint, on others, quite resilient.'

Boyd put a mug of coffee in front on her.

'Thanks.' She read through another report.

Five minutes later, Boyd put his head around the door. 'The handyman has arrived, I'll sit in with you.'

'Give me a sec.' Wheeler sipped the coffee, grabbed her notebook. Uniform had spoken to as many carers as possible, but there had been the usual omissions – people on holiday, off sick and unaccounted for. Plus, there were casual staff who had done the odd day here and there. Wheeler wondered how many people had access to Michael O'Donnell's house. He had done so much to care for his daughter yet still had to rely on many carers over the years. Carers, flexible hours: Aneta Kowalski, Maureen Haig, both had been discounted. She also put a line through another name. Rachal Reid, care assistant, available Saturday to Sunday and bank holidays, was in Ibiza. A hen do had gone awry and the flight home had been missed. She'd called her mum, who in turn had let the station know.

Wheeler flicked to different notes. Vladimir Nazarewich was a handyman in the local community. Vladimir, she read in a hand-scrawled note 'had a bit of an issue with authority'. She recalled what the cleaner, Adele Payne, had said about him: 'It's his eyes, yellow-brown in colour like a cheetah, like he's ready to spring.' Wheeler closed her notebook. Now she would have a chance to meet with him herself.

Boyd stood in the doorway. 'You ready?'

'Yep.' She made her way to the interview room.

Vladimir Nazarewich stood up, he towered over her. He offered her his hand. Firm grip. He made eye contact easily, his eyes were an unusual shade of amber. He wore a heavy crucifix around his neck, the cross the usual way up. Wheeler nodded for him to sit. Wondered if it was the man's height and bulk that had so unsettled Michael O'Donnell's cleaner?

She began the interview.

He answered quickly. Yes, he'd known Michael and Paula O'Donnell. He did odd jobs around the area.

'You've been to their home, you had access to their house?'

'Yes. I went for work, I'd helped Michael with his drains, but in my spare time we played chess. Michael was a great lover of chess. At one time I played for my country. He asked if I could improve his game, if I'd be willing to come and play sometimes, when Paula was upstairs asleep. Maybe we'd have a drink or two. We usually had a game ongoing.'

'I saw an unfinished game in his home,' said Wheeler.

'Probably ours,' said Vlad.

'Did you visit often?'

'I went around maybe six or seven times in the past three months and we played for hours. It seemed like he was desperate for me to teach him all I knew. It wasn't about the malt whisky or the chess for me, it was about the belonging. About being accepted as an equal. I felt like he saw me as more than a hired help to improve his game.'

'And what about Paula?' asked Wheeler.

'I rarely saw her. The first time I visited she was at the window when I walked up the drive. She waved. Of course, I waved back. That happened a few times. She seemed like a sickly princess in an ivory tower. No, she was never downstairs when I visited. I never spoke to her. Occasionally, an ambulance would just be leaving as I arrived.'

'How many people would have access to the O'Donnells' house recently?'

'I've no idea,' said Vlad. 'There were people installing a ramp for Paula's wheelchair and some modifications for the bathroom and wider doors to accommodate it. Nothing unusual. Michael told me that he was worried she might not have the strength to coordinate turning her wheelchair; she tried, Michael said, but got frustrated and wouldn't let him help. I don't know how many folk have been in and around the house. There were quite a few carers.'

'Where were you when Michael was killed?' asked Wheeler.

'I see, so I'm now a suspect? A killer, DI Wheeler? Michael was my friend. He treated me as an equal.'

'Mr Nazarewich, I'm only asking a question,' said Wheeler.

His hand up, palm facing her. 'Leave it. Please. I am used to this approach.'

'I'm sorry? I don't understand,' said Wheeler. 'We are interviewing everyone about this, irrespective of—'

'Their country of birth?'

'Their association with the victim,' said Wheeler. 'It's our job.'

'I help the residents of this community in Mount Vernon, every day. I go out of my way to be helpful. But then the Brexit vote comes in and all I hear is "Bloody foreigners, they need to go back", "Immigrants are no good". That is what I am hearing.'

Wheeler listened.

'And when I say that I am an immigrant they shrug and say, "But you are OK, Vlad, you should stay. It's the rest of them that should be turfed out. The scroungers. But how can this be, DI Wheeler? How can they decide that? It feels like everything I've done has been in vain, all the shit I've taken, all the good I've tried to do. For what? Not to be integrated as Scottish or British but still to be a foreigner. And now a man is dead, my chess-playing friend Michael O'Donnell and you point the finger of suspicion at me.'

'Mr Nazarewich, we're asking everyone who knew them,' said Boyd quietly. 'And if you would be good enough to tell me where you were when Michael was murdered?'

'Are you really asking me if I killed Michael and abducted Paula?' asked Vlad. 'You cannot be serious.'

Wheeler saw a flash of anger and impatience in his eyes; she held his gaze.

'It never changes, does it? I am never accepted. I am always the outsider. I saw Michael on the Thursday evening.'

'Then you were one of the last people to see him alive.'

'And he was alive when I left him on Thursday evening. And Paula was upstairs, as far as I know.'

'You saw her?' asked Wheeler.

'No, but Michael alluded to it. We played chess. I had a glass of malt whisky and then I left early.'

'What time?'

'Around nine.'

'And how did he seem to you?'

'He seemed a little uptight. Jittery. He was quite a fastidious guy, he liked to control things. I think he felt that his daughter's condition was out of his control, so he sought to balance this with having everything else in order. He was very concerned with cleanliness.'

She waited.

'Then I went home. I was alone.' He looked at Wheeler. 'And I resent this. I am an innocent citizen. Why are you trying to make me look guilty? I would like to suggest insensitivity at best and casual racism at worst.'

Boyd leaned forward. 'Sir, we are asking everyone about their whereabouts on the days around when Michael O'Donnell was killed and his daughter went missing, not just you.'

'Are you Scottish?' asked Vlad.

'Yes,' said Boyd.

Vlad turned to Wheeler. 'And you, DI Wheeler?'

'This is not important,' she said.

'Oh, but I'm afraid that it is. How can you possibly know what my life is like and what I am going through?' He paused. 'You have no idea. None. Am I free to go?'

'Of course,' said Wheeler. 'But if there is anything else you can tell us, anything at all which might help us find the killer, I would appreciate it.'

'No,' said Vlad. 'I knew very little about Michael O'Donnell.'

'If there's anything at all you could tell us?' repeated Boyd.

Vlad paused. 'Then perhaps you need to be asking Michael's girlfriend.'

'Do you have a name?' asked Wheeler.

'I don't know her name, he only alluded to her once and by accident. I think they met at the college.'

'The College of Visual Arts?' said Wheeler.

'I got the impression that she may be a lecturer at the CoVA,' said Vlad. He stood to leave. 'I've done my best for Michael. Now I must go back to work.'

'Can I ask you about the upturned crucifixes or crosses in their home?' asked Wheeler.

'They are not to my taste.' He paused at the door. 'To be honest, they were an insult to my beliefs.'

After he had gone, she turned to Boyd. 'Your take on him?'

'I thought that he was edgy and defensive. I didn't like his attitude. Plus, we know that he has a problem with authority.'

'In all fairness,' said Wheeler, 'so do you, Boyd. And just remember the pub quiz at the White Hart. All that new-speak versus old-speak language. And the authority-bashing humour?'

Boyd ignored her and opened the door. Held it for her.

'But a killer?' She sailed through it.

'I don't know,' said Boyd. 'Your take on him?'

'He had no motive,' said Wheeler. 'As far as we know.'

'A grudge?' said Boyd. 'Some perceived slight from Michael O'Donnell? Certainly, after a very polite interview, Vlad wanted to suggest racism. I reckon he's on a very short fuse.'

Wheeler took the stairs two at a time. 'Let's just keep an eye on Vladimir Nazarewich.'

In the incident room the phone rang. Boyd answered, leaned over the desk and grabbed a pen. 'No, he's not here. Can I take a message?' He jotted down a name and number.

Wheeler flicked on the kettle. 'Anything important?'

'A Mrs Marilyn Hawk, Seb's wife. She was just trying to get hold of him.'

'Let's get back to work,' said Wheeler. 'Michael O'Donnell, who appears to be a hero, is getting lost. Let's dig deeper. Who was he involved with and who wanted him dead? And who the hell is this girlfriend from the CoVA, who hasn't come forward?'

Robertson put down the phone. 'Despite the college having something called a "special working Sunday", seems the college principal, Helen McSweeney, has called for the CoVA to be closed as a mark of respect for the missing student. "As a college with a Christian ethos, I feel that this is the right thing to do," is how she phrased it.'

'So, what happens if you're not Christian?' asked a uniformed officer. She was the rookie officer, noted Wheeler.

Wheeler ignored the comment. 'Call Principal McSweeney back, request that all staff remain on the premises until I get there.'

'Ross is on his way,' said Boyd. 'Said he'll be here in ten minutes.'

'About bloody time,' said Wheeler. 'When he eventually arrives, we'll get over to the CoVA, hopefully get a name and speak to Michael O'Donnell's girlfriend. In the meantime—'

'In the meantime,' said Boyd interrupting her, 'here are the contact details for the people who called in demanding only to speak to the detective inspector in charge.'

'About what?' said Wheeler.

'No idea. They wouldn't discuss it with some poor lowlife like me.' Boyd winked at her.

Wheeler picked up the phone and began to make the calls. She was glad of the second coffee Boyd had brought her.

Ten minutes and she'd heard a familiar refrain:

'Michael O'Donnell was a selfless man, nothing short of a saint . . . He adored little Paula.'

'No, he wouldn't have had any enemies, why would he?'

But no one had mentioned the girlfriend and, when questioned, they had seemed incredulous.

'He lived for little Paula. Of course, a man who looked like he did was bound to be of interest to women, but he was a devoted dad. He dedicated his life to her. They were inseparable.'

'Oh my God, this is just so awful. What a nightmare. Michael dead and his little daughter missing. My heart goes out to little Paula. If there's anything I can do to help? Anything at all?'

And then, there were the others, who had nothing to do with Michael O'Donnell.

'I live in Tollcross Road and I want to complain about graffiti which is defacing our area. It's spelled "dEADdOG".'

'I want to complain, in the loudest way possible, about the awful graffiti that is being sprayed in our area, Downfield Street. It's about a **dead dog** and it's an eyesore and I'm trying to sell my flat and it's been sprayed on my garden fence. I want you to do something about it, now! The value of my property is going down and . . . '

'I didn't know the O'Donnells at all, but I'm psychic and I like to think that I am an intuitive person and can help with your investigation. Clairvoyants are very much underrated and I feel that . . . '

Wheeler had reassured all concerned that they were dealing with Michael's murder and that Paula's disappearance was being handled by Missing Persons and that the whole of Police Scotland were aware of the situation. She put the phone down after the umpteenth call. 'A bloody waste of time. Folk moaning about graffiti. Some bloody dead dog shit.'

Seb Hawk stood behind her. 'Who does the Mis Persons? Is there inter-agency liaison?'

'Boyd can sort you out with the details, but yes, the agency has all the information we have on Paula. And, of course, we liaise.'

Hawk drew a chair to her desk, settled himself. 'You mind if I listen in on your chat?'

Wheeler stood, grabbed her coat. 'I'm heading out to the CoVA. Apparently, they have a special working Sunday. You can shadow Boyd.'

Ross walked in. 'I'm just going to have a quick coffee first.'

'No, you're not.' Wheeler strode to the door. 'You're with me.'

'By the way—' Boyd turned to Hawk '—your wife Marilyn just called. She wants you to call her back ASAP.'

Wheeler left, with Ross following quickly behind. As Ross passed Hawk, he stared hard at the journalist.

'Wait up, Wheeler,' said Robertson, looking up from his computer. 'A Jayla O'Donnell committed suicide some years back. Gunshot wound.'

'Get me everything you have,' said Wheeler making her way down the corridor.

Lovers' Tryst #1

8 months earlier

I specifically asked her to help me and she refused. Again. She is colluding with him. She's a colluding bitch.

I know.

She likes to have power over me. She thinks they have it all. They don't.

You have the power.

We do.

Together.

Together.

You know the plan.

Yes.

And?

Game on.

Chapter 17

Nick

She still hadn't contacted him. Nick sent his third text to his mother. 'How goes it, Mum? You around?'

Nothing.

He heard his stomach growl. 'Hud, you want some food?'

'I'm starved,' said Hudson. 'Absolutely famished.'

'Again, with the exaggeration,' said Nick. 'You devoured the crisps I gave you.'

'Truth told, I feel kind of faint, maybe low blood sugar?' said Hudson. 'I think I may possibly be anaemic.'

'Burger and oven chips, OK for you?'

'Make it cheesy chips and I'll get some more cans.' Hudson made for the door. 'Plus, I'll get us a cake for dessert. My treat.'

'That's a first.' Nick spoke to the closing door. He walked through to the kitchen, a list of numbers were on the wall. He looked up Maria Brothcotte, his mum's best friend. Called her. It was answered on the fourth ring.

'Hi, Auntie Maria, it's Nick. How are you doing?'

'I'm good, lovely, how's you? I haven't seen you in ages. How's the studying going? Your mum told me that you're

108

off to art school soon. Brighton, isn't it? You going to be the next Picasso and make your mum a fortune?'

'I'll do my best, Auntie Maria.'

'Good for you, son. Aren't you at the CoVA today? I heard they're having a special working Sunday?'

'I'm working at home,' said Nick.

'Fair enough.'

'I just wanted to have a quick word with Mum, if that's OK?'

A pause. 'She's not here, love.'

'Where is she?' said Nick.

'How would I know?'

'I thought she was with you?' said Nick.

'I haven't seen her since last week, when we both attended Simone's hen night at Arta.'

'She said you two were having a girls' night out last night. And she's staying over tonight.'

'First, I heard of it, love.'

'Said she'd be home tomorrow but would call by lunchtime today.'

'Did she?'

'Where do you think Mum is then?'

The question hung in the air.

'Ah,' said Nick, 'the penny has just dropped.'

'Go on, love.'

'You reckon she's out on a date and didn't want to tell me, 'cause of what dad did to the guy the last time?'

'Could be, Nick. Better safe than sorry. I'm sure she'll be back soon. Hopefully having had some fun. You got something to eat?'

'Yeah, I've just put on some chips and a burger. Plus, Hudson's here.'

'Hudson? Your mum mentioned that waste of space, you want me to come over?'

'No, you're all right. I probably misheard her about her plans, I don't listen to everything she says.'

He heard Maria laugh. 'She did mention that the last time we spoke.'

'Speak to you soon, Auntie Maria.'

'Nick.' She paused. 'I need to tell you that your mum and I had a bit of a falling-out.'

'She never mentioned it.'

'We're not talking. When we were at Arta, we just avoided each other. I'll fill you in some time. Love you, Nick.'

'Love you too.' He ended the call. Took out two plates, cutlery. Tried to focus on food. Put the oven on and put the chips and burgers on trays.

Ten minutes later, Hudson appeared in the doorway clutching more beer and an out-of-date chocolate cake.

'Tell me your mum isn't on her way back?'

Nick updated him. 'She lied to me about being with Auntie Maria. They had a falling-out and aren't talking.'

'You reckon your mum had to lie to you because of what your old man did before?' said Hudson.

'Could be.'

'Either way, she's due back some time tomorrow?'

'Yeah,' said Nick, 'some time.'

'Then you can ask her what she's been up to.' Hudson sipped his beer. 'Yeah, she'll be busted this time. Lying to you.'

'I hope she's enjoying herself. She needs to get her life back.' Nick took out the grater and a thick block of cheddar cheese. 'Cheesy chips, Hud, how come they always make me feel better?'

Hudson sipped his beer. 'You're not worried about her, are you?'

"Course not,' said Nick quietly.

'She's a grown adult out there having a good time. She's probably on a date with some hot dude. Thought she'd keep it to herself.'

'Yeah, I expect so.' Nick began grating the cheese. He felt the reassuring hard punch to the shoulder which had, since their days at primary school, been Hudson's way of showing any emotional support.

Chapter 18

The CoVA

The College of Visual Arts was situated in the east end of Glasgow. It sat in its own grounds, close to Dalbeth Cemetery. Historically, the college had once been part of a grand estate owned by a prominent Glaswegian family. Now, the mansion and some of the land had been transformed into a college for local students. The college took in students who had left school and wished to continue their journey as an artist. The CoVA created pioneering art courses which helped the students prepare for art school. The college did this through teaching, group critique, study visits and self-development/expression. The students created a portfolio of work and deepened their own practice while exploring collaborative working. This prepared them for art school.

Wheeler and Ross drove up the driveway.

'This place must have cost a fortune to build,' said Ross.

'Apparently the Art Space is part of what was originally a Grade II-listed oak-framed former coach house,' said Wheeler.

'Yeah, it feels historic,' said Ross.

'The original part of the building dates from the fifteenth century,' said Wheeler.

'The rest of it is an add-on?' said Ross. 'Like our parking at the station?'

'Yep, apart from a million pound makeover to get it up to speed,' said Wheeler. 'So, not anything like our bloody dilapidated station.'

'You reckon Carmyle Station will fold?' asked Ross quietly. 'It's on the cards.'

'Maybe,' said Wheeler. 'There just isn't the money to keep it going. Plus, it's a bloody wreck of a building.'

'Lucky students here then, to have all this,' said Ross.

'Yes,' said Wheeler, 'but we were pretty lucky to do our police training at Tulliallan.'

'True,' said Ross. 'Training at Tulliallan Castle was pretty cool.'

Inside the CoVA, once they had manoeuvred their way past a prickly receptionist, they went to the principal's office. Helen McSweeney sat at her desk. She was mid-fifties, a small, solid woman with an unusually broad face and short hair.

'I've already spoken to you officers. I'm afraid I can't be more helpful. But I did as you requested. Everyone was happy to stay back, out of respect for Michael. We've had a great response. Only one member of staff insisted on teaching her class.'

'Thank you,' said Wheeler.

'Our students are very upset about this. I am fraught about the impact it may have on their art. In particular, two of our students, the Roach twins, who have had an exemplary year and are set for great things. I fear that they may be too sensitive. They are also models and I believe they have ambitions in that direction but their art is in the same vein as the great Yves Klein or Andy Warhol. Have you see their work?'

'No,' said Wheeler.

'Look.'

They followed her to a wall. Tiny images of the twins' shirtless torsos set in blue paint covered the space.

'You see, they undress and cover their bodies with paint and then they press themselves onto the paper, literally embossing it with their bodies.'

'Right,' said Ross. 'So they just love themselves?'

'Nonsense! It is in the way that the great Yves Klein worked with his "Anthropométries". But with a new, modern, spin. They photograph their paintings, go digital and recreate the images dozens of times. They are both absolutely fabulous artists. Wonderful! And Tala De Luca, another of our students, is also a wonderful artist. I have high hopes for Tala. Even Paula O'Donnell. Her work is incredible. Such vigour. Of course, she has good and bad days, but don't we all? Or her good days, she has such energy! And her art is so very robust.'

'That's not the impression I had of Paula,' said Wheeler.

'No? Well, look at her work. Don't you see the passion? The vigour?' McSweeney paused. 'All of these students are capable of achieving great things.'

Wheeler studied the canvases.

A half hour later and it appeared that Principal McSweeney had told them nothing new. Or at least nothing that would help them with the case.

'This has all been such a worry,' said McSweeney. 'I almost feel that I cannot continue with my own art, my sculpture. And yet, like most artists, I have a deadline to work to.' She crossed to a small sculpture in the corner of her office. 'My latest work *Woman*. It's an exploration of what it means to be a female in our patriarchal society.'

'It's very strong,' said Wheeler.

'Yes,' said McSweeney, 'strong is what I want our students to be. Both Paula O'Donnell and Nick Price applied to Brighton to study art. They would need to be robust to complete the course. As will our students who are applying to Glasgow, Edinburgh, further afield and overseas. They need to find their strength as their art will be criticised. It is the way of it. But sadly, Paula was forced to withdraw her application due to ill health. She was devastated, but her father, Michael, had been quite insistent. He was adamant that she simply couldn't cope with the rigours of art school. Especially one that neces-sitated her living away from home. You see, he didn't believe she could cope without his support. I thought the news might finally break her. And now, of course, with all this tragedy . . . ' She shook her head. 'Awful, just awful.'

Two hours later, they had spoken to all members of staff. 'The cult of the lovely Michael O'Donnell doesn't seem to have spread universally across the college.' Wheeler walked ahead of Ross.

'And Paula seems to be a little spoilt from a few com-ments. So, they are real people not saints after all,' said Ross. 'Although I think the staff were careful not to bad-mouth them too much, seeing as how one is missing, and the other one is dead.'

Wheeler read her notes aloud. 'From Mr Haggerty, Art

History Lecturer, specialising in Modern and Contemporary Visual Art: "Well, Michael was just so arrogant. I mean, I too have a child who has epilepsy. My daughter, Annilese. But could I advise Michael on anything? Could I whit? No offence, and, of course, I'm sorry that he's dead, but the arrogance of the man was breathtaking. Him and his meticulous notes about her diet and theories on her illness.

'Another lecturer, Mrs McCall, Art History Lecturer, specialising in Renaissance Art: "Michael was difficult . . . he was extremely good with Paula, regarding her illness. However, he tended towards interfering when we as tutors encouraged her to push her work in certain directions. I mean, as far as I know, he wasn't a trained artist or an art historian?"

'"Michael was very good-looking but full of it . . . " Mr Balkan, specialising in American Neo-Pop Art. "Really, he was an arrogant sonofabitch. Paula was not a nice girl, granted she had some very special needs but even so . . . unpleasant and demanding. I think she got that from her father. She became much more irritable after she had to withdraw her application to Brighton."'

'What about her tutor?' asked Ross.

'Assistant Principal Robin Kirkpatrick? He's off sick. An accident. I have a note of his return date.'

'So, they weren't necessarily very popular at all, which completely contradicts what the neighbours and Mrs Payne suggested,' said Ross.

Wheeler stretched her arms. 'And no one is admitting to being in a relationship with Michael.'

'You think one of them is lying? That the girlfriend murdered him?' asked Ross. 'And abducted Paula?'

'Let's go see our rebel. The lecturer who insisted on taking her class, she should just about be finishing up.'

The secretary pointed them in the direction of the class where Ms Janine Barnes Olsen was just finishing her lecture.

'You see, the process I follow . . .' Barnes Olsen paused, addressing her students ' . . . the process that I insist on following, to create, is extremely organic. It necessitates that I draw on the elements, the water from the River Clyde, the Glasgow rain, the wind and sleet and snow. All these things combine with the essence of the colour, that is the original pigment. Once I am in the right psychological state, I cast the paint onto the wet canvas, I roll it, stamp on it, cherish it with my hands, pummel it with my fists before leaving it naked and alone to the elements. In many ways, it is like giving birth.' She stood, triumphant. 'Now, you may leave. And remember to go create some unique art. This is a unique Sunday!'

Wheeler and Ross waited while notebooks and pens were packed away, heard the scraping of chair legs as the students stood and filed out through the doorway. Some of them looking back, taking in the sight of another two visitors to the college. Uniformed officers had been there since Michael O'Donnell's murder. They were still compiling information about Paula, the beautiful, fragile girl who had now become the talk of the campus. Wheeler had requested that the officers pay particular attention to information concerning Tala De Luca.

Wheeler watched Janine Barnes Olsen gather her notes. She was small, around five foot one, dark hair cut into an expensive-looking pixie cut. She wore a fitted purple silk dress, patent knee-high boots. Wheeler noted the outsize designer glasses, the distinctive interlocking Cs. Chanel. A long black pearl necklace, again with the double C hung from Barnes Olsen's neck. Whatever the College of Visual Arts was paying Janine Barnes Olsen, Wheeler doubted that it would cover her designer jewellery.

Ross coughed.

Barnes Olsen peered at him over her glasses. 'May I help you?'

Wheeler recognised an Edinburgh accent.

They showed their ID, introduced themselves.

'You don't need to speak with me. I've already spoken to two of your uniformed colleagues. A police presence has been at the college since the tragedy. Your colleagues have asked if I knew Paula's mother, the deceased Jayla. I did not. Principal McSweeney advised us to cancel our classes. I disagreed. It's simply not good enough for the other students to miss out on their coursework just because there has been a death and Paula is missing. Most of our students are applying for art school and need to get decent grades. They simply cannot miss out. It's very unfair. We have these lovely working Sundays. Also, the college has employed additional counsellors, should any of the students need ongoing support. However, I am not heartless, Paula was very well thought of, as was Michael. You probably know that he was a governor?'

'Yes, we do.' Wheeler took a seat. 'And we know that he and someone at the college were close.'

'I see,' said Barnes Olson.

'We think it may have been one of the lecturers here,' said Wheeler.

Barnes Olsen said nothing. Studied her manicured nails.

'I wonder if you could tell me about the last time you saw or spoke to Michael?' said Wheeler.

'Very well. I saw him the evening before he was killed.'

'What time did you leave Michael O'Donnell's house?' asked Wheeler.

'We had an argument and I left his house around two a.m. I went straight home, if you must know. I stopped off for milk at my local garage around two-thirty. No doubt they will have CCTV, if you can't take my word for it.'

Wheeler ignored the sarcasm. 'What did you quarrel about?'

'I'm sorry, but that's private.'

'If you wouldn't mind,' Wheeler insisted.

'We had been in a relationship.' Barnes Olsen crossed to the window, stared out. 'We were lovers. I thought we had a real connection.'

'And?' Wheeler prompted.

'I wanted us to go public about our relationship, Michael was unwilling. I said that I was increasingly irritated at having to sneak around after dark. I'm from a very good family in Edinburgh.' She touched her Chanel necklace. 'And I'm a senior lecturer at the College for Visual Arts for goodness' sake, not some local teacher at a failing comprehensive. Yet, even Paula didn't know about our relationship, she was always in bed by the time I arrived and, of course, I seldom stayed over. If I did manage to stay over, I was unceremoniously bundled out at five in the morning. Often in the dark. What kind of adults live that way? I became frustrated and gave him an ultimatum, either we go public or I inform the other governors of our affair.'

'How did he respond?' asked Wheeler.

'He refused. It was really rather pathetic,' she sighed. 'He was in a particularly foul mood that night.'

'Because?' asked Wheeler.

'Who knows?'

'And so, you left,' said Wheeler.

'I was angry, I wanted him to be truthful. I wanted monogamy, revoltingly dull and pedestrian as it sounds. In short, I wanted Michael to myself. Unfortunately, he felt otherwise. He confirmed my suspicions that he had taken other lovers during our time together.'

'Who else was Michael seeing?' asked Wheeler quietly.

'Oh, if only I knew. I would have confronted them,' laughed Barnes Olsen. 'He made an oblique reference once, when he'd had a little too much wine, to a "friend" who had supported and greatly helped him with managing Paula.'

'Any idea who?'

'No.'

'So, about the other lovers?' asked Wheeler.

'I found an earring a couple of weeks back, it was under the bed. I'd dropped one of my pearl earrings and had knelt to search for it. That's when I found it. Of course, Michael denied ever seeing it before, but I knew it wasn't Paula's style. So, when I got home, I googled it. It's vintage Tiffany's.'

'Do you still have it?' asked Wheeler.

Barnes Olsen crossed to the desk, opened a drawer and took out the single earring. Dropped it into Wheeler's hand.

Wheeler looked at it, gold with a twist and what looked like tiny diamonds. She agreed with Barnes Olsen, it was vintage and it looked expensive.

'Michael liked his little secrets.' Barnes Olsen smiled. 'He kept everything a secret, myself included.'

'Do you know of anyone who would want to harm Michael?' asked Wheeler.

'There were a few people he mentioned who he felt didn't like him much but there was no one that I know of who would wish him harm.'

'Who were the people he thought didn't like him?' asked Wheeler.

'He felt that Arne Van Der Berg, a member of the pastoral team here, was brusque with him and refused to acknowledge Michael's expertise around Paula's condition. He felt that my colleague patronised him, that Arne felt himself to be superior and that he encouraged Paula to go to specific lectures, including those on Frida Kahlo, when she was meant to have been resting.'

'I see.' Uniform had spoken briefly with Arne Van Der Berg. No red flags had been raised. Perhaps just enmity? 'Paula was in one of his groups?'

'Yes, Paula was in one of his little happy-clappy groups. Paula could be tricky. Maybe her illness? She certainly could be angry.' Ms Barnes Olsen walked back to her desk. 'And before you ask, I was here in my studio all day Saturday, working on my pièce de résistance. The principal suggested that some of the staff share studios, but I disagreed.' She led them through to a studio space tucked behind the classroom, again the nutty smell of turpentine. 'I think it's important that we all have our own space.'

'Sounds like something Hawk would say,' whispered Ross. 'The revered Seb Hawk. The *married* Mr Hawk.'

Wheeler ignored him, walked on. Saw that Barnes Olsen's pièce de résistance was a painting. The figure closely resembled Michael O'Donnell, but his form had been made grotesque and misshapen. Across his torso, a number of red slashes.

Wheeler knew that the full details of how Michael had died had not been released to the press. She would check out Barnes Olsen's alibi. Surely the college had CCTV?

'Impressed? I think it speaks for itself, don't you?' Ms Janine Barnes Olsen smiled. 'It's a very robust depiction, granted, but nevertheless it captures the essence of who Michael was and, if I'm being completely congruent, it is a symbol of unrequited love.'

'It's certainly interesting,' said Ross.

Barnes Olsen peered at him. 'I'm quite empathetic. Are you sickening for something? Maybe a lost love? Some man or woman you are holding a torch for?'

Ross blushed, looked at his shoes. Studied them as if they held the answer to her question.

'Sorry to be so abrupt but when I mentioned unrequited love, you flinched, only an infinitesimal movement but I read your body language. My father is a psychologist, so I'm well versed. Care to expand? Perhaps you and I are kindred spirits, each chasing an elusive lover?'

'Back to the case in question.' Wheeler walked towards one of the huge paintings. 'So, this one would have been done when Paula was on the course?'

'Yes, it's possible she could have seen it if she'd come to my studio but to my knowledge she was never here, and I never taught her directly. She was Robin Kirkpatrick's student. His specialism is Fauvism and, as you know, Mr Van Der Berg was her link to the pastoral support team.'

'And this here?' Ross indicated a trail of dark red liquid which had been smeared across the painting.

'Looks like blood I know but it is pigment mixed with rain and water from the River Clyde. Left outside, the wind and elements combine to interact with the canvas. They imbue it with their energies.'

'Still looks like blood,' said Ross. 'Maybe we should get it analysed?'

'Naturally, if you must be so tirelessly suspicious,' said Barnes Olsen, turning to Ross, 'but I don't want it damaged.'

Wheeler noted that Janine Barnes Olsen affected a pout as she waited for Ross's attention. She wondered at someone being able to flirt so obviously so soon after their lover's murder.

'I don't think there's any need to have it removed,' said Wheeler.

'My creative process happens quickly, an extremely organic progression.' Barnes Olsen smiled. 'I specialise in death. Recording it. Celebrating the journey to the other side. No matter how dark the subject matter.'

'Like satanism?' asked Ross. 'What about the upturned crucifixes in Michael's home?'

'That may be part of a conversation, certainly not it all. The crucifixes were part of an ongoing dialogue I believe he had with Paula's mother, Jayla. It was a discourse on the nature of being worthy or unworthy, a dynamic that existed between them. My work is completely different. But one of the things I do believe in is spirit possession, which I know some students follow. And yes, some students identify as satanists, Hudson Lennox being one. Others identify as Christians, atheists, agnostics. Whatever. Just as some students identify as non-binary. It's an open dialogue.'

'Sorry?' said Ross.

'Some of our students don't identify as being male or female,' said Barnes Olsen.

'It just gets crazier and crazier,' said Ross.

'Christ, Ross. What century are you living in?' said Wheeler quietly.

Ross shrugged. 'I'm just saying.'

Wheeler walked behind Barnes Olsen. Saw the huge painting. The canvas depicted a woman leading her army into war. She was on a chariot, wore a long cloak. Around her neck, Celtic jewellery. Wheeler immediately recognised the figure. 'Boadicea,' she said. But the figure had been cast to resemble Janine Barnes Olsen.

'I prefer Boudicca, DI Wheeler. I see myself as charging into battle, here at the College of Visual Arts, for my art and for my other work, to represent what is happening to humanity. And, of course, the jewellery I make for relatives and friends of the dead.'

'If I remember correctly, Boadicea wasn't victorious,' said Wheeler. 'There were tens of thousands killed in the conflict.'

Barnes Olsen sighed. 'You misunderstand, Inspector. It is her rebellious spirit that I hope to emanate. Death is always around us, it surrounds every part of our lives. I work with its energy. This here—' she climbed a ladder and gestured to another painting '—this relates to the death of Caroline Langonberg.'

Wheeler knew the case well. Caroline Langonberg had been a well-known Scottish model, who had been killed at her wealthy boyfriend's estate on the outskirts of Milngavie.

'And this star here, this explosion of energy, is the emergence of spirit into another realm. Caroline's sister has asked that I help the family remember her this way. I make jewellery for grieving families, including the Langonbergs. They provided me with some of Caroline's ashes. The time and date of her death will be inscribed into the silver backing. This, of course, is all done off campus but the paintings I do here.'

'Caroline Langonberg was brutally murdered, and no one, as yet, has been charged, so her killer is still out there,' said Ross.

'Yes, but her body was found. Her spirit took flight into the universe at a specific time. The pathologist knew when exactly she died, it was in her report. And I plot my canvases and create my jewellery with the same precision.'

'And this was the death of Malcolm Brauer.' Barnes Olsen pointed to another canvas. 'His poor mother came to me last month on the anniversary of his death. She believes, as I do, that a person can be possessed by spirit. She's working closely with spiritualists and other mediums to contact him.'

Wheeler stared at the canvas. Said nothing. Malcolm Brauer had been one of the victims of a homophobic psychopath who had killed four young men before being caught. It had been one of Wheeler's first cases as a detective inspector. She remembered Malcolm's mutilated body, how young and vulnerable he had looked in death. It was an image that had haunted her for years afterwards. She stared at Barnes Olsen, but the tutor refused to meet her gaze.

'Now, what do you think of my work?' Barnes Olsen turned her attention to Ross, smiled.

'It seems exploitative,' said Ross.

'Then you don't understand it, Inspector Ross. I venerate the dead. I record their lives in paint and in the jewellery for eternity, so in a sense they remain with us. Don't you understand?'

'No, I'm afraid I don't,' said Ross.

'I think I see what you mean.' Wheeler tried for the middle ground. 'So why did the families of Caroline Langonberg and Malcolm Brauer come to you in particular?'

'Because, Inspector Wheeler, I celebrate all deaths,' said Barnes Olsen.

'But you don't record them all?' said Wheeler.

'No. Only some,' said Barnes Olsen.

'Just the families who can pay?' said Ross.

'I am making a living, DI Ross, just as you are. You prey on these deaths. What do you make a year as a detective inspector?' she snapped. 'I'm guessing many thousands?'

'I work for that money,' said Ross.

'You feast on desolation. You are a dark carrion crow, Inspector Ross. It is apt that you have dark hair. Like the crow, you need death to survive. You depend on the deceased, exploit them and luxuriate in their lurid detail. Tell me you don't sit around the bars on a Saturday night and boast about your job, about apprehending the murderous psychopaths who kill?'

'I don't think I need to justify myself to you—' Ross began.

Barnes Olsen cut across him. 'Oh but you do, because you take a salary for it. A salary that comes out of our pockets, our tax payers' pockets. I pay your wages.'

'I beg to—' started Ross.

'Then you'd do it for free would you, Inspector? You'd hover around corpses for a hobby? It gives you a vicarious thrill. Doesn't it?' Barnes Olsen smiled.

'I don't make trinkets out of the ashes of dead bodies to sell to grieving relatives or artwork purporting to help them heal,' said Ross.

'I am helping them with the bereavement process,' spat Barnes Olsen. 'The grieving process needs support to work through the five stages of bereavement – denial, anger, bargaining, depression and acceptance. It can be an extremely difficult time for those left behind.'

Wheeler handed over her card. 'If there's anything else you think of, Ms Barnes Olsen, please don't hesitate to contact us.'

'I'm having a public exhibition of these works at the Open Gallery if you're interested? It's entitled, "That which is Immortal, sings in our hearts for Eternity".'

They left.

Outside, Ross turned to her. 'What a bloody piece of work that woman is.'

'While you were your usual charming self,' said Wheeler.

'Would you though?' asked Ross.

'Would I what?' said Wheeler.

'Would you do this work for free, if you know, you didn't need the money? I think that it's important to know what you want in this life.'

Wheeler shook her head. Didn't answer, instead she strode towards the car.

Ross stood where he was, the snow setting around him. 'Wheeler, I asked you a bloody question.'

Silence.

His mobile chirped a text. *Ross, where are you? Why aren't you returning my messages? I thought we'd had a good time the other night? Aubree xxxxxx PS Let's get together soon! Love you.*

Ross cursed quietly, shoved his phone back into his pocket. Followed Wheeler to the car.

Chapter 19

Evening

In her flat in Great Western Road, Aubree Rutherford checked her mobile for what felt like the hundredth time; Steven Ross still hadn't returned any of her text messages. She flicked back her long red hair and called her cousin.

'Seb?'

'Yep.'

'I just wondered if I could come over for a bit? I want to run something by you.'

'Sure, Aubree. When suits you?' said Hawk.

'How about now?'

'OK, I'm just finishing up my notes here at the station,' said Hawk. 'Meet you back at my flat?'

'Thanks.'

Thirty minutes later Aubree stepped out of the taxi and walked to Seb's flat. Inside, she noticed that some of the paintings had been completed. 'You're kidding me?' She was incredulous. 'How did you get all this done?'

Hawk handed her a chilled glass of Prosecco. 'This is a good space, Aubree. Creative. It's just what I need. Marilyn has been trying to get in touch again. It's good to be here in Glasgow.'

'Marilyn's never going to let you go.' Aubree's voice was hard. 'You know that, don't you?'

'She'll soften in time,' said Hawk quietly.

'I doubt it. You know exactly what she's like. You were her husband and till death do us part and all that shit. And you know how vicious she can be. I'd be careful if I were you. Especially if you intend dating again. At least warn whoever you are dating, tell them what she can be like.'

'Aubree, you shouldn't talk about her like that, especially—'

'Especially, what?' She smiled.

'Nothing.'

'No, go on. Spit it out. What you were about to say was, especially since I got myself into trouble with my ex-boyfriend?'

'Supposed boyfriend,' said Hawk.

'He was my boyfriend! I don't care what the fuck he said.'

'You did what you did,' said Hawk. 'You weren't well at the time.'

'I was perfectly well. I let myself into his apartment and—'

'You shouldn't even have had his keys!'

'He dropped them. So, I had entry and I decided to let myself play.'

'No one could have been well if they did what you did,' he said quietly. 'That animal should still be alive today.'

'It was already poorly. I did it a favour.'

'Aubree, I think that you—'

'Let's change the subject, cousin. Shall we?' Her voice,

high, brittle. 'Let's keep this pleasant. We are family, remember? And besides, I seem to remember Marilyn accusing you of being controlling.'

'So, what is it you wanted to talk about?' said Hawk quietly, sipping his wine.

'I hope I've not come at a bad time?' She laughed. 'I could go away. Would that be more convenient?'

'You're my cousin, there's never a bad time. Say it, girl!'

'I think I'm in love,' said Aubree, perching on the edge of a sofa.

He waited.

'Aren't you going to ask me about him?'

'I'm waiting for you to tell me,' said Hawk.

'His name is Steven,' said Aubree.

'Ah, right.'

'We've been together on and off over the past few months and now I think we need to make it more permanent.'

'Is this the cop I bumped into leaving your flat?' said Hawk.

'Jesus, you met him in my flat?' said Aubree.

'You were asleep,' said Hawk. 'I took you out for breakfast afterwards.'

'Then you know he's gorgeous?' said Aubree.

'I know that he doesn't seem that interested in you if he was sneaking out.'

'He has to get up early for work.'

'Right. I met him again at Carmyle Police Station.'

'You're working with him?' Aubree stood, began pacing the room.

'You know the commission I had to write a book?' said Hawk.

'Yeah.'

'Well it's a book based on the police force, shadowing them, documenting their work, but in a semi-fictional way.'

'Kind of like in *The Wire*, the American show?' asked Aubree.

'Not quite as cool,' said Hawk.

'Woah, you just told me that you get to work with Steven Ross every day? I think that's very cool.'

'It's not as exciting as you make it sound,' said Hawk. 'You like him?'

'Love him.'

'And it's reciprocated this time?'

'Definitely. He told me the other night.'

'OK, I believe you.'

'I'm on my way to work,' said Aubree. 'But I could hang out here for a bit? What are you up to this evening? Maybe at some point we could hook up with Steven?'

'I'm writing up my notes and getting in some food,' said Hawk.

'What are you cooking?'

'I'm getting a takeaway,' said Hawk. 'Pizza.'

'That's not like you,' said Aubree.

'You don't know everything about me, Aubree, little cousin.' He walked her to the door. 'Besides, it's not just any old pizza.'

'Ha, I knew it!'

'A new gourmet pizza place has opened. Esposito's.'

'Oh, the pizzas are so gorgeous but so expensive,' she wailed. 'And I'm pretty peckish and don't have to be at work right away.'

'I'll treat you one evening.' He opened the door.

'Hint taken. You'll have a think about what I should do about Ross?'

'Of course. Let me mull it over.'

'While you're eating your gourmet pizza?' She paused. 'Alone?'

He held the door open. 'Good food never hurt anyone, Aubree.'

Chapter 20

Wheeler and Ross

They were both tired and frustrated at the lack of progress in the case. They had left the station and travelled across the city in silence. Finally, Ross broke it. 'You want food?'

'Your shout,' said Wheeler.

'Fine, but in that case, we're having curry,' said Ross.

'Whatever,' said Wheeler.

'You're pissed off with me,' said Ross.

'Rubbish.'

'You are. Because I called Janine Barnes Olsen out on her scam.'

'Why couldn't you just leave her alone? She's a grieving witness. A heartbroken lover.'

'She's not fucking grieving, Wheeler. She was flirting. Or did you just decide not to notice?'

'Because I was trying to empathise with the woman, but you took the discussion in a whole new direction. It was bloody unprofessional, Ross. If you want to know the truth.'

'She's full of bullshit. That whole art thing and the fucking jewellery. What the hell was that about? At best, it's exploitative.'

'She's trying to record their deaths in a meaningful way. God knows, it may help the devastated families,' said Wheeler. 'Who knows if it helps them, why should we judge?'

'Christ, she's exploiting them for her own bloody financial means. Why can't you see that, Wheeler? Are you even thinking as a detective now? Your judgement seems to be off-kilter.'

'You are way out of line, Ross.'

'And it's the same with Seb Hawk, he's bloody exploiting our process as detectives. We have absolutely zero use for him at the station. He does not need to be embedded in our team. We can one hundred per cent do without his—' Ross put his two index fingers in the air, making them into quotation marks '—art or whatever he fucking calls it.'

'Don't bring him into it.' Wheeler stared out of the window. Watched the snow fall.

'Why not? He's part of the problem,' said Ross.

'You are full of anger,' said Wheeler. 'I don't understand why?'

'Maybe.' Ross paused. 'But he likes you.'

'For God's sake, Ross. Concentrate on the bloody investigation. What age are you?'

'What about him shadowing us though? Because of a fucking book? I mean how self-serving and egoistic is that?'

'Hawk sits in on the meetings out of professional interest. He wants to absorb our process.'

'He's a useless idiot.'

'He's an artist,' said Wheeler.

'He likes you,' Ross repeated.

'Again, this rubbish! Ridiculous,' said Wheeler. 'What age are you? Fifteen?'

'He does though. Do you like him?'

'For God's sake, Ross, give it a bloody break.'

'Turns out I'm not hungry after all,' said Ross.

'Me neither. Let's just let it go.'

Ross dropped her close to her flat in the Merchant City.

In her flat, Wheeler poured a glass of chilled Chardonnay, put on a CD. An old favourite. *Ah Um* by Charles Mingus. As 'Better Git It in Your Soul' filled the room she felt her shoulders relax. She was pissed off with Ross, he should have known better than to think that she had been taken in by Janine Barnes Olsen. And all that 'are you thinking as a detective' shit. What the hell was the matter with him? If anyone was the consummate professional detective, it was sure as hell her. Not for the first time Wheeler wondered if Ross even had it in him to be a really good detective inspector. He was still only acting after all. She opened her folder of case notes. An hour later she was ravenous. She wandered through to the kitchen, opened the fridge; only a raw beetroot, wrinkled and abandoned. The freezer had the remnants of a chip, frozen, shrivelled. She couldn't be bothered calling for a carry-out. She topped up her glass and settled back down to read. Tried not to think of Ross. Or the takeaway curry he was probably eating. What the hell was happening to them? They used to be a team. And she cared about him a great deal.

It was unmistakable, a short sharp knock on her door. Well maybe Ross had reconsidered? She hoped so.

Seb Hawk smiled. 'That new gourmet pizza place, Esposito's, was having a sale, buy one get one free. Buffalo mozzarella, fresh herbs and white truffle shavings on one. On the other, wild mushroom and cream sauce with ricotta.' He paused. 'I didn't get chips, you'll be pleased to know.'

'Great,' she lied. She smelled the food

'I went for the *frites*, instead.'

She heard her stomach growl. 'Right, I'll get us some wine.'

'Seems a fair trade-off.'

'Red or white?'

'My dear Kat Wheeler.' He smiled. 'You are a complete philistine.'

'Mr Seb Hawk, I think you'll find that I've never denied it,' said Wheeler.

'Red with pizza. Always.'

'Yeah. Right.'

'What are you having, Wheeler?'

'White.'

'Really?'

She paused in the plating of the food long enough to give him a cold, hard stare.

'I'm silenced,' he said.

'About bloody time.'

They settled with the food and wine.

'So, you want to get me up to speed?' said Hawk.

'We went to the college, spoke to a Ms Janine Barnes Olsen.'

'Go on.'

'She was a piece of work,' said Wheeler.

'Because?'

'She accepts commissions to do work for the grieving families of the murdered. She incorporates their ashes into jewellery.'

'Based on Police Scotland's cases?' asked Hawk.

'Yep.'

'It's macabre.' Hawk took out his notebook. Began scribbling.

Wheeler sipped her wine, reached for another slice of pizza. 'This pizza is amazing.'

'Glad you like it.'

'I love it.'

'Tell me more about Janine Barnes Olsen,' said Hawk.

'She thinks she's the reincarnation of Boadicea. Or channelling her spirit.'

'Boadicea? You've got to be kidding me? What's all that about? Does she see herself as the warrior queen of a British tribe?'

'She has an exhibition coming up, "That which is Immortal, sings in our hearts for Eternity". What do you think?'

'Barnes Olsen sounds interesting, if a little eccentric, but aren't all artists?'

The CD finished, and Wheeler changed it to Ike Quebec's *Blue & Sentimental*. She finished her slice of pizza. 'I think you might have liked her.'

'OK, I hear you. Did Ross warm to her?'

'No. He couldn't see her attraction himself. She told him that he wasn't open to spirit. They clashed.'

'Ross seems to make a habit of that. And you?'

'She was fine. Sometimes folk do weird things. I didn't get the jewellery at all, sounds ghoulish.'

'But if you were close to a family member?' said Hawk.

'And your cousin?' said Wheeler, changing the subject. 'Are you close to Aubree?'

Hawk shrugged. 'We took diverse paths, we see things differently. She was quite ill for a time.' He paused. 'But she's fine now. She's at Strathclyde University doing a Masters in Criminology Research Methods. That's the upside.'

'OK,' said Wheeler. 'So, she has a good mind and is using it. What's the downside?'

'She thinks that she's in love with a detective.'

'That's not a great start. To anyone's love life,' said Wheeler. 'I don't envy her that.'

'No,' said Hawk quietly. 'But I do believe that he led her on to believe that there was something between them, then when she mentioned her feelings for him . . . well, I caught him trying to sneak out of her flat.'

'That doesn't sound very promising,' said Wheeler.

'No.'

'And you?' asked Wheeler, shifting in her seat. 'What was your path?'

'I went to university, then into journalism. We both escaped our backgrounds in our separate ways.'

'When did you get to fall in love?' Wheeler sipped her wine.

'Only once. I married young. It was a mistake. We split up a long time ago.'

'Divorced?'

'No, just never got around to it. And I never fell in love again.'

'Right.'

'But I think I just found someone I could love.' Hawk reached for the last slice of pizza. 'You?'

Wheeler rose, took the dishes through to the kitchen. 'Then good for you. You should go after her. Presuming it's a her?'

'Yeah,' said Hawk, looking after her as he finished his wine. 'It's a her.'

Later, as she saw Hawk out, Wheeler noticed the smell of paint and turpentine again and how familiar it now felt. She liked Seb Hawk, liked the fact that he was a painter, that he was a journalist. That he enjoyed food. Loved jazz. Wheeler didn't believe in omens, good or bad. But merely noted facts, observed them, stored them in her memory and moved on. She wondered about Ross. He'd changed recently. He seemed guarded. She used to think that they were close, perhaps she was wrong? She bloody hoped not. He didn't seem to like Seb Hawk. While she on the other hand . . .

Chapter 21

Tala

Her green Doc Martens lay abandoned on the floor. Tala sat crossed-legged on her bed; the quilt had been made for her by her grandma De Luca. Tala knew that she should call her gran, maybe even offer to walk the dog again. But Tala knew that she couldn't do that, what she was about to do was so much more important. Her laptop was open in front of her, the screen blank save for one sentence. One command. PLAY. She heard Autumn coming up the stairs, heard the exasperation in her voice. 'Tala, you were supposed to vacuum the house and for goodness' sake why do you have to keep your door locked? Once, Tomas was caught in your room but he's four years old, for God's sake, what harm could he do? And now you barricade yourself in in a very melodramatic way. Honestly, if you could just get off your bloody high horse for a second and help me with the laundry. And how dare you leave my son alone? You really are the most irresponsible piece of shit on the planet.'

Tala was silent.

'Do you hear me, Tala?' Autumn's voice was irate. The

141

door handle was being rattled but Tala knew that the lock would hold. It always did. The Moderator had recommended one which she could buy from Amazon. One that teenagers like her were using to keep themselves safe from parents and siblings all over the world. She ignored Autumn, put on her headphones and listened to the music they had sent her.

The dEADdOG community were the only people who understood her, who really got her. They got how torturous it was to not fit in, especially with your own family. She didn't want to be in this world. A world of hypocrites and liars. She wanted to be free where she could be herself. If this world was all that was on offer to her then she would reject it. She listened to the demonic music, she was at one with the nihilism it represented. She didn't want to live if she was merely existing. If she couldn't be a great artist then what was the point?

'You could be a nurse,' a career advisor had once suggested when she'd still been at school. 'You could be in the entertainment industry, working in the background. Perhaps not a star, we can't all be stars, you know?' The list had gone on and on, careers she had no interest in. Tala dug her fingernails into her palm. Felt the pain. She thought of Francesco Soule who was exhibiting some of his paintings at the college to inspire young artists. She thought about the bursary for the most promising student at CoVA to go study in Florence for three years. She knew that it would never in a million years be her. She stared at the screen. She had found her tribe. Tala felt her breathing return to normal. Leroy had posted a picture of his tattoo. The outline of a wild dog dug into his thigh. It was blistered and bloody but still it had the discernible outline of a dog.

Tala knew that Leroy was three steps ahead of her in the programme. He'd said that it was beautiful, him being so tantalisingly close to death. 'Not yet,' he had sent her the message, 'not yet.' Leroy had his prearranged date too. At the thought of Leroy, she instinctively placed a hand over her heart. She loved him. Twinned souls. If the boy at college had been really interested in her, if he hadn't slept with her then told her about a girlfriend, maybe she wouldn't have been so attracted to Leroy. But life unfolded as it was meant to. She thought of the artefact her gran had, the triskelion, which symbolised birth, death and rebirth. How her gran always kissed it. Yes, thought Tala, life would unfold as it was meant to and so would her death.

Chapter 22

Monday 14 December

Press conference

Boyd sat to the left of Robertson on the stage. He wished that Wheeler had taken the gig; Stewart had asked her to, but she'd managed to dodge it. Boyd knew that he wasn't a natural at public speaking. He felt himself begin to sweat. Not least because he was grimly aware of the facts: they had nothing new to report on the Michael O'Donnell murder and Paula was still missing. Also, earlier that morning, the son of Sarah Price had come into the station to register his mum as a missing person. Boyd sighed, Michael O'Donnell's murder, and now Sarah Price's disappearance; Wheeler had informed him that she reckoned that potentially they may have been lovers. And so far, no one had come forward with any credible sightings of Paula. Classmates from the CoVA had offered to help with the search, asking if they could do anything at all. But police were already combing the area next to the college grounds, including Dalbeth Cemetery.

He cleared his throat, spoke to the assembled press. 'This morning Sarah Price was reported as missing . . . '

Ten minutes in and he drew their attention to Paula and Michael.

'Police Scotland officers at Carmyle Police Station are still appealing to the public for information in tracing Paula O'Donnell who is missing from the Mount Vernon area. She was last seen attending a class at the College of Visual Arts. She was wearing thick black tights, a denim skirt and a black woollen jumper with a heart pattern on the front. She usually wore a gold pendant of a kitten playing with a ball of wool.

'Anyone with information on any of these individuals are requested to contact the police on any of these numbers.' He recited the familiar numbers, hoped that someone would hear the appeal and get in touch.

For the next half hour, they fielded questions from the press. Both sides knew that pickings were slim.

Back at the station, they were half an hour in and Boyd had answered his fourth call. He sighed. 'An elderly lady has just called us to report some boys who were cruel to a fox cub she'd been feeding. Her house is over by Hamilton Road, Mount Vernon.'

'With the best will in the world,' said Robertson, 'doesn't she know that we're kind of busy right now.'

'A Mrs Ruby De Luca,' said Boyd.

'De Luca?' asked Wheeler 'We met up with an Autumn De Luca outside Michael's house. She was a neighbour of his and her stepdaughter, Tala, attends the college. Now Sarah Price is missing, and her son Nick attends the CoVA too.'

'Nick provided a DNA sample of his mother, earlier,' said Boyd. 'He brought in both her hairbrush and toothbrush. He's gone to stay with his dad, over by Glenshee Street.'

'Glenshee Street? Where that lassie went missing years ago?' said a uniformed officer. 'What was her name?' She paused. 'Zoe Wishart? She was a trainee beauty therapist, wasn't she? Same course as my wee cousin is doing.'

'Get me the address for Ruby De Luca,' said Wheeler. 'In the meantime, I want to speak with Nick Price.'

The phone rang again; Boyd answered and began scribbling down notes.

Wheeler stood. 'Ross, let's get over to Tollcross and speak to Nick Price. There's too much centred around the CoVA. And if his mum was seeing Michael O'Donnell—'

Boyd put the caller on hold. 'Wheeler, I'm speaking to a guy who's just seen the appeal for Sarah Price. His name's Bernie Morrison. He met her at Balloch. Says there was another guy there, Frankie Fermin. Sarah seemed nervous of him.'

'I'll speak to him,' said Wheeler, then she paused. 'The pathologist at Michael O'Donnell's house mentioned a guy name of Frankie Fermin.' She listened to Bernie Morrison, took notes. Finally finished the call. 'Well, it's a breakthrough at last.'

The atmosphere in the room changed.

Chapter 23

Tollcross

Wheeler parked in Glenshee Street, outside a neat row of terraced houses. There was a beaten-up red Fiesta parked outside one. They had no option but to park too close to it, boxing it in. They made their way through a gravelled garden to the door of the house. She pressed on the bell. It was opened quickly.

Wheeler and Ross showed their ID. Introduced themselves.

'I'm Nick. I already brought some of Mum's stuff to the station earlier.'

Wheeler saw the pale face, took in the hesitant body language. Nick Price had a mass of curls and a nervous, lopsided smile. She knew that the police needed to have Sarah's DNA should they find any evidence or worse, her body. She kept her voice soft. 'Thank you for that, Nick. We appreciate it.' Wheeler studied Nick. He hadn't quite grown into himself. He was around five foot eleven and would perhaps fill out in time, but he still had gangly limbs. Dark hair, clean shaven, wearing skinny jeans. But it was his voice which was unusual. It was very deep for someone so young.

'Come on through.' Nick led them through to a living room dominated by a huge television screen.

'Sorry it's a bit spartan. Dad's a big racing fan, it's his passion.' Nick sat on the sofa. 'Along with any other kind of gambling. He spends half his life in casinos. Mainly the Golden Key.'

'Any idea who the red Fiesta belongs to, only we've boxed it in?' said Ross.

'No worries, it's mine,' said Nick. 'And I'm not going anywhere.'

'A member of the public has come forward after we appealed for information,' said Wheeler. 'He said that he spoke to your mum on Saturday evening.'

'Who?' asked Nick.

'A man called Bernie Morrison.' She paused. 'Do you recognise the name?'

'No, never heard of him,' said Nick.

'He said your mum was at Balloch train station,' said Wheeler gently.

'News to me,' said Nick, absent-mindedly picking at a ragnail.

'There was another man travelling on the same train who got off at the station. His name is Frankie Fermin. We're trying to locate him. Mr Morrison said your mum seemed a little nervous of him.'

'None of this makes any sense,' said Nick quietly. 'She never mentioned any of it.'

'Your mum was waiting at Balloch train station,' said Wheeler. 'She'd travelled from Glasgow Queen Street.'

'Why would she be at Balloch?' said Nick.

'We wondered if she'd ever mentioned visiting someone out that way? Mr Morrison said she mentioned the Queen

148

Elizabeth Forest Park and the West Highland Way. He got the impression she was heading to Drymen? To meet someone?' asked Wheeler.

'She never mentioned going to Drymen. Or Balloch.' Nick paused. 'Are you sure it was my mum?'

'We can't be absolutely certain, but the description is pretty accurate, other than the clothes you said she was wearing,' said Wheeler. 'When Mr Morrison spoke to her he said that she was wearing a black dress and coat. Black boots. Not the black jeans and flat shoes you mentioned.'

'Doesn't sound like Mum,' said Nick. 'She always wears comfy shoes and trousers. Jeans at the weekend. When I left her, she was wearing her Christmas jumper. It had a Rudolph face on it.'

'Could you perhaps check her wardrobe, Nick? When you get home? I'll send a car to take you back.'

"Course.'

'Do you know if your mum was seeing anyone?' asked Wheeler.

'No, I tried to encourage her to date,' said Nick. 'I mean I won't be here for ever. I'll be off soon and she'll be on her own.'

'She didn't mention anyone at all?' prompted Wheeler.

'No,' Nick bit his thumbnail. 'But . . . '

'But what?' asked Wheeler.

'She might not have told me. Dad . . . ' Nick paused. 'Dad has a way of eliciting information which he doesn't necessarily need to know.' He looked at Wheeler. 'Once, a while back, Mum was going on a date and I was staying with Dad. He demanded to know where Mum was going. I didn't want to tell him, but he forced it out of me.'

Wheeler waited.

'He bullied me until I told him. Dad can be like that. He has a bloody awful temper.'

'And then?' prompted Wheeler.

'And then Dad went to the restaurant and confronted Mum and this man and they had a flaming row and Dad broke the guy's nose. Mum was horrified.'

'So, after this encounter, she never told you if she was dating?' said Wheeler.

'It was safer for her not to,' said Nick. 'She was probably just trying to protect me.'

'Go on.' Wheeler waited.

'And there was another time, he followed us up to a birthday party in Balmaha. It was another student's party, Tala De Luca's, but Dad insisted on going up there just to check if Mum was meeting up with someone.'

'I completely understand,' said Wheeler. She paused. 'Did you get on well with your mum?'

'We argued quite a bit over the years, but more recently, say in the past six months, we got on a lot better.'

'Why was that?' asked Wheeler. 'What changed?'

'I'm going to be off soon,' said Nick. 'Ms Barnes Olsen reckons I could make it big in the art world.'

'Your art tutor seems to have a fascination with death,' said Ross.

'Someone said her baby daughter died years ago and she never got over it. Might only be a rumour. We all think she's nuts. But then all artists are eccentric in their own way, aren't they? Plus, she's a pretty good tutor. Very supportive.'

'So, you're off to art college?' asked Wheeler.

'University. The School of Art at Brighton University. I'm hoping to get accepted into the BA Fine Art Painting. It's a three-year course,' said Nick. 'Depends.'

'Why Brighton?' said Wheeler.

'I love the place. What is there not to love? The water, the English Channel? The Lanes, with all their cool shops and art galleries? And, to be honest, I need to get away from Glasgow. After Mum and Dad split up, she kind of dedicated herself to bringing me up. Dad was hardly what you would call present for me as a parent. But I need some freedom now, and Mum needs to pick up the threads of her own life.'

'Did you know Michael O'Donnell?'

'I never spoke to him.'

'And Paula?' asked Wheeler gently. It looked like Nick Price might cry.

'We shared a few classes. Some days, she seemed exhausted from her illness. She seemed very frail. On other days, pretty robust.' He paused. 'But she is a fantastic artist.'

One foot tapped in agitation.

Wheeler took out the gold Tiffany earring that Barnes Olsen had given her. 'Do you recognise this?'

Nick looked at it. 'It's Mum's. Dad gave it to her before I was born, when they first got together. She said it was the only decent thing he ever did for her. He'd had a big win on the horses and had a blowout. Spent most of it on himself, Mum said, but she got these. I think they are from some store called Tiffany?' He stared at her. 'Where did you get Mum's earring?'

Again, Wheeler noticed Nick Price's foot tapping in agitation.

'It was handed in to us,' said Wheeler. She wasn't lying but she didn't need to tell Nick Price the whole truth at present. That was if Barnes Olsen was telling the truth herself. 'Do you mind if we take your mum's laptop when we run you home?'

'No, of course not.'

Ten minutes later and they were ready to go.

She stood. 'Thanks very much for speaking with us, Nick. I'll send a car for you.'

Outside, Ross turned to her. 'How did you guess Sarah Price and Michael O'Donnell were lovers?'

'It's all in the mix, Ross. Now let's go see Ruby De Luca.'

'The old woman who called in about a bloody fox?'

'That's the one,' said Wheeler walking ahead. 'Let's go find out if she can give us anything.'

Chapter 24

Ruby De Luca was exhausted. She hadn't slept well at all at the hospital for the past few nights and was glad to be home. All that to-ing and fro-ing and nurses gathering around beds. Fussing. But she knew that it hadn't just been the hospital staff keeping her awake, she'd been fretting about her granddaughter. Tala hadn't been her usual self in recent months, she'd sounded increasingly depressed and Ruby knew what that meant. Suicidal tendencies. And attempts. It wasn't the first time she'd visited Tala in hospital after the poor girl had swallowed a load of painkillers. Ruby knew that her son Marc had a high-powered job, of course, she got that, she truly did, but his father Enzo had worked hard all his life and had still been there for his son. But Marc worked away and was often holed up in some bloody five-star hotel and Tala was left to her own devices. Ruby was sure that Tala was neglected by her stepmum. That Autumn was no good. Between working full time as a bloody fitness coach, caring for her son Tomas and her ongoing beauty appointments, Tala got little, if any, attention. Autumn had made it clear that Tala was an inconvenience, even though the poor girl had lost her own mother. And she was at that very sensitive age when anything could happen. Ruby hoped Tala wouldn't try to overdose again. Or get pregnant. She just wanted her to have a nice normal life. Ruby had voiced her concerns to Marc, the last time he'd called, but he'd shrugged her off with a 'Don't interfere, Mum.' And eventually she'd had to let it go. Marc had also accused her of stream of consciousness talking. That was the most hurtful accusation. Marc had insinuated that she was losing it. Well Ruby knew that she bloody wasn't. But how cruel that a child who you'd given birth to, nurtured and kept alive for all those crucial years, now wanted to discard you as something old and useless. An irrelevance. Ruby glanced at the photograph of Enzo. She wished to hell he was still here with her. He would sort this bloody mess out.

Ruby took hold of the three-spiral artefact they'd bought from Newgrange on their honeymoon. The triskelion symbolised birth, death and rebirth. 'Enzo,' she said, speaking to it, 'Can you sort this out for me? Marc is being a bloody arse, I don't know who the hell he takes after. Some throwback to past generations. And I'm very worried about little Tala.'

Ruby kissed the triskelion twice before putting it down. She crossed to the window and drew back the curtains, saw two uniformed police officers in the street. Well, she knew what they would be asking about. She watched the two men make their way up her neighbour's garden path. She chewed on her bottom lip. She'd have phoned it in before if she hadn't been taken into hospital. She'd seen it all and heard their language from her front room. The two boys, the Roach twins. They were despicable, always had been. Some people were just born bad. Rotten to the core her mother would have said. She hoped Tala didn't ever get caught up with either of them. If she took up with that nice Nick Price, well, that would be fine. Absolutely fine, but the evil twins had the looks, someone mentioned that they'd been signed to a model agency. One of the big, London-based outfits. She hoped to God that they had, it would get them the hell away from the area and Tala.

Ruby lifted her little dog and hugged her. 'Are you hungry, angel?'

Her doorbell rang. That would be the two men in uniform, but she was puzzled, she hadn't seen them leave her neighbour's house. Ruby carried the dog through to the bedroom, placed her on her little dog bed. 'You stay here and be a good girl. I'll be back soon, darling.' Ruby closed the bedroom door. Made her way through the hall. She opened the door a fraction, kept the chain on. Saw a tall woman with short blonde hair and a man behind her, dark hair, pale blue eyes, handsome. The same long lashes as her beloved Enzo had, God rest his soul.

'Mrs De Luca?' the blonde woman asked.

Ruby waited.

'I'm DI Wheeler and this is DI Ross, we'd like to come in and have a chat with you, if it's convenient?'

Ruby checked the police ID. Studied it. 'Can't be too careful, nowadays.' She closed the door, undid the chain. 'Now, I know why you're here. Take a seat and I'll explain.'

Ruby seated herself. 'I need to have the window of my bungalow open, see, I feel the heat bad. It's the heart medication, makes me too hot. I'm just out of hospital, the Royal Infirmary, yesterday. It's like a furnace in there. I felt like I was a lobster in a big pot of boiling water.'

'I'm sorry to bother you,' said Wheeler.

'It was last week. And I heard them you see, talking

155

about some game. I know about games, my late husband was a sporting commentator, boxing mainly, and he covered many of the big matches but he still managed to be there as often as he could for our son, Marc. But then Marc does have a big job, means he travels across the world. But they are awful those two.'

'Who?' asked Wheeler.

'The evil boys, the twins.'

'Mrs De Luca, we're asking residents if they heard or saw anything about—' said Ross.

'I'm getting to that, young man. Remember your manners!' said Ruby. 'Well, one twin, I think it was Brock, said to the other "So, what do you think?"

'"About what?" said the other. I think it must have been Bradley.'

'"The game. The football result." Ruby paused."It was f—ed from the start." That's the kind of language he used. Then he saw it.'

'What?' asked Wheeler.

'The fox cub. The one I called in about?'

'"Oh, look a sh—ty fox." Again, with the language,' said Ruby. 'Brock and Bradley Roach are eighteen, with blond hair and blue eyes. They look angelic, but they are both devils incarnate. "Little b—, mange-ridden sh—t," said one. "Game on," said the other.' Mrs De Luca frowned. "We have a skinny little football."'

Wheeler listened while Mrs De Luca gave a blow-by-blow account of the conversation between the Brock twins. She sounded like a professional sports commentator. A neighbour of Wheeler's had watched all the boxing matches on television when she had been growing up and he had been babysitting her. She remembered that his favourite commentator had been someone called Enzo De Luca.

'"When it bleeds, can we catch disease off it?" says Bradley.

'"Go for it," said Brock. "And this one's for Nick fucking Price." And he kicked the poor wee thing so hard it, it went flying into the air.'

Wheeler tutted. 'Shocking.'

'Well I heard it shriek, poor little thing. I used to leave milk and a sandwich out for it. They say jam sandwiches help with the mange. I felt responsible, it was making its way to my garden. So, I went forward to the window. I'd held back a bit on account of them being evil. And they saw me and raised their middle fingers. Called me a nosey old witch. Well then doesn't young Nick Price turn into the lane and nearly collide with them. Nick had to brake hard, his bike was nearly over the twins. "What you two losers up to?" he says.

'"Wee game of footie," smirked the twins.

'"You certainly need the practice," said Nick.

'"F—you," the twins replied.' The woman looked at Wheeler. 'Again, with the language. Those two can't express themselves without resorting to language. Shitty little runts.'

Wheeler waited.

'Nick turned towards the creature, bent over the poor wee thing. "So then, you two are prize dickheads," he said and that sent them off on one. Then the twins were both facing up to Nick. "Who are you calling a dickhead?" One put his face in Nick's face. It was horrible. Then that youngster Paula, who was always wearing long-sleeved jumpers even in the summer, she came down the road in her motorised wheelchair and saw the three boys just facing off. I thought there was going to be a fight. I was so worried about her. Well, Nick faced up to the deplorable twins and I daresay Nick can handle himself?'

'Go on,' Wheeler.

'"You OK?" Paula asked the twins. One of them was bleeding at that point.

'One twin lunged at Nick, grabbed him by the throat.' The elderly lady fell into fight commentator again.

'Nick fell back a step, steadied himself as the other one lunged at him and thrust his fist into Nick's face, caught him with a right hook, just below the eye. Nick flinched but drove forward, throwing a random punch in the direction of the twin, he turned just before it landed, and it caught him between the eyes. The twin stood for a brief second before he crumpled onto the concrete, like a brown paper bag, his body hitting it at an unusual angle.

'"God's sake, Nick!" said little Paula, looking scared. 'What've you done? He's hardly breathing, you could have killed him. You're a lunatic. I hate you!"

'I thought otherwise,' said Mrs De Luca. 'I thought that Nick had been quite the hero.'

'"Run," little Paula had whispered to the other twin. Hoping the little git would get away.' Mrs De Luca was lost in the memory of the fight.

'Then what?' said Wheeler.

'Then the twin spoke. He said, "Piss off, retard, who asked you?" and eventually the other one got up. He'd just been badly winded. To tell you the truth, Inspector, I was glad Nick had floored him. As good-looking as they are, the twins are evil. I don't like them one little bit.'

'Yet they were set upon by Nick Price?'

'Well, whatever they did to the poor little fox cub, they deserved it. My late husband Enzo was a devoted family man, wouldn't hurt a fly. Loved animals. But he was a sports commentator and he always said that there needed to be "balance" in the game. Well, to my understanding, they kicked the creature half to death, they got what was coming to them. There's some sort of balance in that.'

'What can you tell me about Michael O'Donnell?'

'Why are you changing the subject?' said Ruby. 'I thought you were here to talk about the incident with the fox cub and the three boys fighting?'

'We're here to ask if you saw or heard anything on last Saturday afternoon?' said Ross.

'I don't understand. I've been in the hospital. The Royal Infirmary. Did I not make that clear?' said Ruby. 'I thought it was about the boys,' she repeated and trailed off. 'Nick gathered up the injured fox cub and rode off with it. I think he would have taken it to one of the animal shelters.'

'We'll investigate what happened to the little fox,' said Wheeler gently. 'But in the meantime, we'd also like to ask you if you can tell us anything about Michael O'Donnell?'

'Lovely man, devoted to little Paula. She studies art, doesn't she, at the same college as my granddaughter, Tala, the CoVA? Poor wee thing, it gives her an interest, doesn't it? Takes her mind off her illness. Gets her out and about. Otherwise, what would she do? Shrivel up and die without her dad's support, I'd guess. Or hang about with those dreadful twins, even when they called her a "retard". They don't even like her. She just doesn't seem strong enough for this world. And her having no mother, that was just too bad. I didn't know Michael's wife at all, she passed before I moved here. Remind me again, why are you asking about Michael?'

'He was murdered on Saturday,' said Wheeler.

'No!' Ruby fidgeted with the edge of her scarf. 'Awful. This world is godless. Godless! How is poor little Paula doing?'

'She's missing,' said Wheeler quietly.

'Oh my God, the killers have taken her. Oh, my goodness.' She peered at Wheeler. 'Have you interviewed the Roach twins? I'm not saying directly that they are killers, but if anyone round here would be capable of it, I'm sure it would be those two evil boys. I warned Tala to stay away from them. I think they had a fight with one of the governors at the CoVA.'

'Go on,' said Wheeler.

'I don't know what it was about. There was an open evening and the twins were drunk and Tala said they had words with one of the governors.'

'Was it Michael O'Donnell?' asked Wheeler.

'Tala didn't say who it was. I didn't even know that Michael O'Donnell was a governor until Tala mentioned it.'

'I met a Mrs De Luca outside Michael O'Donnell's house,' said Wheeler.

'That would be my daughter-in-law, Autumn. I'm sure she would be poking her nose in.' Ruby paused. 'I don't expect Tala was with her?'

'There was a little boy, a toddler, with her,' said Wheeler. 'I think maybe I caught a glimpse of Tala, a way back.'

'I could have guessed as much. My daughter-in-law doesn't much care for her stepdaughter. Autumn cares as little for Tala as I do for my daughter-in-law. And poor little Tomas gets caught up in all this, the little pet.'

'Do you have an address for the twins?'

'Not an exact address but I'm pretty sure their poor mum has a house over by—'

'Don't worry, we'll find it and send uniform,' said Ross.

'We'll visit them ourselves,' said Wheeler. 'Mrs De Luca, did you know Nick Price's mother, Sarah?'

'No, not at all. Why?'

'She's been reported missing.'

'Oh, dear God, no.' Ruby sat down heavily on the sofa. 'I need a drink.' She reached for the sherry bottle. Took a long measure and held it in her mouth before swallowing. Then she took another long mouthful.

'Can I get you anything, Mrs De Luca?' asked Wheeler. 'Can I call someone?'

'No, pet. Thank you. My carers will be here shortly.' She paused. 'But, if you could, keep a lookout for my grand-daughter, Tala.'

'Because?'

'Because like most teenagers, she's struggling and I fear for her.' Ruby wiped her eyes. 'I think I need to go for a lie-down.'

'Of course,' said Wheeler. She stood. 'Just another quick question, do you know a local handyman called Vladimir?'

'Vlad? Yes, I know him. Looks like a fighter. He's a walker. Goes out every night for a stroll around the area. Unusual eyes. He did some maintenance for me, on and off over the years. He was good with Tala when she was young. Used to make her laugh. Made daft faces. He has my phone number and I have his. He can be called upon. My son Marc's useless with his hands. Not practical at all, to be honest. Marc is a bloody useless at DIY. His father would have been ashamed of him. On many levels.'

'Did Vlad ever mention the O'Donnells or Sarah Price?'

'Not that I can recall.'

Wheeler handed the woman her card as she and Ross made their way out.

'What is it with you?' asked Ross. 'That we need to go and see everyone ourselves? She's just a little old lady living on her nerves. And worried about her grand-daughter.'

'Call it being professional,' said Wheeler.

'I'm not feeling great,' said Ross.

'Christ, are you hungover again?' said Wheeler. 'Then it's your own bloody fault.'

Ross said nothing. Fingered a hospital appointment card in his pocket. Almost began a conversation. Decided against it.

Wheeler's phone registered a text. *The station. Boss wants you back ASAP.*

Inside her bungalow, Ruby crossed to the phone. Dialled and waited. Heard it go through to the answering machine. 'Tala, it's Gran. The police have just been here. Poor Michael O'Donnell has been murdered and little Paula's missing. Did you know? And if so, why didn't you tell me? I might be old but I'm not out of it. I told them about the fight with the revolting Roach twins and Nick Price over the little fox cub. They were asking me about Nick Price's mum. Apparently, she's missing too. Do you know her? Give me a call back. Tala, I'm worried about you. Love you, darling girl!'

Ruby dialled another number, spoke calmly into the receiver. 'Marc, it's your mum. If you don't get back to me ASAP, I will bloody well disinherit you. You heard me.

I know you have gambling debts so it's your choice, son, take it or bloody leave it.'

The cottage

The medication was wearing off. Her tongue felt swollen and sore as she felt around her mouth. Some teeth were missing. She felt the raw, bloody space where they had been. The softness of tissue around the space. Touched her lips, felt the wet of saliva. She was dribbling. She felt small and vulnerable. She began to cry.

Chapter 25

Carmyle Station

Bradley and Brock Roach

Wheeler scrolled down their Twitter feed on her mobile phone – @Blue-eyedBrock&Bradley. 'Nothing but pictures of them posing and pouting. And pictures of their art. Fucking hell, these two are in for models. I mean really? Really?' She glanced at that morning's edition of the *Glasgow Chronicle*. Page two was devoted almost entirely to pictures of the two boys, shirtless, posing on the bonnet of a swish car, at some exotic beach, all ripped muscle and what looked like shimmering baby oil.

'They have a reputation for violence?' asked Boyd.

'Yes, according to Ruby De Luca, so I want to have a quick word with them ASAP,' said Wheeler.

'Based on what?' Stewart stood at the door. 'You were supposed to do the press conference earlier, Wheeler.'

'Anyone can do the press conference,' said Wheeler. 'Boyd and Robertson made an excellent job of it, by all accounts.'

'The point is I told you to do it,' said Stewart.

Wheeler was aware of Seb Hawk quietly taking notes. She hoped that the usual spats of the station didn't make it into the book. Or if they did, that at least no names were attached.

'So, where are you off to now?' said Stewart.

'To talk to the Roach twins,' repeated Wheeler.

'Because?' said Stewart.

'Because they may well be involved in this case,' said Wheeler.

'Because an old lady didn't like them, and they weren't nice to a *vulpes*?' asked Stewart. 'I've been updated.'

'A what?' asked Ross.

'A bloody fox,' said Wheeler.

'Why didn't the boss just say that then?' said Ross, under his breath. He glanced at Hawk, who was jotting down notes in shorthand. 'This place is getting very fucking weird.'

'An anonymous phone message came in while you were out,' said Boyd.

'And?' said Wheeler.

'A student of CoVA was attacked last year, name of Craig Brennan. Apparently, it was pretty bad. No one was ever done for it.'

'I wonder if it was the Roach twins?' said Wheeler. 'If they beat up another student of the CoVA last year? Plus, they may have had a run-in with a member of staff and have had issues with Nick Price. I think we definitely need to have a chat with them.' Wheeler stood, saw the hieroglyphs Seb Hawk was using, hoped that they would get a look at the book before it was published. Doubted it. 'I'm betting that the governor of the college the twins had a run-in with was Michael O'Donnell.'

'Go careful,' said Stewart, scrolling through the news-feed on a computer. 'Apparently, according to STV, the Roach twins are the next big UK models. Their manager has informed the media that they have quarter of a million followers on their Twitter feed, loads of followers on Instagram and Facebook. If they aren't involved, we don't need a social media backlash against the police. Plus, their artwork is selling fast.'

Wheeler did not remind him that the last time he had uttered that phrase he had been wrong. What she should do is not go careful but go strong. She grabbed her coat. 'Ross, let's go.'

Thirty minutes later, Wheeler rang the bell.

One of the twins answered, she had no idea which one. He was wearing a tight T-shirt and denims. She couldn't swear to it, but she thought a little foundation and mascara. Perhaps a touch of lip gloss.

'And you are?' asked the twin. 'If you're double glazing bores, we're not interested.'

They flashed their ID. 'Detective Inspectors Wheeler and Ross,' she said. 'May we come in?'

The twin smiled. 'Are you a fan of ours, old girl? Or is this a professional visit?'

Wheeler resisted the urge to slap him.

A voice from the back. 'Brad, who is it?'

'Polis, Brock,' Bradley shouted back before standing aside and letting them enter.

In the living room Wheeler met the other twin. Brock was eating a steak, taking great gulps of it in between slugging from a bottle of Diet Coke. 'So, what's up, man?'

'We're investigating a murder,' Wheeler started. 'Michael O'Donnell.'

'Yeah, he was a governor at CoVA,' said Brock. 'I heard he'd been snuffed.'

'Very sympathetic,' said Ross.

'It's all in the news,' said Bradley.

'We barely knew him,' said Brock. 'He has a retarded daughter.'

'He has a daughter suffering from epilepsy and related complications,' said Wheeler. 'A young woman who is now missing.'

'Yeah, I read that Paula's done a runner,' sniggered Brock. "'Cept she can't run.'

'I didn't know her well,' said Bradley, laughing.

'She tried to hang out with the cool guys at college,' said Brock.

'Who are?' asked Wheeler.

'Us,' sniggered Brock. 'But we ignored her.' He made an L-shape with his thumb and forefinger. 'She's a loser.'

Bradley smiled.

'I understand that you've recently had an altercation with Nick Price?' said Wheeler.

'Oh that, it was a misunderstanding. It was a one-off. We're never in trouble. Didn't you read the piece about us in the local paper?' asked Bradley. 'We're model students in more ways than one. Plus, we are shit-hot artists.'

'Our art is terrific, everyone thinks so,' said Brock. 'Plus, we're about to make it big time as models. We're going stratospheric. You'll look back and be grateful that you even met us.'

'Tell me about the last time you were in Mount Vernon?' said Wheeler.

'I get it, that old witch De Luca called you, didn't she? About the shitty mange-ridden fox? And then the wheelchair cruiser, Paula, who has a crush on my brother here, turned up and put her oar in,' said Brock.

'Where were you last Saturday?' asked Wheeler.

'Here.' They spoke in unison.

'Can anyone verify this?' asked Wheeler.

'Us,' they chimed perfectly.

She watched as the twins pointed to each other and laughed. They were their own alibi. How very convenient. There was something about them, the smugness, the effortless good looks. But it was their eyes that she most recognised. Vladimir Nazarewich had unusual coloured eyes and the expression in them didn't trouble her. But the expression in the eyes of the Roach twins did. Cold. Dead. Whether the twins had done anything up until now, she had no doubt that in the future they would commit crimes. Handsome as they were, their real persona shone through their eyes. Ruby De Luca was right, they were potential killers. The trouble was, was Michael O'Donnell their victim, or were their victims somewhere in their future? Wheeler knew that she could not count on Ruby De Luca's bias, convenient as it may be, to expose the killer.

'So, love, if you're quite finished?' Brock made for the door.

'What can you tell me about Craig Brennan?' asked Wheeler.

'Oh, not all that shit again,' said Brock. 'Does that old witch never stop telling lies? She's nuts. His attack had nothing to do with us and if she says otherwise, we'll fucking sue. We have an agent, management and we're properly represented.'

'Do you live here alone?' asked Wheeler.

'Yeah, our mum has a holiday home in Malaga. She spends most of the year out there.'

Wheeler couldn't blame her, what must it be like living with these two narcissists? 'When you were at the open evening for the college, you had words with one of the governors.'

'Yeah, so?' said Brock.

'Was it Michael O'Donnell?'

'Nope, we had "words", as you say, with the crazy lecturer.'

'Who?'

'Ms Barnes Olsen. She's right into religion, upturned crosses,' said Bradley. 'Satanism or St Peter's cross.'

'How so?'

'Some biblical dude wanted to be crucified upside down, seems he didn't feel equal to Christ. And Christ was crucified right way up, but I reckon she's a witch and the upside-down crucifix is satanic.'

'Way out of line, that shit,' said Bradley.

'Agreed.' Brock sipped his Coke, smiled a too perfect smile with unnaturally white teeth. He smirked at Ross. 'How much do you two make? What's your annual salary?'

'None of your business,' said Ross.

'That right? Only we've just signed a modelling contract that's going to make us millions. Plus, with our artwork selling like bloody hot cakes, people like you are going to have to come through our people in future if you want to talk to us.' He looked at Wheeler. 'Including you, darlin'.'

'People like me will go straight through anyone who gets in my way in a murder investigation, including you two,' said Wheeler. 'Is that absolutely clear?'

The twins stared at her.

'Well?' growled Wheeler.

'Clear,' said Brock.

'Clear,' said Bradley. 'Sorry.'

Outside, Wheeler and Ross walked to the car.

'Little shits,' said Ross.

'Little sexist shits,' agreed Wheeler.

In the car, she took a call. Ended it quickly. 'The result of Michael O'Donnell's autopsy has confirmed what we suspected. He was stabbed to death. Then gratuitously slashed. So much we know already.'

'Look at this.' Ross passed her his phone. She scrolled down the Twitter feed. A series of tweets read:

@Blue-eyedBrock&Bradley

Just had a visit from @police Scotland. Very scary #policeintimidation #speakout #innocent #useyourvoice

Next up:

@Blue-eyedBrock&Bradley Horrified to find out that a precious member of our college is missing! Let's find Paula O'Donnell, a student from @CollegeofVisualArts We need specialist help. Let's fundraise to bring someone in! A professional! Would be awesome if @ChetAustin was on board to #justfindpaula

Wheeler watched as the heart symbols reached over five hundred in less than a minute. The likes and shares multiplied into tens, then reached the hundreds. And then moved quickly upwards.

'Fuckssake.' She handed the phone back to Ross. 'Little buggers. So this is now all about them. Bloody narcissists. And who the hell is Chet Austin?'

'Some American bounty hunter. He has his own TV show,' said Ross.

'That's all we need,' said Wheeler.

'I know,' said Ross.

'But whoever he is, he has no jurisdiction here,' said Wheeler. 'So, there's no need to worry.'

'I hope you're right and this doesn't disintegrate into a social media mess,' said Ross. 'You know how bad that would look for the station.'

Chapter 26

dEADdOG

Tala

Tala ignored the message from her gran, pulled her laptop towards her on the bed. Her stepmother was at work. This was her secret time. Tomas was at nursery. She was meant to be at college, but this was way more important. She opened the site. She had been accepted to the next level. She held the acknowledgment open as long as she could, revelling in the excitement. All too soon it disappeared, but she'd seen it. She knew that she was finally a full member of the dEADdOG community. That finally, she belonged.

Now she had to do as they asked. She had to plan her own death, her 'suicide' the others would call it. The uninitiated, the ill informed. Who the hell cared about people who were pretending. She was real. The group was real, and they would show doubters that they were the real thing. What was it the Moderator called it? Congruence. Real on the inside and the outside. I Am Nothing, she repeated to herself. I.A.N. Their mantra. I am Nothing. I am Nothing. It was the only thing that made sense to her.

She thought of her birth, her impending death and her rebirth. What did the uninitiated know of death and rebirth? Nothing. Her life was nothing now, but after death she would be reborn. She'd felt guilty about her gran, but she couldn't respond. This was way too important. She hoped that she'd meet her mum on the other side.

Tala let the harsh music wash over her, become part of her. Thought of last term when Assistant Principal Kirkpatrick had asked her to stay behind after class. 'Maybe we could go for a walk? Talk about the Fauvist painters, or indeed any painter. In particular, Georgia O'Keeffe. I think your work resembles hers. At least it could be, in time, as great.' Him, in his fifties, shaved head and tweed jackets. Loud trainers. Like he was a teenager in his head. What did he want with an eighteen-year-old art student? Tala knew. She'd seen another student at the front of the class flirt with him. But it was her, Tala, who he had asked to stay behind, asked if she could call him Rob. Tried to put his arm around her. Kiss her. She hated that he was coming back to the college. Dreaded it.

But, she reminded herself, that unpleasant incident was then, and this was now. And what she had to get on with was planning her goodbye. Her final goodbye.

While she waited for her next instruction, Tala took out her sketch pad. She quickly completed a rough sketch of Leroy from his profile picture. She faithfully captured his calm smile, the serenity of his expression. Her sketch was sharp and accurate, she had looked at his picture a hundred times. She picked up her phone, photographed the sketch and posted it to the group.

TALA: Good luck when your special day comes. You will look beautiful. As always. Love you, Tala. See you on the other side.

A few minutes later, his response.

LEROY: Yes, we are soul mates. We will soar towards the stars together.

Moderator:

dOGdEADdOGdEADdOGdEADdOGdEADdOGdEADdOG
dEADdOGdEADdOGdEADdOG**TALA**dEADdOGdEAD
dOGdEADdOGdEADdOGdEADdOGdEADdOGdEADdOG
TALAdEADdOGdEADdOGdEADdOGdEADdOGdEADdOG
dEADdOGdEADdOGdEADdOGdEADdOGdEADdOGdEAD
dOGdEADdOGdEADdOG**YOURSOULMATEISLEROY**
dEADdOGdEADdOGdEADdOGdEADdOGdEADdOGdEAD
dOGdEADdOGdEADdOG**TALA**dEADdOGdEADdOGdEAD
dOGdEADdOGdEADdOGdEADdOGdEADdOGdEADdOG
dEADdOGdEADdOGdEADdOGdEADdOGdEADdOGdEAD
dOGdEADdOGdEADdOGdEADdOGdEADdOGdEADdOG
dEADdOG**TALA**dEADdOGdEADdOGdEADdOGdEADdOG
dEADdOGdEADdOGdEADdOGdEADdOGdEADdOGdEAD
dOGdEADdOGdEADdOG**TALA**dEADdOGdEADdOGdEAD
dOGdEADdOGdEADdOGdEADdOGdEADdOGdEADdOG
dEADdOGdEADdOGdEADdOG**TALA**dEADdOGdEAD
dOGdEADdOGdEADdOGdEADdOGdEADdOGdEADdOG
dEADdOGdEADdOGdEADdOGdEADdOGdEADdOGdEAD
dOGdEADdOGdEADdOGdEADdOGdEADdOGdEADdOG
dEADdOGdEADdOGdEADdOG**TALA**dEADdOGdEA
DdOGdEADdOGdEADdOGdEADdOGdEADdOGdEADdO
GdEADdOGdEADdOG**YOUWILLSOARTHROUGHTHE
UNIVERSEATEXACTLYTHESAMETIME**dEADdOGdEA
DdOGdEADdOGdEADdOGdEADdOdEAdOGdEdEADdOG
dEADdOGdEADdOGdEADdOGdEADdOG**TALA**dEADdOG
dEADdOGdEADdOGdEADdOGdEADdOGdEADdOGdEAD
dOGdEADdOGdEADdOGdEADdOGdEADdOGdEADdOG
dEADdOGdEADdOGdEADdOGdEADdOGdEADdOGdEAD

dOGdEADdOGdEADdOGdEADdOG**TALA**dEADdOGdEAD

dOGdEADdOGdEADdOGdEADdOGdEADdOGdEADdOG

dEADdOGdEADdOGdEADdOGdEADdOGdEADdOGdEAD

dOGdEADdOGdEADdOGdEADdOG**KNOWTHATYOU**

HAVEBEENCHOSENdEADdOGdEADdOGdEADdOG

dEADdOG**TALA**dEADdOGdEADdOGdEADdOGdEADdOG

dEADdOGdEADdOGdEADdOGdEADdOGdEADdOGdEAD

dOGdEADdOGdEADdOG**TALA**dEADdOGdEADdOGdEAD

dOGdEADdOGdEADdOGdEADdOGADdOGdEADdOG

dEADdOGdEADdOGdEADdOG**TALA**dEADdOGdEADdOG

dEADdOGdEADdOGdEADdOGdEADdOGdEADdOGdEAD

dOGdEADdOGdEADdOGdEADdOGdEADdOG**TALA**dEAD

dOGdEADdOGdEADdOGdEADdOGdEADdOGdEADdOG

dEADdOGdEADdOGdEADdOGdEADdOGdEADdOG

TALAdEADdOGdEADdOGdEADdOGdEADdOGdEADdOG

dEADdOGdEADdOGdEADdOGdEADdOGdEADdOGdEAD

dOGdEADdOGdEADdOGdEADdOGdEADdOGdEADdOG

dEADdOGdEADdOGdEADdOGdEADdOGdEADdOG

TALAdEADdOGdEADdOGdEADdOGdEADdOGdEADdOG

dEADdOGdEADdOGdEADdOGdEADdOGdEADdOGdEAD

dOGdEADdOGdEADdOGdEADdOGdEADdOGdEADdOG

dEADdOGdEADdOGdEADdOGdEADdOG**TALA**dEADdOG

dEADdOGdEADdOGdEADdOGdEADdOGdEADdOG

REJOICEINTHISMESSAGEdEADdOGdEADdOGdEAD

dOGdEADdOGdEADdOGdEADdOG**TALA**dEADdOGdEAD

dOGdEADdOGdEADdOGdEADdOGdEADdOGdEADdOG

dEADdOGdEADdOGdEADdOGdEADdOG**TALA**dEADdOG

dEADdOGdEADdOGdEADdOGdEADdOGdEADdOGdEAD

dOGdEADdOGdEADdOGdEADdOGdEADdOGdEADdOG

dEADdOGdEADdOGdEADdOGdEADdOGdEADdOGdEAD

dOGdEADdOGdEADdOGdEADdOG**TALALEROY**dEAD

dOGdEADdOGdEADdOGdEADdOGdEADdOGdEADdOG

Anne Randall

dEADdOGdEADdOGdEADdOGdEADdOGdEADdOGdEAD
dOGdEADdOGdEADdOGdEADdOGdEADdOGdEADdOG
dEADdOGdEADdOGdEADdOGTALAdEADdOGdEADdO
GdEADdOGdEADdOGdEADdOGdEADdOGdEADdO
GdEADdOGdEADdOGdEADdOGdEADdOGdEADdOG
LEROYTALAdEADdOGdEADdOGdEADdOGdEADdOG
dEADdOGdEADdOGdEADdOGdEADdOGdEADdOGdEAD
dOGdEADdOGTALAdEADdOGdEADdOGdEADdOGdEAD
dOGdEADdOGdEADdOGdEADdOG

176

Chapter 27

Carmyle Police Station

Wheeler stood in front of the information boards and studied the photographs of Paula O'Donnell. Paula looked like a beautiful little doll. Eighteen years old with an elfin face, brown eyes protruded from high cheekbones. Her dark hair had been cropped close to her skull. Wheeler knew that Paula weighed around eight stones and was five foot six. She stared at the image – the upturned nose, the sweet smile. A young and very beautiful Audrey Hepburn. 'She looks like she should be starring in a Disney film,' said Ross. 'Only one with a happy ending.'

'She looks like a film star. Angelic,' said Boyd. 'She has this gazing thing going on, like they have in the old paintings of saints and martyrs, the soulful look as they are being taken up to heaven or transfixed with passion for some deity. Like somehow their suffering has elevated them to some kind of a supernatural state.'

Wheeler looked again at the photograph. Paula did indeed look like an ethereal beauty. Her lips were set in a perfect Cupid's bow, her dark soulful eyes turned mournfully towards the camera. Very beautiful.

'What do we really know about her?' asked Robertson, coming into the room and dumping a stack of papers on his desk. 'Remind me because she feels like she's fading fast.'

'What do we think, team?' asked Wheeler.

'I reckon she's dead,' said Boyd quietly. 'She looks too fragile to have lasted this long. I read the reports – numerous fits, suicidal tendencies, couldn't keep her food down. How could she still be here?'

'Unless her abductor is somehow keeping her alive?' said Ross.

'The human spirit can be very strong when it comes to survival,' said Robertson, holding up two large notebooks. 'These arrived when you two were out visiting the Roach twins. Paula kept two diaries, "Normal for CoVA" and "Diary Alien".'

'"Diary Alien"?' asked Wheeler.

'I think she felt a little like a freak, sometimes very frail, and, like many teenage girls, she didn't like her appearance,' said Robertson. 'Despite the fact she looked fabulous.'

'I've had a quick look at the CoVA diary,' said Robertson. 'Brock Roach teased her a lot.'

'So far so usual for him,' said Ross. 'Little shit.'

Wheeler took up the "Diary Alien". Read aloud, '"I sometimes think that I don't belong here on this planet. In this life. I am an alien, too small to be fully formed and yet I'm here. I look at pictures of Mum and Dad and struggle to see myself in them. Did they adopt me? And if so, whose child am I? Aliens? Brock told me that because Mum was foreign, Brexit will mean that I should go and live in Amityville. I like the idea of other foreigners like Vladimir Nazarewich being made to return to his own country. I feel suffocated by my life.

"'I spoke to Ms Barnes Olsen. She is small with short hair. I think she looks a little like me. Perhaps we are both from an alien race?'"

Wheeler picked up the second diary.

November

Boat-face McSweeney was way out of line today. She asked me what I thought of her stupid new sculpture. Her prize shit. A sculpture of some woman. Apparently, it defined the feminine. Bullshit.

I couldn't tell her the truth, obviously, so I said, 'I think it looks great.'

Boat-face corrected me. 'She. I told you about her provenance, Paula. I told you all about her history and meaning.'

I could tell she was cross, she stared straight at me as if she had special powers to bend me to her will. She droned on and on. I thought of the great art I'd seen. Of the fantastic lecture about Frida Kahlo and women like her.

Boat-face still droned on.

But I wasn't listening.

'Paula!' She spoke with irritation.

When I saw Brock and Bradley making signs behind her back, I knew that Mr Van Der Berg, from the Pastoral Centre was on his way. They would have seen him through the doorway into the corridor. Mr Van Der Berg always comes to collect me in my wheelchair. And they always make fun of this. And of him.

'What I mean, Miss McSweeney,' I said to Boat-face, 'is that I couldn't listen when you were talking. I just felt too faint.' I sniffed.

McSweeney looked at me. 'Paula, why are you crying?'

'Ms Barnes Olsen was giving me grief for not feeling well and stopping to rest in the corridor, so I'm feeling very fragile.'

'Indeed, I was not,' said Ms Barnes Olsen from the doorway.

I kept my head down. I didn't want to get into trouble. And then Boat-face McSweeney asked Ms Barnes Olsen if she would accompany her into her office.

Wheeler stopped reading. 'Well, Paula certainly seems to have had a handle on the twins and their behaviour.'

'Plus, she hated McSweeney.'

'And dobbed Barnes Olsen in it too,' said Ross. 'Sounds as if she didn't much like anyone.'

'Barnes Olsen said that Paula was "tricky",' said Wheeler. 'That she could be angry.'

'Perhaps Paula knew that they didn't really care for her? Plus, she would have been struggling with a great deal of pain. Heart-breaking,' said the rookie officer.

Wheeler read on through other excerpts.

Diary #1: My dad is the biggest hero ever! He just bought me tickets to see the Rubes! And I get to go backstage (in my wheelchair, I know how lame is that?) but it's backstage to meet the lead singer, Madison De La Fontaine. I can't wait.

Wheeler thought of what the pathologist Hannah Scott-Fletcher had told her: 'The Rubes have now arranged for some of their fans who have disabilities to meet them backstage.' So, Paula O'Donnell had been scheduled to meet the band. Wheeler also recalled that Hannah had mentioned Madison having extra security on the door of their King Tut's gig because she'd been stalked by Frankie Fermin.

'Boyd, did you get any update on a Frankie Fermin? Guy who was on the train with Sarah Price?'

'Christ,' said Boyd. 'Sorry, Wheeler.' He flicked through his notes. 'I did. Frankie Fermin is registered with Parkhead Psychiatric Hospital. He's a complete fantasist. Gravitates towards women, tries to make small talk. Completely socially inept. The hospital says he's annoying, rude and quite overbearing but ultimately harmless. He talks of trying to sue the Rubes and other bands. He's completely delusional.'

'Right, well if they're sure?' said Wheeler.

'They seemed pretty certain,' said Boyd.

Wheeler returned to the diary.

My dad is just the loveliest man in the universe. I know he doesn't get the Rubes, but he recognises that I do. They played T in the Park last year for God's sake. I watched it on YouTube. The crowds loved them, and Madison De La Fontaine just let herself fall into the crowd and surfed it. They all held her and passed her through them until the song finished. It was so beautiful. And now Dad has arranged for me to go backstage to meet her. Omg. Omfg! Dad, you're the greatest. Not that I'd tell you that. As you know I'm a teenager. A stroppy one at that, as you tell your friends. I know. I've overheard you. But I know you love me. Ditto.

Diary #2: Was at the art club today. God, but Nick Price is an absolute arse. Could not be any shittier. It's only a matter of time before he goes off the rails. Nick knows I occasionally use a wheelchair but let the door go in my face. I now have a bruised knee. He's a cunt.

Diary # 3: So, some big shot artist name of Francesco Soule is running this competition to see who is the 'most promising' student at the CoVA. I bet it will go to one of the bloody Roach twins. Not that their work is anything brilliant, but they look photogenic and isn't that all that matters in some of these competitions? I was thinking about entering an art competition in a glossy magazine, but they asked for a photograph, so I didn't bother. Why are these things always linked to what we look like? I don't agree that we should win prizes for our looks. I know I look like Audrey Hepburn and that Dad says 'talent will out' but I'm not convinced. It all seems so contrived.

Diary #4: I had a rough day today. My meds don't seem to be working too well and I'm exhausted. There was an incident around old Mrs De Luca's place about an orphaned fox cub. Mrs De Luca is Tala's grandma and she is a lovely woman. I don't think she deserves sulky little Tala as a granddaughter. Anyway, the Roach twins were kicking – yes kicking – the poor wee fox and Nick Price intervened. It would have been the least he could do, given his background. It shows though that maybe he has a decent side. At least around animals. Those two Roach boys though. What could they have been thinking? I heard that they'd been humiliated about their poor performance on the football field, but really to take out your frustration on a poor defenceless creature? What kind of morons are they? Yes, I know, they are super sexy but still. But still. They're fuckwits. Bradley hates me, called me a retard. Didn't tell Dad.

Diary # 5: I'm making my own version of an inverted cross. Ms Barnes Olsen says that it needn't be specific, but I think that if you are going to go to the trouble of making a cross then it must mean something. I won't tell anyone what my cross represents, that would be way too lame, but the person involved will know that I'd love to see them crucified to death, upside down. They would not be worthy of anything else. #unworthy #justgiveitup #die

Diary # 6: I'm not sure about this cross thing. I think bad things are going to happen to me. I read that if you provoke Satan then it may come back to you. I spoke to Ms Barnes Olsen and she said that it's just art. Nothing sinister will happen and not to worry. She makes jewellery out of the ashes of dead people.

Diary #7: Dad has that guy coming around today to play another chess game with him. I don't understand why. Dad is a member of the chess club at college. Why does he need him? I hate those guys. They pretend to play chess or whatever, but I know they are just drinking my dad's good malt. They should buy their own. I'm scared of the one called Vlad Nazarewich, he makes me nervous. I think Brexit is a good thing. Dad says no, but why not? Dad told me not to bring it up with them, it's too sensitive an issue. Not that I ever go down when Vlad's here. His yellow eyes scare me.

Wheeler looked at the last entry. What did it tell her? Why was she scared of Nazarewich? And who was it that Paula had made the cross for, who was it that she wanted dead?

Ross crossed to the kettle. Made two coffees. He took one for himself, put the other mug on Wheeler's desk. 'The paper says they've been inundated with people offering to help but no actual fresh leads.'

Wheeler scrolled down the front page of the online newspaper, the *Chronicle*. 'I see the Grim Reaper has done himself proud.'

The headline screamed,

**Police Admit That They Have No New Leads on
Missing CoVA Student Paula O'Donnell!**

Concerns are growing for the teenager who was abducted from her home in the quiet residential area of Hamilton Road in Mount Vernon some time on Saturday afternoon. Friends of the popular student at the College of Visual Arts have insisted on joining the police search around the area where Paula was last seen.

Local celebrities, including artists and models Brock & Bradley Roach, have backed a crowdfunding Kickstarter campaign to pay for specialist help to be brought into the case. The #justfindpaula campaign now has tens of thousands of followers. The specialist help they suggest is USA bounty hunter Chet Austin who has reported that he would be 'delighted and honoured to follow the trail of the killer who abducted little Paula'.

'We need to get someone professional on board before it's too late,' said Brock Roach. 'The local police have nothing, so bringing in Chet Austin seems like a no-brainer.'

'The little shits, there's no way they can do this during an ongoing investigation,' said Ross, grabbing his jacket. 'I'm going to see them.'

'Ross, for God's sake, sit down,' said Wheeler. 'Of course, there's no way the twins will get this through, our legal team will be all over it. It's nothing more than a publicity stunt. This isn't about finding Paula or even Michael O'Donnell's killer. It's a publicity campaign for the twins and the American bounty hunter, Chet Austin, who's just some low-rent reality television guy.'

'I've met Chet Austin,' said Seb Hawk quietly. 'He operates out of Phoenix, Arizona. Makes a better salary than most bounty hunters in the state. Big guy, wears a handlebar moustache and a Stetson.'

'Does he ride a bloody horse?' asked Boyd.

'He does,' said Hawk. 'Often.'

Robertson scrolled down through the twins' Twitter feed. 'So far, their tweets about the campaign have nine thousand likes and three hundred and seventy shares. And counting. Let's look at Chet Austin's site.' He flipped to @ChetAustin who had been copied into the tweets. 'He's responded to @Blue-eyedBrock&Bradley.'

'Saying what?' asked Wheeler.

'Honoured to be asked to come to UK to help @ policescotland with their investigation. Thanks to @Blue-eyedBrock&Bradley for the invitation #justfindpaula.'

Stewart stood in the doorway. 'I've just had a phone conversation with the superintendent and to be quite sure, I can report that he was not impressed. His first word were, and I quote, "Have you seen this shit?"'

Wheeler saw that Hawk's note-taking had quickened. He was recording everything.

'Plus, there's this,' said Robertson, sitting back from his computer. 'The tech guys have unlocked Sarah Price's laptop.'

'Go on,' said Wheeler.

'Sarah Price had multiple debts. Looks like she was struggling to pay them off, a credit card sitting at four thousand pounds, an overdraft coming in at just under two thousand and three personal loans amounting to £13,300.'

Wheeler listened.

'Sarah Price's salary was £30,465 a year less tax. Her debt was around £19,300. Plus, her mortgage was £625 a month.'

'Plus, bills, electricity, gas, council tax, water, food,' said Robertson.

'She wasn't coping, was she?' said Ross.

'Certainly not financially,' said Wheeler.

'Could she have faked her death for insurance?' asked the rookie officer. What if she and her ex, Ian, were in this together? He takes care of the son and she goes missing so they get a payout from insurance? Then their son, Nick, goes off to college or university.'

Silence in the room.

Finally, Robertson spoke. 'Unlikely. Let's just keep an open mind and all that,' he said. 'Let's keep digging.'

Chapter 28

11.30 p.m.

Wheeler was exhausted, she knew that she was not thinking straight. Her go to at these times was the computer. Let faceless technology feed her facts, let the information stay with her and then sometimes, later, when she was doing something completely mindless, like the laundry, the stats and her cop mind would come together and there would be a small but important link or discovery.

Wheeler looked at the information from Missing Persons in Glasgow. Were Paula O'Donnell and Sarah Price part of a bigger picture? And no one seemed to know that Sarah Price and Michael O'Donnell had been lovers. And what about Zoe, the missing beauty therapist? Wheeler scrolled down the long list. Statistically speaking, some were already dead, and their bodies would be missing for ever, others would turn up at some point, their corpses discovered in some woodland or waste ground, or dredged out of the River Clyde. Others wanted to remain missing, while some would be found, safe and well. Those might well be reunited with loved ones and the wheel of life would continue for them.

Wheeler kept reading, scrolling though the information, letting it settle around her. She needed time to think. Not just about Michael O'Donnell and his missing daughter, Paula. Or Sarah Price. She needed time to consider the missing in Glasgow. She read on.

Eighty-nine-year-old Manny Ulrich had gone missing from his nursing home in Rutherglen.

Evie Evenguard, nineteen, who'd attended the CoVA and had left after one term. Evie hadn't been a party girl, hadn't been a drinker or a drug user. She had been described by the former headmaster of her school as, 'A superb student. One who will excel at life and any challenges it may throw at her. A natural to gravitate towards law, her sense of justice was unparalleled.' And Joanne Reilly, sixteen, another student at the CoVA, who'd disappeared two years previously after having an argument with her father. Zoe Wishart, a trainee beautician, who'd disappeared a couple of years ago, on her way to meet a friend. She had vanished close to Ian Price's home.

Wheeler compared the missing women. Evie was five foot seven with dark hair cut into a short bob. Paula, five foot four with short brown hair. Joanne, five foot three and wore her blonde hair long. Sarah Price was five foot two inches in height, of curvy build, with short blonde hair. Zoe was a redhead. What were the facts telling her? That there was a link or were all the disappearances merely random?

Sarah Price. Had she been involved with the death of her lover, Michael, or was she also a victim of the killer? And what about Paula O'Donnell? The clock was ticking.

Wheeler felt a headache kick in and she gave up, she stood and stretched. She knew that she was exhausted and so she gathered her things and left. Outside, beyond the glare of the station's strip lighting, was welcome nightfall. She glanced up at the stars, calm in their ordered universe. Imagined that they twinkled back their support. *Keep going, you will find the killer.*

Will I? she wondered, slamming the car door. Her head ached, her throat was sore and, more than that, more than any physical ailment, she knew that the team had nothing. Sweet FA. They were all tired, and they needed something, a breakthrough to give them hope and energise the case.

She drove through the snow, on down London Road, on past Belvedere Village and the Sir Chris Hoy Velodrome. The radio blared Christmas songs as she drove towards the Merchant City, and her flat in Brunswick Street. She loved the area, with its high-end cocktail bars and exclusive designer shops, which sat cheek by jowl with partly demolished buildings, their insides gaping and bare in the freezing cold. Also, the old-fashioned bars where music belched out until the small hours and patrons congregated outside the doorways in groups, sucking on damp cigarettes, exhaling smoke fumes into the night. Wheeler didn't want any of that, at this moment she just wanted to curl up on the sofa with a glass of wine and listen to her go-to musicians – Thelonious Monk, Sonny Rollins and Hank Mobley. Cosiness, that was what she was craving. And maybe a takeaway pizza from the Italian restaurant opposite her. With extra mozzarella. Pure comfort food. But she needed it.

Ten minutes later, Wheeler slowed the car in front of the heavy wrought-iron gates. As they rolled back she drove into the inner courtyard. The copper tubs held their usual ivy and evergreens. The old stone was hidden beneath a thin layer of snow. As she took the stairs she could smell the now familiar nutty aroma of turpentine from the flat opposite hers. As she made her way to the landing, the door opened. 'Are you still in work mode, Wheeler, or can you take a break?'

Wheeler paused, 'I'm shattered, Hawk.'

'Then you definitely need to take a break. Have you eaten yet?'

'No, I haven't—' she paused '—but really, you don't need to always be offering to feed me.'

'Then why don't you come in for a quick drink?' He smiled. 'Let's have an off-record chat. I can make you a coffee or something stronger?'

She paused. 'Today's been a shit day and tomorrow, as you well know, isn't shaping up to be any different.'

'I'm not asking you to move in, just to have a quick drink.' He grinned. 'Really, is it too much to ask from a neighbour?'

'You're not just a neighbour. You're a colleague who is recording every step and misstep of my team.'

'I'm a journalist, merely an observer of police procedure, and hopefully I'll report it in the proper context. I'm really not out to do a hatchet job on you or your colleagues, trust me, Wheeler.'

Wheeler looked at his mischievous smile. 'Fine, a quick drink then.'

'Now what can I get you? I'm drinking Pernod but what would you like?'

'I'd like a Chardonnay,' she said. 'A large glass please.'

'Then that is what you shall have.' He disappeared into the kitchen and Wheeler was left alone in the room. A number of large canvases had been brought in since her last visit.

He reappeared. 'Here we are, one Chardonnay for you and another Pernod for me.'

Hawk's flat was identical to hers in that both were light and airy. His was also sparsely furnished, mainly mid-century, but it was the artwork which really interested her. The huge canvases. Full height oils, maybe around the six-foot mark and glorious in colour and form. 'They're beautiful,' she said. 'Really, honestly, beautiful.'

'You're too kind but I only paint to relax. It's just a pastime of mine and most of them are still unfinished. I brought them over from Aubree's flat.'

Wheeler strolled over to one. It was impressive in both its height and composition and it was the closest to the work of her favourite artist, J. D. Fergusson, in quality as she had seen. 'Gorgeous.'

'I'm glad you like them. I have an exhibition coming up at the Art House Gallery later this month. There's going to be a drinks reception on the opening night, if you'd like to come? I'd love you to see them properly hung in a gallery space, they'll be more impressive.'

They were impressive now, thought Wheeler. 'I don't know, I may be working.'

'What makes you need to be at the station all of the time? I've noticed that you're rarely home. Surely it should be a team effort? I mean, work–life balance and all that shit.'

'You've seen our workload.' She sipped her wine, noticed again that it was far superior to what she had back in her own flat.

'I have and it's my turn to be impressed but I don't think anyone does their best when they are on the job 24/7.' He paused. 'Anyway, it's not up to me. I've made a few nibbles, I often pick on them if I am working overnight on a painting. Tempted?'

Wheeler was hungry. 'I'd love some.'

'My pleasure. I love cooking but it's never better than when I'm sharing food. Eating on one's own is never the same.' He changed the CD. 'Sonny Rollins' *The Bridge* all right to keep you company while I'm away?'

'Sure.' Wheeler stood and studied the paintings.

'Have you tried that new place, Bar 7 & An Angel?' he called through from the kitchen.

'Where's that?' said Wheeler. 'Is it in the Merchant City?'

'The one with the black and gold mosaic entrance,' said Hawk.

'Fabulous entrance, but no, I've never tried it.'

'We should go,' said Hawk. 'Perhaps I could treat you when the case is finished?'

Wheeler sipped her wine, felt the knot in her shoulders unravel. Wondered just when the case would be over and if they would have a positive outcome.

A few minutes later he returned from the kitchen with a wooden platter.

'Wow. They look amazing.'

'It's nothing. Here, eat.'

Wheeler looked at the food and her mouth watered. 'What are they?'

'A mixture. Tiny arancini, which are risotto balls with an arrabiata dipping sauce. Slivers of fig, Camembert and red onion tart, mini Halloumi bites with pear and savoury choux buns with Gruyère and wild mushroom.'

'Fantastic,' said Wheeler.

'I find it relaxing to cook. It's similar to painting in that you take the raw ingredients and try to create something else. And like shadowing you guys at the station, I take the raw material of your days and distil it into a book. I take the essence of what happens and make it believable for the reader.'

'Believable?' asked Wheeler in between mouthfuls.

'Understandable, might a better description.'

'OK.' Wheeler helped herself to a tiny Halloumi bite. 'These look delicious.'

'I need to tell you about my cousin, Aubree,' said Hawk.

'Go on.'

'OK,' said Hawk slowly. 'I told you that she was in love with a detective.'

'Yep.' Wheeler heard the change in tone, knew that whatever he was going to say was serious.

Hawk sipped his Pernod. 'She's in love with Steven Ross.'

Well, so that's what's been on Ross's mind, thought Wheeler. 'Really? And is Ross in love with her?'

'That's where it gets complicated,' said Hawk. 'She's pretty sure that he is. I'm not sure if he's interested and just wants to take it slowly or . . . '

'Or he's just not that into her?' said Wheeler.

'You can see my predicament,' said Hawk. 'I work alongside Ross, but Aubree's my cousin.'

'Complicated,' said Wheeler, helping herself to one of the savoury choux buns. Finished it. Added a sliver of tart to her plate before she looked up. 'Well, Ross hasn't mentioned anything to me, but that's nothing to go on. He knows that we're neighbours. If you like, I'll have a friendly chat with him, if that's what you're wondering? See what I can find out?'

'I just don't want to see Aubree heartbroken,' said Hawk. 'She reacts badly.'

'Fair enough,' said Wheeler, biting into the tart. 'Wow, this is fantastic. You sure you just didn't buy them from the new deli?'

'Scout's honour,' laughed Hawk.

She was on her second glass of wine when a text came through. Hawk was recounting a self-depreciating but amusing tale of how his poor sense of direction and chronic inability to map-read had impeded him while driving across America's fabled Route 66.

'So, I was heading from east to west, seems reasonable, doesn't it? I began at Illinois, made it through to Missouri and thought I had the hang of it, I only needed to get to the next place, Kansas, but then I took a wrong road . . . ' Hawk had paused mid-sentence when her mobile chirped. 'Do you need to take that?' He stood. 'I can wait in the kitchen if it's confidential?'

She glanced at the message. It was from Ross. *You around?*

Wheeler paused. Knew that it wouldn't be case-based, Ross probably just wanted to come over. Saw another text come through. *You want company?*

She smiled at Hawk. 'No, I just need to send a quick text.' *I'm fine. See you at the station tomorrow.*

She let the phone slide back into her pocket. 'Carry on, I'm enjoying your adventures. You were going to Kansas, when you took the wrong road.'

'Not only the wrong road,' Hawk laughed, 'a bloody disastrous road. As I said, I was meant to be heading to Kansas but got disorientated after staying up all night playing poker with a guy known as Heaven Sent. You can imagine what he supplied. And could he play poker? My head wasn't on straight the next morning and there was no one else up at that time for me to ask, so I just headed out. Ended up in Arizona.'

'Is that when you encountered Chet Austin?' asked Wheeler.

'What a bloody nightmare,' said Hawk. 'Austin was on the trail of Dalston Weinkert and he was closing in on the fugitive. Weinkert had been hiding out in . . . ' And so he continued.

It was 3 a.m. when Wheeler eventually crawled into bed. A few hours in Hawk's company felt like she'd been on holiday for a week. She thought of his other adventures on Route 66, and of the year he had spent painting in Antibes. He told her that he had spent the summer in Golfe-Juan, a resort on the Côte d'Azur, which had echoed the artistic journey of Fergusson. Suddenly Wheeler's own life seemed rather small. But Hawk had been very generous. 'You do the real work. Beside you, I feel like a dilettante.'

The truth, Wheeler felt, lay somewhere in the middle ground. She felt very attracted to Seb Hawk, but what she wanted to know, what she hadn't asked him, was where was his wife, Marilyn? Was it true that it had all been a mistake? And could she trust him to tell the truth?

Chapter 29

Tala had finally revealed all to the dEADdOG community. Her entire story. She'd gone further back and included why she struggled with her four-year-old stepbrother, Tomas. How his mother, Autumn, was the reason her dad had left her mother. How her dad had had a stupid fling with his then personal trainer, Autumn Novak. How bloody clichéd. And then Autumn had got pregnant and her dad had left her mum and bloody married Autumn. Do the maths, Tala wrote. Compare the salary of a personal trainer (*junior* personal trainer) of around £25,000 and living in a shared flat, with the salary of Tala's dad (she knew it was over £200,000, the arms trade paid well) plus a large five-bedroom detached house in Mount Vernon. It had been a no-brainer for Autumn. Five foot seven and a size eight, blonde ponytail and so much younger than him, she was a walking cliché. Plus, there was the perma-tan from the time spent in the salons. So, right on cue, Dad had left Tala's mother. The fights, the arguments, the name calling. It had been a mess. After he left, Mum had stayed focused on Tala and had begun making a life for them both. That was, until the night her car had slid off the road on ice. She had been killed instantly. And now Dad spent all his time working abroad while Autumn expected her, Tala, to look after Tomas.

Now Tala had another task to do for the Moderator. A supreme act of defiance that would allow her to enter the sacred annals of time. Before that though, she had to offer two sacrifices. One, she had to destroy something that she loved. Later, herself.

Tala turned on the music, put on her headphones. Rewatched the violent images. She was completely desensitised, and it felt great, but they had warned her that she would have to be diligent and stay strong. Topping up the videos and music would help her do that. They had informed her not to speak to the uninitiated, the outside world, the non-believers. She couldn't speak to her gran. The music thundered in her ears, the violence played out before her. She was numb. She felt strong, emboldened. She would soon be gone to her glory. She would smite something she loved. Smite, she liked that word. Leroy had told her about it. He was about to smite his stepdad. An old biblical word. Not that she was religious. It depended on the Moderator. Only the Moderator could decide if she was worthy of the next level. And then she received it. His reply. Her hands shook as she pressed, *open*.

cONgraTUlatiONs
iT'S yOUr cHOiCE, tALa
cHOoSe wELL
and
aCT with the fULL aUthoRITY
oF

a
dEADdOG
sOCIEty mEMbER

Tala felt a ripple of excitement. The Moderator trusted her, this was to be her choice. The Moderator had approved of her. He knew that she was serious, that she could be trusted. She sat back on her bed, rested on the stupid cushions her stepmother had put there. This was her time to decide. For this moment in time, she was God. And she would savour it. And to hell with Autumn and the rest of the ambulance-chasing sharks who had crowded around to keep her alive last year. And the previous years, when she had wanted to die. It had not been an accident or an oversight. They had intentionally dragged her back to a world that she didn't want to live in. And now she had to do it all over again. She didn't want to live in this shitty world. Why would they force her to remain here? She would never be a great artist, so what was the point? Tala thought of the birthday party weekend that her father had sprung for her, six months earlier. The cottage up in Balmaha. Everything had been paid for, and it should have been perfect. She'd had her hair dyed, her black jeans and Ramones T-shirt were edgy and provocative. She should have looked great for the guy she was in love with. They'd been together for one night. She hadn't realised that he already had a bloody girlfriend. He'd told her, confessed. She'd felt used. Then swarms of midges had descended and had curled and buzzed around her and bitten her relentlessly. She was allergic to them and what was supposed to have been a great weekend had meant that she had looked swollen, boiling hot and ridiculous. She had let herself down. She had felt used and stupid and ugly. Why hadn't she known that he had a girlfriend? What was wrong with her? And then she had cried in front of everyone. Pathetic. 'I am nothing,' said Tala quietly, 'I am nothing. I.A.N.'

Chapter 30

Tuesday 15 December, Morning

The buildings of the hospital loomed ahead of him. Ross walked on, quickly made his way inside. Took the stairs to the required floor. Tried not to gasp with each floor. Shit, he wasn't as fit as he thought.

'Shortness of breath?' the cardiac nurse asked him, when he arrived.

'Yes,' said Ross. He watched her write this information down.

'My GP insisted that I come here. I only went in to get some information on the tightness in my chest.' Ross paused. 'Do I have heart problems?'

'It could be that you have,' said the nurse, 'but not necessarily.'

'My dad died of a heart attack,' said Ross. 'I know that these things can be hereditary.'

'Since your father had a heart attack,' the nurse continued, 'we have to carefully consider your medical history.'

'Right now, I feel fine,' said Ross.

The nurse put down her pen, glanced at her notes. 'Except for the pain around your heart?'

'I don't have it all the time,' said Ross. 'So, what are you suggesting?'

'That we investigate. Heart attacks and other conditions, such as angina, reflux acid, etc., are similar in that they share certain symptoms.'

'I was sick the other morning,' said Ross. 'Acid reflux, I reckon.'

'Go on.' The nurse took up the pen again.

'But I had been drinking the night before.'

'Excessively?' she asked.

Ross thought of the shots of tequila he'd consumed at the White Hart pub on Friday night and decided to be frank. 'Yes.'

'Give me a ballpark number.' The nurse waited.

'Quite a few,' said Ross. 'To be honest, I lost count.'

'We need to set up a series of appointments for you to access imaging and blood tests,' said the nurse. 'That way, we'll have a better, more informed picture of what is happing to you.'

'OK.' Ross felt defeated. All that gym work, all that running. Now it was just down to this. Genetics. His gran on his mother's side had died of heart attack. His father too. Was that all he was, just a bag of DNA, scheduled to explode at a certain time? 'So, there's no way of knowing today?'

'No. You may have some issues or a cardiac condition. We'll find out.' She peered at him. 'Are you a healthy eater?'

'On and off,' he lied.

'Uh huh,' she continued writing. 'Smoker?'

'No,' said Ross.

'Alcohol consumption, apart from the other night? Usually excessive?'

Ross looked at the floor. 'I'm a cop.'

'I'll take that as a yes.' She peered over her glasses at him. 'Units consumed per week?'

Ross knew that medics usually doubled the amount of alcohol units patients admitted to and halved the amount of exercise they said they did. So, he did the maths on her behalf and presented the sanitised version.

'There may be several contributing factors to your condition,' said the nurse, noting the information.

'Which are?' asked Ross.

'Emotional stress being one of them,' said the nurse. 'Have you been under any additional stress recently?'

'No,' said Ross.

'Nothing happened say, in the last year or so?'

'Well, my dad died,' said Ross.

'That's quite a factor. Anything else? No new love affairs or recent break-ups?'

Ross said nothing. He thought about his feelings for his father, his rage against his mother and her second fucking husband. How he blamed them for his father's unhappiness, depression and excessive drinking. Not to mention his feelings for Wheeler.

'No,' he said.

'A surge of emotion can trigger hormones and stress,' said the nurse, 'which can have a big impact on the heart.'

'So, I'm an emotional mess, a time bomb just waiting to go off?' said Ross.

'The heart can only deal with stress hormones for a certain level of time. Then it gives up. It's exhausted.'

'But it's not fatal?' asked Ross. 'I mean time heals and all that malarkey?'

'I'm afraid it can be fatal, if left untreated,' said the nurse.

'The heart tries to keep going but may fall into cardiogenic shock through exhaustion. You may be suffering from Broken Heart Syndrome, in which case you may experience difficult arrhythmias. This can damage your heart and potentially lead to a heart attack.'

'Why didn't I even know about this?' said Ross.

'You know about it now.' The nurse closed the folder on his information. 'We'll get to the bottom of this for you. Don't worry.'

'Great,' said Ross. 'That's good to know.'

'I'll get you booked in for an angiograph,' said the nurse.

'Which is?' asked Ross.

'Nothing to be concerned about,' said the nurse. 'We just inject some dye into your blood and then we administer medication to increase your heart rate to mimic exercise and we can see how your blood vessels are doing. In the meantime, I want to give you a course of statins, aspirin and beta blockers.'

'I don't want to take anything immediately,' said Ross. 'Until I know for sure.'

'Why not?'

'I don't like taking medication,' said Ross. 'Especially if it's not needed.'

'You would only be taking it for three months,' said the nurse. 'Until the results of your angiograph are available.'

'And if it's all clear?' asked Ross.

'Then you can stop the medication right away,' said the nurse.

'But I would be taking beta blockers, aspirin and statins for three months. All of which have side effects, don't they?' said Ross.

'But they will keep you safe,' said the nurse.

'I'm not sure,' said Ross. 'The thought of having all those drugs in my system for months makes me feel uncomfortable.'

'Right,' the nurse sighed heavily, 'in that case I'll give you this.' She handed over a spray.

He glanced at it, read 'Sublingual'. Put it in his pocket.

'If you get chest pain again spray once under the tongue, wait five minutes. If the pain continues, spray again. Wait five minutes and then a third spray. If the pain continues, call an ambulance. Right away. Got it?'

'Got it,' said Ross.

'I'll be in touch,' said the nurse.

Ross left the hospital, headed for the deli closest to Wheeler's flat. He needed some breakfast to console him. Bloody hell. What a fucking morning.

Chapter 31

Wheeler's flat, Brunswick Street, Merchant City

The intercom buzzer sounded as Wheeler was finishing her shower. Since she'd had a late night at Hawk's she'd allowed herself an uncustomary lie-in. It was Ross. 'I brought us breakfast.' She opened the door to find Seb Hawk leaving his flat on his way downstairs. 'On my way out for breakfast. I love Café Romano, they do the best croissants, pain au chocolate and café au lait but then you probably know that already, don't you, Wheeler?' said Hawk.

She was aware that Ross had turned into the landing and was watching Hawk. She felt herself blush for no reason. Hawk smiled and looked at the coffee and rolls Ross held. 'Ah, you brought us all breakfast, DI Ross, how thoughtful.'

Ross ignored the smile. 'Enjoy your breakfast, wherever it is.'

'I'll leave you to it.' Hawk moved past Ross.

Wheeler closed the door behind them.

'He's always so bloody full of himself, isn't he? Bloody Seb Hawk. He made me feel like the tea boy.'

'Jesus, Ross, he was only joking, for goodness' sake.' She took the fried egg rolls and put them on a plate. 'Come through, these look great.'

'They're from the new takeaway.'

'I know,' said Wheeler.

'Not quite the artisan coffee and croissants I heard Hawk offer.'

'Geez, Ross. Get a grip,' said Wheeler. 'I just met him on the landing.'

'Yeah, in your robe,' said Ross.

She slapped his arm, hard. 'You got me out of the bloody shower.'

'So, were you busy last night?'

'Yeah.'

Ross looked at her. Waited.

'I was having drinks and tapas with Hawk,' said Wheeler.

'He was here?'

'No, in his flat, he's such a good cook and he made the most delicious food.'

'I'll bet,' said Ross.

'Bloody hell, Ross, the tapas were terrific.'

'Right.' Ross cut through her. 'I get it. He can cook. I don't need the bloody details.'

'He was showing me his artwork. He's an incredible painter,' said Wheeler. 'His work's stunning, really fabulous.'

'Great,' said Ross. 'Just great. But isn't that a conflict of interest?'

'How so?' she asked.

'You work with him, Wheeler.'

'He's observing us for a book, muppet. What is the

matter with you? Are you jealous that he's now part of our team?' She watched Ross reach into his pocket and bring out some kind of a spray.

'Is that another hand sanitiser?'

'No.'

'What then?'

'The thing is, Wheeler, I need to have a chat—'

Wheeler's mobile rang. It was the station. She listened to the message. Flicked it off. 'Let's go, Ross. There's been another murder.'

'Where?' asked Ross, quietly putting away the spray.

'Villa in Blackcroft Gardens.' She glanced at him, saw that he hadn't started on his egg roll. 'You can finish that on the way to the car.'

'Yeah, whatever,' said Ross, following her. 'I think I just lost my appetite.'

'God, you are getting even more sensitive.' Wheeler walked on. 'Steady on, partner.'

Chapter 32

Ross drove.

'You OK?' said Wheeler. 'Only you seem very quiet?'

'I'm fine.'

Wheeler left him to it. If he was sulking because she'd spent the previous evening with Seb Hawk, then that was his problem. They had always been close but come on, really? She couldn't have a drink with a colleague? She waited until they approached the scene before she spoke. 'Sounds vicious.'

'Nightmare,' said Ross.

'The dead guy was a medic and an academic. He was renting the house.'

'Unlucky for him,' said Ross. 'All that medical knowledge and it didn't keep him alive.'

Wheeler looked at him. 'What the hell is wrong with you?'

'Nothing, I'm just saying,' said Ross.

'That he was a medical doctor and somehow that information was meant to keep him alive?'

'Just that you never know when your time will come.'

'Stop being so bloody melodramatic, Ross.'

He said nothing.

The victim's house was obvious, given the amount of emergency vehicles parked outside. Wheeler noted that the crime scene had been secured and the familiar army of forensics, police and SOCOs were mapping the place and photographing every angle. She approached the uniformed officer. 'What do we have? Do you have a name for our victim?'

'Dr David Buckley, a London GP and academic. He was on sabbatical for research. Late forties. He rented this place after splitting up with his partner last year. The partner stayed in London. The dog-walker says Dr Buckley was a lovely, gentle man. She's not coping at all well. She found him this morning. Came in to work and the victim was lying on the floor, his head a bloodied mess. She's outside with uniform having a cup of tea in a car; she'll be back in presently.'

'Where is the dog?' asked Ross.

'No idea. Name of Toby. A Bernese. The dog-walker said it was missing when she arrived.'

'Who owns the property?' asked Wheeler.

'It belongs to a Mr Anthony Stephens. It had been for sale, but he'd taken it off the market.'

'Because?'

'Until house prices stabilised.'

'Where is Mr Stephens now?'

'He's at the station.'

Wheeler left her and continued towards the officer issuing the familiar covering. She checked the door, there was a lock and a bolt, but nothing had been forced. Just like in the Michael O'Donnell murder. Whoever the killer was, the door had been opened to them. Inside the house, the air was stale with violence and blood. It was as if the building itself was in shock. The hallway was long, and the parquet flooring gleamed with polish. Apart from the blood smears. It looked like the victim had been dragged from the door, through the hallway and into the bedroom at the end of the corridor. Dr David Buckley's body lay beside his bed. Blood covered the pulpy mess of what would have been his face. Hannah Scott-Fletcher was again the pathologist in attendance. She looked up as they entered the room. 'I'm just finishing up, Wheeler. Hi, Ross.'

'What do we have?' asked Wheeler. She struggled to ignore the smell. Saw Ross cover his mouth with his hand.

'From first impressions, it's just as it seems,' said Scott-Fletcher. 'Our victim was attacked and battered to death with a heavy object.'

'Looks brutal,' said Ross.

'Yes, it was. He had no chance at all. He was hit from behind; my guess is that he let whoever it was in and turned to lead them through the hall and then he was struck. The damage to the back of his head is substantial.' Scott-Fletcher stood. 'Do you want a close look before I get him taken away?'

Wheeler leaned forward. Dr David Buckley was lying on his back; a black halo of dried blood surrounded his head. His jaw had been hit with such force that it had rearranged the bottom part of his face, giving him the look of a macabre ventriloquist's doll. He had been wearing a tracksuit and trainers and they were crusty with blood. 'I hope at least whoever did this to him left their DNA. This much blood, surely they must have?' said Wheeler quietly.

'I hope so, Wheeler. I hope so.' The pathologist sounded fatigued.

'Busy day, Hannah?' asked Wheeler.

'Busy days. We're two staff members down, plus in the evenings my partner Madison's out gigging. The Rubes are doing really well but, so far, I'm averaging four hours, maybe four and a half hours sleep tops, every night. It's wreaking havoc with my love life. Maybe I should be single?'

'Nightmare,' said Ross.

Wheeler wasn't sure if he meant being single or the sleep deprivation. There was something off about Ross, she wasn't sure what it was. But she couldn't worry about his moods or love life right now, she had more than enough on her mind. She saw that he was staring ahead, he never could manage more than a cursory glance at a corpse and was even worse at post-mortems. Not for the first time she wondered if he would stay the course as a DI.

She spoke to the pathologist. 'Do we have an estimated time of death?'

'Difficult to be precise but the body is bloated and there is discharge from both the mouth and nose.'

'Which tells us what?' asked Ross, still not looking at the corpse.

'That it's been between three to five days,' said the pathologist. 'Certainly, uniform says that our victim, Dr Buckley, was one of the good guys according to the dog-walker. He did local community work, helped raise hundreds of pounds via sponsored bike rides for the refurbishment of the local art college, the College of Visual Arts.'

'So, he was linked to CoVA?' said Wheeler. 'So was our other victim, Michael O'Donnell.'

'Then you have something to work on,' said the pathologist.

Wheeler looked around her. The place was swarming with SOCOs, sifting, bagging and photographing; surfaces had been dusted with fingerprint powder.

'DI Wheeler.' A voice from the hall. 'You need to see this.'

Wheeler walked into the hall. A bronze statue of a whippet, about 40 cm high by 20 cm wide. It was a handsome statue, except that it was smeared in dried blood. The statue had been processed by the SOCO and now it was being carefully removed.

'So, the killer took the statue from outside the front door and battered him with it?' said Ross from the doorway.

'Yes,' said the SOCO. 'Looks like it happened that way.'

'So, any good news for me?' said Wheeler, returning to the pathologist.

'Sorry, but I'll need to get back to the lab,' said Scott-Fletcher, standing. 'That's where the real magic happens.'

On her way out, Wheeler passed a uniformed officer. 'Anything else you can tell me?'

'No CCTV covering this stretch of the road, sorry, DI Wheeler.'

'Any indication that Dr Buckley had been robbed?' asked Wheeler.

'The dog-walker says no; the victim's wallet and mobile phone are in the living room on the table. There's nothing to suggest the attack was motivated by robbery.'

'Great,' said Ross. 'Just bloody great. We have nothing to go on.'

Wheeler strode on. 'Stay focused, Ross. This is what being a detective is all about.'

Back at the station, Boyd updated her on the Michael O'Donnell case. 'The area had been targeted by Just-Conservatory, a conservatory/double glazing firm in recent weeks.'

'Get on to them, find out who was in the area,' said Wheeler. 'In the meantime, where's CCTV of the area?'

'Nothing,' said Boyd.

'The road at least?' she said.

'You know as well as I do residential coverage doesn't always throw up much,' he said.

She couldn't contradict him. It was fine to want CCTV, to want the killer to be caught on camera sauntering away from the crime scene, their face uncovered and immediately identifiable. Realistically, she had to face facts, in many residential areas this resource was not available.

Details of the new murder case were already on the information board under the name, Dr David Buckley. A picture of him had been placed centrally on the board. Before becoming a bloated corpse, David Buckley had had deep grey eyes and an open honest face. Underneath the picture were scant details. Wheeler updated the team: 'Dead three to five days. He had been on sabbatical to complete some research papers. He was in his late forties. He lived alone after splitting with his partner. He liked Indian food and walking holidays, preferring to stay in hostels to big hotels. He cared greatly about the community in general and humanity. He was vegan and a practising Buddhist,' she said finishing up. 'He loved animals and had one dog, Toby, a Bernese, which is missing.'

'Anything else?' asked Stewart.

'He raised money for CoVA,' said Wheeler, turning to Boyd. 'Get on to the college. Find out if David Buckley knew Paula and Michael O'Donnell.'

'Will do.' Boyd picked up the phone.

'Paula O'Donnell's mobile phone has been traced to a restaurant dumpster out by Partick,' said Robertson. 'Vegan Heaven.'

'Anything useful on it?' asked Wheeler.

'Nothing. Looks clean. The tech team is still working on it.' Robertson read from his notes. 'The staff at Vegan Heaven didn't know either Paula or Michael. No link.'

'Then it was probably dumped,' said Ross.

'Sarah Price's ex, Ian Price,' said a uniformed officer loudly. 'He did time in the Bar-L for murder. Look at this.'

Wheeler was behind him at his desk.

'What am I meant to be looking at?' Ross joined them.

The officer ran his finger under the information on the computer screen. 'Ian Price. Did time for murder back in 2008. Killed a guy, name of Nigel Thorogood. He told his victim, "Don't you know? This is how evil people die."'

'Sounds a lovely guy. So, he taunted his victim before he killed him?' said Ross.

'This was what he said to his victim. The man was treated by paramedics, but Nigel Thorogood died shortly afterwards,' said Boyd.

'And now his ex is missing.' Wheeler grabbed her coat. 'Right, Ross. Let's go have a chat with Ian Price.'

'He's staying over at Sarah's house, ostensibly to take care of Nick,' said Robertson.

'Right,' said Wheeler. 'I'm on my way.' She paused. 'It's a long shot but can you check Dr Miriam Studley's research on epilepsy? I saw it in Michael O'Donnell's home. Just as an add-on? And any other research?'

'Will do, Wheeler.'

'Thanks.' She was out of the door.

Chapter 33

Mount Vernon

They were less than ten minutes into their chat.

'I was a different person back then,' said Ian Price.

Wheeler had been informed otherwise. Burglary, resisting arrest, a list of misdemeanours. 'Go on.'

'I was young and daft. I thought crime was the way forward. I thought I was going to be the next gangland hero. I was obviously mistaken.' Ian Price leaned towards her, his eyes narrowed, his huge hands clasped in front of him. 'DI Wheeler, I did my time and learned my lesson, you have to believe me. Now I've moved on.'

'Remind me of the details.' Wheeler waited. 'What led you in?'

'Things got out of hand,' Price said. 'I was looking for "an in" and heard Nigel Thorogood was running with some very heavy guys, drugs, extortion. The usual.'

'And that's when you came in?' said Ross. 'You offered your services?'

'Nigel Thorogood owed good money on bad debt. He thought he could take the piss and get away with it.'

'So, you went after him,' said Ross. 'You joined the heavy guys?'

'Thorogood eventually tried to face me down, so I had no option. That was my role, to make folk pay for taking the drugs and not paying their dues.'

'So, you became an enforcer?' Wheeler snapped.

'If you want to call it that, then, yes.' Price laughed. 'But I've learned my lesson, I'm totally legit now.'

'And many of your "clients"—' Ross cupped his two forefingers into quotation marks '—heard you say, "This is how evil people die."'

'It was a phrase. It sounded good. I didn't mean it.' Price smirked. 'Well, at least not all of the time.'

'Until you met up with Mr Thorogood?' Wheeler prompted.

'Nige was a dreamer. A professional numpty. He was up to his ears in debt. And, as a gambler, I know you pay your debt, or you pay the fucking consequences,' said Price.

'Nigel Thorogood was a human being,' said Ross.

'He was an idiot,' said Price. 'He thought he could take the stuff, outwit the organisation and make a profit. He needed to know the real fucking deal. What did he think was going to happen?'

'So, you murdered him?' said Ross.

'He had to go,' said Price.

'So, you killed a dreamer? Well done. Very courageous slashing someone so defenceless to death,' said Ross.

'You don't get it, do you?' said Price. 'You don't live on the street, do you? You don't know the fucking rules. You're a fucking snowflake.'

'Rules?' said Ross. 'If someone is armed and his opponent

isn't then it's a fair fight? Doesn't seem very fair to me. Looks like a lamb to the slaughter.'

Price shrugged. 'Life of milk and honey, you lot live. Life's not fair. Besides, as I'm sure you know, I did my time. I was, if I say so myself, an exemplary prisoner.'

Wheeler looked at her notes, 'Apparently you took a number of classes on self-improvement while you were incarcerated.' She reeled them off, 'Computing for beginners, advanced computing and developing IT solutions. Quite the IT student, weren't you?'

'So fuckin' what?' said Price.

'And now Michael O'Donnell is dead. Murdered in a very similar fashion to Thorogood,' said Wheeler. 'And your ex-wife, Sarah Price, is missing.'

'So? Again, fuck all to do with me.' Ian Price lit up a cigarette. Puffed on it furiously. The smoke filled the room.

'And you say you haven't seen her recently and you hadn't met Michael O'Donnell, but you met at the college, the CoVA open night.' Wheeler kept her voice reasonable. She wasn't going to mention the earring yet.

'I didn't say I didn't know O'Donnell. I knew of him. Yeah, he was maybe at the open night, but everyone associated with the college was there. They were all milling about, can't say I remember him specifically. I was a bit tipsy. I'd had a few drinks, but why not? I work hard.'

'Were Sarah and Michael close?'

His eyes narrowed. 'No idea. You tell me. Were they?'

'Where do you work, Mr Price?' asked Wheeler.

'I do odd jobs in the community.'

'Go on.'

Ian Price swallowed. 'A bit of gardening here and there.'

'In this weather?' prompted Wheeler. 'It's a bit cold for gardening, surely?'

'Winter gardening, clear-ups. Window cleaning, DIY. You name it, I can turn my hand to it.' Ian Price glared at her. 'Odds and sods. I make a living. Claim the odd benefit.'

'And presumably you have a client list we could look at?' asked Wheeler.

'No, never bother with the paperwork, it's all word of mouth,' said Price. 'It's not a fucking crime is it?'

'Were you jealous of Michael O'Donnell?'

He stared at her. 'No, I bloody wasn't.'

'You sure?' asked Wheeler.

'Positive,' said Ian Price.

She watched him glance down at his large hands.

'You can see how it looks, can't you, Mr Price?' said Ross. 'Tricky at best. You have a reputation for being quite the jealous character.'

'So, you reckon I knew Michael O'Donnell was shagging Sarah and I killed him? For fuckssake. I killed him and now I've stashed her dead body under my floorboards? Then get yourself a warrant and go look. You won't find anything. In fact, don't bother with that, let's all just take a minute to get to my place and I'll lift the floorboards myself.'

Twenty minutes later, Wheeler and Ross left.

'No point,' said Wheeler.

'I disagree,' said Ross. 'I think we should have torn his place apart.'

'Right, so you'd have gotten a search warrant for ... what exactly?' said Wheeler.

Ross said nothing.

'There's nothing at his home, no dead body of his ex-wife

and certainly no clues about Michael O'Donnell,' said Wheeler. 'Ian Price was way too cocky.'

'He could have been bluffing?' suggested Ross.

'I don't think so,' said Wheeler. 'What he offered us was a look at his place; what we must find out is where else he has access to. A lock-up, or a garage? We need to find out more about him and how he funds his gambling habit, how he earns enough money to fund his lifestyle. It sure as hell isn't gardening.'

Wheeler's mobile rang. It was Robertson. 'Dr Miriam Studley was an academic, specialising in epilepsy and the effect it has on families.'

'Go on,' said Wheeler.

'She died two years ago.'

'Suspicious circumstances?' She waited while he read the report.

'Skiing accident in Gstaad.'

'Find out about Dr Buckley's work,' said Wheeler.

'Will do.'

'Thanks, Robertson.'

'There's more.'

'Go on.' She waited.

'David Buckley sat in on a few meetings with Michael and Paula O'Donnell.'

'Good work, Robertson. Follow it up.' Wheeler killed the call.

Lovers' Tryst #2

6 months earlier

Why the fuck did you do it?

I was stupid drunk. An idiot.

That's not good enough.

I know.

I need to know that I'm the most important person to you.

You are. You know that.

Doesn't look like it.

I said I was sorry a million times.

And as I've said. It's not enough.

I'll do anything to make us good again.

You should.

But what you are asking is a lot.

Why? You've done it before. To a stranger. I saw you. I was just passing by, but I saw. Sheer poetry.

Zoe was a mistake. I got carried away. It was the spur of the moment. I took too many risks. This time she can be traced.

Last time she could too. The Zoe situation hasn't gone away. They could still find her.

It was a mistake. I should have been more careful.

You had no self-control. These things take self-discipline.

I have control now.

I taught you that.

I know.

If there's a will . . .

I know.

Are you going to do it?

Yeah.

You need to do it to make it up to me. You know that don't you?

I know.

We two are soul mates. We're alive in this time and place for a reason. We have no need for the other rules. Their pathetic rules. Fuck them.

I want to be free.
Then live freely. You have done so already.
I know. So, what now?
Game on.

Chapter 34

The Incident Room at Carmyle Police Station

'Sarah Price told her friend, Maria Brothcotte, that she was on Kik,' said a uniformed officer.

'What the hell is Kik?' asked Robertson.

'An instant messaging mobile app,' said the officer.

'Geez, I can't keep up,' said Robertson.

'You register and can be anonymous. You can chat, send photographs, message and a lot more. And no one knows who you are. No one knows your name, the country you're in, your address, nothing. You're completely anonymous.'

'Freaky,' said the rookie officer.

'Or safe?' said Boyd.

'What else did the friend say?' asked Wheeler. 'Anything we can use?'

'Not so much, she was in tears. Said she felt guilty that they had fallen out. She said they hadn't talked in a while. She said that Sarah had mentioned a boyfriend. No names. All hush-hush. But he had a poorly daughter.'

'Michael O'Donnell?' said Wheeler.

'She reckons it could have been. She says he was demanding and a very particular parent.'

'Right.'

'Maria said that Sarah had split with the controlling guy and had joined some online dating agency, Looking4Love, she reckons it was called. Said she couldn't be sure, she can't really remember.'

'Get onto them, find out if Sarah joined and who she was communicating with, also if she was meeting up with someone.' Wheeler grabbed a coffee and carried it through to her office. Fired up her computer. She glanced out of the window, saw a truck pick up waste from across the road; dusk was just beginning to descend. There was a thick layer of snow which had settled already. As the truck pulled away, she saw a bulky object on the pavement on the other side of the road. She stared at it. She was sure that it hadn't been there a few minutes ago. She squinted through the window. What was the large lump? Was it a dog? she thought. Had it been hit by a car?

Ross came through the door.

'Come over here a moment,' said Wheeler.

He was beside her in a second.

'What the hell is that?' said Wheeler.

'What?' said Ross.

'Look, across the road. Is it me or is it a dog? Or . . . ?'

He made for the door. 'Only one way to find out.'

They were downstairs and out of the station in seconds. They sprinted across the road and stood over the lump.

'It's a dead dog,' said Wheeler.

'Yes,' said Ross. 'But its head . . . its head is . . . '

Wheeler stated the obvious. 'Its head is missing. It's been decapitated. What on earth happened?'

'How the hell did it get here?' said Ross.

'I think it was dumped here, across from the station.

I think we were meant to find it.' Wheeler nudged her boot into the animal. Poked around a bit.

'Jesus,' said Ross. 'Leave it alone. It's fucking gross.' He took out his little bottle of hand sanitiser. Sprayed a few drops on his hands. Rubbed them together furiously.

Wheeler continued to press her boot into the animal carcass; eventually it shifted slightly, and an object became visible. 'Look at this, Ross.'

Ross leaned over the animal, peered into the open throat of the creature, where an object had been buried. 'An inverted cross,' he said and reached again for the hand sanitiser. 'Jesus.'

'We found what they wanted us to find.' Wheeler scanned the area. There was no one in sight. She took an evidence bag from her pocket and carefully picked out the bloodstained cross, avoided moving the carcass. There was something written on the cross but she couldn't make it out. It was saturated with blood. She glanced at the animal. Its brown, white and black fur was getting wet. Snowflakes were already starting to cover it. She touched it with a gloved hand. 'It feels frozen.'

'It would be, out here,' said Ross.

'No, I mean properly frozen. Like it's been in a freezer. I'll get uniform over to move this, we can't leave it out here.' She glanced at both sides of the road. The lights changed, a few cars and lorries made their way carefully through the heavy snowfall. A large HGV came towards her, lights in the cabin sparkled a Very Merry Christmas. Yes, she thought, you too. Have a Very Merry Christmas.

'Right, Ross,' she said. 'Let's get this back to the station. I feel like we've just had a very personal calling card.'

Chapter 35

Three hours later

'So, what's with the decapitated dog?' asked a young officer in uniform coming into the room.

'A satanic offering?' offered Boyd.

'Maybe just a prank, really nothing more?' said Hawk, just entering the room.

Silence.

'Bit of a coincidence,' said Ross staring at Hawk. 'The fact that it was deposited opposite the station. Plus, the fact that it had an upturned cross in its throat, sort of gave the game away. With regard to it being just a prank, that is.'

'I didn't know that,' said Hawk. 'Apologies.'

'Animal sacrifice, do you think?' asked the rookie officer.

'Did they kill it to tell us something?' said another officer.

'If you did want to leave a calling card like this, how would someone even get hold of a headless animal?' said an officer at the back of the room.

'Unless you killed it?' said Robertson. 'In some countries, dogs are meat. Dinner.'

'My boyfriend threatened to order dog meat when we

were travelling in Vietnam,' said a uniformed officer. 'I said I couldn't kiss him if he'd eaten it. Urgh, even the thought of it makes me want to bloody retch. We have two rescued greyhounds. How could he?'

'So, the whole thing is what?' said Ross. 'A satanic warning to us? Or a bloody dietary recommendation?'

'Satanism is a recognised religion,' said Wheeler.

'Come again?' said Ross. 'They want to sacrifice animals to intimidate us?'

'Remember the very freaky Ms Barnes Olsen said that there were students at the CoVA who identified as satanists?' said Ross.

'A bloody affectation,' said Boyd. 'There's no rebellious spirit any more. Fucking comfy, middle-class, stay-at-posh-hotels-when-on-holiday students identifying as satanists. Give me a fucking break.'

'Possessed by spirits? Like in *The Exorcist*?' asked Ross.

'A lot of people, from many religious and spiritual backgrounds, believe in spirit possession,' said Wheeler.

'You think whoever took Paula is leaving a warning about her?'

Wheeler sighed. 'I have no idea if this is a present from the killer, the abductor taunting us or, frankly, if there's been a leak and some prankster knows about the crosses and this is just one almighty wind-up and time-wasting exercise.'

'What about Vlad?' said the rookie officer. 'Vladimir Nazarewich?'

'Because he wears a cross? Hardly a bloody crime,' said Ross.

'I'm just saying. He wears a crucifix and believes in all this religious stuff. And there was an upturned cross in the poor dog.'

'Are you crazy?' said Ross.

'Bloody hell,' muttered Robertson. 'You are more of an idiot than I ever thought.'

'I'm not remotely religious,' said the rookie. She held her hands up. 'I'm just saying, I'm just wondering. That's all.'

'I'm curious about the whole satanism thing,' said Wheeler.

'I hate it,' said an officer. 'Just looking at the pictures gives me the creeps. The torturous faces on the figures. Gross.'

'If it's a prank, then who? One of the kids at the college? The Roach twins, maybe?' said Robertson. 'Is this something they might do?'

Wheeler took a sip of coffee, gave herself time before she replied. 'I don't think the Roach twins did it. They strike me as handsome and artistic but are they devious enough to organise a decapitated animal being delivered to the station?'

'I don't know, Wheeler,' said Ross. 'They have an average of A- in their grades at the CoVA.'

'Fair point but are they resourced enough?' said Boyd.

'Then who?' asked Wheeler.

There was a silence.

'The College of Visual Arts' said Wheeler. 'I think the truth lies there.'

'So, who at the college? One of the staff?' said Boyd.

'Or a student?' Wheeler finished her coffee. Her stomach felt empty and acidic. Too much coffee, no food. A headache kicked in. 'Which leaves it wide open.'

'What about Tala De Luca?' asked Ross.

'You think she could be the culprit?' Wheeler reached into her handbag.

'I think that there is something about her that's disturbed,' said Ross. 'Her gran, Ruby De Luca, asked us to keep a lookout for her. Suicidal, so nothing to lose?'

'So, Tala De Luca has Paula? Or she's playing some game with us, pretending that she had her?' Wheeler rooted around in her bag for painkillers. 'Uniform spoke with her. Came up with nothing.'

'I don't know, Wheeler,' said Ross. 'There's something about Tala that's off. Her stepmum said that she was manipulative and all that running away the other day, a little bit theatrical, don't you think?'

'She's a teenager,' said Wheeler. 'That's what they do.'

'I'm aware of that, but she's a disturbed teenager. Her stepmum, Autumn, told us as much, when we met her,' said Ross. 'And a disturbed teenager can lead to problems.'

'Go on,' said Wheeler.

'What if Tala is caught up in this whole thing?' said Ross. 'What if she has abducted or killed someone else?' said Ross. 'What if she's targeting the vulnerable? Including a dog?'

Wheeler sat back in her seat. 'Tala murdered Michael O'Donnell and abducted Paula?'

'A possibility?' said Ross.

'I'm not sure it makes sense,' said Wheeler. 'Tala's way too slight to have done it herself and even with an accomplice, what would be her motivation?'

'She certainly could have had an accomplice,' said Ross. 'And we don't know the why yet.'

Wheeler popped open the foil on two painkillers. Swallowed the tablets dry. 'Fair enough. You dig into that and I'll see you tomorrow.' Her phone rang. It was forensics. 'The message carved into the cross is "dead dog".'

'"Dead dog"?' she repeated.

'Yes, Wheeler, but spelled dEADdOG.'

She noted it down.

'And another thing.'

'Go on.'

'The dog was a Bernese. It was microchipped. Name of Toby, belonged to—'

Wheeler interjected, 'Dr David Buckley.'

'Yeah, right. You need his address?'

'No, we already have it,' said Wheeler.

'The dog had been kept in a freezer.'

'I imagine that it was taken when its owner was murdered. And kept as a present for us.' She finished the call. Looked at the team. 'Well, guys, the dog was Dr Buckley's and you know some of the new graffiti we have been seeing across the city?'

Boyd groaned. 'Which lot of graffiti, Wheeler? There are hundreds of new additions.'

'dEADdOG. The stuff folk rang in to complain about.'

'Oh, that shit,' said Boyd.

'Well, it was carved into the cross lodged in our animal sacrifice. And the dog has been kept in a freezer since the doctor's murder.'

'Right, I'm on to it,' said Boyd. 'I'll see what I can find. Maybe some psycho saw it on the wall and copied it.'

'I want to know who or what the dEADdOG is and the significance to this case,' said Wheeler. 'If anyone needs me, I'll be in my office.' She strode towards the door. Let it slam behind her.

Chapter 36

Tala had waited an hour before reassuring herself that her stepmother wouldn't attempt to burst into her bedroom again. She sat on the side of her bed and switched on the stupid Disney lamp Autumn had bought her for her eighteenth birthday. The woman had no understanding, no grasp of who Tala was. Her father wouldn't let Tala bin it.

She opened her laptop, accessed the site and the familiar videos. Stuck her earphones in and pressed play. The experience hit her like a drug. It was an hour before she was numb enough to begin the next challenge.

She lifted the needle; the thread was already in place. Carefully she began to stitch the outline of a dog. Thought of her gran's triskelion from Ireland, the three circles, symbolising life, death, rebirth. They were all interconnected. There was no real life, only existence. No real death, only a pause until the whole cycle began again. Tala hesitated, took in the video, the exquisite pain, the torture. Death. Welcome numbness spread throughout her as she continued to weave the needle through her flesh, creating the dog. The dEADdOG. Finally, she'd found a pack to which she truly belonged. A flicker of a thought made its way into her mind. What if she didn't go through with it? She felt her resolve falter for a split second before she reminded herself that the Moderator had said this might happen. Had advised that she watched the videos more often, listen to the music and repeat the mantra. I Am Nothing. I Am Nothing.

Chapter 37

Wheeler was still at her desk when she heard a text come through. It was Ross.

You still OK for tonight?

What the hell is tonight?

Your birthday present? Remember?

Wheeler took a moment. Shit. Months ago, on her birthday, Ross had presented her with tickets for a jazz concert. At that time, she thought that she couldn't wait. Now though, they were in the middle of a case. She felt herself torn between staying at the station and working on or giving herself the evening off to enjoy the music.

Boyd stood in the doorway, hand on the light switch. 'You still here? Only Ross said something about swanning off to some jazz concert. Told him I'd rather rip out my own heart and eat it than go to one of those things. Turns out I don't need to, he got the tickets for you.' He flicked the light off then on again. 'Isn't it time for you to scram?'

'I'm just finishing up.' Wheeler gestured to the pile of paperwork scattered across her desk.

'It will still be here tomorrow.' Boyd crossed to her desk and began tidying the papers. 'You need to be fresh for this case, too much tunnel vision and you'll probably miss something crucial.'

She slapped him on the arm.

'Ow.'

'That's rich coming from you.'

'You know I'm right.' He smiled at her. 'You look exhausted. Take the evening off and come back in the morning refreshed.'

Wheeler sat back in her seat. Her eyes were strained, the painkillers hadn't erased the headache and she was going around in circles with the endless paperwork. 'Of course, you're right.'

Boyd paused. 'Can I have that phrase recorded for posterity? I mean I hear it so little around here.'

Wheeler threw one of the balled-up notes at him.

An hour later and she was sitting in the cavernous building, transfixed. If she had to take time out from the case, this was a fantastic way to do it.

Beside her, Ross. 'What would you like to drink?'

She barely heard him.

'Wheeler.'

'Chardonnay.' She sat forward on her seat. 'Isn't this brilliant?'

Ross looked up at the guy playing the sax, the suit, the sound. It was all lost on him, but he had known that Wheeler would love it. He made his way to the bar. 'A large Chardonnay and a pint of Heavy.'

'We don't do pints of Heavy. We only do craft beers.' The bearded barman tried to hand him a hand-written menu in swirling calligraphy.

Ross ignored it. 'Right. Let's just make it a bottle of Chardonnay and two glasses,' said Ross.

'Forty-five pounds, eighty pence,' said the bartender.

This has to be fucking worth it, thought Ross, taking the tray. He ignored the 'gratuity' section of the bill and took the drinks back to Wheeler.

'That looks nice,' said Wheeler

'It should be,' said Ross.

'Because?'

Ross looked at her, saw the open face. 'Because you are worth it, and this was for your birthday.'

'Get a grip, Ross.'

'I already have a grip, Wheeler.' He raised his glass. 'Cheers.'

'Cheers,' said Wheeler absent-mindedly. 'So what do you think about the set?'

The music intensified and thundered out through the venue. He watched Wheeler relax and find solace in it. Watched the guy on stage and the aura that surrounded him. Ross looked across the crowd and saw Seb Hawk at a table near the stage. He sipped his wine. 'Wheeler, look, your friend Hawk is in the front row.'

She saw. 'So?'

'Doesn't it mean something to you? That he is here, listening to this music? The music you love?'

'I guess.' She glanced at him. 'So, you have a new girlfriend?'

'Nope,' he said.

'Doesn't the name Aubree Rutherford ring any bells?'

Ross ignored the question, busied himself with staring at his glass.

She took the hint. 'Sorry for asking.'

Ross swallowed. He was well aware that he was trying to impress Wheeler. Also, Hawk being in the audience pissed him off. During the break he ordered food for them and another bottle of wine. This time he left a generous tip. Perhaps it would bring him luck.

Chapter 38

The Hospital

Ross parked up and walked towards the sprawling build-ing. It was yet another visit. The tests had been done and he was waiting for the diagnosis. It was the same nurse he had seen previously. He hadn't drunk excessively the night before, at the jazz concert. He'd stuck to wine in preparation for this morning.

'Well, you haven't had a heart attack.' She greeted him with a smile.

'That's good to know,' said Ross.

'Your arteries aren't blocked, but blood flow has been reduced.'

'Because?'

'We believe that you do indeed have Broken Heart Syndrome,' said the nurse.

'Right,' said Ross. 'You mentioned it before.'

'It's a heart condition that is brought on by a number of factors, including physical stressors, an operation and some kinds of medication.'

'I'm not on any medication,' said Ross.

'I know, I'm just giving you an outline. In your case it may be caused by stress.'

'I haven't had any particular stress,' said Ross.

'Including,' she continued, 'the death of someone you have loved. Such as your father. The symptoms are similar to a heart attack, chest pains, for example.'

'I'd never heard of Broken Heart Syndrome before you mentioned it the other day.'

'It's also referred to as Takotsubo cardiomyopathy and the good news is that it's temporary. Symptoms are treatable, and you will recover.'

'So, it's not fatal?' said Ross, relaxing. 'That's excellent news.'

The nurse paused. 'I'm afraid that in rare cases it can be. There can be complications, such as heart failure and low blood pressure among others.'

'Right,' said Ross. 'So, it's back to square one.'

'Are you a particularly anxious person, or prone to depression?' asked the nurse.

'Maybe a little anxious,' said Ross

'Did your GP suggest anything?'

'Not yet. Is it something I should be thinking about?' said Ross. 'Will these symptoms return?'

'There's a chance that without medication, they will reoccur,' said the nurse.

'Go on,' said Ross.

'It's usually more common in women than men.'

'Right,' said Ross.

Thirty minutes later he left the hospital. 'Bloody Broken Heart Syndrome. Takotsubo cardiomyopathy.' He needed to breathe the fresh air and forget about the sanitised version available at the hospital. He stepped out into the cold air, took out a small bottle of hand sanitiser and squirted his palms. He didn't trust hospitals, they were full of sick people and germs. He walked on.

Chapter 39

Carmyle Police Station Car Park

Wheeler pulled up in front of Ross, opened the door.

'So, Michael O'Donnell's sister-in-law has flown in from New York?' said Ross getting in. 'I got your text.'

'Yeah, we're on our way to speak with her. She got in a couple of hours ago. Name of Kirsten Rivera. I researched her sister's death.'

'Yeah.'

'Single gunshot to the head. Suicide,' said Wheeler.

'Right.'

'By the way, thanks so much for last night. I loved it.'

'Then it was worth it,' said Ross.

Thirty-five minutes later she turned the car into Moray Place; ahead was the house.

'Wow. Is she renting this for the visit?' said Ross. 'Impressive.'

'She owns it,' said Wheeler. 'Apparently rents it out for holiday lets.'

'Looks like Kirsten Rivera has some money. What do you think this would go for?' asked Ross before answering his own question, 'More than we can afford on a police salary.'

'It was built by Alexander "Greek" Thomson,' said Wheeler. 'He favoured the horizontal lines and the geometry of Greek architecture. Thomson apparently modelled the terrace on the Stoa of Attalos II of Athens.'

'Stoa?'

'Covered walkway,' said Wheeler.

'Right,' said Ross, pressing on the bell. 'Here's hoping she has something new to tell us.'

The door opened. 'I overheard you. I'm afraid I don't have anything new to tell you, but welcome to my modest home.'

Modest it wasn't, thought Wheeler. They followed her through the hall into a large room. It boasted what looked like hand-blocked wallpaper and a glorious amount of original art. Wheeler couldn't help but notice a small framed sketch from her favourite artist J. D. Fergusson. It was part of the *La Vie En Rose* editions and she knew that the sketches cost upwards of £3,000. She tore herself away from the artwork. Saw Ross watching her. Wheeler positioned herself on the sofa. 'Thank you for seeing us so quickly.'

'I couldn't bear to come to the station. Police stations are so depressing.'

'They can be grim,' said Wheeler.

'And besides, I have this place. I kept a holiday home here in Glasgow,' said Rivera. 'Initially to be near Jayla and little Paula. But now I find myself having to sell it. The artwork too. Financial difficulties.'

'I'm sorry to hear that,' said Ross. 'It's a beautiful place.'

Wheeler studied the woman. Kirsten Rivera was tall,

maybe five foot ten or eleven and broad. Her face was extraordinarily graceful, smooth like a carefully planed mask. But it was her poise which struck Wheeler most forcibly.

'I'm sorry about Michael O'Donnell's death,' said Ross.

Rivera shrugged. 'Michael O'Donnell? I could have done without seeing him for an eternity.' She stared at them. 'I'm sorry if you think that harsh but I'm nothing if not honest.'

'This is obviously a difficult time for you,' said Wheeler.

'Only as far as Paula is concerned. I didn't care for Michael. Not one bit. Now, what updates do you have on Paula's abduction?'

'I'm afraid there's been little progress although we are following a number of lines of inquiry,' said Wheeler.

'Even to you, Inspector, that must sound lame?' said Rivera.

Wheeler didn't contradict her. 'Do you have any idea where Paula might be? A particular friend or a boyfriend?'

'You're kidding, right? Michael was adamant that his child was too young and too poorly to have a boyfriend. That said, she was alone in the house for a few evenings a week. Maybe she had someone over? Just because Michael didn't approve, doesn't mean Paula wasn't active. She is beautiful. But I guess it would have to have been secret. As to special friends, Michael dissuaded most people from coming to the house, citing Paula's need to rest as a reason. I'm afraid that I have no useful information to give you. At least not up to date. If I knew where Paula was, I'd have called already.'

'Then at least, can you tell me the significance of the upturned crosses?' asked Wheeler.

'My sister, Jayla, gave Paula the crosses to protect her.' Kirsten Rivera bit her lip, her eyes welled up.

'Are they satanist?' said Wheeler.

'We are, broadly speaking, a family of believers but not as you would understand it. Those crosses were to keep Paula safe. But we are also open to other faiths.'

'Like satanism?' said Ross.

Kirsten Rivera paused. 'Let's just say we are integrative.'

Wheeler took out a photograph of the cross with the engraving dEADdOG. 'This was left outside Carmyle Police Station. What can you tell me about it?'

'I can tell you that it's from my sister's collection,' said Rivera. 'You see the carving? These represent red-rimmed eyes. That was a particularly important part of her collection. The symbolism of tears. This life we have as human beings is all about suffering.'

'And the word dEADdOG?' asked Wheeler, sharing another photograph.

'I have no idea what that refers to.' Rivera glanced at the photograph. 'What is that creature?'

'It was a dog which had been decapitated,' said Wheeler. 'A pet.'

Rivera shrugged. 'I don't know much about animal sacrifice. Pretty gruesome, if you ask me.' She folded her arms, crossed one leg over the other. Her foot tapped in agitation.

Wheeler saw a change in the woman's face. Noted the body language.

'But it might be a message?' said Ross. 'An animal sacrifice?'

'If you say so,' said Rivera. 'But really, animal sacrifice isn't my area of expertise.'

Wheeler watched the woman. She listened to the intonation in her words; she didn't believe her about not knowing about animal sacrifice. Her face came alive when she spoke about it. So, what else was Kirsten Rivera hiding? 'Did Michael ever mention Sarah Price?'

'The man never told me anything. Now, presumably you have all the data about Paula,' said Rivera, 'so why are you here?'

'We are investigating Michael's murder,' said Wheeler. 'Anything you can tell us may be helpful.' Again, Wheeler noticed the slightest of movement when she mentioned the word 'murder'. If she had to pin it on body language alone, she thought that Rivera was delighted that Michael was dead. What she had to find out was how much Rivera knew.

Rivera sighed. 'Very well then, let's talk about the man. Michael O'Donnell was a psychopath.'

'Go on,' said Wheeler.

'He beat Jayla. Regularly. Yes. Detectives, he used to yell at her that he would beat it out of her.'

'Beat what out of her?' asked Ross.

'Our religion.'

'Which is what?' asked Ross.

'Integrative,' said Rivera.

'And by integrative, you mean what exactly?' asked Ross.

'None of your damn business,' said Rivera. 'That's personal to our family and is unrelated to this case.'

'How can you be so sure?' asked Wheeler.

'You can take my word for it, Michael O'Donnell beat my sister half to death.'

'We didn't find any evidence that Michael was involved in domestic violence,' said Wheeler.

245

Anne Randall

'No, you wouldn't because he was a clever son of a bitch. Whiplash, falls on the stairs. She was too scared to report him. He killed my sister, I'm certain of it,' said Rivera. 'He probably had enemies, I suppose one of whom may have snatched my niece. Michael was an awful man. Hideous.'

'The police inquiry reported that your sister died as a result of a self-inflicted gunshot wound,' said Wheeler.

Rivera cut through her. 'Surely you don't believe that? Even as a police officer? You must know that evidence can be tampered with, that sworn statements can be lies?'

Ross said nothing.

'Jayla would never have killed herself, she simply wasn't the type,' stated Rivera.

'Depression can—' Wheeler began.

'She suffered from post-natal depression, DI Wheeler, but she wasn't suicidal,' said Rivera. 'Believe me, I knew my sister.'

'In her medical records her GP suggested otherwise,' Wheeler said quietly.

'Then they are simply wrong,' said Rivera. 'Jayla did suffer badly after Paula was born but she had a warrior soul. Plus, I know for a fact that Michael didn't help at all. Not one bit.'

'Because . . . ?' Asked Wheeler.

'Because Jayla realised, too late, that she had married a shit. A real fuck-up. Previously Jayla had trusted her gut instinct. After she had Paula, she changed, she got softer but life with Michael brought her down. It was like he eroded her bit by bit, piece by piece. He wanted to take away her personality and finally he did. I told the police all this at the time. He killed her. I would bet my life on it.'

246

'I read all the reports,' said Wheeler. 'There was nothing in them to substantiate your claim.'

'There wouldn't be,' said Rivera. 'That way it went down in the stats as a suicide. If it had been reported as a murder, they'd have had to clear it. And clearance rates are mighty important for you lot, aren't they?'

'A suspicious death is always investigated,' said Ross. 'Thoroughly.'

'Yes, perhaps you like to think that, but I'm sorry, DI Ross, I don't have the same faith in police procedures as you do. I had my suspicions about the officer in charge. I read the stats. Am I wrong to find the number of unsolved murders and missing people on Police Scotland's casebook alarming?'

Wheeler thought of the list she had compiled.

Rivera paused. 'Michael had a very strong hold over Jayla. He may not have pulled the trigger himself, but he would have goaded her into it. He often told her she was worthless. Michael killed Jayla as sure as the River Clyde flows through Glasgow.'

'Go on,' said Wheeler.

'Well, I reckon Michael bought the gun. It's easily done in the US. I could go down to any gun store in Long Island and pick one up.'

'Ms Rivera, I can assure you it's not quite so easy here in Glasgow,' said Ross.

'Really? I'm damn sure it is, so don't give me that bullshit, cause I ain't buying it.'

'I can tell you that—' Ross began again.

She cut through him. 'The gun wasn't registered, was it? And do tell me that there's been no other fatalities due to unregistered guns in Glasgow since Jayla died? You lot are friggin' hopeless. You were hopeless at investigating her murder then, and now you can't even find her missing daughter. Useless.'

Ross stood, looked at Wheeler. 'We should go.'

Wheeler remained seated. 'So, Michael O'Donnell obtained a gun. What happened next?'

'Michael got hold of the gun on the black market, then begins in on Jayla. He berated her, belittled her and poured scorn on her until she was ready to believe him, that she was useless and that her baby would be better off without her. He said that she was an unfit mother and a danger around Paula. He threatened her that he would have her sectioned after her diagnosis with post-natal depression, that he would testify in court that she'd hurt Paula.'

'That couldn't happen,' said Ross.

'Paula had fallen on a couple of occasions and hit her head. Michael began to document the falls, however small. Paula was a clumsy child. He relentlessly bullied Jayla, suggested that she had abused Paula and that was the reason she was such a poorly child. He constantly researched shaken baby syndrome and made notes comparing Paula's illnesses with the symptoms. He repeatedly told her that he held all the cards. He was such an absolute bastard. He drove her over the edge. The idea of losing Paula would have made Jayla depressed and desperate. She was the love of her life, the only real anchor.' She swallowed. 'Then it was a short step to, well, just go ahead and put everyone out of their misery. He set her up with a gun, then afterwards used his looks and pseudo charm to convince people that he was a nice guy. He convinced them that he was devastated and that he was the grieving widower who rose to the occasion of sole parenting his daughter.

You must have heard during your investigations just how wonderful he was?'

Wheeler thought of all the platitudes: 'Nothing short of a saint, a wonderful man, so devoted, so good-looking.'

'He seemed to be very popular,' said Ross.

'Certainly, Michael had a hold over people. He was very good-looking and charismatic, that's why Jayla initially fell in love with him. The erosion of her spirit was done carefully and manipulatively over time. And always behind closed doors.'

Wheeler watched Kirsten Rivera carefully. She was obviously fired up and her body language was restless. Was she on a mission to discredit Michael O'Donnell? To pin the death of her sister on him? They had heard from various sources that Michael O'Donnell had been a dedicated and loving dad. A governor at the college. And yet some colleagues at the CoVA had suggested otherwise.

'Now what are you doing to find Paula?' asked Rivera. 'You need to look at the College of Visual Arts, there are sinister goings on in that place. Sinister people.'

'We've spoken to most of the people at the college, both staff and students,' said Wheeler.

'Three female students have gone missing in the past five years,' said Rivera.

'I know,' said Wheeler quietly, 'Evie Evenguard, Joanne Reilly. And now Paula.' She thought of Zoe, the trainee beautician, who was also missing.

'You need to be looking at the college. They are responsible for Paula's disappearance, I'm sure of it. The same thing happened in the States.'

Wheeler waited.

'Kids go missing and there is such a furore and then

everyone other than their families move on and they are all but forgotten.' Rivera swallowed back tears. 'I don't want this to happen to Paula. I feel that Jayla is now lost and forgotten. Michael, I don't care about. Let his killer dance on his grave. I'll dance too. It will be revenge for what he did to Jayla but please don't let the same thing happen to her daughter.'

'We've spoken to the principal of the CoVA, Helen McSweeney, about the missing girls,' said Wheeler. 'It's all still under investigation.'

'You ask that sleazebag, Robin Kirkpatrick, what he thinks about all this,' said Rivera.

'He has been off after a car accident, he's back today,' said Wheeler.

'Then you ask him about Paula's disappearance. He hated her. Hated the fact that she was so talented. He was jealous of her. I mean,' said Rivera, 'he picked on Paula. Tell me, what kind of an asshole picks on a kid? And a sickly kid at that?'

'We will talk to him,' said Wheeler.

'And speak with a guy name of Carsten Louyar. He's a carer at the care home Jaya helped out at. You ask him about his take on all of this. Please? It's not just me. I'm not alone here. He suffered too, with Hurricane Sandy. He knows about suffering. You go ask him."

Wheeler finished the interview.

Outside, Wheeler turned to Ross. 'Your thoughts?'

'She hated Michael O'Donnell, I think she resented the closeness he had with Paula and blamed him for the death of her sister.'

'Who was clinically depressed according to the medical notes,' said Wheeler.

'So, she's on a bit of a vendetta to frame him posthumously for the death of her sister?' said Ross. 'And the integrative religion, what was that about? And the refusal to explain.'

'She didn't seem at all surprised by the arrival of the decapitated dog,' said Wheeler.

They walked through the snow to the car. Wheeler held her face up to the soft snowflakes. 'This weather is pretty magical.'

'Only for folk like you who prefer the winter,' muttered Ross as he slipped on a particularly slushy part of the pavement.

'Bah humbug.'

'I saw you noticing the artwork,' said Ross. 'They were from that artist you like, weren't they?'

'Yeah, J. D. Fergusson.'

'How much?' asked Ross.

'Around three thousand, I reckon,' said Wheeler, walking on.

'Fine,' said Ross quietly. As they approached the car he glanced at her. 'You fancy a coffee?'

'Let's go meet up with Robin Kirkpatrick,' said Wheeler.

'Lucky us,' said Ross. 'But bear in mind that I never do my best work on an empty stomach.'

She turned to him, smiled. 'Just remind me again, Ross, just when do you do your best work?'

'Shut it you. Just drive.' He slammed the door of the car.

The Cottage

She tried to call out. Heard herself lisp, when there had never been one before. Felt the space where the tooth had been and began to cry. She listened, but the two dogs

251

weren't in the place. She tugged at her constraints, pulled and heaved at them until her wrists and ankles were bloodied and raw. Felt her heartbeat thunder in her chest. Wanted to curse the dogs into eternal hell. Found her voice and screamed obscenities at the blank wall.

Chapter 40

Assistant Principal Robin Kirkpatrick stood at the door of his office. 'I'm sorry not to have spoken with you before now. I'm just back today.'

Kirkpatrick was early fifties, around five foot five and wore a smart tweed jacket and jeans. Bright trainers. His head shaved. But it was the waxy pallor and the bloodshot eyes that she noticed most.

'Do you feel up to this?' said Wheeler.

'This college is my life, Inspector. It's what sustained me through the dark times. The thought of returning to my duties was my one constant. My motivation.'

'What can you tell me about Michael O'Donnell and his daughter Paula?'

'Michael, I barely knew. He appeared to be somewhat overprotective of Paula, some might say obsessively so. To be honest, I had very little time for him. He was a bore.'

'Did he ever mention Sarah Price?'

'No.'

'And what can you tell me about Paula?'

'Pretty little Paula? She is—' Kirkpatrick flicked his

253

hand in a gesture of distaste '—a mediocre artist at best. Her work lacks nuance or flow.'

'We've just come from talking with her aunt, Kirsten Rivera.'

'Oh dear, the conspiracy theorist? I do wonder about her mental health. She came to my office many years ago and demanded that I take special care of "poor little Paula".'

Wheeler noted the change in tone.

'She made all sorts of outrageous claims about Michael. That he had killed his wife and was dominating Paula. Ridiculous stuff. The woman is obviously deranged. Completely nuts.'

'And you refused?' asked Wheeler.

'Of course, Paula wasn't my sole responsibility. I have many students to mentor. Then I went online and discovered that Kirsten Rivera is a concert hall witchcraft performer who claims voodoo and spell-making to be part of her act. Apparently, she tours the US as Queen Crow.'

'You don't have a good relationship with Paula?' asked Wheeler.

'Not in the slightest. She is without artistic talent or much personality. Some days she can be incredibly feeble, others quite robust. But talentless, in my opinion. Although she is very pretty.'

'I see,' said Wheeler.

'But, I can show you some of her painting, if you like?' Kirkpatrick moved to the back of the room, selected a canvas from a pile and held it up. 'Paula's art, for what it's worth. And I daresay comparatively little.'

Wheeler stared at it. The dramatic abstract painting was a mass of energy and angry welts. The colours were a mix of black and red. 'What can you tell me about it?'

'I think she felt emboldened to express her anger at her medical condition. I knew from her pastoral support lecturer, Mr Van Der Berg, that she felt imprisoned by her condition, she couldn't join in with friends at clubs or indeed be capable of all that her peers were achieving. Van Der Berg really encouraged her to express herself emotionally through painting. He told her that art was a medium through which she could truly transcend her physical restrictions. I mean, how ridiculous is that? What the hell was the man thinking? Certainly, he isn't an artist. And Paula has little discernible talent whatsoever. At least in my opinion.'

Ross coughed. But the tutor was on a roll.

'Art, Van Der Berg told Paula, elevates what can be a mediocre existence, in Paula's case a restricted way of life, into something much more precious and timeless.' He paused. 'Ridiculous. And this—' he gestured to the painting '—is the drivel that is produced when that kind of rhetoric is espoused.' He paused. 'I wouldn't want you to think that I am dismissive of my students. On the contrary. I do have some exceptionally talented students, Tala De Luca being one.' He crossed to another canvas. 'Look at this. Isn't this incredibly promising? What a bloody talent and yet so young.'

Wheeler looked at the painting. 'Lovely. Influenced by Georgia O'Keeffe?'

'Yes, I think so, but what breadth of scope, what use of colour. Such a different approach to Paula's childish paint splats.'

'I guess they're all just kids,' said Ross.

'If there's anything else?' asked Kirkpatrick.

'What can you tell me about the other missing students, Evie Evenguard and Joanne Reilly?'

'I never knew Evie. She was only here for one term and didn't take any of my classes. Of course, I heard that she was missing but she had gone to Strathclyde at that point. Law wasn't it?'

'And Joanne Reilly?' asked Wheeler.

'Oh, Joanne was a pretty little thing,' Kirkpatrick murmured.

'Thing?' repeated Wheeler.

'It's only a turn of phrase, DI Wheeler, I meant no harm. You women are all so touchy now.' Kirkpatrick glanced at Ross. 'Us blokes need to mind our Ps and Qs, eh? Your colleague here seems a bit of a ball-breaker. No doubt you've had to keep her in line.'

'She's my boss,' said Ross. He stared at Kirkpatrick. 'Do you have a problem with that?'

'Joanne Reilly?' said Wheeler. 'What do you know about her?'

'She was a good enough painter, albeit in the abstract, non-figurative tradition.' Kirkpatrick shrugged. 'She hung about with Craig Brennan for a while, lucky boy. I don't know what young people call it nowadays, perhaps they had a *thing*.'

'You sound bemused?' said Wheeler. And also, jealous, she thought.

'I am if I'm to be honest, she was really quite striking, physically, and I think she could have played the field a little and it may have given her a little bit of perspective on life.'

'She was sixteen,' said Wheeler.

'I know, old enough to get married and consider having children. So, your point, DI Wheeler?'

'You seem very interested in her,' said Ross.

'What, a man can't look?' Kirkpatrick chuckled. 'Is that what you're saying? I may be middle-aged and recovering from an accident, but I'm not dead.'

'You were her tutor,' said Ross.

'Quite, DI Ross, but only her tutor. Not her father, who I gather she had quite the fractious relationship with, wasn't that why she ran away from home? Perhaps you should go speak to Peter Reilly, see what he has to say for himself. Apparently, he was a sanctimonious, domineering bully.'

Wheeler had read the interviews; both parents had reacted to their daughter's disappearance very differently. The mother, who lived in New Zealand with her new partner and their two children, had been tearful and distraught. She had flown over immediately and had insisted on joining in with the search. Peter Reilly, on the other hand, had been incredibly angry and had constantly carped and bitterly blamed the police for not doing enough.

'Craig Brennan was attacked last year,' said Wheeler. 'What do you know about the attack?'

'I imagine that Craig may have falling-outs throughout his life,' said Kirkpatrick. 'He is a deeply disturbed and secretive young man.'

'Did he report the assault?' asked Wheeler.

'Not at first.' The lecturer limped towards his desk. Sat down heavily on a seat.

'Go on,' said Wheeler.

'It's difficult to explain . . . ' said Kirkpatrick.

'Just do your best,' said Ross, taking out his notebook.

'No, you misunderstand. It's not because it's of a sensitive nature, it's because the individual involved wouldn't divulge the true nature of the attack,' said Kirkpatrick.

'You see, Craig was attacked but he refused to name his assailant.'

'But you think he knew them?' said Wheeler.

'I most certainly do,' said Kirkpatrick.

'Was he intimidated by them, too scared to report them?' asked Wheeler.

'It went beyond fear. He was terrified, he could barely speak. Refused to cooperate. Wouldn't say much to the police, or his parents.'

'And were the perpetrators ever found?' asked Wheeler.

'No. Craig was nearly blinded. He was in hospital for three weeks. His face had been smashed. I believe that he was fearful for his life. I don't know if it's in the reports, but an upturned cross was found beside him.'

Wheeler glanced at Ross.

'The boy refused all support and wouldn't say a word about it,' Kirkpatrick continued. 'He said he just wanted it all to go away.'

'And did it?' asked Wheeler.

'Things quietened down for him, at least there were no further attacks. His friends stood by him, but he left college soon after, refusing to take his exams. A great pity, he was a bright talent. One of our most experimental students. He had been provisionally accepted by two prestigious art schools. But it all came to nothing. I heard a rumour that he had taken to carrying a gun for protection. I've no idea if it was gossip or not. About six months ago, I overheard one of the students mentioning something about dead dogs. A group called the dead dogs. A rock group perhaps? A secret society?'

'I've seen the graffiti around the area,' said Wheeler. She was not going to mention the cross found in the dead animal. She would withhold that information.

'Yes, I noticed some the other day whilst driving – dEADdOG. I heard one student talking when I was marking papers with the window open. Students used to congregate around the bus shelter for a smoke. They thought we'd all gone home. Some of their voices drifted upwards. I used to listen in. Quite illuminating what they thought of us tutors and also who was having sex with whom.'

'Do you have any information about the dEADdOG group?' asked Wheeler. 'A list of names?'

'No, I told Principal McSweeney and she spoke to the students one morning at assembly, primarily about transparency, but of course these societies, if it was one, are secret by their very nature and us hoary old lecturers are the last to be included.'

'Who do you think attacked Craig Brennan?' asked Wheeler.

'I couldn't possibly speculate.'

Wheeler tried and failed to keep the impatience from her voice. 'Mr Kirkpatrick, this is important. Anything at all you can tell us would be a help.'

'Very well, then, if you insist in being tiresome. If I were to *imagine* who might be involved in such a thing, I think the Roach twins may have been involved. Maybe Nick Price. Those types of boys. Rough types.'

'Really? Why would the three of them be together? I thought they didn't get on?' asked Wheeler.

'They certainly used to be best friends,' said Kirkpatrick. 'They exhibited together, early days. I think they must have had a falling-out later.'

'What about Michael O'Donnell? Did they ever have a run-in with him?'

'Not that I know of, but I can't be sure.'

'And Paula O'Donnell? Was she part of the group who congregated beside the bus stop?'

'I only heard the voices. I didn't see them, there is no view from here, it's obstructed.'

'Tala De Luca?' Wheeler persisted.

He stood. 'I'm sorry, I don't know. As I said, I didn't see them. Perhaps it's nothing. I'm feeling a little tired. I think that I may have overdone it, returning to college so soon after my accident. But, as I said, this place is my life.'

'I do hope you're not overdoing it,' said Wheeler, standing. 'Do you by any chance know where Craig is now?'

'Oh, I heard that he works in some bar in the Merchant City.'

'Which one?'

'Something about an angel, a mosaic entrance.' Kirkpatrick sighed. 'Now I really must get on.'

'Well, thank you for your time, Mr Kirkpatrick, I appreciate it.'

'No doubt you can find your own way out,' said Kirkpatrick, staring out of the window.

'Before I go,' said Wheeler. 'Do you know anything about upturned crosses or crucifixes?'

'I imagine you might like to talk to our voodoo queen Rivera about that. Also, one of our lecturers, Ms Barnes Olsen, supplements her income by making jewellery from the ashes of the deceased. A macabre pastime. But, of course, our lovely Barnes Olsen would not need to stoop to this revolting pursuit if she were a more accomplished artist, whose work actually sold in galleries.'

Wheeler and Ross left.

Outside, Ross turned to Wheeler. 'He was a piece of work.'

'Gave me the creeps,' said Wheeler.

'Tell me we're off for coffee?'

'What do you think?' Wheeler walked on. Then she turned to Ross. 'Bar 7 and an Angel has a mosaic front. It's got to be the bar where Craig Brennan works.'

'Merchant City?' asked Ross.

'Yeah.'

'You're the expert on trendy wine bars,' said Ross.

'How much time do I have to peruse new bars, muppet?' said Wheeler.

'I thought that maybe you and Hawk would have had time to visit a few.'

'Very funny. You just couldn't resist, could you?' said Wheeler.

'Fair dos. A cheap shot,' said Ross. 'He just irritates me.'

'I can tell. What do you reckon the cross found beside Craig means he's linked to these cases?'

'Fairly high.'

'Me too,' said Wheeler.

Chapter 41

During the summer months, the twelfth-century church was popular with tourists, who trod the worn, internal one hundred and seventy stone steps happily. Once at the top of the tower, they could stand well back from the safety barriers and gaze over the city. Beyond the barrier, the old stone wall was unsteady and a fund for the restoration of the church had raised only £3,000 of the £170,000 that was needed. Part of this was to replace the rusting fire escape which had been hastily erected in the 1970s after fire had damaged the church.

Today, the church was deserted. As the weak sun shone over the old building, a figure could be seen standing deathly still while balancing on the outermost corner of the wall. The figure was silhouetted against the grey light. Tala, thin and vulnerable against the sinister gargoyles who surrounded her, repeated the mantra, 'I.A.N., I.A.N.' She thought of Leroy and the rest of the group, all at varying stages of the tasks. 'Leroy,' Tala whispered into the wind. 'Wait for me.'

That morning she had slipped out of bed, dressed in

dark leggings and a T-shirt. She'd quickly laced up her boots and made her way downstairs, through the kitchen and out the back door. She'd been gone in seconds. Autumn and Tomas were already out. Not that they would care where she went.

A wind got up and tugged and pulled at her flimsy T-shirt. The hail seeped into her clothes making them heavy and wet. She felt as if she were being dragged down by the hand of God. For a moment, she thought that she may lose her balance and fall but she righted herself. Then her leg began to cramp. She stared at the long drop. It seemed very far indeed down to the graveyard below. 'I am nothing,' she whispered to herself as the wind howled around her. 'I am nothing. I. A. N.'

Later, when it was over, she stood in the old graveyard and spoke to her mum. Told her about her new family. How they understood her. Tala's mobile rang. Her gran again. Tala made to ignore it, but something prompted her; her mother had been very close to Gran de Luca.

'Hello?'

'Tala, darling. Where have you been? I've been worried sick.'

'Just busy, Gran. There's a lot going on.'

'I know, pet, I know. I just need to have a quick chat. You know the money my beloved Enzo left me? It was to go to your dad eventually, but I've changed my mind. I'm giving it to you. It's to support you while you're going through art college. Then later, while you're trying to get your art into galleries.'

Tala thought of the dEADdOG and that she wasn't going to be around much longer. 'Gran. I don't want it. I can't use it.'

'But Tala—'

She killed the call. Saw her gran's number flash up again. Ignored it. Put the phone in her pocket. Thought about her mum again and how she had always encouraged her with her artwork. Tala began to cry.

Chapter 42

Bar 7 & an Angel

On the drive over, Wheeler had spoken to Boyd.

'Judging by the notes, there's no way Craig Brennan wanted to take it further,' said Boyd.

'Was Michael O'Donnell ever involved? Paula implicated? What about Tala De Luca?'

But Boyd had come up with no links, nothing to connect them. 'All negative, Wheeler.' She'd ended the call.

'Perhaps this attack wasn't connected to our case?' said Ross.

'We still have to chase it up,' said Wheeler.

'This must be home ground for you,' said Ross, as they approached the intricate black and gold mosaic at the entrance.

'I told you, I've never been here.'

'Hawk probably has,' said Ross. 'You know what he's like.'

Wheeler walked on. 'Stop being petty. It isn't you, Ross. Just concentrate on the case.'

A young blonde, heavily made-up waitress eyed Wheeler. Wheeler knew she didn't fit the demographic for the trendy place. She flashed her badge and asked to speak to Craig Brennan.

'Oh of course, detectives. If you would like to take a seat, I'll get him to come down.'

They sat at one of the tables; Wheeler glanced at the menu on display. Would she take Hawk up on his offer to come here? She noted the hand-cut truffle chips, home-made butternut squash gnocchi. Braised rabbit with forest mushrooms and whipped potatoes. 'What the hell are whipped potatoes,' she asked Ross.

'No bloody idea, maybe mashed potatoes?' said Ross. 'Food is getting very bloody posh. I mean they are spuds. Just spuds. Why make it more complicated?'

'Not just that, they have sour cream and cream cheese added,' said the receptionist who appeared beside them. 'I took the liberty of bringing you some iced water with Sicilian lemons.' She put the tray down.

'Thanks,' said Wheeler. She took a sip.

'Sicilian lemon water tastes just like ordinary lemon water,' said Ross.

When he came down the stairs a few minutes later, she saw that Craig Brennan had tried for a swagger. Wheeler took in the neat asymmetrical haircut. The skinny jeans with turn-ups and the obligatory craft beard.

'Mr Brennan, do you mind if I ask you a few questions about the attack at the CoVA?' said Wheeler.

Brennan shrugged. 'There's nothing to say. It was random. Whoever it was attacked me from behind, I didn't see a face.'

'But you heard their voices?'

'I was on the ground, they were beating me. Blood was pouring from my head. I was just trying to get away. I was nearly blinded you know. Do you have any idea how that feels?'

'But you heard them talking,' Ross insisted.

'I heard a few words. Muffled,' said Brennan. 'They didn't make any sense.'

'Go on,' said Wheeler.

'I told the police everything at the time,' said Brennan. 'Look I don't want to get into it all again.'

'I'd appreciate a little more of your time,' said Wheeler.

'Look, can I get back to work now?' said Brennan. 'Only the manager doesn't like us to be off duty for too long.'

'I'll have a word with her if you like?' said Wheeler.

'I'd rather you didn't.'

'Is there anything else you can tell me, Mr Brennan, anything at all?' asked Wheeler.

'It's all over now, it's history. I just want to forget it.'

'I appreciate that, but this is a murder inquiry,' said Wheeler. 'Michael O'Donnell is dead.'

'I already told the police, I didn't know him.'

'He was governor of the CoVA.'

'I still didn't know him,' said Brennan. 'I never paid attention to governors. They came and went. I mean they're not paid, they're not lecturers and they're not staff.'

'His daughter, Paula, is missing,' said Wheeler.

Brennan sighed. 'Yeah, I saw that on the news.'

'She's very vulnerable,' said Wheeler.

'You think I didn't notice that when she was in class?'

'What can you tell us about her?' said Ross.

'Nothing,' said Brennan quietly.

'You were in the same class,' said Wheeler.

'She was just, you know, very frail, but beautiful. It took a lot out of Paula to even make a painting. I often told her that I thought she had incredible talent. She was quite shy, blushed. She was embarrassed. Once, she squeezed my hand. She was a really lovely girl.'

Wheeler looked at him. 'What about the upturned cross left beside you?'

'No idea. Freaky thing. I heard it was to do with satanism.'

'Or the Petrine cross, is it a symbol of humility?' said Ross.

'I've no idea. As I said, it's not my thing.'

'Was it Paula's?' said Wheeler.

'How would I know? Ask around the campus.'

'We're asking you,' said Ross.

'Figure it out. You are meant to be the bloody detectives.'

'You were attacked, Mr Brennan, but don't you want to get the person who did it?' said Wheeler.

'That's your job, isn't it?'

'Not if you can't help us,' said Ross.

'Listen.' Brennan smiled. 'I know you'd love me to stay out here and you know, chat, but I have work to do. Then again, don't you two?'

'We spoke to Assistant Principal Kirkpatrick,' said Wheeler.

'That old perv? Always ogling the girls.'

'He told us that you knew Joanne Reilly, the girl who disappeared.'

Brennan looked at his feet. 'I knew her a bit.'

'Mr Kirkpatrick suggested that you two were dating.'

'No, we never dated. We were just friends.'

She heard the change in his voice, the adoption of a faux casual tone.

'Do you have any idea where she is, what happened to her?' she persisted.

'No idea,' said Brennan. He looked at the floor.

She saw the ghost of a smile cross his face for a split second.

'Sorry to repeat myself,' Brennan continued, 'but isn't that your job?'

'Mr Kirkpatrick mentioned that there had been a rumour that you procured a gun as a means of self-defence,' said Wheeler.

'Rubbish. Just absolute bullshit,' said Brennan. 'Why don't you people just get out there and do your job instead of hassling innocent folk who have already been through enough?'

'I'd very much appreciate it if you could tell me about it,' said Wheeler. 'Mr Brennan, we have a murdered governor of the CoVA and a missing student.' She saw Brennan flinch when she mentioned a missing student. 'I need to get to Paula before she dies. If you know anything at all, please tell me.'

Brennan sighed. 'I heard my attacker use a name. He chanted it, "dEADdOG", like in a little riff or song. "Small d, capital EAD, small d, capital OG!" He chanted it as he beat me. And there was a girl's voice too. Her voice was much softer but she still sang along as she pounded into me.'

'Did you recognise either of the voices?' asked Wheeler.

Brennan stared at his hands. 'No,' he said softly.

Wheeler didn't believe for a minute that Craig Brennan hadn't recognised the voices of his attackers. He knew but was too scared to tell. Who were these people? 'Any idea of the significance of dEADdOG?'

'It's when animals take their own life,' said Brennan. 'Like the way, in some areas, dogs jump to their death.

They commit suicide. You know Overtoun Bridge, near Dumbarton?'

'Yes,' said Wheeler. She had read the stats. Hundreds of dogs had jumped to their death there. Some believed it was scent that drove them over, others that the spirits that inhabited the place lured the dogs to their deaths. Either way, it hadn't made for comfortable reading.

'Animal suicide,' said Brennan, 'is rife there. And we are all animals.' He looked directly at Wheeler.

'Yes,' Wheeler agreed, 'we are all animals. But we are not all suicidal.'

Brennan stood. 'I'm done here.'

'Mr Brennan,' she called to him, but it was too late. Wheeler watched him stride through the reception area and deliberately slam the door behind him.

She turned to Ross. 'He's lying. He does know something about the missing girl, Joanne Reilly. I saw the body language. Clear as day. It contradicted what he said. Plus, I'm positive that he knew his attackers. He knows way more than he's letting on.'

'So why not tell us? You reckon he's involved in Joanne Reilly's disappearance?'

'I think he's terrified. I just don't know of what or who yet.' She stood. 'Let's go.'

'At least tell me we're going for food?' said Ross.

'We're going to see the carer,' said Wheeler, leading the way.

Chapter 43

dEADdOG

The Moderator worked quietly on the review of Tala De Luca's progress. He watched the video she had sent of herself on the roof of the old church. Then self-harming. Then the other ones. Tala had shared such a lot. She was such a good little student of the dEADdOG society, such an easy student.

He had already decided on her special date. The twenty-fourth of December.

He scrolled through the images of the Bernese, Toby. In images one, two and three, the dog looked adorable. The Moderator smiled. Then he added three more photographs, the dEADdOG process. The final picture was a photograph of the dog after death, the cross already in place.

He posted online to Tala.

I have left a tOkEN of my cOMMITmEnT to you in a pUBliC area. The dead dog was collateral damage from an uNBELIEvEr who struck out in aNgER. The dog became a symbol of his hAtE but I have transformed it into a unifying symbol of our commitment to our community. One must

271

die so that the rest of us will live for eternity. There is nothing else. Life, death, rebirth, dEADdOG.

dEADdOGdEADdOGdEADdOG**TALAYOURSPECIAL DATEIS24THDECEMBER**dEADdOGdEADdOGdEADdOG
dEADdOGdEADdOGdEADdOG**24THTALA**dEADdOG
dEADdOGdEADdOGdEADdOGdEADdOGdEADdOG
TALAdEADdOGdEADdOGdEADdOGdEADdOGdEADdO
GdEADdOGdEADdOGdEADdOGdEADdOGdEADdOG
dEADdOGdEADdOGdEADdOGdEADdOGdEADdO
G**TALA**dEADdOGdEADdOGdEADdOGdEADdOGdEAD
dOGdEADdOGdEADdOGdEADdOGdEADdOGdEA
DdOGdEADdOGdEADdOGdEADdOGdEADdOGdEADdO
G**YOURSPECIALDATE**dEADdOGdEADdOGdEADdOGA
TALAdEADdOGdEADdOGdEADdOGdEADdOGdEADdOG
dEADdOGdEADdOGdEADdOG**TALA**dEADdOG
dEADdOGdEADdOGdEADdOGdEADdOGdEADdOGdEAD
dOGdEADdOGdEADdOGdEADdOGddEADdOGdEADdOG
dEADdOGEADdOGdEADdOGdEADdOGdEADdOGdEAD
dOG**TALA**dEADdOGdEADdOGdEADdOGdEADdOGdEA
DdOGdEADdOG**TALAYOURSPECIALDATEIS24TH
DECEMBER**dEADdOGdEADdOGdEADdOGdEADdOG
dEADdOGdEADdOGdEADdOGdEADdOGdEADdOGdEAD
dOGdEADdOGdEADdOG**TALAYOURTIME**dEADdOG
dEADdOGdEADdOGdEADdOGdEADdOGdEADdOGdEAD
dOGdEADdOGdEADdOGdEADdOGdEADdOGdEADdOG
dEADdOGdEADdOGdEADdOGdEADdOGdEADdOGdEAD
dOGdEADdOGdEADdOGdEADdOGdEADdOGdEADdOG
dEADdOG

Chapter 44

Wheeler and Ross pulled up outside Carsten Louyar's flat. 'So, this is the guy Kirsten Rivera said we ought to talk to?' said Ross.

'Yep, he's a carer at the home Jaya used to help out in,' said Wheeler, getting out of the car. She rang the bell. 'Let's hear what he has to say about her.'

Carsten Louyar led them through to the living room. It was sparsely furnished, there was no sign of a television, only a small radio on a shelf.

'Would you like a tea or coffee, some water perhaps?' asked Louyar.

'Water would be great, thank you.' Wheeler glanced at a montage of photographs on a cork pin board. A birthday card, a picture of a small child. In another photograph, the same brown-eyed toddler and his parents. Underneath, *Mummy and Daddy.*

Wheeler had been in houses overrun with insects, houses where she didn't want to sit on sofas stained with numerous unidentifiable substances, houses where she had wanted to don a protective oversuit so that neither her skin nor her clothes would need to touch the furniture. This spartan flat was the opposite. Everything had been scrupulously cleaned, the room smelled of bleach to such a degree that it caught at the back of her throat and for a moment she thought she was about to sneeze. She swallowed quickly, sat on a hard, wooden chair.

Louyar returned carrying a tray, glasses, a jug of water. 'I'm ashamed of this place, Inspector Wheeler. You see we had to leave our home in Amityville quickly, the speed with which Hurricane Sandy blew through our neighbourhood was insane. We had no time to pack our belongings. When we arrived to stay with my aunt, Jace, my son . . . ' his voice faltered ' . . . our son, contracted pneumonia and died. What you see is my wife's need to create order, to control her environment and to sterilise everything continuously. I know what you must be thinking. I am a qualified doctor, now working as a care assistant. My wife had returned to university part-time to continue her studies in architecture. She was a genius. Now, what do we have to show for ourselves? Nothing. Jace is gone, and my wife has retreated into herself. Grief has consumed her.'

He poured water into three glasses. 'What would you like to know?'

Wheeler leaned forward. 'Did you know Michael and Paula O'Donnell?'

'Not particularly well.'

'What about Jayla? Michael's ex-wife, Paula's mum?'

'Yes, I knew Jayla. She died in very tragic circumstances.'

'We spoke with her sister, Kirsten. She seems to have a different view on what happened to Jayla.'

Louyar studied his hands. 'There were some people who said awful things about Michael, but I think his heart was broken.'

Wheeler sat forward on the chair. 'What did they say?'

'That he had driven her to it. Some even said that he had been in the room with her when she shot herself.'

Wheeler heard the pain in his voice. 'Were you close to Jayla?'

'We became friends; she came for coffee sometimes. She was a good person. She helped out at the care centre and always had a smile and a hello.'

'And Michael?' asked Wheeler.

'I didn't know him so well. He popped into the care centre to pick up Jayla sometimes. But he was mainly just looking after his daughter.'

'Their daughter,' said Ross.

'Yes, their daughter,' agreed Louyar.

'Did you ever meet Paula?' asked Wheeler.

'No, I knew that she was very poorly and was hospitalised on a regular basis. But Jayla spoke of her often, she was a devoted mum.'

'Didn't Jayla want to be home with her daughter instead of Michael?' asked Ross.

Louyar shrugged. 'I don't know. I never asked her, and she never said. I just supposed that they'd worked the finances out for themselves, which way was best for their family.'

'That's not true!'

Wheeler turned. Mrs Louyar was standing in the doorway, wearing a dark-green cotton nightgown.

'You go back to bed, darling,' said Louyar gently.

'I heard you talking. Michael O'Donnell is not a nice

man. You should ask him why he insisted on looking after Paula and not leaving it to Jayla. You ask him!'

Louyar walked to the doorway. 'Lovely, I'll finish off with the police.'

'Police? Why are they here?'

Wheeler could see that the woman was wide-eyed and obviously heavily sedated.

'Jayla kept her baby well. Paula was a strong toddler. Robust even. Sure, she had a few knocks but she was healthy. It was only after Jayla died that little Paula really deteriorated. The rest was all lies. Lies and deceit.' Mrs Louyar began sobbing, her voice rose. 'I know what it is like not to be able to keep your baby safe!'

'If you don't mind, excuse me a moment.' Louyar took his wife gently by the shoulder. 'Darling, have a lie-down. I'll make supper later. Have a little sleep.'

'I was dreaming about Jace.' Mrs Louyar allowed herself to be led from the room. 'He was singing that little song he used to sing, do you remember? Do you even remember?'

'I do, my darling, I do,' said Louyar.

'Can you remember the melody?' Mrs Louyar's voice sounded feeble and she looked like she might faint.

Wheeler heard him softly sing a child's nursery rhyme. A song of care and safety and love. Wheeler wasn't sentimental at all, she had never been broody. She knew for a fact that these emotions wouldn't touch her at all. She swallowed hard.

A few minutes later Louyar re-entered the room. 'My wife has gone to sleep. Now, I will tell you all I can and then if you could go? I need to rest. I am tired.'

'Did Jayla ever suggest there was any trouble in the relationship?' she asked.

'Never, that I know of.' He paused. 'Although she was clumsy.'

'With the residents?' asked Ross.

'No, not at work,' said Louyar. 'Never with the residents.'

'Then?' prompted Wheeler.

'Jayla had a black eye once and bruising on her arm many times. She often wore a short-sleeved tunic and they were visible. When I asked her, she said she'd been in a car accident. Whiplash, she said. Another time, she said that she had fallen.'

This chimed in with what Kirsten Rivera had told them, thought Wheeler. It also confirmed that Michael O'Donnell liked to control situations and people.

'I know some of the staff had suspicions,' Louyar continued, 'but honestly she never suggested or hinted even for a moment that anyone had hurt her.'

'Did you know anything about the upturned crosses in their home?' asked Wheeler

'No, we were never invited to her home. I got the impression that Michael wanted it to be the preserve of him and his daughter. I'm sorry not to be more of a help.'

After a few more questions, Wheeler thanked him, and they left the sparse flat. Outside it had started to snow again; still they took their time walking to the car.

'I could barely breathe in there,' said Wheeler. 'I don't know how he can.'

'It's his wife. Maybe loyalty to her?' said Ross. 'You know loyalty, right? It's when people care for each other and hang on in there.'

'Besides you and your little hand sanitisers, you have a cheek to talk about having a bloody obsession with hygiene,' said Wheeler.

They reached the car, he turned to her. 'Food?'

'I know that despite feeling overwhelmed with sympathy for this case and for the grieving Louyars,' said Wheeler, 'your appetite will kick in and you'll want to stop off and eat.'

'I'm starving,' admitted Ross.

'Right,' said Wheeler. 'A quick sandwich and let's get on with the case.'

'I need to refuel. Like a racing car. Quality,' he boasted. 'Formula One. Pretty much like a Ferrari.'

'You are sadly delusional, Ross,' she laughed, closing the car door. 'More like a clapped-out old banger.'

An hour later and she had eaten a cheese roll, drunk a cup of coffee. Ross had consumed a macaroni pie and chips, two Americanos and an empire biscuit.

'You feeling better?' she asked.

'Yeah, thanks,' said Ross. 'I'll drop you at the Fairfield Hotel. You sure you'll be OK on your own with MacCullagh?'

'Ross, I'm meeting an old colleague, who's an award-winning journalist. How risky can it be?'

'I'm just saying,' said Ross.

'I know about the availability of guns from our viewpoint. He's been on the streets, talking to the gangs. He can tell me what their view is, especially around unregistered guns.'

'You want me to come in with you?'

'Shift. Stop trying to mollycoddle me. Get yourself back to the station and check up on our bloody case.'

'You around later for a takeaway and some wine? Or are you cosying up with that Lothario Hawk?' Ross smiled. 'Another bloody journalist.'

'Focus on the job, Ross.' Wheeler walked towards the hotel. She heard a text come in. Seb.

The station is dead without you. You free for dinner later?

She ignored it. Dropped the phone back into her pocket. Made her way towards the hotel.

Chapter 45

The Hotel

The Fairfield Hotel was situated between the Buchanan Galleries shopping centre and the Royal Concert Hall. Its prices, if not standards, were high. She walked into the bar. It was as she remembered, all gilt and plush velvet. In the background soft muzak. He was already ensconced in a leather tub chair. An empty glass in his hand. 'Any joy with your case?' he asked.

She quickly updated him on everything, finishing with, 'Any views on dEADdOG?'

'Never heard of it. So, what do you need me for?' asked MacCullagh. 'Specifically?'

'Michael O'Donnell's sister-in-law believes that he killed his wife, Jayla.'

'Because?' said MacCullagh.

'Long story short. Previous cases of clumsiness towards the child. Sister says he wanted to frame the mother around harming her daughter. A co-worker says Jayla often had bruises.'

'Anything concrete?' asked MacCullagh.

'Other than her conviction?' said Wheeler. 'No.'

'She hated him before her sister's death?' said MacCullagh.

'Yes.'

'People construct all kinds of fantasies. Your take on the sister-in-law?'

'Extremely angry,' said Wheeler.

A waiter approached. Wheeler ordered coffee. MacCullagh ordered a double whisky.

'And the daughter?' MacCullagh asked when the waiter had gone. 'What about Paula?'

'She's still missing,' said Wheeler.

He paused. 'You still single, Wheeler?'

'And planning to keep it that way.' She looked at him. He had gone to seed. A thick gut dropped over his belt and his chin had a flabby echo.

'A woman with your looks should be thinking about settling down. And at your age, maybe the old biological clock is kicking in?' He laughed. 'Tick-tock and all that shit?'

Wheeler stared at him.

He tried for a laugh. Failed.

She let the strangled sound hang in the air.

'Sorry, so you're not broody. Never have been?' His voice light, nervous.

The waiter arrived with their drinks.

'I've never needed a mini-me.' Wheeler picked up her coffee cup, sipped the strong liquid. 'How goes it with the new assignment?'

'Changing the subject?' he asked.

'Nothing more to be said, I don't think that I'm the type. Married life works for some, you included.' Wheeler paused. 'How is Monique? And the kids?'

Anne Randall

'I'm divorced now.' He stared into his whisky. 'Since last July. It's been a fucking nightmare. Plus, not seeing my kids every day kills me. It's like a knife through my heart. I feel like I can hardly breathe.'

'Sorry to hear that,' said Wheeler.

'Monique got a better offer. Seems being the wife of a journalist wasn't as cool as being the partner of some big shot in film production. She has an indoor pool now. The kids are at private school. Her life's complete.' He gulped his drink. 'Without me.' He gestured to the waiter.

Wheeler saw the tears begin to form in his eyes. She pushed on, 'So, about this case.'

'Are you at least dating, Wheeler?'

Oh, dear God, she thought, now it was supposed to be her bloody turn to share. 'What's it to you?'

'That guy, the one in your team?' said MacCullagh.

'There are quite a few guys on the team,' she said.

'Yeah, but one of them is in love with you.' MacCullagh sipped his drink. 'And you know it.'

Wheeler was beginning to regret the meeting, it was disintegrating into a lonely-hearts confessional.

'The tall, dark-haired guy, what was his name?'

'No idea.'

'Supports Raith Rovers.'

'God, is that how you boys identify each other? By your bloody football teams?'

'Pretty much,' admitted MacCullagh.

'Still no idea,' said Wheeler.

'You're lying, Wheeler,' said MacCullagh. 'He has a three-legged dog.'

Wheeler sipped more of her overpriced coffee. 'Steven

282

Ross, I guess is who you are referring to. Supports Raith Rovers and has a three-legged mutt.'

MacCullagh smiled. 'That's him. That's the one.'

'He barely tolerates me.'

'You are shit at lying, Wheeler. He's in love with you and do you know what?' MacCullagh sipped his drink. 'I think you know it. Now the question is—'

'Christ, can we shelve the romantic advice?' said Wheeler. 'We're here to talk about a case. You know, the one I called you about?'

'The question is, are you in love with him? Is it reciprocated?' he asked.

Wheeler looked at MacCullagh, heard the pain in his voice. The suffering. What was it about men like him, they couldn't seem to function without someone beside them.

A waiter approached.

'Another?' MacCullagh asked her.

'No, you're all right, thanks.'

'Fair enough. I'll have another.' He turned to her. 'Who was the CIO in the case? The dead woman?'

'The Chief Investigating Officer was Peter Morgan.' She paused. 'I've heard rumours that towards the end, he wasn't up to the job.'

'That right?' said MacCullagh. 'He was out of it. He was an absolute coke head. He swore it made his thinking process sharper and made him a better cop. Of course, I will never say that in public.'

'I know,' said Wheeler.

'Morgan may well have messed up. He did on many occasions. At other times, the man was an absolute genius.'

'You think he might have missed this one as well?'

'It's a possibility,' said MacCullagh. 'What did the pathologist's report say?'

'That Jayla died of a single gunshot wound.'

'You studied the photographs from the crime scene?'

'Of course.' Wheeler thought of the pictures, of the leakage that had surround Jayla O'Donnell's head. Brain matter had coated her hair and lay across the room. It had been a horrendous sight.

'Your question is, did she pull the trigger herself?'

'The trajectory says she did. I want to know how easily she could have acquired a gun?' asked Wheeler.

'Your crime is going back a bit, but, as things stand now, if money's tight, a used gun will set you back less than a hundred pounds. If you need to look cool, spend more and get a Beretta 9000 with a silencer; if you're a tough guy and need to look the part, there are shotguns, machine guns and pistols available. The Glock 9mm is popular. If you're at the top of the pecking order and running a serious outfit, Uzis and fully automatics are the way to go. The criminals out there are far better armed than you lot, I'm afraid. For a few thousand, you could get yourself an AK-47 assault rifle. Five were uncovered last month in Ayrshire.'

'Yeah, I heard about that,' said Wheeler. 'And that the bigger outfits don't hold their own guns, they have keepers who'll stash the guns at their place, a lock-up or a garage, a hut in the garden if necessary.'

'Keeping it in manageable segments,' agreed MacCullagh.

Wheeler was thinking of Ian Price. A spot of winter gardening or DIY wasn't keeping him in betting money at the Golden Key Casino. She'd had uniform pay a visit to the Golden Key. Turns out Ian was a regular, lost an average of £80 an evening. That was close to £600 week, well over £2,000 a month. She was pretty sure that the occasional DIY/gardening job didn't support that habit.

'What did Michael O'Donnell do for a living? You reckon he was mixed up in this? A keeper?'

'Mainly he was a carer for his daughter and a governor at her college, the College of Visual Arts. There had been an incident with a student suspected of carrying a gun last year, Craig Brennan.'

'You spoke to the kid?'

'Of course.'

'And?'

'He denied it.'

'The area surrounding the CoVA is controlled by the Broad gang, you might know some of them?'

Wheeler nodded. 'The ring leader was Pauly Wilkie who was arrested last month for murder. His brother Shane is in charge now. But the members are getting younger. Teenagers are being drafted in, often as young as twelve or thirteen. They know the neighbourhoods, they are out on their bikes at night.'

'Often ferrying a gun for another gang member. Some of the bigger operations use kids to rent out a gun. The gang can't afford their own gun, so they hire one for a night.' MacCullagh sipped his whisky. 'So, I hear that upturned crucifixes and maybe satanism are also in the mix?'

That information had been kept back from the press. Wheeler didn't ask who he'd heard it from. Police Scotland wasn't exactly watertight. 'More leaks than the bloody *Titanic*,' she muttered. 'Yes, those artefacts were found in Michael O'Donnell's home. And one beside Craig Brennan.'

'You think Paula's abduction is to do with some cult?' said MacCullagh.

'I don't know. Carmyle Station was also the recipient of a decapitated dog.'

'Sick fuckers,' said MacCullagh.

'And shoved into the poor creature's unfortunate throat, was an upturned cross.' Wheeler paused, 'If Michael O'Donnell did kill his wife, what are the chances of posthumously convicting him? Slim, I'm betting?'

'Not necessarily,' said MacCullagh. 'Gartcosh.'

She knew all about the Scottish Crime Campus in Gartcosh, North Lanarkshire. Knew that it pioneered forensic techniques. Knew that it got incredible results.

'I've just come from a meeting with a tech from Gartcosh. They've had an upgrade.'

'Go on.'

'Whereas before the boffins used to swab a gun for DNA, they now dismantle the whole thing completely. Every component is stripped bare and individually tested, so any microscopic particles, skin, sweat, blood or any matter which had seeped into the gun, is recorded and identified. This is anywhere, the magazine, the grip or the chamber. Then—'

'The information is recorded in the National Ballistics Intelligence Service,' said Wheeler, standing. 'So I just need to track down the gun used and get it retested?'

'Shouldn't be too difficult for someone as capable as you, Wheeler.'

As she left, she glanced across the room. MacCullagh was already at the bar. She watched him order again. Knew that he was drinking too much, that the absence of his wife and kids had left a hole a mile wide that he didn't know how to fill. Her phone beeped a text. Ross.

You have food? I can go get a takeaway? She read it quickly before dropping the phone back in her pocket. Ross wanted to meet up but the words of MacCullagh were too close, too relevant. *'He's in love with you . . . The question is, are you in love with him? Is it reciprocated?'*

Wheeler ignored the text. Heard another come through. Ignored that too. She had a case to solve. She just had to get the hell on with it.

Chapter 46

Home

She eventually left the station and felt weary as she climbed the stairs to her flat. The idea of a home delivery and an hour or two to herself, thinking about the case, seemed a good option. As she climbed, the aroma drifted towards her and she heard the music, the sax soar on Sonny Rollins' 'St Thomas'.

As she approached her door, Hawk appeared on the landing. 'I've been cooking again, you want to come in and have a taste? It's for Aubree's birthday tomorrow but I always let it cool overnight. It gives the flavours time to develop and deepen. Come and tell me what you think of it. Besides, I've finished the first draft of the first chapter on Carmyle Police Station; you can give me your opinion.'

'My mind's still on the case,' said Wheeler.

'Then forget it for a while, let your subconscious use it. Take some time out and approach it with fresh eyes tomorrow.' He paused. 'I sent you a text earlier.'

'I haven't checked messages.' She smiled.

Wheeler followed Hawk into his flat; there was

something infectious about his enthusiasm and half an hour of her time wasn't going to hurt anyone.

Inside the flat, the smell was intense. He poured her a chilled glass of wine, placed a small amount of food onto a red and gold plate, poured on a sauce. 'Baked courgette fritter with marinara sauce. Try.'

It was incredible. 'Wow, pretty spectacular. Where did you learn to cook like this?'

'From my family. I think food is the language of love. If I love someone I want to give them my very best. And in partnership with the wine it creates little bubbles of happiness in an otherwise stressful day. Listen,' he said, 'try a little of this. The pairing of cream and caramelised scallops with cauliflower purée goes extremely well. And here, try this wine with it. Just a drop.'

She accepted the food and sipped the wine. The partnerships were fantastic. 'I wish I had the patience and the ability to cook like this.'

'Then I'll teach you,' said Hawk. 'It takes practice but after that, only artistic flair.'

'I'm not sure—' said Wheeler.

'Pardon me for interrupting you but anyone who appreciates the beauty of Thelonious Monk, Sonny Rollins and Hank Mobley, while simultaneously deciphering the clues and patterns of killers, is indeed an artist. Here let me show you a finished painting.'

It was in his bedroom, leaning against the far wall. She studied the painting, the colour, the broad brushstrokes. It was breathtaking. The woman looked strong and sensual. The expression in her eyes, one of a warrior. Wheeler again likened his style to that of her favourite painter J. D. Fergusson. 'Beautiful.'

289

Hawk was beside her. 'I'd like to paint you one day, if you'd permit me?'

Wheeler glanced at the painting, took in the romance of the setting. 'I couldn't do it justice; your model is very poised and elegant.'

'The model, Margie Trammain, is a bus driver in Edinburgh. When I saw her, I knew immediately that she had elegance. When I first asked her to pose, she refused. It was only after asking her persistently for maybe two or three weeks that she knew that I was serious. As to elegance, I believe that all women are intrinsically elegant. It is the artist's job to record it accurately. And you, Wheeler, have more elegance than most.'

She felt herself blush, as she studied the painting, 'It reminds me of a Fergusson paining, *La Terrasse*?'

'Yes, he was a fine artist. I'm impressed by his handling of the paint, it's very loose, very sensual and, in a sense, it captures one very special moment of existence. And strong women often dominate his paintings. And you have such strength. Which is why I would like to paint you.'

'Many of his models wore hats.' Wheeler laughed. 'I don't own one.'

'There are many without hats. Many without clothes. His paintings of his partner Margaret Morris were spectacular. As for his paintings of the nude, they lacked the overt formality and sombre tones that many artists reserve for this oeuvre. His gift to us as artists was to—'

Behind them the sound of a throat being cleared.

Hawk turned.

Ross addressed Wheeler. 'Your place was in darkness, so I just followed the smell of food.'

'Ah, what a good little detective you are, DI Ross.' Hawk

smiled. 'Of course, I left my door open too, which may have helped. May I offer you some food? Wine?'

Ross held up the pizza boxes. 'We're good. Thanks.' He glanced at Wheeler. 'Aren't we?'

'The local chippy does pizza? I wouldn't have thought that they would have, but what do I know?' said Hawk eyeing the boxes.

'The queue was around the block for the posh place, so I doubled back to the chippy.'

'The posh place, as you call it, is very good. I find it helps if you make a reservation in advance for dining there and phone in an hour or so in advance for takeaways. If you're sure you won't have any food, then I'll show you out. We don't want your pizza to get cold.' Hawk paused. 'There's nothing more *revolting* than cold pizza.'

Ross turned to say something. Stopped.

Wheeler put down her wine glass. 'That's fine, let's go discuss the case.'

In her flat, Wheeler collected the plates and cutlery. 'I wasn't expecting you.'

'I sent a text. I didn't notice you slipping out of the station.'

'I didn't slip out, Ross.'

'Anyway, isn't he a bloody show-off?' said Ross.

'Hawk? What makes you say that?'

'All this writing and painting and blah di fucking blah cooking. It's all a bit flamboyant.'

'He's a journalist by trade, it's his job, muppet.' She sipped her wine. 'And painting is his hobby.'

'What's with the fancy food?'

'I think it's good to be able to cook. Not everyone lives on takeaways, Ross.'

'I can cook. I made macaroni cheese the other night.'

'Yeah,' she laughed, 'out of a can.'

'And who the hell doesn't like cold pizza? What kind of a freak is he?' Ross took a slice of pizza. 'And I overheard that he wants to paint you. Surely you're not going to let him?'

'How long were you standing there, eavesdropping?' She watched the blush begin at his throat and work its way up his face.

'Let's get on with the case. You went to see MacCullagh, get me up to speed.'

And so, she told him everything that they had discussed. But as she ate the stodgy pizza and drank the mediocre wine (her own wine, she reminded herself), her mind drifted back to Hawk and his exquisite flat. He made it all seem so effortlessly elegant, so easy to live well and to cook well. If nothing else, Hawk intrigued her. Sure, he was handsome, that went without saying, but that had never been the pull for her. There had to be more. Hawk had something that she was drawn to. And his paintings were beautiful. His cooking was sublime. Would she pose for him? She wondered what a portrait of her would look like.

' . . . and so, I reckon that we need to be looking for someone who . . . ' Ross paused, looked at her. 'What do you think?'

'Yes, I agree.' She fudged it. She'd been daydreaming about art and Hawk and good food. Get a grip, she silently admonished herself. 'Your take on the case?'

'You were miles away.'

'I'm tired, Ross.'

'Or were you just in the other flat?' He pushed the rest of the cold pizza away. 'I think we're done here.'

She stood. 'Fine, OK.'

She heard the door slam behind him. After clearing up, she went into the bathroom and began to brush her teeth and, ten minutes later, crawled into bed. Tomorrow morning, she would go for a long run before work. That always sorted her out. Then, when she was at the station, she would find a quiet corner to ask Ross what was bothering him. Was it Aubree? Was that the problem? Or was it tension about going for some promotion? Either way, Ross was most definitely not his usual easy-going self. She thought about one thing Hawk had mentioned. She still hadn't read the first chapter of his book about shadowing the team at the station. But tomorrow was another day, she reminded herself as she closed her eyes.

Chapter 47

Thursday 17 December

Wheeler was talking to Dr Buckley's business partner, Dr Bridges. Hawk sat across from her, listening on the speakerphone. Taking notes.

'Is there anything at all you can tell me about Dr Buckley?' said Wheeler.

'He was a well-respected GP, and a partner here at the Health Centre. He had recently split from his long-term partner, Mary-Ellen Patterson.'

'We've already contacted her,' said Wheeler. 'She hadn't been in contact with Dr Buckley since they broke up.'

'He was a very private person. He didn't say much but I got the impression that the decision to split had been his and that's why he arranged a sabbatical. He took a year off, ostensibly to write up a research paper but also, I think, to give Mary-Ellen time to grieve. He was like that, a thoughtful man. He was also a keen cyclist and did upwards of a hundred miles a week. He enjoyed opera. I knew him well enough through work but not personally. If I'm being honest, I thought of him as Dr Buckley, not David.'

'When was the last time you spoke with him?' asked Wheeler.

'About a week ago. I needed to update him on some personnel changes here at the Health Centre.'

'Did he mention if anything was out of the ordinary?' asked Wheeler.

'No, on the contrary, he was quite chipper. He sounded much more upbeat than usual and I wondered if he had perhaps met someone. He really was rather jolly during our conversation.'

'Would you have any idea who he might have been seeing?' asked Wheeler.

'None, I'm afraid. As I said, Dr Buckley was an extremely private man. The only way we'd even managed to meet Mary-Ellen was by chance at the opera one night, *The Marriage of Figaro* if I remember rightly. My wife and I bumped into them quite by accident.'

'You didn't socialise together?'

'No, as I said, he didn't socialise much at all. Outings to the opera, chess and his bike riding. He raised quite a bit of money for local charities. Loved dogs. Always dog walking. He got them from rescue centres. The whippet he loved. Now dead, unfortunately. '

Wheeler thought of the statue of the dog that had been the murder weapon.

'The new one, the Bernese, Toby, he was besotted by him. Absolutely besotted.' He paused. 'I presume the dog is being cared for?'

'I'm afraid the dog's dead,' said Wheeler.

'I see. How awful.'

'You were telling me about Dr Buckley.'

'Yes, he was incredibly diligent. That's not to give the

impression that he was a bore, quite the opposite. He was very interesting and fabulous at chess. It's just that he was almost completely self-sufficient. He really didn't need people, or at least very many, to complement his life. This is an awful shock. I know you can't divulge too much but do you have anyone in the frame for this?'

'I'm afraid I can't comment on an ongoing investigation,' said Wheeler.

'Of course,' said Dr Bridges.

'Did Dr Buckley ever mention feeling fearful? Did he suggest that there was anything wrong?' asked Wheeler.

'On the contrary, he seemed settled and relatively cheerful. He was enjoying living albeit temporarily in Glasgow. He'd attended Glasgow University many years ago and had a real soft spot for the place. He mentioned playing chess frequently.'

'He was a member of the chess club at the College of Visual Arts,' said Wheeler.

'I imagine he might have been, he loved the game.'

'Did he ever mention Michael O'Donnell, a governor at the college?'

'No, but as I said he wasn't someone who craved friendship. He was very autonomous.'

Wheeler could feel her frustration: if Dr Buckley was so independent, so self-contained, then why were both he and his beloved dog dead? There had to be something. 'Take a minute, think back over your conversations. Anything at all would be helpful.' She waited.

'Now I recall that he did mention that he had run into someone, I think he said that the person was connected to the college. He didn't care for the individual as far as I remember. He thought that they were rather objectionable.'

'In what way?'

'Dr Buckley was very circumspect. He only alluded to the fact that the person was rather pompous and opinionated.'

Wheeler thought of the staff. Barnes Olsen, Kirkpatrick, McSweeney or Van Der Berg? 'Did he mention any names at all?' she asked.

'None, he was the soul of discretion,' said Dr Bridges. 'Now, I am so sorry to cut this short, but I really must go. I have a surgery to run and, as dreadful as it sounds, I need to think about a replacement for Dr Buckley.'

'Before you go,' said Wheeler. 'Did Dr Buckley ever mention a man, name of Vladimir Nazarewich? He was known as Vlad, and was handyman in the area?'

'I'm afraid not, no.'

'Vlad was a chess player.'

'Is this person pertinent to your investigation?' asked Dr Bridges. 'Sorry, I shouldn't ask.'

'Can you tell me about Dr Buckley's research?'

'Not much, it was his own pet project and pretty much off-limits. But wait a minute, he did discuss it with another specialist, Dr Emelda Owen. She's on a silent retreat at present. She'll be back soon. Shall I get her to contact you?'

'If you would.' Wheeler thanked him and ended the call. She turned to Hawk. 'Does this show you how frustrating police work can be?'

'That right, Wheeler?' he replied distractedly.

'Yes.' She saw him scrolling down his phone.

'You're not the only woman who's frustrated. Seems like our detective Ross isn't replying to any of Aubree's texts,' said Hawk. 'And it's her birthday week.'

'Ghosting – isn't that the preferred name for it now?' asked Wheeler. 'In new speak?'

'It's bloody bad manners, in old speak,' said Hawk. 'Sounds like Aubree's better off without him.'

Wheeler couldn't contradict him. She dearly wanted to speak up for Ross, but she knew that as a boyfriend, he had at best a patchy reputation. At worst . . . well she didn't even want to go there. She really hoped that Ross was sorting himself out. She also hoped that he knew that she was there for him.

Chapter 48

The College of Visual Arts – The Pastoral Centre

'Try to curb your impatience' was what Mr Van Der Berg had always told him. 'Pace yourself, Nick.'

Nick Price sat at one of the tables, in front of him a cup of tea.

'I am so sorry for what you are going through, Nick. I know the disappearance of your mum must be a very difficult time for you,' said Van Der Berg.

'Thanks,' said Nick.

'I know it's not the same by any measure, but I too have experienced loss. The loss of my partner, Josh.' Van Der Berg stared at his hands. 'He died in an accident a year ago.'

'I'd no idea that you were gay, Mr Van Der Berg.'

Van Der Berg glanced at Nick. 'It's not something I broadcast.'

'Then you're ashamed of it?' said Nick.

'No, never. But at the CoVA, I think that I must be careful. But I trust you, Nick. You were always mature.'

'I trust you too.' Nick briefly touched the lecturer's hand. 'And I'm sorry for your loss.'

'It's OK, but I just wanted to tell you that I know some-thing about loss. That I am also bereaved.'

Nick paused. 'Mr Van Der Berg, how can you be a pastoral support team member?'

'I don't understand?' said Van Der Berg.

'As a member of the pastoral support team, you are left alone in a room with vulnerable young people,' said Nick. 'Young men like me.'

'I'm afraid I'm not sure what you mean, Nick?'

'Who else knows about your homosexuality?'

'Why does it matter?' said Van Der Berg.

'I'm just wondering if the board of governors know?'

'Do they know that I am gay?' asked Van der Berg. 'Why on earth would it matter?'

Nick stood. 'It would matter to my mum. She isn't a fan of homosexuality. She's a practising Christian.'

'Then I hope you can—' started Van Der Berg.

'What?' spat Nick. 'Keep your filthy little secret for you?'

'It's not a secret. I would never want Josh to be a secret.'

'What are you asking me to do?' said Nick.

'Only to keep what I told you in confidence,' said Van der Berg. 'To hold a respectful boundary.'

Nick's voice softened. 'Why would I lie for you, Mr Van Der Berg?'

'I'm not asking you to lie, Nick.'

'It certainly sounds like it.'

'We are both human beings and we are both experien-cing loss.'

'Mum's not dead. My mum is not dead. How revolting of you to imply that she is,' said Nick. 'You need to be ashamed of yourself.'

'I didn't say she was, only that her being missing is a type of loss.'

'And as for your touching me, Mr Van Der Berg. That felt like a violation.' Nick paused. 'I feel like I have been abused.'

Van der Berg stood. 'But I didn't touch you, Nick. I only said . . .'

The door opened and Principal McSweeney entered.

'Is there something I can help you with, Principal?' said Van Der Berg.

'I need to have a quiet word, Mr Van Der Berg. Am I interrupting anything?'

'No, we're fine,' said Van Der Berg. 'We're just having a quick chat.'

'I'm sorry but there is something I would like to discuss, Principal McSweeney,' said Nick. 'It's concerning my mother's faith. I have concerns about Mr Van Der Berg being at liberty to mix with vulnerable young people, especially males. Given what I've just encountered. I feel used. Dirty. Like an old tissue.'

McSweeney looked at Van Der Berg.

'I can assure you, Principal, that none of this is true.'

Nick stood. 'Then don't believe me, Principal McSweeney.'

Mc Sweeney gestured. 'Sit down, Nick, please.' She glanced at Van Der Berg. 'If you'll excuse us, Mr Van Der Berg, I'll talk with you later.'

There was a small sound like a breath escaping from Van Der Berg. He lifted his mug and stood.

Once Van Der Berg was gone, Nick looked at Principal McSweeney. He felt elated; if what he was about to do could even leave a small indelible stain on Mr Van Der

Berg's life that would be something. He mentioned, tear-fully, reluctantly, the inappropriate touching. He knew that Van Der Berg was on his way out. After doubt had been cast, the college could say that it was down to cuts, to finance, to a reshuffle. Anything.

Later, as he left the college, Nick passed through the car park. Mr Van Der Berg was sitting alone in his car. Nick walked towards it, rapped his knuckles on the top. 'You chose your path, Mr Van Der Berg, and I chose mine.'

'But why are you doing this, Nick? Why? Is it grief? Anger is one of the stages of loss, as is denial and depression. What can I do to help you?' Van Der Berg called after Nick.

But Nick ignored Van Der Berg. Kept walking. Smiled to himself.

Chapter 49

The Station

Wheeler put down the phone. 'Kirsten Rivera just called in.'

'And?' said Ross.

'She forgot to mention it when we were at her house. Didn't know if it was important. Paula was to inherit money from her mother when she turned eighteen.'

'Right,' said Ross, crossing to the coffee pot. 'So far so normal.'

'She's going to inherit two hundred thousand dollars.'

Ross stopped pouring his coffee. 'Bloody hell. That makes a big difference.'

'If she was going to strike out on her own, have a more independent life, two hundred grand would certainly help her move towards it.'

'But if she's dead, who does it go to?' asked Ross.

'Her father.'

'And since he's dead, who to?'

'To Kirsten Rivera.'

'Then, there's motive,' said Ross. 'She did mention that she was having to sell her house and artwork. Financial difficulties.'

'Keep an open mind,' said Wheeler, turning back to her reading. She was sifting through the transcripts of Michael O'Donnell's Facebook posts. She had asked the tech department to isolate the posts referring to Paula's health. She read them quickly. 'Michael O'Donnell seemed very bloody angry,' she said to Ross. 'Look at this.'

I am going to sue them for misdiagnosis. The NHS has been negligent in diagnosing Paula. I know that she is special, that she is unique, but they have a duty to find out what is wrong with her and treat her accordingly. This may provide her with enough money, so that when I am gone, she can live independently. She was incredibly poorly yesterday, I feared that I would lose her. The ambulance staff were, at best, mediocre. I think the NHS struggles to attract quality staff. One of the paramedics was barely comprehensible. She muttered something about Paula's fitting being unusual and about her needing to finish her shift and no overtime being available. I ask you, when my daughter had almost passed out on the floor and that imbecile is wittering on about overtime?

Wheeler scrolled down:

And later I had a meeting with Paula's GP and a Dr David Buckley sat in. He's merely a London-based GP who has relocated to write up some paper, no doubt a vanity project. I heard on the grapevine that he was licking his wounds after a failed love affair in London. Tosser. He fancies himself as a chess buff. I've seen his chess technique. Amateur.

Later he had written:

The lovelorn and exiled Dr Buckley had the temerity to suggest that Paula wasn't suffering from a rare case of epilepsy but perhaps something more psychological. He insinuated that she needed a psychiatrist. I was dumbfounded by his arrogance. He is the one in need of psychiatric help.

And later,

He had the audacity to suggest that Paula should have a boyfriend. My child is far too naive to experience this. The man is ridiculous. Worse, he is a monster.

Wheeler sat back in her chair. 'So, the person Dr Buckley thought arrogant was Michael O'Donnell.'

'And now they are both dead,' said Ross. 'Where do we go from here?'

'I've read Paula O'Donnell's Twitter feed and Instagram posts. There seems to be nothing more interesting than cute kittens and picture of sunsets.' The phone rang. 'Wheeler.' She listened. Started taking notes. Eventually put the phone down. 'The tech team have got into Sarah Price's Facebook and other social media accounts. Sarah had been meeting up with someone called Rob Carter and she had copied his profile from a dating website and stored it in a Word document. Trouble is, the online dating agency Looking4Love doesn't actually exist.'

'Someone lured her into a fake website?' asked Ross.

'Yes, but apparently Looking4Love looked very slick, very professional,' said Wheeler.

'Surely she'd have checked Facebook, Instagram, etc. to see if her date was real.'

'All you need is an email account and you can call yourself anything or anyone,' said Wheeler.

'So, we have absolutely no trace to her? No idea where she might be?' said Ross.

Wheeler's phone rang again. 'Dr Chowdry's downstairs.'

'Let's go see the epilepsy specialist,' said Wheeler.

He was seated in the interview room. He was small and rotund, he was mid-fifties and wore a perfectly fitted grey three-piece suit, purple silk tie held in place by a gold tie pin.

Wheeler introduced herself and Ross.

'I must apologise for not coming to see you earlier, I was at a family wedding in New York.' The doctor peered at her. 'Is Paula O'Donnell dead?'

'Honestly? I don't know,' said Wheeler.

'It seems certain, unless her abductor has her specific medication.' He paused. 'I read online that two students from the college are crowdfunding for a bounty hunter to be brought over from the US to find Paula. Is this true?'

'The Roach twins,' said Wheeler. 'The students are, unsurprisingly, very upset; however they have no access to police files or this case, despite what they may think.'

'Troubling times.' Dr Chowdry sat back in his chair. 'Now, how can I help?'

'I'd like your opinion on Paula O'Donnell's illness and also your views on her father, Michael. There are conflicting accounts. Michel wrote in his notes about a paramedic, who suggested that Paula's seizures were unusual. Michael gave no clue to his or her name. Paula also attended the epilepsy clinic at the Royal Hospital for Children in Govan . . .' Wheeler paused ' . . . and some of the other parents—'

He cut across her. 'They weren't complimentary about her?'

'No, they weren't. I just wondered if you could enlighten me?'

'And presumably furnish you with a straight yes or no answer?' said Dr Chowdry.

'If possible,' said Wheeler.

'I'm afraid that's not possible, Inspector Wheeler. A concrete diagnosis of epilepsy is not quite so simple. We collate various types of information around both the causes and the nature of the seizures.'

'There isn't a particular test you can do?' asked Ross.

'Not one which in my mind is conclusive,' said Dr Chowdry. 'Tests can include an EEG, a CT scan, an MRI scan, Pet, SPECT.'

'Right,' said Ross.

'Sorry, Inspector Ross. My wife is always reminding me that I talk too quickly and sometimes explain too little. An EEG is an electroencephalogram, a CT scan is a computerised tomography. MRI you're probably familiar with. The SPECT we often use in difficult cases, such as Paula's, when the EEG and the MRI fail to determine the area in her brain where the seizures were initiated. There are many scans available, plus of course the regulatory blood tests, but I'm afraid despite a battery of tests we could neither confirm that Paula O'Donnell was epileptic, nor deny it. The range of symptoms she presented with were very diverse, also her fitting was erratic in how it occurred, and this made it impossible to say for sure.'

'But your gut instinct, Dr Chowdry?' asked Wheeler.

'My dear DI Wheeler, I am a scientist, I don't believe in all that gut instinct mumbo-jumbo. But I will tell you one thing.' Dr Chowdry sat forward, hands clasped together in front of him.

Wheeler waited.

'I believe that Michael O'Donnell was utterly convinced that his daughter had an extremely rare type of epilepsy and dedicated his life to proving it. My main concern was his psychological state. He was determined to prove that his daughter was "one in a million".'

Wheeler had heard that phrase before. Two of the carers had said it. No matter what Paula suffered from, she had to be unique.

'Now, if you'll excuse me?' said the doctor. 'I need to get back to my patients.'

'Of course, you must be busy.' She paused. 'Did you know Dr David Buckley?'

'No, sadly our paths never crossed but I read his research paper in the *IJEP*, "Withdrawal of AED. Risk factors – a review". He offered some very profound insights.'

'The *IJEP*?' asked Wheeler. 'The *International Journal of Epilepsy*?' She had seen research papers in Michael O'Donnell's home.

'Yes, the late Dr Buckley had great insight in his academic publications. I'm absolutely certain that he was a consummate professional in his role as GP, but he was also a great academic. He could present very complex material in an easy-to-access way. He is a great loss to the medical profession.'

'And AEDs, if I remember correctly from Michael O'Donnell's notes, are antiepileptic drugs,' said Wheeler.

'Correct,' said Dr Chowdry, standing and crossing to the door. 'In many cases, over seventy per cent of epileptic seizures can be controlled.'

'By diet alone?' Ross sounded sceptical.

'Mainly by medication,' said Dr Chowdry. 'Or perhaps, a combination of both.' He closed the door behind him.

Wheeler thought back to the journals she'd seen at Michael O'Donnell's house. She flicked through her notebook. In between the tomes on satanic worship and literature, Michael O'Donnell's study had contained research papers. Plus, Michael, Paula and David had known each other and all had links to the CoVA. But what was the link between the death of Michael and David? And what about the fake dating agency site which Sarah Price had joined? The tech team were already working on it. Wheeler made the call. 'Have copies of all the research papers David Buckley was working on brought to my office, ASAP.'

Lovers' Tryst #3

Three Months Earlier

How long have we been dating now?

You don't remember?

I'm testing you. Well?

A year.

Do you think anyone suspects?

No.

Good. Let's keep it that way. Do you remember how we met?

Online. Social media. I remember the photographs you PM'd me. Breathtaking.

I do take a mean selfie.

Then I came over.

You had to be quick. Furtive.

Anne Randall

I was.
And now we are one.
So now what?
Game on.

Chapter 50

Carmyle Station

The incident room was busy; the acute sense of focus was undercut by the smell of stale coffee. Boyd had made yet another pot of black coffee and hadn't troubled himself to clean the three mugs that resided on his desk and were filled with varying amounts of discarded beverage, some of which had green mould floating on the surface.

Wheeler glanced at the rookie officer. She looked washed out. 'You OK?'

'Yes, of course.'

'Only you look pale,' said Wheeler.

'I just don't like looking at those things, they give me nightmares.' The rookie gestured to the pictures of the inverted crosses. 'But, I'll be fine, honestly.

But, thought Wheeler, she didn't look fine. Every cop in Police Scotland must have a thick skin, if you wanted to be part of the MIT then you needed to look at the photographs: of strange inverted crucifixes, of murder victims, of crime scenes and carnage. And while retaining a sense of humanity, also be able to file the individual, somewhere in your brain, under victim, and everything in their home, everything they may have held dear – a favoured dress, a mug – as potential evidence. It was a balancing act between empathy and compassion for the victim and a clinical detachment. In previous cases she had privately thought that she had some concerns around Ross, but the young officer looked shell-shocked, as if the act of investigating was taking too much out of her instead of focusing her. Most cops, if they were successful, were invigorated by the chase, but she looked depleted.

Wheeler updated the team on the fake dating website. 'The tech team are trying to trace it.' Also, her chat with Dr Chowdry.

'So, we don't even know for sure that Paula O'Donnell is epileptic?' asked Boyd.

'Apparently there's no one definitive test. Only a battery of tests and even then, sometimes nothing conclusive,' said Wheeler.

'Poor girl,' said a uniformed officer. 'Such a lot to go through at such an early age.'

Wheeler's phone rang. 'Yes?' She listened and jotted down the information. Ended the call. 'The same saliva has been identified on the dog torso, the cross found in its throat and in Michael O'Donnell's home.'

'Go on,' said Ross, shutting down his computer.

'A complete DNA match for Ian Price,' said Wheeler, making for the door.

'Bingo,' said Boyd. 'Now I take it you two are going to tootle off and apprehend our killer and grab all the glory? You'll leave us minions to keep going? Talk about Santa's little helpers.'

But Wheeler and Ross were off out of the door before he could finish.

Chapter 51

Glenshee Street

Nick Price followed his father into the living room, where the huge television had been switched on. The news blared out at him.

' . . . Also, teenager Paula O'Donnell is still missing, her father, Michael's murder inquiry remains ongoing, although the trail appears to have gone cold for Police Scotland. DCI Stewart had this to say, "We are following up various leads . . . but urge anyone who has any information to come forward . . . "'

The next news segment: 'A dog walker has unearthed a bloody scarf at the site where trainee beautician Zoe Wishart went missing almost two years ago. The scarf had been buried but the owner reported that the dog dug "furiously" at the site. The scarf was discovered on the route Zoe would have taken to the bus stop. Police and forensics are examining the evidence now.'

The commentator paused. 'In other news, police are still appealing for information about missing woman Sarah Price. Mrs Price was last seen at . . . '

His mother's face stared out at him. He heard the news commentator continue to appeal for witnesses.

Nick put his hands over his ears. 'I don't want to hear this.'

'It's a fact Nick,' said Ian. 'You need to face it.'

'It's nothing yet. They don't know what happened. If anything. She could have hit her head, she could be suffering from amnesia. We don't know.' The hysteria in his voice was apparent. Nick slumped into a chair. 'Dad, you just can't be sure.'

'Listen, I'm not trying to be harsh but face facts. Not that your mother and I got on, but I will say in fairness to her that this isn't like her. She was very clingy and co-dependent around you. She ignored all those years of anger and rage. Remember when a teacher thought you had Attachment Disorder and that you should have been diagnosed? And your mum just laughed? She was bloody besotted with you. She can't see past you.'

'Rubbish.'

'Plus, you've never bothered to have a decent go at our relationship.'

'Who would? Given you for a father?'

'She excused you everything, your shit temper, what happened to the poor wee dog and—'

'The bloody dog wasn't my fault!'

'I just wonder if she . . . '

'What?' said Nick.

'Well, you hear about mothers and sons and the bloody weird bond they have.'

'So?' said Nick.

'So,' Ian continued, 'what with you going away to art school in Brighton, maybe your mum couldn't face being on her own. Plus, you need to think of the finances. You're going to inherit a lot of money when your mum dies. Her life insurance is worth close to—'

'Fuck off,' shouted Nick.

'You read these stories in the press and who knows?' said Ian. 'You've been her entire life for so long now, maybe she couldn't see a way forward without you. Without being a mum.'

'You're not laying the blame for her disappearance at my door,' said Nick. 'You're off your bloody head. Mum would never have done it for the insurance.'

Ian shrugged, sipped from a can of lager. He'd been assured that no guns were needed for the following twelve hours. A truce to honour the funeral of Glasgow gangster Big Rab McMullion. All guns were on the lock-down until tomorrow, but then things would probably kick off. But that meant that Ian could get drunk tonight.

'So where were you when Mum disappeared?' asked Nick.

'You know bloody well where I was,' said Ian. 'With you.'

'I was at the gig at King Tut's until gone eleven.'

'So?' asked Ian.

'So, I wasn't back at yours until after midnight,' said Nick.

'You little shit.' Ian stood, threw a punch.

'It takes one—' Nick caught the punch, twisted his father's arm, held him down and then smashed a fist into his face. 'That's for being a bastard father.'

A faint sound of the doorbell ringing. Both of them were oblivious to it.

Ian struggled to breathe. 'Wise up, son. Your mother's missing, perhaps dead. God knows what happened to her.

You need to get a grip and stop being so bloody adolescent. You're a fucking snowflake, just man the fuck up.'

'Hey, I'm the one who's being realistic.' Nick released his grip. Walked into the kitchen.

'Your mother's no doubt dead. You're in denial. It's one of the five stages of grief, I read it on the internet. Denial, anger—'

Nick grabbed a carving knife and lunged at his father. 'You cunt.'

The doorbell rang again. In the background the television reporter ended his segment and the weather report began. 'Happily, for many, there will indeed be a white Christmas as snow is expected . . . '

'You little fucker, you owe me everything.' Ian put both hands up in defence, deflected his son's attack and punched Nick in the face. Watched the blood start.

'You bastard. Look what you've done to me.'

'You fucking asked for it.'

The sound was unmistakable. Someone was now hammering on the door.

'See that's the fucking nosey neighbour, you made enough racket that she's come round,' spat Ian. 'Go and sort it out. For fuckssake, get rid of her.'

A few seconds later, Nick opened the door. Two figures he recognised showed their ID.

'Hi, Nick. We'd like to speak to your dad. Is he here?'

Nick stood back.

Wheeler and Ross entered.

Chapter 52

Carmyle Police Station, Evening

Ian Price had been adamant that he was innocent. Completely innocent. He had been informed that he would be spending the night in a cell to reconsider.

Ross glanced at yet another text from Aubree. *Why are you ignoring me? Are you frightened of what we have together? Axxx PS I love you. I know you feel the same way. You told me, remember?*

Ross crossed the room and switched on the kettle. Contemplated his choices. Number one was that he left the force and went up to the house in Pittenweem that he had inherited from his father. Maybe he could become a photographer? He used to be pretty talented in that area. Number two, he could apply for promotion and move away from Carmyle Station and Wheeler. Would it be best to just do that? To stay on track, get his career in line and leave her behind? He knew that he was thinking about how much time he had and who he wanted to spend it with. Wheeler, without a doubt. But that might not be an option. Especially since the arrival of Seb Hawk. Realistically though, even before Hawk's

317

arrival, had them getting together even been option? Ross poured a coffee. Took it back to his desk, glanced around. Took out a flask from his bottom drawer, poured a tot of whisky into the mug. What did they have? What did he and Wheeler have that was worth pursuing? Attraction? Yes, definitely. He knew more than enough about her to recognise that she spent time with him through choice, not always through necessity. Knew that they'd been lucky, they had what the force called 'the thing'. The glue that made some partnerships work, without it, nothing. Only colleagues. Less than the sum of their individual parts. Whatever attraction he'd had with Aubree the other night and whatever Wheeler had with Hawk, he was sure that it wasn't even close to what they had together. Ross poured another tot of whisky into his coffee. With Wheeler, he had a feeling of inevitability, that they would at some point get together. Maybe he would need to move stations, move into a different specialism, but in the long run, it would be about them getting together, *being* together. And wasn't that the real point?

And then the little voice in his head repeated, *Except for the new guy. Seb fucking Hawk.*

Ross had, that morning, torn open the letter, another bloody hospital appointment. Fine. Broken Heart Syndrome. Just his luck. He wasn't over fifty, or a female, but still he'd managed to get it. For fuckssake, what was the matter with him? He glanced at the spray in his desk drawer, what had the cardiac nurse told him? 'One burst under the tongue. If pain persists, wait five minutes and administer a second. If pain persists, a third. After that, call an ambulance, ASAP.'

Ross sipped his whisky-laced coffee. His mother and father hadn't had a functioning relationship, so no great role models there then. He thought of Aubree. What was going on there? He'd been drunk that night but that wasn't an excuse. He was flattered that someone like Aubree had been interested in him. She was gorgeous. But he was ignoring her texts. He knew that his heart wasn't in it. He knew that she definitely wanted more but also that he certainly didn't. He wondered what she wanted. He knew what he was doing, he was avoiding talking to the one person he needed to talk to. Wheeler.

That small, critical voice again. *What if you tell Wheeler how you feel and it's a no? How do you even get back from that?*

What then? Ross knew that there was a big wide world out there, which he could explore. If he was well enough. Broken Heart Syndrome, the nurse had explained, was like a heart attack with regards to the symptoms, including chest pain and shortness of breath. He thought of the pizza, the chips, the fried egg rolls. The drinking. His father had been an alcoholic. Whisky. Ross put his mug down. A moment later he picked it up again. Finished the contents and poured another whisky. Another text came in. He glanced at it. Aubree.

Ross, we need to talk. Call me! Love, Aubree xxxxxxx PS I've seen a ring I like!

He walked through to Wheeler's office. Saw the ubiquitous Hawk sitting across from her, scribbling as per fucking usual in his notebook.

'How goes it?' Ross kept his tone casual.

'Bloody Ian Price is denying everything,' said Wheeler. 'Even though the DNA match is a hundred per cent.'

'Let him stew in the cells,' said Ross.

Hawk looked up from his notebook. 'Yeah, that's what DCI Stewart said.'

Ross ignored him. 'You need a lift home, Wheeler?'

'I'm here for another couple of hours, Ross. You go on ahead if you like?' She picked up the phone, dialled.

'I can give you a lift,' said Hawk, 'I'm here for a bit. I can write up my notes here.'

'OK,' said Wheeler. 'I'll go back with you.'

'No, you're all right,' said Ross. 'I've got a mountain of paperwork too. I'll get you in a couple of hours. I'll take you home, Wheeler. You'll be safer with me.' He tried for a laugh. Heard it die in his throat.

Wheeler began her conversation. 'Is that the SSPCA? I need some information about an animal.'

Hawk stood. 'Well if that's all agreed with you two guys, I'll head back to the flat now. I'm having a quick drink with my cousin, Aubree.' He glanced at Ross. 'Seems like some dickhead she likes is ghosting her.'

Wheeler spoke into the phone. 'So, no fox cub was brought into your centre on or around those dates?' She listened for a second.

Ross watched her scribble down the answer. Heard her thank them.

He left her to it.

Chapter 53

Chantelle Ward and Kim McGroarty, cousins, were making their way back from visiting the Scotia Bar, via an impromptu birthday party at their friend, Aggie's. They tottered gingerly towards the bus stop in the High Street, their progress hindered by a couple of factors. One, they were both wearing their best five-inch platform heels and the slush and ice didn't make that such a great experience. Two, they were both extremely drunk, having begun earlier in the evening with a couple of half-price cocktails and packets of crisps at a city centre bar before going on to the Scotia where the two guys they were hoping to 'casually bump into' drank. A night out meant they couldn't afford food. It was an either/or situation. Either go for dinner or go out drinking; the latter had been chosen as their best way forward. As it turned out, the guys hadn't shown, but they'd gamely waited their time, casually rebutting all other flirtatious advances, until it was time to leave. The cousins were known for their tenacity. Among their other attributes. But now they were completely and unmistakably drunk. And the party at Aggie's hadn't added to their sobriety as Aggie had provided music, wine and laughter.

But, unfortunately, her sixteen-year-old son and his friends had earlier laid siege to the fridge. So, again, no food.

'Oh, look at that,' Kim stopped, looking up into the night-time sky. 'It's snowing really hard, it's so gorgeous at this time of the year, isn't it? Very Christmassy. I just love it.'

Chantelle ducked out of the road and into the side street, wobbling perilously on the sleeted cobblestones. 'Sorry but I'm going to vomit, Kim, hen.'

'Fuck sake. Again? How much is there left? It's not like you ate much. A few crisps.'

'Still, feeling shit. Here's fine. It'll need to do.'

Kim watched her cousin barf up the cocktails, rum and Cokes she'd consumed, plus a couple of glasses of red wine. She watched their bus, in the distance, pull away from the stop and take off. Shook her head. 'Nae money for a taxi, hen, still, the walk home will do you good. You'll be sober, by the time you get back to your dad's.'

'Can't face walking, Chantelle.'

'Too bad.' Chantelle wedged her diamanté clutch bag tight under her armpit and with her other hand guided her cousin towards the street lights. 'Mon, hen. You're doing fine. You'll be okay, now it's all sicked-up. I always feel better once it's up.' They made their way towards the opening of the side street.

Ross and Wheeler were sitting at a red light close to the Royal Infirmary.

'That was a long couple of hours, Wheeler. More like four.'

'You know the job. I was reading notes about Dr Buckley. He was an accomplished academic. I think that's what annoyed Michael O'Donnell. That's why he was so snippy about him in his notes.'

'You want to grab something to eat? Maybe a pizza or a curry? Your choice.'

'Not tonight.'

'You sure? I'd quite like a quick chat.'

She turned to him. 'About what?'

He thought about Aubree. About his hospital appointments. About Broken Heart Syndrome. About Seb fucking Hawk. About them getting together. 'Nothing in particular. Just a chat. It's been a while?'

'It's been a split second since you spoke, and I am sitting right here. Shoot.'

'No, I need to think a bit first,' said Ross.

'OK, we'll talk tomorrow. I need to walk and think and take in some air. My head is buzzing with the case.'

'And how much to share with Hawk, no doubt?' said Ross.

'Leave him out of it,' said Wheeler. 'Why is he even so much on your radar? What is it with you? He's a nice guy.'

Ross stared ahead.

'I'll jump out here.' Wheeler undid her seat belt. 'See you tomorrow, sunshine. Have a good evening.'

'We could get a takeaway?' said Ross.

'No thanks. I just need to walk for a bit.'

'You sure? On your own?'

'Sure,' said Wheeler. 'And by the way, I'm a grown-up, remember? I can go for a walk on my own.'

'My treat for the food?' Ross persisted. 'It might not be up to Hawk's standards, but it served us well before he arrived.'

Wheeler smiled. 'Do you even know how nuts you sound?' She stepped out of the car, closed the door and took off towards the Royal Infirmary. She needed to walk in the cold night air to help her think straight. Ahead, to her left, was the Necropolis. Part of her wanted to wander around the ancient dark cemetery, but her cop radar said no. The cold night air was welcome and as she walked gentle snow drifted into her face. Ahead, a group of young men joshed and shoved each other. She passed them, heard one call out, 'Hello, gorgeous. You not talking then?' She ignored them, crossed the road. It was a short walk to her flat in the Merchant City. She heard the group say their drunken goodbyes, figured they'd be fist-bumping each other. Home to mothers or wives or girlfriends, their bravado to be replaced at breakfast by a crashing hangover. The pavements were almost deserted; she was glad of the silence. She thought of Michael O'Donnell and his daughter and of David Buckley and the animosity between the two men. She thought of Sarah Price and her affair with Michael O'Donnell, and of the fake dating website, wondered what the tech team would come up with. She heard something in the silence behind her, a change in the atmosphere. Her cop radar was always on, a quick glance. Nothing that she could see but was someone there? In the shadows, hidden in a doorway? She walked on. She thought of another bloody headline she'd seen in a newspaper, the theory that Sarah Price had gone looking for a new life. That she had been heavily in debt and had simply 'disappeared'. That whatever the police were suggesting was remiss, that Sarah Price had disappeared by choice, because hadn't she lied to her son about where she was going? Wheeler didn't buy it. Her gut instinct told her that whatever had happened to Sarah Price had not been of her own doing.

Wheeler did not subscribe to the idea of auras. Sure, she knew that some people did and that they believed they could read a person's aura or energy and decipher if someone was good or bad. She didn't believe in any of it. Nor did she believe in ghosts or the harbingers of gloom. Or the power of the inverted crosses in Michael O'Donnell's house or satanism. She believed that horror lived in the individual, not the geographical location. She walked on, turned over the evidence in her mind. Mulled it over and over. Still her gut instinct told her that someone was behind her. Following her. Watching her. Another quick glance behind her. Nothing. Was she imagining it? Her head felt like it was about to burst.

She tensed as she passed more graffiti, dEADdOG. Sensed, more than heard, someone behind her, turned again. Nothing. Only the blurred outline of the traffic moving slowly through the snow. Her nerves were frayed, there was no one behind her. Ahead a street light. She walked towards it and was about to step directly underneath it when a figure sprang out of the shadows in front of her. Wheeler glimpsed the hammer as it came towards her, the blur of an animal face, a dog face, grinning at her. She opened her mouth to cry out. Tried to marshal her kickboxing skills. But too late. Felt herself fall. The assailant began to drag her, she dug into the frozen ground, tried to scream, heard nothing.

Chantelle was first on the scene. She saw enough. 'Hey, you! What the fuck do you think you're doing? Eh?' She saw a figure in the doorway, lying on her side. Eyes closed. The man stood over her, one arm behind him.

'The fucker's hiding something,' she whispered to Kim as she quietly slipped off a high-heeled shoe, a five-inch hell of a weapon. 'Well if the bastard thinks he's sticking around, I'm fucking up for him. Bastard'n coward to attack a woman.'

Kim removed a shoe too, another solid platform of pain. 'Right, Chantelle, hen. We're fucking going to do him. And do him proper. The bastard. And he's wearing a mask too.'

'Cowardly fucker.'

'Come ahead, then,' they shouted in unison, marching towards him, brandishing their weapons.

The assailant paused before turning and sprinting through the alleyway. Disappeared.

They stood over the body. 'She's in a bad way. Let's have your phone,' Kim shouted, 'mine's out of charge.'

Chantelle rummaged in her bag. Handed it over.

Kim punched in the three digits. 'Ambulance', she demanded, explained briefly that there was an unconscious woman on the ground with a bloody wound. Gave her location. Repeated it, before muttering a terse, 'Get yerselves over here now. Super pronto. Move it! And get the polis too!' Ten minutes later she finished the call.

Chantelle and Kim slipped out of their coats and layered them over Wheeler. Chantelle took off her wool scarf, folded it and placed it carefully underneath Wheeler's head. 'What kind of a sick fucker does this?'

'Jesus, hen,' said Kim. 'Hanging's just too fucking good for him.'

'If we hadn't come along . . . ' said Chantelle.

'Don't think like that, hen. She's going to be OK. The ambulance and polis will be here soon.'

'You think mibbe we should look for a name and phone a husband or a partner?' said Chantelle.

'Fair dos,' said Kim. 'Don't disturb her though.'

Chantelle slipped a hand into Wheeler's pocket, took out police ID. 'Jesus, she's a copper.'

'Fuck sake,' said Kim. 'We need to keep an eye out.'

'How's that, doll?'

'Maybe it's been a hit,' said Kim. 'Know like an organised hit.'

'He wanted to take her out?' said Chantelle.

'Aye,' said Kim.

'Christ, mibbe he's still here.' Chantelle looked around the side street. Focused herself. She held her platform shoe in her hand. Poised. Ready.

Kim mirrored her. 'Then he'd better come mob-handed, cause the bastard's in for it if I see him again.'

Chapter 54

Glasgow's West End

Ross walked his dog though the freezing night air, enjoying the softness of the snowflakes on his face. The dog trotted along beside him, her three legs easily keeping up with his stride. She wore a smart tartan coat and a matching tartan harness. Ross walked towards the Kelvingrove Art Gallery. He paused in front of the building as the dog sniffed, her nose deep in whatever scent the frozen ground held. He looked up at the impressive building, which was illuminated against the night sky. He knew it was one of Wheeler's favourite places, probably her absolute favourite place. He walked on, thought of their chat in the car and how ridiculously petty he had been. Why? he asked himself. He knew the answer, he was jealous of her friendship with Hawk. Why didn't he just call her and apologise? He flicked on his phone, texted. *You still up?* Knew she would probably be sitting in her flat with a glass of wine and going over the evidence. Nothing. Tried again. *You about?* No answer. Maybe he had it wrong, maybe she was listening to her precious jazz and was miles away. The image crept unbidden into his thoughts, Wheeler with Hawk. Ross replayed the scenes, reliving his embarrassment when he'd turned up at Wheeler's flat with a bloody takeaway pizza, when she and Hawk had been eating hand-made tapas. Had she only left his place and taken Ross back to her flat through loyalty or, even worse, pity? He thought of Hawk, journalist, painter, cook. A guy most of the station agreed bore more than a passing resemblance to George Clooney. Ross wondered what he could offer Wheeler, as opposed to Hawk. The comparison didn't comfort him. Not one bit. He walked on.

And what would he tell her?

That he loved her?

That he was seriously thinking of leaving the force? That what she had suspected all along was that his heart wasn't completely in it? That although he liked the job, he was pretty sure he didn't love it.

He walked towards the River Kelvin, crossed the Partick Bridge. The dog trotted obediently beside him. The ghost of the Western Infirmary hospital loomed large. It was no consolation that the site was now part of Glasgow University's expansion. To him, the area would always be the hospital. He texted Wheeler again. *You sure you don't want company?*

Waited in vain for a reply.

Was Wheeler falling in love with Hawk? Ross felt the pain around his heart begin. He fingered the spray in his pocket. Decided against it. Told himself to keep walking. A few minutes later he turned into Byres Road, walked the length of it, then onto Great Western Road, before making his way back through Kelvingrove Park. He glanced across

to the gallery again. He wanted to give Wheeler a meaningful Christmas present. She loved the Colourists, J. D.
Fergusson in particular, and he knew that they sold prints
of his work in the gallery. Then he thought on. Something
better. An actual painting was beyond him, they sold for
thousands of pounds, but a sketch was affordable. Wheeler
had said that sketches cost around £3,000. Ross knew that
buying one was only possible because of his inheritance.
Ross thought of his father, said a silent thank you to him
for the money and the house.

Back at his flat, he towelled the dog dry and gave her a
supper of gravy bones and cold roast chicken. He settled
himself with a glass of red wine, opened his laptop and
searched J. D. Fergusson, artwork for sale. *La Vie En Rose*
popped up. He glanced out of the window, the snow was
falling thick and fast. Very festive, he thought. Wheeler
loved this time of the year. Whatever she was doing,
however she was spending her evening, he hoped that she
was happy.

Chapter 55

Tala

The task had been designed specifically for her. At every stage, the Moderator had asked for allegiance. Demanded that she prove that she was worthy of the task. Worthy of being part of the group. She'd had to fill in endless questionnaires about her lifestyle, habits, history. They knew that she was sexually inexperienced. Had only had one 'boyfriend' who had been more of a friend. Had only slept with one guy. Once. Hadn't realised that he had a girlfriend. She had been vegetarian since she was eight.

She'd already eaten raw meat. Had smuggled it into her room, swallowed it piece by piece and videoed herself while she did it.

Give yourself wholly to the most undeserving. Give willingly to someone you know who will abuse your gift. Take strength in knowing that you are in charge. Take strength in nihilism. Know that ultimately life is meaningless. Take strength in that. Kill what you love.

YOU ARE MEANINGLESS. ANYTHING ELSE IS A LIE. CELEBRATE NIHILISM. TELL YOURSELF HOURLY:

I AM NOTHING. REPEAT: I AM NOTHING. I. A. N.
REPEAT.

Tala had slipped out of her bedroom window, landed
lightly on the grass and began the familiar journey which
would take her an hour.

She had been walking for forty minutes when she saw
them.

Three men, obviously drunk. They were in their thirties.

She felt herself wobble. They smelled of alcohol and they
hadn't shaved. Part of her wanted to run, to return to the
safety of her home, but a bigger part of her, the stubborn
part, reminded her that SHE WAS NOTHING and that
everything else was a LIE. I.A.N. I.A.N. REPEAT.

'How you doing, doll?' asked one of the men.

'You're looking good,' said a second.

The first man reached for her, began to paw at her
breasts. The other two laughed. She heard the drink in
their laughter. It made her skin crawl. She thought of Leroy.
Pulled herself away. No, her redemption wasn't in these
guys. She sprinted past them, easily skirted them.

'Hey.' One made to follow. 'Come on you little tease.'

'Fuck you,' said Tala.

'Hey!'

But she was too fast, she took a corner, glanced behind
her but they hadn't followed.

In her rucksack, she had a can of accelerant, matches and
a can of petrol for backup. She pulled her hood up, a scarf
hid the bottom of her face and she wore gloves. Finally, she
arrived at her destination.

The Art Space within the CoVA was timber-framed.
Of course, it had been treated, but not to withstand
what she was about to do to it. She closed her eyes. 'Leroy,

I know you have done similar, we will go through this together.'

Tala set her phone onto record. Videoed herself before panning back to the scene behind her, watched the fire begin, the flicker of flames in the dark night. Later, when she was on a secure connection, she would send it to the Moderator. They would know that she was serious. This would be in the papers tomorrow. It was her destiny.

She began to run.

An hour later and she was home. She opened her laptop and posted on the site. Then she streamed the local news. The bar scrolled across the bottom of the screen

'Fire has broken out at a popular art college in Glasgow, the Centre of Visual Arts.'

The newsreader updated her. 'Firefighters rushed to a fire at the prestigious college in the East End area of the city after a concerned member of the public saw the flames from their home and immediately called 999. The Scottish Fire and Rescue Service crews were on site within fifteen minutes. They quickly tackled the blaze and early indications suggest that most of the building may be saved.

'A spokesperson for the SFRS said: "We're battling the fire and given the intensity of the heat, we don't want the internal structure to collapse. We hope that we can get the fire under control before that happens."

'Around forty firefighters remain in attendance at the college. Police Scotland and the Scottish Ambulance Service are also at the site.

'A spokesperson from Police Scotland had this to say: "Police Scotland will work with the SFRS Investigation Unit to establish the cause of the fire. We have no further information available at this time."'

Tala continued to stream the news.

'The Art Space, part of the College of Visual Arts, is housed in a Grade II oak-framed former coach house. The building, reputedly originating from the fifteenth century, is listed. A million-pound improvement programme was completed only last year.'

She watched as the camera cut to a tearful Principal McSweeney. 'This is an absolute tragedy. Thank goodness the building was empty at the time. If this accident had happened when any of the students and staff had been inside it would have been unimaginable.'

The camera panned out. 'We can now speak with Francesco Soule, an internationally renowned artist whose exhibition was currently showing at the centre.'

'I am absolutely devastated about this,' said Mr Soule. 'As Principal McSweeney has so rightly stated, had this occurred during classes there could have been fatalities and for that, I am immensely relieved. That said, this is nothing more than a tragedy for the community and the students involved with the centre.'

'I believe that you had a number of artworks on display there?' asked a reporter.

'I had fifteen paintings on display. I'm extremely upset that they may be destroyed.' Francesco Soule tailed off. Coughed. Cleared his throat. 'The paintings were part of my ReachOut tour where my work is exhibited in smaller art colleges to inspire the young artists of today. I look at the students' work from each college and select the one who is the most talented. I then award a bursary for them to study, work and live in a world-class institute in Florence for three years to develop and refine their art.'

'And had you chosen one of the students from the College of Visual Arts?'

'Yes, that has already been agreed. The student, whose work is outstanding, will be informed as soon as possible. Today has been a harrowing day for all concerned with the college. I would at least like to spread one piece of joy to the community. Tala De . . .' He stopped himself. 'Apologies. It's late and I'm in shock. I've spoken out of turn.'

'Principal McSweeney, there has been talk of starting a crowdfunding page to help the centre.'

'I wasn't aware of that, but it sounds like a good idea, although I am very hopeful that the majority of the centre will be saved. The Fire Service were on site very quickly and are working tirelessly to control the blaze. Later, there will need to be an emergency meeting of the governors and academic staff to consider the options and the best way forward for our community. Understandably everyone is in considerable shock. It is an outstanding old building with fine exposed timbers, a part-vaulted ceiling and a fine library with a fantastic range of art books. Of course, now that it will be closed for some time, we will need to consider what to do next.'

Tala streamed the comments coming through on her computer:

MATTIO: *Finché non è il mio turno* (until it's my turn).

FANTINE: *Pour toujours* (for ever).

ANA SOFIA: *Nos vemos en el otro lado* (see you on the other side).

335

INES: *Eu vejo o quão bem você fez. Minha próxima vez* (I see how well you did. My turn next).

ALEXEI: Друг мой, я приветствую вас за вашу храбрость (My friend, I salute you for your bravery) Алексей.

Tala cried, she was with her new family, one who cared for her. But where was Leroy? She checked online. Nothing from him. She turned to another news channel.

She heard her mobile ping. Ignored it. Knew what it would be – the students on social media sharing the video on Twitter, Facebook and all the rest. No doubt expressing their 'devastation'. Including the twin arses themselves @ Blue-eyedBrock&Bradley.

She glanced back to the screen. 'The fire . . . '

Wondered again about Leroy in Chicago. Waited. Nothing.

Tala glanced at her mobile, a text from Hudson Lennox. How did he even have her number? She guessed that Nick Price must have given it to him.

> *Have u seen the news? Awful. Plse don't be 2 upset.*
> *U got the prize!!! How amazing!* 😊

Tala rewatched the news segment. How could she have missed it? She felt her heartbeat quicken, she was going to Florence! She'd won the prize. She glanced at the screen. Saw the fire. What the hell had she done? She closed her eyes, wished that her mother was here with her now. She would help her. She would know what to do.

Chapter 56

Friday 18 December

DCI Stewart stood in front of the team. 'DI Wheeler was admitted to the Royal Infirmary at 2.24 a.m. this morning. She was the victim of an apparently random attack while walking home. Unfortunately, there is no CCTV covering the area, but we have a description from the two women who found Wheeler. Her assailant was male, wearing a mask of a grinning dog and was of slim build. He was wearing trainers and jeans and a fleece top. That's all they had. Both women said he seemed of average height but they didn't get a good enough look.'

The room was silent.

'Wheeler didn't have her car. It was lucky that there were two members of the public, who just happened to find her at that time. They saw off the assailant.'

'The two women?' asked Robertson.

'Ms Chantelle Ward and Ms Kim McGroarty were on a night out. After they discovered Wheeler on the ground, they were on high alert and saw off her assailant. They called an ambulance and police and kept watch over her until the emergency services arrived.'

'How's Wheeler doing?' asked Boyd.

'I was with her until an hour ago,' said Stewart. 'She's sedated and is understandably quite groggy. When she comes around fully, we'll find out what she remembers. There are two uniformed officers waiting outside her room.'

'I thought she was getting a lift home with you, Ross?' said Hawk. 'What the hell was she doing in a bloody dark side street?'

'I dropped her close to the Royal Infirmary,' said Ross.

'Why didn't you take her home?' asked Boyd.

'Was it too far out of your way?' asked Hawk. 'Jeez, Ross, you are one lazy shit.'

'She said she needed to walk,' said Ross. 'She said that she wanted to clear her head.'

'Walk? In the fucking snow?' asked Hawk. 'She needed to walk home in a snowstorm?'

'Yes, she bloody did,' spat Ross.

'Here's your problem,' said Hawk, 'you're a lazy arse. You snuck out on Aubree after she told you about her feelings. And now you've dumped Wheeler in the middle of the night. You are one almighty fuckwit.'

Ross stood. 'Fuck you.'

Hawk matched him.

Boyd shot out from behind his desk and stood between them. 'Cool it, you two. Wheeler is in the best place for her.'

'You couldn't be bothered making sure she got home safely?' said Hawk.

'She insisted on getting out of the car,' said Ross.

'She's a copper and in the middle of a major murder investigation,' said Hawk. 'And she's not in any danger?'

'Perhaps the attack was unrelated?' asked the rookie officer quietly.

'Why? Why pick on her?' spat Robertson.

Ross made for the door. 'I'm going to see her.'

'Sit down, Inspector Ross,' said Stewart. 'There are two officers on site already.'

'But, I'm closer to—'

Stewart cut across him. 'You are *closer* to DI Wheeler?'

Ross said nothing.

'She's part of the team, DI Ross. Our team. We *are* a team, remember?'

'Except that you dumped her in the middle of the city,' said Hawk.

'You're not even part of this team. You are a fucking parasite,' spat Ross. 'You barely know her. Oh yes, I forgot, you're neighbours. And you can cook, so well fucking done you. That's going to keep her safe.'

'I am here to record your fucking mishaps. So, fuck you,' said Hawk. 'And you give me plenty to write about, *Acting* DI Ross.'

'Wheeler was close to home, she said she needed some air before turning in.' Ross spat out the words. 'You bloody know what she's like. Fiercely independent. Who the hell do you think you're talking to?'

'You're a lazy arse,' repeated Hawk.

Ross lunged at him, caught him above the eye. Hawk reeled for a second then righted himself. Smashed his fist into Ross's stomach.

Ross doubled over, gasped.

'Cut it out!' Stewart roared, marching towards them. Stood between them arms outstretched. 'If this goes any further, it will be a disciplinary matter. Ross, you are way out of line. And, Hawk, may I remind you that you are here as a courtesy? Remember that. Both of you. Now get the fuck on with your jobs.' He glared at the rest of the team. 'Briefing at midday today. In the meantime, get me up to date with everything. Michael O'Donnell's killer is still at large, his daughter Paula is missing, feared dead. Sarah Price remains missing after joining a non-existent dating site, and Ian Price is locked in a cell and refusing to say a word. Meanwhile Dr Buckley has been murdered and we have nothing. Can I repeat that? Nothing. Sweet FA. Now Wheeler has been attacked and is in a bad way. Is that enough for you all or do I need to spell it out? Get off your arses and get results. We'll reconvene at 12 noon, sharp.'

Hawk looked at Ross. 'DI Ross, when Wheeler gets back here, she'll have her back covered, we'll make sure that she's supported. We'll all be looking out for her.'

Ross visibly relaxed. 'Yes,' he agreed,' I think—'

'You on the other hand,' Hawk cut across him, 'after yet another selfish debacle, who'll be looking after you? Tell me, who would really care if you never came back, who would miss you?'

Again, Ross lunged for him.

'Enough,' said Stewart. 'It's like dealing with two bloody children. Now both of you listen to me. I for one am not convinced that Wheeler's attack was in any way random. She's getting closer to the truth, to our killer and this was a warning shot. If Chantelle Ward and Kim McGroarty hadn't come along at the time they did, I believe Wheeler would have been killed.'

'You think we should see Wheeler getting attacked as a fucking positive?' Ross couldn't keep the disgust from his voice.

'She was getting too close to the truth! Be objective,

analytical. It means that she was making progress,' said Stewart.

Ross sighed.

'And you should have kept a bloody eye on her,' Hawk snarled.

'Cut it the fuck out,' said Stewart. 'Ross, this is a dangerous job, the closer we are to the truth, the more a killer will fight back. I'm surprised that you're not thinking like a detective. I believe Wheeler's attacker wanted to kill her, but I don't think for a moment that in future he or she would hesitate. They were interrupted, that's all.'

'They can't attack us all,' muttered Boyd.

'I am not prepared to let any of my officers be harmed in any way. What I need you all to do is to go over what Wheeler was working on, what leads she was following. Ross, you take the lead.'

Hawk said nothing.

Stewart made for the door. 'Twelve sharp, team. Get onto it!'

Chapter 57

Midday

Ross could feel it. The atmosphere in the room was charged. The resentment. The accusation. If he was trying to decide about staying on and seeing the job through or quitting the force altogether, this was certainly his moment to bloody take stock.

'Since we no longer have DI Wheeler to update us on our progress – and I do hope we have made some,' said Stewart, 'can you update us, DI Ross?'

A voice from the back of the room, someone who'd just entered. 'That won't be necessary, Ross.' Wheeler strode into the room. Her black eye shone in the harsh lighting, there was a dressing on the side of her face, her scalp visible as hair had been shaved on the right side, but her determined stare and the familiar confident gait told them not to argue.

They did, anyway.

'You shouldn't be here,' said Boyd.

Wheeler turned on him. 'Who says? You a doctor suddenly, Boyd? Did I miss your graduation? Sorry about that. Was it a blast?'

'I think under the circumstances, Wheeler,' Ross continued. 'That—'

'You a doctor too, then? How come you never mentioned it, Ross? When did you find the time to retrain?'

'I'm just saying that, I feel that in the—'

She cut across him. 'I don't want to hear what you feel, Ross. I want to know what you think. I've been discharged. Get over it.'

'Were you discharged?' asked Robertson. 'Or did you discharge yourself?'

She rounded on him. 'And what the hell difference does it make?'

Silence. She let it settle around the room. She glared at everyone, daring them to either contradict or challenge her. No one did. 'Then let's get the hell on. I spent a long time recently reading Dr Buckley's notes and I'm pretty certain you and Boyd aren't up to the job of being a GP. Now, what have I missed?'

Thirty minutes later, she held up her hand. 'We need to get on. Both men are dead but two women are out there, still missing. Let's go.' She quickly recapped on the case and what they were facing, rapidly issued orders and finished with, 'OK, let's go to it, move it.'

She waited until they had all left, saw that he'd held back. 'Ross, I don't want any of your schmaltzy apologies. I heard that Hawk was giving you a hard time about it but he's wrong. You and I both know that.'

'Who told you?' asked Ross.

'You don't need to know. I have friends. Plus, you're a good detective.'

'Right.'

'In the early hours, Stewart was talking. He talks a lot

when he's stressed. Probably thought I was out of it and I was in some ways. Perhaps I couldn't respond so much but I heard him. He really rates you. You need to know that. He referred to you as one of the best guys on the team.'

'Then this isn't going to be what you want to hear,' said Ross.

She waited.

'I'm seriously thinking of resigning. I've had a bit of a health scare. Broken Heart Syndrome.'

She listened to him tell her the news. Said nothing. What could she say? More importantly, what was she supposed to say? What did he want from her? Because she knew from the expression in his eyes that he wanted something in response, she just didn't know what.

He glanced at her, waited. Finally, he left.

A second later, Boyd put his head around the doorway. 'Boss wants to see you in his office now.'

'Got it.' She stood.

Boyd held the door for her.

'Geez, what's with the manners, Boyd?'

'Don't get used to it,' he said, ushering her gently through. 'It's only going to happen whenever you get mugged.'

Wheeler walked on. 'Pleased to hear it, otherwise I'd think you were losing your touch.'

'Quite,' said Boyd.

Wheeler stood outside Stewart's office and gave herself a minute to process what Ross had just told her. He was thinking of resigning. She was damn sure he should reconsider. But Broken Heart Syndrome? What the hell was that? It sounded as if it should be in a Mills & Boon novel. For fuckssake what was Ross on about? She'd google it when she had a minute to herself. But not here, not in the station. Ross would never hear the end of it if the lads got hold of the phrase. But there was something about his demeanour when he'd told her. He was serious. Something was going on for him. But she knew that she couldn't let him leave, she would miss him way too much. She snapped back to the case in hand as the door opened and Stewart ushered her in. She knew that the media guys were doing a reconstruction around Michael O'Donnell's murder and Paula's disappearance which might help jog people's memories.

Wheeler saw Hawk slip into the room. Realised that while she was in principle OK with the idea of him shadowing them, in practice it was becoming tiresome for the team.

'DI Ross left you or rather abandoned you in a vulnerable position last night,' said Stewart.

'If there's nothing else, boss? Only I need to be getting on.'

'A vulnerable position, DI Wheeler,' he repeated. 'Hawk has asked that this incident be included in the book. No names, of course.'

She walked towards him. Leaned into his face. 'Sod it, sir. I am not ten years of age. This thing with Ross is going too bloody far. I do not need a chaperone to walk me home. I live in this city, remember? I was born and brought up here and if walking home alone constitutes a vulnerable position then we have a hell of a lot more to worry about than Michael O'Donnell's and Dr David Buckley's murders and the disappearance of Sarah and Paula.' She paused. 'And no, I don't want the incident to be included in the book. Now if we're finished?'

Hawk moved to open the door for her. In the hallway she turned to him, expecting him to follow her. Instead she heard the door close firmly behind her.

Now what the hell were Hawk and Stewart discussing in her absence? She walked back to her office. Ross was waiting.

'Wheeler, I am so sorry that I left you last night. I—'

She cut over him. 'Don't even try going there, Ross. I walk the city 24/7. I don't need or require your attention or protection. Now, it was either random, or the attack was related to this case. Either way, we need to get on with it and stop messing about. I am not a damsel in distress, despite what the team are pretending.'

'I just mean that I feel guilty—'

Wheeler lost it. 'Again with the feelings, what is wrong with this station? With this team? I'm all for congruence, empathy and even sympathy but good police work, solid police work is about analytical thought process, for fuck sake, get on with it. OK?'

He paused. 'Sure.'

'So, what do we have? Not in some bloody touchy-feely universe. Tell me about the real world.'

Wheeler's phone rang. It was the tech department. 'Wheeler, we've just sent you an email re. some of the data on Michael O'Donnell's iPad. I think you'll find it interesting.'

'I'm onto it.' She fired up her computer, opened the file. Saw the sexual details of the information. Naked bodies. Compromising situations. 'Shit.'

'Look at this, Ross, the tech guys have come up with this – these videos of Autumn De Luca and Sarah Price look like they were recorded without the participants knowing.'

'Hidden cameras,' said Ross. 'Michael O'Donnell wasn't the man he pretended to be.'

Wheeler sat back in her chair. 'Boyd,' she yelled, 'you and Robertson get over and interview Autumn De Luca, she's been lying to us.' She turned to Ross. 'You and me, we're going to speak to Ian Price. We have concrete proof. Since Sarah and Michael were an item, Price might not have been a fan.'

Ian Price was waiting in the interview room. Wheeler began. 'We have evidence that your ex-wife, Sarah Price, was seeing Michael O'Donnell.'

'That right?' said Price.

'You knew that they had a relationship?' asked Wheeler.

'If you're asking if I knew that she was a slut, then yeah, I did know. I just didn't have all the names.'

'She was single,' said Ross. 'Wasn't she allowed to date?'

Price slammed his fist into the table. 'We were married. She was my fucking wife. Till death do us part and all that shit.'

'So, when did you first suspect that they were having a relationship?' asked Wheeler.

'I was always suspicious around her,' said Price. 'I told you she was a tart.'

'About Michael O'Donnell,' said Wheeler. 'When did you suspect?'

'Last summer, there was some eighteenth birthday party, Tala De Luca I think the kid's name was.'

'And?'

'Sarah was going to run Nick, but I knew that Michael O'Donnell would have been dropping Paula off and hovering in the background. I knew that he would have been around. Convenient. Very fucking convenient for him and Sarah to get their shit together. So, I insisted on taking Nick up there.'

'Where was the birthday party?' asked Wheeler.

'Can't recall. Up in Balmaha or thereabouts, bloody back of beyond if you ask me. And the midge bites were awful,' said Price.

Wheeler noted the area. Recalled that Nick Price had mentioned walking in that area too.

An hour later and Ian Price had given them nothing. He was absolutely adamant that he was innocent.

'Your DNA places you at Michael O'Donnell's house,' said Ross. 'Yet you claim that you were never there.'

'I've been framed,' said Price. 'Knock yourself out going over my place. You won't find anything.'

'We are going over your place,' said Wheeler. 'And your car. Anywhere else we should be looking?'

Price smiled. 'That's your job to find out, sweetheart, so why don't you just crack on and do it?'

Chapter 58

The Cottage

The wintery sun shone over the landscape. Fresh snow covered the old cottage and the setting around it. Should an estate agent be marketing it at this time, they would refer to it as magical.

Inside, the woman had experienced a few lucid moments when the drugs had waned, and she felt her body, heavy and damp and sour with sweat. But in these moments, the experience had stripped away layers of life, of memories and history that she no longer needed. In those few seconds, she felt transported to a bright world of consciousness. It was in those brief illuminating seconds that she heard snatches of conversation. Or thought she did. But discussions from her past swirled around her and she couldn't be sure which were real, and which were imaginary.

The door opened and one of the dogs padded towards her. A syringe in its hand. This dog was rough, its eyes watching her, waiting for her to flinch. This seemed to please the dog. The other dog came to watch. She felt the pierce of the syringe. What were they doing with her? Then she was in a plane, high above the ground and she felt her stomach clench as she fell through the air and suddenly she was alone in a forest. Monkeys were chattering above her, and birds with bloody eyes were watching her. She tried to run from them, to escape. But her mind was a kaleidoscope of terrifying fragments. On the table, a laptop, open. A repeated word she hated:

dEADdOG

dEADdOG

dEADdOG

dEADdOG

Chapter 59

'You're kidding me? So, Ian Price just walks?' asked Boyd. 'How does that even bloody happen?'

'His alibi holds out. CCTV at the Golden Key Casino says he was there when Michael O'Donnell was killed,' said Wheeler. 'His bank card has debits from the bar there too. He was gambling when Michael O'Donnell was murdered. Done and dusted.'

'He claimed his DNA was smeared onto the cross,' said Ross. 'Swears he was set up.'

'We don't have anything to keep him,' said Wheeler. 'Doesn't mean we don't keep an eye on him. In the meantime, Autumn De Luca confirmed that she'd had an affair with Michael O'Donnell. Says she had no idea that he was filming her in his bedroom.'

'And she lied to us because?' asked Ross.

'She said that she was afraid her husband would find out,' said Wheeler.

'What about Sarah Price?' asked Ross.

'Autumn was oblivious to the fact that Michael was having numerous affairs.'

'Same as the CoVA lecturer, Barnes Olsen?'

'Yeah,' said Wheeler. 'Autumn did confirm though, that Tala had her eighteenth birthday party in a cottage in Balmaha, at Bird's Eye View,' said Wheeler. 'And that Ian Price had dropped Nick off there. Michael was staying at a B & B in the area to be near Paula, in case she fell ill.'

'So?' said Ross.

'I think that it's important,' said Wheeler. 'They were all there at a specific time.'

'That they all went to Balmaha?' Ross waited.

'It's just over twenty miles from Glasgow. But more to the point,' Wheeler said, 'Ian Price is hiding something. The forensic guys found sand on the rim of his tyres. There's no sand in Glasgow.'

'But there's a beach in Balmaha,' said Boyd.

'And the area's good for walking,' said Ross. 'Maybe he went for a walk on the beach? Parked up?'

'It's remote,' said Wheeler. 'What if Ian Price is keeping Sarah hostage there? It's a remote enough place. I also wonder if Ian Price is a keeper?'

'Go on,' said Ross.

'I spoke to a colleague, MacCullagh. I suspect that Ian Price may be a keeper of guns.'

'Because?' said Ross.

'His background. I don't believe all the "I've gone legit" shit. Plus, the fact that his lifestyle can't possibly be funded by the odd gardening job. Certainly not the frequent casino visits. Plus, he fits the profile, an ex-con but someone who isn't under surveillance. A wannabe in other words. Not a big player but happy to play a supporting role. The remote location of Balmaha would be ideal. Plus, Nick Price is a walker. Could be Ian had to collect or drop Nick off from various locations before and after a walk. The perfect cover. He may well already know the area. Tala De Luca's party was there. Balmaha is only eleven or so miles from Balloch, is close to both the Queen Elizabeth Forest Park and the West Highland Way. Sarah Price mentioned all those places to Bernie Morrison. Ian Price had a knowledge of the cottage at Balmaha.'

'It all seems tenuous,' said Ross. 'A bit piecemeal?'

'Sarah is still missing. Balmaha is remote. Ian Price is obsessive about his ex-wife. We know that he was stalking her up at Balmaha at Tala De Luca's eighteenth party. Plus, there's the phoney dating site she joined. And remember all the IT courses Ian Price took while he was in jail? How difficult would it be for him to set up a fake dating site? Post an anonymous leaflet through her door, especially when there were other companies targeting the area? The tech team went through his computer.'

'And?'

'Nothing yet,' admitted Wheeler. 'But they need time.'

'I'll check out cottages for rent in the area,' said Ross. 'See if the name Price comes up.'

'I'll read over Dr Buckley's research papers.'

Half an hour later and she had the reason David Buckley had been a threat to Michael O'Donnell. 'Dr Buckley was less than supportive of both Michael and Paula O'Donnell.'

Lovers' Tryst #4

Now

How great does this feel?

Fantastic. Free. Amazing.

We are gods in our own universe.

Anne Randall

God-like. All powerful.
It's like a drug.
Better than drugs.
I feel super-human.
Me too, like I could take on the world. The best adrenaline
rush ever.
We will take on the world.
And win.
Game on.

354

Chapter 60

Evening

Wheeler heard a knock at the door. Ross walked in.

'What are you up to?'

'Still reading the case notes.'

'What have you discovered?' said Ross.

'Remember when Principal McSweeney said that both Paula and Nick had applied for the same art school in Brighton?' said Wheeler.

'Yes,' said Ross. 'They were both accepted but Paula had to withdraw her application due to ill health. Paula was devastated but Michael had been quite insistent. He was very concerned about her.'

'And there was a series of invited speakers, the Open Lectures,' said Wheeler.

'So, what?' said Ross.

'How was Paula so knowledgeable about the content of the lectures on Frida Kahlo? She mentioned them in her diary.'

'Nick or one of the other kids told her?' said Ross. 'Or it was online?'

'I checked, nothing was made available on the internet.

The guest speakers are compiling a book about their lectures, it will be on sale next year in the campus shop,' said Wheeler. 'All profits will go to college funds.'

'What are you getting at?' said Ross.

'I think Paula attended those lectures. Think about it, she had good days and bad. Plus, her art was "robust". I think she was allowed to go to the lectures, rather than attend her weekly resting/counselling sessions with Van Der Berg. I think Van Der Berg let her off. Barnes Olsen told us already. Don't you realise what this means?'

'Uniform spoke with Principal McSweeney. Mr Van Der Berg has resigned.'

'Because?'

'A student made a formal complaint about inappropriate touching. Apparently Van Der Berg has gone back to his parents in the Netherlands.'

'That's convenient,' said Wheeler. 'He's out of the way. Who was the student who complained?'

'Uniform didn't get a chance to find out. Principal McSweeney had to rush out to a meeting. They're going to follow it up.'

'Good. I think I know who it might be,' said Wheeler.

'How could Paula have managed to get to the lectures?' asked Ross. 'Given that she was so poorly and needed to rest?'

Wheeler let the question hang in the air.

'You think she wasn't as ill as we thought?' said Ross. 'Or that she had help?'

'Remember Robin Kirkpatrick said that Paula could be quite robust at times? I also think she had great determination. Plus, she was about to inherit a lot of money, giving her the chance to be independent. To move to

Brighton and reinvent herself. She wasn't ill all the time. Remember the energy in her paintings?'

'Leading to the question, was she abducted, or did she abscond?' The full realisation of what Wheeler was implying hit Ross. 'You are kidding me? You think she killed her father and then calmly walked out of the house, covered in his blood? Just so she could inherit a lot of money and go to art college? And no one saw her?'

'I don't think she worked alone, I think she had an accomplice.'

'There is no forensic evidence that she was involved in his murder. Or anyone else's for that matter.'

'Her prints were everywhere in the house. And the door was unlocked.'

'The cleaner said there were only two keys, both of which were still in the house.'

Wheeler stared at him. 'Anyone could have taken a key in to be cut. It's not like you even have to give your name. But, if it was someone who already had a key?'

'So, just supposing Paula isn't as ill as we have been led to believe and can walk? The word "robust" came up often.'

'Remember the paramedic's report which said he thought that Paula's seizures were unusual? And Dr Chowdry who said that despite the tests, they couldn't ascertain that Paula was definitely epileptic? Plus, Michael referred to her as "one in a million"?' Wheeler said.

'Yeah,' said Ross.

'Well, I think we got it wrong. I think that was a euphemism for saying they didn't believe either Paula or Michael. They thought that Paula was faking it and Michael was facilitating her illness.'

Ross took a moment. 'So, what are you suggesting?'

'Munchausen by Proxy,' said Wheeler. 'Because it fits, Ross. We thought that there was no link to Paula, but there was. Don't you see, Dr Buckley was writing a paper on a specialist subject and the initials were MBPS. I overlooked it while focusing on epilepsy. It was Munchausen by Proxy and the common abbreviation is MBPS. Paula consistently failed her electroencephalographs, and while Dr Chowdry kept an open mind, that's when Dr Buckley became interested. He was suspicious.'

'I thought that failing an electroencephalograph wasn't conclusive,' said Ross. 'That Paula could still be epileptic.'

'Yes, but put the rest of it together, some of the ambulance crew were suspicious, but they couldn't challenge her, but they were less than sympathetic,' said Wheeler. 'And Dr Buckley's notes are also less than supportive.'

'There was no absolutely convincing evidence,' said Ross. 'The trouble is, she may have had different types of epilepsy. And it didn't show on her EEG.'

'Of course, but let's look at it the other way,' said Wheeler. 'What if she was faking? What if she had been told, no groomed, since childhood, to fake her illness? And kept heavily medicated since before she could remember? What if this is a case of Munchausen by Proxy? What if Michael kept Paula a prisoner in her own home for all these years? What if he told her repeatedly that she was sick? Fed her the lie ever since she was small and kept her heavily drugged? Medication which all have side effects.'

'Bloody hell,' said Ross.

'Think,' said Wheeler. 'What age was Paula?'

'Eighteen,' said Ross.

'Yes, eighteen, but Michael said she was psychologically much younger. He always referred to her as a child, he never acknowledged she had grown up,' said Wheeler. 'He kept her suspended in that early adolescence. He thought that she was too young to have a boyfriend. Even the cleaner called Paula a child, as did Vlad.'

'This just coming through,' said Robertson from the doorway. 'The DNA found at Dr Buckley's house . . . '

They waited.

'Michael O'Donnell's. A full match.'

'Bloody hell,' said Wheeler. 'Michael O'Donnell killed Dr Buckley?'

'Because they disagreed over Paula?' asked Ross.

'Because the dynamic was changing?' suggested Wheeler. 'Paula was changing. Was she trying to move away from Michael's control? Dr Buckley's support would have facilitated that. And in a very public way.'

'Where do you think Paula is now?' asked Ross.

'All we have to go on is a cottage in Balmaha and sand on Ian Price's car. Let's start there.' Wheeler grabbed her coat.

Chapter 61

Tala

She heard him at her door. The animalistic snuffling sound he always made. Normally it angered her but given she was about to leave him, she opened the door. 'Come on in, Tomas.'

Tomas wandered into the room, his head high, the beatific smile on his face.

'I need to get some research done. You understand?'

Nothing in reply, save an attempt at a cuddle, arms outstretched.

She picked him up and sat him on her knee. 'I need to do some research on another country, wee man.'

Tala searched on her computer for news of Leroy. Had he taken the ultimate challenge? She checked her phone. A myriad of messages from students and tutors, telling her that she'd been selected. Plus, dorky Hudson Lennox had texted her again.

Tomas cuddled into her. She touched his hair. 'You and me Tomas, we're going to be apart. I'm going on a long adventure.'

She watched his face break into a smile.

'To Italy, wee man, to Italy. But first I need to do something.' She pressed send.

Message Board

TALA: I feel scared. I can't do this. I don't want to. I want to leave the group?

She sent the request. The screen flashed.

dEADdOGdEADdOGdEADdOGdEADdOGdEADdOG
NOTALAdEADdOGdEADdOGdEADdOGdEADdOGdEAD
dOGdEADdOGdEADdOGdEADdOGdEADdOGdEADdOG
dEADdOGdEADdOGdEADdOGdEADdOGdEADdOGdEAD
dOGdEADdOGdEADdOGdEADdOGdEADdOGdEADdOG
TALAYOUAREWEAKdEADdOGdEADdOGdEADdOG
dEADdOGdEADdOGdEADdOGdEADdOGdEADdOGdEAD
dOGdEADdOGdEADdOGdEADdOGdEADdOGdEADdOG
dEADdOGdEADdOGdEADdOGdEADdOGdEADdOGdEAD
dOG**TALA**dEADdOGdEADdOGdEADdOGdEADdOGdEAD
dOGdEADdOGdEADdOGdEADdOGdEADdOGdEADdOG
dEADdOGdEADdOG**WEAKTALA**dEADdOGdEADdOG
dEADdOGdEADdOGdEADdOGdEADdOGdEADdOGdEAD
dOGdEADdOGdEADdOGdEADdOG**TALA**dEADdOGdEAD
dOGdEADdOGdEADdOGdEADdOGdEADdOGdEADdOG
dEADdOGdEADdOGdEADdOGdEADdOGdEADdOGdEAD
dOGdEADdOGdEADdOGdEADdOGdEADdOGdEADdOG
dEADdOGdEADdOGdEADdOG**TALAREMEMBERWEARE
FAMILY**dEADdOGdEADdOGdEADdOGdEADdOGdEAD
dOGdEADdOGdEADdOGdEADdOGdEADdOGdEADdOG
dEADdOGdEADdOGdEADdOGdEADdOGdEADdOGdE
dEADdOGdEADdOGdEADdOGdEADdOGdEADdOG

TALAISACOWARDdEADdOGdEADdOGdEADdOGdEAD
dOGdEADdOGdEADdOGdEADdOGdEADdOGdEADdOG
dEADdOGdEADdOGdEADdOGdEADdOGdEADdOGdEAD
dOGdEADdOGdEADdOGdEADdOGdEADdOGdEADdOG
dEADdOG**TALAISLETTINGHERFAMILYDOWN**dEAD
dOGdEADdOGdEADdOGdEADdOGdEADdOGdEADdOG
dEADdOGdEADdOGdEADdOGdEADdOGdEADdOGdEAD
dOGdEADdOGdEADdOGdEADdOGdEADdOGdEAD
dOGdEADdOGdEADdOGdEADdOG**TALAWHOWENT
BEFORE?**dEADdOGdEADdOGdEADdOGdEADdOGdEAD
dOGdEADdOGdEADdOGdEADdOGdEADdOGdEADdOG
dEADdOGdEADdOG**TALA**dEADdOGdEADdOGdEADdOG
dEADdOGdEADdOGdEADdOGADdOGdEADdOGdEAD
dOGdEADdOGdEADdOG**TALAYOUAREPARTOFOUR
FAMILY**dEADdOGdEADdOGdEADdOGdEADdOGdEAD
dOGdEADdOGdEADdOGdEADdOGdEADdOGdEADdOG
dEADdOGdEADdOG**TALA**dEADdOGdEADdOGdEADdOG
dEADdOGdEADdOGdEADdOGdEADdOGdEADdOGdEAD
dOGdEADdOGdEADdOG**TALA**dEADdOGdEADdOGdEAD
dOGdEADdOGdEADdOGdEADdOGdEADdOGdEADdOG
dEADdOGdEADdOGdEADdOGdEADdOGdEADdOGdEAD
dOGdEADdOGdEADdOGdEADdOGdEADdOGdEADdOG
dEADdOGdEADdOG**OURSISTERTALA**dEADdOGdEAD
dOGdEADdOGdEADdO

TALA: I want to stop now.

MODERATOR: yOU cANNOT lEave the gROUP. iT is
iMPOSSIbLE. yOU hAVE cOMMItTED your life to it. You have
committed to our rULES. You encouraged LuCaS and ALi to
fulfil their dESTINY and now you wish to break your pROMISE?

Shaking, Tala typed: Leroy, are you out there? Are you online? Can you talk to me? Please?

Thirty-five minutes passed before he was online.

LEROY: I can't talk right now, Tala. I'm in the middle of a TASK. What's the matter? I saw your request. I thought we were in this together? Have you lost faith in us?

TALA: I'm scared.

LEROY: Be strong! Remember what you agreed? Remember how happy you were to find this group? To be part of it? How can you renege now? What kind of a person are you? I don't think I like you any more. I thought that you were one of us. Now I'm not so sure. I thought that you and I shared a destiny? Is that over? Your choice.

TALA: I just feel frightened. And different. I've got a chance to get away. A chance to leave home and go to Italy to study. Plus, I've inherited money from my gran. Things have changed. I want to try again.

LEROY: We are all afraid. But it is important to see it through. It's immensely important.

ALEXEI: оставайся сильным (stay strong).

SIMMY2: You just need to stay strong!

JAN USA: What's with the wobble? I don't get you. I thought we were all in it together? Like family?

EMILIO: *Débiles!* (Weak)

LEROY: The Moderator has provided graffiti around our cities to give us encouragement. To remind us that we are part of a bigger community, that we are not alone. Why do you ignore this support? Haven't we all supported each other? Be strong.

Tala wiped away her tears. Scrolled through earlier messages.

MATTIO: *Finché non è il mio turno* (until it's my turn).

FANTINE: *Pour toujours* (for ever).

ANA SOFIA: *Nos vemos en el otro lado* (see you on the other side).

INES: *Eu vejo o quão bem você fez. Minha próxima vez* (I see how well you did. My turn next).

The group had accepted her, they had made her feel connected and less alone in the world. What had changed and why did she feel like betraying them? Tala thought of her mother, how proud she had been of Tala's artwork. How proud she would be that Tala had won the prize and would be studying in Italy. She cuddled Tomas, felt him squirm in her arms.

A message from the MODERATOR:

tHErE iS A sPEcIAL pLAcE wHErE yOU wILL bE wELCOmED aS pArT oF tHe sOCIeTY. gO tO tHiS pLAcE tOMORrOW nIGhT. yOu wIlL fInD pEAcE aNd aCCEpTANcE. sTAy tHErE uNTiL yOU feEL sTROnGeR. aND tHeN lEaVE. tEIL nO oNe wHeRE yOu aRE gOInG.

Tala typed quickly: Promise.

Moderator: tHE aDDrESS will flash on the screen for a fEW sECONDS. dO nOT write it down. mEMORISE it. yOU will aRRIvE by sEVEN o'clock tOMOrrOW night. tELL nO oNE.

But Tala didn't need to memorise the address. She already knew it. Bird's Eye Cottage. The same cottage that she'd had her eighteenth birthday party.

She closed her laptop, put it into her rucksack. Ten minutes later she was out of the house and running through the frozen streets. She thought of what she would have to abandon to accept the prize. She would have to turn her back on the dEADdOG community. How could she do that? Especially since two people had gone over to the other side? She thought of her gran De Luca, how much she loved her. She thought of the prize she was about to get at CoVA. But the group? Was she strong enough to leave? Tala ran on through the snow and squall. Thought she heard a whisper on the wind. It felt like her mother was murmuring to her, advising her what to do. She ran on.

Chapter 62

Five minutes into their journey Wheeler heard Ross begin to complain.

'Bloody hell, December in Scotland,' Ross fumed as they sat behind a gritting lorry.

Her mobile rang. It was Boyd. 'I've just spoken with Principal McSweeney. The student who complained about Mr Van Der Berg was Nick Price.'

'Shit,' said Wheeler. 'Have you spoken to Van Der Berg?'

'I can't reach him. His parents said he rang them to say he'd resigned but that he wasn't going home to them, after all. He told them that he had gone off fishing. He said that he needed to be alone for some thinking time. But he isn't answering his phone.'

'Keep me informed.' She killed the call, turned to Ross. 'Van Der Berg has resigned and is now missing. Nick Price is bloody responsible, and you are worried about a gritting lorry?'

Ross said nothing.

'Can you at least try to get a grip? You're worrying me!' She dialled quickly, the phone was answered on the second ring.

'Principal McSweeney.'

Five minutes later and Wheeler finished the call. 'Nick Price had been flagged up by a former teacher as having an inability to attach.'

'Go on.'

'Attachment Disorder is when kids, young kids, don't form an attachment with their parents or caregivers.'

'And?'

'It can lead to a lack of empathy and a sense of distance from what other people experience.'

'So, he couldn't understand how Van Der Berg might feel about his actions?'

'Or didn't care,' said Wheeler.

When they turned off towards the village, the traffic all but disappeared.

'So where to now?' said Ross.

Wheeler googled short-term and holiday lets. Took on-board the research that Ross had already done. 'I've found that Bird's Eye View Cottage, four-bedroom, has been let for the previous month and won't be available until the twenty-first of January.'

'OK.'

'I'm going to call the owner,' said Wheeler. 'That's the same cottage where Tala De Luca had her eighteenth birthday party.' Five minutes later she ended the call. 'The cottage has been let to a Mr Price. Everything was done online, all payments and deposits too, so the owner never actually met him.'

The car slid on ice and veered off the road and almost into a hedge.

'You want me to drive, only you don't seem to be getting the hang of it?' said Wheeler, smiling.

'Shut it, you,' said Ross. 'No one likes a smartarse. Tell me again, which bloody cottage are we looking for?'

'Bird's Eye View.'

They drove down a ridged track. There was a beaten-up red Fiesta parked outside the house. 'That's Nick Price's car,' said Wheeler. 'Kill the engine. Now.'

'Should we call for backup?' said Ross.

'We don't know if anything is happening yet,' said Wheeler. 'Nick might be in there with his mum. Or his dad. Or both.' She left the car and crouched between the bushes and made her way towards the cottage. There was a light on, but the blinds were closed and only a splinter of an orange glow came through them. She snuck up to the door and quietly tried the handle. Locked. She skirted around the side of the building, avoiding the gravel and kept to the frozen grass. At the back of the building there was a long narrow garden leading into a dense woodland. A small wall of less than a foot was between her and the garden. She stepped over it. Listened. The wind made it difficult, but she thought she heard the trace of a noise. The sound of a voice, high and hysterical. She heard Ross behind her.

She crept forward, peered through the tiny slats in the wooden blinds. She saw enough. The syringe lying on the counter, a stained trail on the tiles which suggested something had been dragged through, something leaking a dark substance. Blood. She saw a shadowy figure at the far end of the hall, saw it move between rooms. She turned to Ross, whispered, 'Call for backup. Now.'

Ross grabbed his mobile. The light shone in the darkness, no bars. 'No reception.'

'Go back down the path, back towards the car,' whispered Wheeler.

'I'm not leaving you,' said Ross. 'I left you once before and it didn't go well.'

'Very fucking funny,' she said. 'Go!'

He waited.

'Go,' she hissed. 'And request an ambulance. Sirens off!'

'Right.'

'And Ross?'

'Yeah?'

'You need to get the fuck over my attack. Not your gig, OK?'

'OK.' He retreated soundlessly down the path.

Wheeler crouched under the window and watched. Inside, the masked creature was moving swiftly between the rooms; she saw it carry a pair of pliers. And a few seconds later she heard a scream, so loud and terrified that she knew exactly what it was: the sound of torture.

She glanced around quickly; she'd no idea if Ross would have to walk further to get a signal. Another scream and then a plea for mercy. Mocking laughter. She teased the window open, slipped through it and was on her feet in seconds. The smell was unbearable, and she instinctively clamped a hand over her mouth. Moonlight streamed through the open window and she saw the cause of the stench. Wheeler doubled over and fought the urge to retch. Instead she steadied herself and moved towards the door. She could hear a drugged voice muttering and crying. The voice subdued now, pleading for her abductors to release her.

Wheeler heard a noise behind her. 'They're on their way.' Ross silently climbed through the window. Immediately gagged. 'Oh no, what the fuck is—'

'Ignore it,' she hissed, 'It's the remains of an animal,

keep moving.' She led the way past the animal, its mouth stretched open in an agonising silent howl.

'Why is there a fucking decomposing fox cub in this cottage?' asked Ross.

Wheeler glanced at him, 'Work it out, Ross.'

They crept through the corridor. On a shelf an open laptop. Wheeler recognised the words. dEADdOG dEADdOG dEADdOG dEADdOG

'Jesus,' said Ross.

Wheeler pulled on a glove. Scrolled down. Saw that whoever was working from the laptop was the Moderator. Saw that they had created multiple online profiles, including LEROY, ALEXEI, SIMMY2, JAN USA, EMILIO, MATTIO, INES. Wheeler glanced at the online dialogues between all these people who did not exist and one student who did. Tala. Wheeler read on. Switched to another online stream, raced through the information.

Looking4Love
Profile picture of CJ200
Unclaimed treasure

Home: The wonderful Drymen and also St Andrews, Scotland. (Although the above picture was taken while I was on holiday in Rethymnon, Crete. Hence the tan. I am now somewhat paler.)

About me: Height 6' 2" (187 cm)

Hair: dark/ going on for salt and pepper

Eyes: Blue

Body type: Muscle-ish (200 lbs)

Past Relationship? Ended amicably when she accepted a (long overdue, in my opinion) promotion to New York.

What am I looking for? To find the love of my life. I'm a hopeless romantic!

Children? No, but I don't mind if you have any. (Or how many.)

Religion: Not sure about the whole God thing but I'm open to discussing it, if it's your thing.

Star sign: Pisces. Romantic. Bit dreamy.

Wheeler moved away from the laptop, she'd seen enough. She inched her way forward; she could smell the coppery smell of blood, guessed that the cottage had traditional thick stone walls, which meant that smells and odours were contained within the old place. As she stole towards the door on the far side of the hall, unmistakable odours hit her. Urine and faeces. Whoever was behind the door had not been allowed access to a toilet. They would have only one reason to keep her in such a state.

They were going to kill her.

Chapter 63

Wheeler grabbed the handle and threw open the door. A figure in a dog mask was positioning the pliers into the mouth of the tethered mess on the bed that was Sarah Price.

'Police!' yelled Wheeler, bursting into the room. 'Hold it right there.'

'I don't fucking think so.' The figure leapt away from Sarah before tucking its head down into its chest and barrelled into Wheeler, forcing her to stagger backwards.

Fuck, thought Wheeler. That voice. She recognised it. She righted herself, turned, raised her right foot shoulder high. She was glad of her strength, her army background and kick-box training. Her boot caught the creature in the throat. It dropped to the ground.

Ross bent to cuff it. As he straightened up, from somewhere behind her, a second masked figure ran into the room, raining a baseball bat into the side of Ross's temple. Ross sank to the floor groaning and the figure sprinted towards the bed, grabbed the already full syringe from the side table.

Wheeler intervened. 'No fucking way.' She lunged at the creature, tore at its hand. The syringe dropped to the floor. The creature grabbed the bat and ran at her. Wheeler kicked out at it. The blow landed on its shoulder.

'Fuck you! This is my gig,' the creature squealed and hurled the bat directly at her. Wheeler stepped to the side too late, it caught her a glancing blow above her right eye. The creature sprinted towards the door, while a dazed Ross slammed his foot hard against its shin, failed to bring it down. Wheeler ignored the blood running into her eye and ran forward.

'You OK?' shouted Ross.

'Fucking little shits,' Wheeler shouted and ran into the hallway.

The figure turned on her, pulled a Stanley knife from a pocket.

Wheeler felt the sting of the cut. Lunged at the creature, grabbed the wrist, twisted it hard. Once, twice and then the knife dropped. The figure kicked out and tried to twist away from her grip. Wheeler held on, forced her assailant around. Grabbed the handcuffs. Used them.

The cursing was loud, like a banshee's evocation of evil.

Wheeler caught her breath before pulling off the mask. 'Jeez.' She couldn't take it in. She tried to process it.

'Bloody hell,' said Ross. 'Why?'

'Why the fuck not?' spat Paula O'Donnell. 'You don't think I should be here? Really? You don't know what shit I had to put up with for years.' She glanced across at Nick. 'What we've both had to put up with, but you lot never intervened, so we just had to do it for ourselves. Do you have any answers?' Paula glared at Wheeler. 'Do you have any idea what my life has been like? A living hell.

An absolute fucking living hell with that grotesque monster of a fucking father. And his shitty cohort, Sarah.'

'If you killed him, you'll go to prison for it,' said Wheeler. 'And for this.' She gestured towards the bedroom door.

'Prison will be a walk in the park compared with the shit I've had to put up with,' said Paula. 'They kept me a juvenile, an adolescent.'

Nick smiled at Ross. 'You hear her? Isn't she an absolute doll? My bitch of a mother tried to break her, it only made her stronger.'

Wheeler went through to the bedroom. Sarah Price was obviously heavily sedated. The blood around her mouth was crusted. Wheeler stood in front of her. 'Sarah Price? Sarah, can you hear me?'

Sarah blinked.

'Geez,' said Wheeler. She saw lights through the blinds.

Outside, the backup had arrived, lights flashing into the black wilderness.

The uniformed officer took the handcuffed Paula; her partner took Nick. Wheeler watched silently as the drugged woman was quickly assessed before being lifted onto a stretcher and carried to the ambulance. Out of respect, or perhaps habit, she followed the stretcher outside. Nick Price was getting into one police car. Paula O'Donnell into another. He glanced across to the stretcher. Looked back at Paula and smiled. Wheeler saw the look that had passed between them. If she'd had to describe it, it would be glee. Unbridled glee. She watched him make a sign. LT. Saw Paula mirror him. LT.

'Little shits,' Wheeler repeated.

'See, this is why we probably shouldn't have kids,' said Ross.

'We shouldn't have kids?' Wheeler nearly choked. 'We shouldn't have fucking kids?'

'I mean,' Ross retracted hastily, 'we both shouldn't bother, too much trouble. I don't mean together. You can never tell how they might turn out.'

She stared at him. She thought that maybe, just maybe, Ross was losing his mind. If, during the chaos and violence, Ross was thinking about them having children, then he'd definitely lost the plot.

Chapter 64

Vladimir Nazarewich stood in the shadows, ahead of him the orange sodium lights leached over the road. He had been taking his usual night-time stroll. Regardless of the time of night, he'd never been stopped on any of his walks, never had anyone try to intimidate him. Probably because of his height and bulk. He had inherited both from his father. Nothing more or less, he thought, only the unique DNA mix that is bestowed on us all. His mother had taught him chess. How to outwit an opponent. How to take them down. Quietly, successfully. He'd noticed the girl, with her familiar long dark hair and heavy green boots. He'd watched her run, saw her trip on something and stumble before righting herself and carrying on. From his place in the shadows he saw her wipe her eyes. Tears. Upset. He waited until she had moved off before quickly, quietly following her. He trailed her to the old church, saw her scramble over the locked gate and on through the grave-yard, then skirt around the back of the building. He crossed the frozen ground easily. Made his way through the graves, followed her to the back of the church. Here in the shadows it was darker, only a pale moon offered just enough light that he could watch her slim body climb, saw her slipping on the rusty fire escape. Heard her mutter in exasperation. Saw her head towards the roof. He followed her. Saw her creep towards the edge. Heard the wind howl and cry around him as he quietly followed her. Quickly, he lunged at her, heard her scream, but the sound of it was caught on the wind and immediately extinguished.

Ruby De Luca woke from a nightmare, her heart pounding. She'd been dreaming about Tala, that something horrible had happened to her. Ruby reached for her triskelion. Made a silent plea to her dead husband. Please Enzo, please not Tala. Ruby kissed the three circles, life, death, rebirth. Ruby heard the noise, took a second to register it. The phone ringing. Who was calling her at this time of the night? She hoped it wasn't that nice policewoman DI Wheeler to tell her something awful had happened to Tala. She steadied herself before she answered the phone.

'Mrs De Luca?'

She recognised the warm voice. 'Vlad?'

'I have your granddaughter.' He paused. 'She's not in a good state.'

'I imagine that she might not be,' said Ruby. 'Please bring her home to me. Can you?'

'Of course.'

Ruby sat on her sofa and poured herself a sherry. She thought of her granddaughter, Tala, and her pain. Of her son, Marc, and his denial. Felt herself get so angry that she did not know where to place it. Instead, she poured herself another drink. Cursed her son. Longed for her husband. Finally, Ruby heard the bell. Opened the door. Vlad brought her granddaughter in. She saw that Tala was in shock.

'What's wrong, darling? You can tell your old gran.'

'I can't tell you. It's too big.'

Ruby glanced at Vlad. Saw the distress in his face. Took stock. Knew that it was bigger than a little misadventure. 'Right, angel. I know the very fucking person you can tell.'

'Gran, you swore!' said Tala.

'Abso-fucking-lutely, darling.' Ruby took the card from the drawer. 'Her name is Wheeler. I'm going to call her. She'll sort it.'

Vlad turned to leave.

Ruby patted his arm. 'Thank you, Vlad. I can't tell you how much I appreciate this. You'll come in for a sherry next time? We'll talk?'

He nodded.

The phone was answered on the second ring. 'I want to speak to DI Wheeler. It's Ruby De Luca. Tala's gran. I need her to come and talk to my granddaughter.'

'I'm afraid DI Wheeler is busy.'

'I insist,' said Ruby.

'I'm sorry but DI Wheeler isn't available at present.'

'Then make her available.' Ruby settled herself down for the conflict; she knew how to win a fight. Thirty-five minutes later Ruby heard what she wanted to hear.

'DI Wheeler, how can I help you?'

An hour later Wheeler and Ross sat in Ruby De Luca's living room.

'Go on, Tala,' said Wheeler gently. 'You can tell me anything.'

Wheeler listened to the litany of abuse, the online bullying, the list of challenges. Tala refused to say what the last challenge would be.

'Finally leading to death?' said Wheeler quietly.

Tala nodded.

'Can you find these evil people?' asked Ruby.

'I know who is in charge, who the Moderator is,' said Wheeler.

Tala began to cry.

'Don't worry. I know who he is,' said Wheeler. 'And I know that because we have just taken him into custody.'

Tala sobbed loudly. 'But there are others involved. I just feel so angry with myself. They are in danger. Some have already gone.'

'No one else is involved,' said Wheeler. 'The Moderator invented all of the other participants. There was no group. No one has died.'

They talked for another twenty minutes. Tala agreed to go into the station the following day. In the meantime, she opened her laptop and logged into the dEADdOG site. Wheeler saw the destruction, recognised all the postings from Nick Price's laptop.

She took the laptop.

Outside, she turned to Ross. 'Your thoughts?'

'Bastards doing this. Forcing Tala to wake up at silly hours, self-harm and watching scary videos to disorientate herself,' said Ross. 'The guy who ran this kind of shit is seriously messed up. What did he get from wanting her to hurt or kill herself?'

'A godlike power,' said Wheeler. 'That's what it is. Godlike.'

'Except he's the devil,' said Ross. 'Satan incarnate. Both him and Paula.'

379

'You OK?' said Wheeler. 'Only you look shattered?'

'Probably just need an early night.'

'Instead it's back to paperwork at the station,' said Wheeler, leading the way. She paused. 'Why don't you go on home and have some downtime. Maybe a takeaway pizza and wine?'

He paused. 'Well, the dog hasn't been walked in a couple of hours. My neighbour usually does her but she's out with a friend tonight. I'd really appreciate it.'

'Go,' said Wheeler.

He paused.

Wheeler did not make a habit of it but she moved towards him. Hugged him. He hugged her back. They held each other for a couple of seconds before she drew back. 'Now, shift, go home.'

He stood back.

'Stay safe, muppet,' she whispered.

He smiled. 'You too. Don't get mugged again.'

She slapped his arm.

'Ouch, that hurt.'

'Glad to hear it. Now, shift. Go home.'

Chapter 65

Aubree flicked back her long red hair and walked into the close. She made her way to Ross's flat door and took out the keys. Inside, she took a moment to pet the three-legged dog who had come to her, tail wagging. 'You're a good girl, aren't you?' She bent to pat the dog. 'And Ross told me that you mean the world to him. I took his keys when he stayed over. Now we can meet up properly.'

The dog ran to her bed, retrieved a toy, brought it back. Put it at Aubree's feet.

'Unfortunately, he doesn't feel the same way about me, little doggy. So, in a way, you and I are in competition with each other.' She tugged hard at the dog's ear, heard her whine in pain.

'Aren't we, you little bitch?'

The dog had her tail between her legs.

'Now, you and me, we're going on a little walk.' Aubree reached for a tartan lead which was hanging up behind the door. 'It's a bridge, the Overtoun Bridge, near Dumbarton. Doggies love this bridge. They launch themselves over it often. To their deaths. I'm sure you will love it too.' She attached the lead to the dog's collar. 'Let's get on then. We have a date with destiny, don't we, you little shit?'

The three-legged dog walked obediently beside her, her tail still between her legs. They made their way outside.

Ross drove towards his flat just in time to see Aubree appear to take the dog for a walk. His dog. His mind scrambled. Just how did she get access to his flat? Did his neighbour Mary give her the keys? But he knew that Mary was out with a friend, which is why he'd left the station early. And if Mary had let her in, why didn't Mary tell him? He stopped the car. 'Aubree! Wait up.'

She heard him, he knew she did, but she bundled the dog into her car and took off.

'Fucksake!' muttered Ross as he started the engine. 'What the hell does she think she's doing?' He followed her through a red light, on through the snow-covered streets. She was stuck behind a lorry at a red light when he caught up with her. He jumped out, tried to open her door. Locked. He ran to the lorry in front, showed his ID. 'Stop here. Stay here. Don't even try to bloody move.'

Five minutes later and she had nowhere to go. He had hemmed her in from behind, the lorry in front. 'Nowhere to go, Aubree,' he shouted through the door. 'And if you try to move, I'll have uniform onto you in a fucking heartbeat.'

She opened the door, threw the dog out.

'What the hell were you doing?' asked Ross.

'I was just taking her to Overtoun Bridge, near Dumbarton. You know it? I thought she could launch herself off into the next world. Or at least out of ours. Maybe you'd have time for me then, Ross?'

'Fucksake, Aubree.' Ross held on to the dog's collar.

Aubree pressed central locking. Stared ahead. Once Ross had given him the all clear, the lorry moved off. Aubree drove on.

'Fucking psycho nutjob,' muttered Ross, scrambling the dog into his car. 'Lunatic.' He felt the dog's front leg, she had landed badly. 'The emergency vet for you, girl,' he said. He grabbed his mobile. Spoke to the vet. 'Yes, she was thrown from a car. She hurt her leg. Yes, I'll be there in twenty minutes.'

An hour later and the vet had stitched the dog's leg. Ross took the antibiotics from him and paid.

Chapter 66

Hawk sat on his sofa, Wheeler was in the chair opposite. Between them a bottle of Merlot, some finger food and some tiny nibbles.

'Can you make the preview evening of my exhibition?'

'Yes, I probably can. The case is being prepared to be passed to the Procurator Fiscal.'

Hawk reached for a couple of macadamia nuts. 'You know that I'm attracted to you, Kat.'

She waited.

'But I'm not in love with you. At least not yet. Too soon but . . . '

Wheeler took a sip of wine. Thought about what he had said, took another sip. Realised that it was more of a gulp. She put her glass down and studied the finger food. Slices of Brie and fig, tiny pastry cases of melted cheese and Jalapeños, rounds of mini guacamole bruschetta.

'What I am aware of, though, is that you already have someone who is quite clearly in love with you.' He refilled their glasses.

Wheeler nearly choked. She coughed discreetly and

sipped more wine. The alcohol was going to her head and she let it go there. She reached for a bruschetta. But surely not this again? What was it MacCullagh had said about Ross? What was it with these guys?

'You don't know?'

'It's news to me. I think maybe your information isn't quite on the ball. Gossip can be a terrible thing. What have you heard? God, if it's from Boyd at the station, don't listen to a thing he says. He's definitely nutty. Love him but he's crazy.'

'I haven't had the pleasure of discussing you with Boyd.'

'Well, that's probably a good thing. He's great but he's a bit rough round the edges.'

'But Boyd isn't in love with you.'

'No,' she snorted, 'he's not. Thankfully. He's in love with his fiancée.'

'So, who does that leave?'

Wheeler sighed. 'Fine, Sherlock. You tell me.'

'Ross.'

'What has he been saying? Honestly.'

'He said nothing, but I see the way he looks at you.'

'Rubbish.'

'Not so dismissive, Kat. The man is in love with you. I really don't mind if you want to reject him but please be aware that it is so. If we are to go ahead with any kind of a relationship, and I am interested in one, then it's with a clean slate.'

'Ross in love with me? You are clearly mistaken.'

'I see the way he looks at you.'

'You don't know him. He looks at a macaroni pie and chips with adoration. And pizza as if it's some kind of food for the gods. Really, we're just friends. Good friends. I love him. He's devoted to his wee dog.'

'But *he's in love* with you. Are you certain you're not in love with him as opposed to loving him as a friend?'

Wheeler sipped her wine, averted her gaze. This wasn't the kind of evening she'd envisaged; it was becoming too deep too soon. She reached for a slice of cheese. Finally, she spoke. 'What do you make of Ross?'

'You're avoiding the question.'

'I don't know,' she sighed. 'You and I have only known each other for five minutes and now all this deep probing into feelings.'

'I just wanted to clear up a nagging suspicion. If we were to get to know one another better, and I hope that we do, I just wanted to clear the air if there was potentially a third person involved.'

'What do you want me to tell you?'

'The truth.' He sipped his wine, watched her over his glass. 'Ideally, I'd like to hear that you are aware that Ross has feelings for you but that they are not reciprocated. If that were the case, I would pursue you until you agreed to go out to dinner with me. I know of the most fabulous pop-up Lebanese restaurant, part of an exclusive supper club. It's only going to be there for one night, but it will be magical, all fairy lights and beautiful food. A wonderful experience. I'd love you to be there with me.'

Wheeler finished her wine. 'And Ross?'

'I think the man is an imbecile. He larks about at the station. Turns up for work hungover. Eats shit, all that fried egg roll nonsense. And the revolting and cheap takeaway pizza. I think he's a waste of space, to be honest.'

'Do you?' said Wheeler. 'He's a good friend of mine.'

'Yes, I know that. Of course, I do. But if we become close, and I envisage we will, he will have to go his own way. No popping round for late-night drinks with you. Or bringing you his dreadful, soggy, takeaway pizza. Of course, I understand that as colleagues he has to be at the station, but that would be the majority of the contact you would have with him.'

'You envisage all of this?' spluttered Wheeler.

'What I offer is a more sophisticated lifestyle, one in which you would be very comfortable. I shall paint you and we can go to exhibitions together. I assume Ross has never accompanied you to one previously?'

'No, he hasn't. Not that it's ever been a problem. I don't need anyone to hold my hand. I'm a grown-up.'

'So, you see, you are better to have him merely as a colleague and perhaps he may move off to another station. Or resign altogether. I fear that his heart is not really in the job.' Hawk paused. 'I would still love to paint you, if you have the time?'

Wheeler stood. 'I'll think about it but I doubt it's going to happen.'

'Do you need to go right now?'

'Work to catch up on.'

'Really, at this hour?'

'I'm a cop.' She made for the door. 'And I don't appreciate you trying to tell me who to see. And when.'

'I only meant—'

'You've said more than enough. I'd shut up now if I were you.'

In her own flat she pulled out a CD, selected the track. Hearing Horace Silver's 'Peace' soothed her. She went through to the kitchen and poured herself another glass of wine. Took it back through to the living room, switched off the light and sat in the dark. The window blind hadn't been drawn down and outside she watched the street lights shine and the snow fall quietly. A couple passed, arm in arm under an umbrella. Ross. Steven Ross. Of course, she knew that there was an attraction. Of course, she had enjoyed the banter with him. But what Hawk had alluded to, no, what he had said outright was that he thought that Ross was in love with her. He could be wrong, and she could dismiss it, but something about the way he said it, the confidence, made her take notice. He was serious. And if he was right, what then? What were the implications for them working together in the team? She knew that she was avoiding the real question which Hawk had asked her. How did she feel about Ross? Was she in love with him? MacCullagh had asked as much.

How did she feel about Hawk? He had certainly gotten under her skin. She liked him. If she were being honest, she was very attracted to him. Not just physically but intellectually. He was a brilliant artist and a fantastic cook; he had an engaging way of looking at the world which made her fell less cynical, less jaded. She had wondered if they'd make a good couple. But now, she knew that it wasn't a possibility. All that telling her what to do, who to see, and how often and under what circumstances she would see Ross. Fucking ridiculous. What century was the man living in? But Ross. Steven Ross. She sighed, drained her glass and went back to the fridge for a refill. Heard a couple of texts come through.

Seb. *It was lovely to see you tonight. Sweet dreams. Sxx*

Ross. *You around? I'm outside with a takeaway pizza and garlic bread. Could bring them up? Have wine too. What says you? Plus, I've got the dog with me. She's had a trauma, needs company.*

Wheeler padded through to the hall, buzzed him in.

'This better be quick, I'm shattered.'

'How long does it take you to eat pizza and a bit of garlic bread?' he said, walking into the flat. The dog trotted beside him.

'Twice as long as it takes you to just inhale it,' she laughed as she poured him some wine. Sat opposite him. Helped herself to a slice of pizza. 'You got extra cheese.'

'Yeah, mozzarella.'

'Bloody good call. What's with the dog visit?'

He told her. And about Aubree's destination. The Overtoun Bridge.

'Fuck sake. Psycho bitch!' said Wheeler.

'I know. Aubree's crazy. She threw my dog out of the car. The emergency vet was £579, but the dog's worth it. Aubree's a fucking nutjob.'

'An excellent escape,' said Wheeler. 'Intending to kill a little dog. What a shit. And the dog. Poor wee love.' She reached over and patted the dog. 'Here, love, have a bit of cheese.' The dog swallowed the treat.

'You OK?' Ross asked.

'Yes,' she said, munching the pizza. 'I'm fine. By the way.'

He waited.

'This pizza is bloody good. Thanks for bringing it over.'

'Anytime,' said Ross.

'I'll call you on that.'

'Please do.'

'I was thinking of Hawk,' said Wheeler.

'Yeah?'

'I'm getting to know him properly.'

'Right,' said Ross.

She heard the tension in his voice. 'And he's quite controlling.'

Ross just about choked on his pizza. 'Bloody hell, good luck with him being controlling around you!'

'Yeah, wish him luck.'

'He's got no fucking chance,' laughed Ross.

'Yep,' said Wheeler.

'So what about Paula and Nick?'

'They'll spend a long time in prison. They're both only eighteen, they might learn.'

When Ross had gone, an hour and a half had passed, Wheeler still sat alone with her thoughts and the music of Silver, Monk, Rollins and Brubeck, until it was gone four. At which point she went to bed.

Chapter 67

Saturday 19 December, 5 p.m.

Wheeler and Ross sat across from Dr Emelda Owen.

'Dr Buckley wanted to publish his theory on what has previously been known as Munchausen Syndrome by Proxy. It was going to be a controversial piece in which he would dissect what he had observed in action,' said Dr Owen. 'He sat in on some of Paula's sessions, just as an observer, and spoke with Michael O'Donnell privately. He recognised the signs, quizzed him and Michael became hostile.'

'But why did Michael kill him, surely, he could have just let it go?' said Wheeler.

'Dr Buckley was extremely tenacious, he played the long game. About his cycling – an award – for long-term grit. He wouldn't have forgotten or ever given up. Anything he believed to be worthwhile, part of his life's work had to be acted upon and a conclusion drawn. He recognised the dynamic that was being played out between Michael and Paula,' said Dr Owen. 'He would have brought it to light and confronted it. He wanted justice to be done for the daughter. Unfortunately, too much damage had been done.'

'And he would have known that Paula would finally turn on her father?' asked Wheeler.

'It's well documented when the children get older. When they reach young adulthood and find the strength to be angry and to access that anger, they use it.' Dr Owen paused. 'Hate and anger and resentment are a pretty volatile cocktail.'

Wheeler thought of the paintings she had seen at the CoVA. Paula O'Donnell's art had been called robust but was full of anger. The welts of red. She recalled the angry ridges made in the wooden doors by her wheelchair. What must it have been like to have been kept suspended in childhood as she was becoming a young woman? 'Michael always referred to Paula as a child,' said Wheeler. 'Someone who was unable to date.'

'Yes, that's typical. And yet Paula was eighteen. Old enough to be married, to join the armed forces. To have a child of her own,' said Dr Owen. 'Paula was no longer a child.'

Wheeler thought of the young woman she'd wrestled to the ground, who had been quite slight, but it was the rage which had propelled her. Wheeler would never forget the guttural growl that had emanated from Paula as she had hurled herself, like a slight battering ram, into Wheeler.

'Years of rage had made her strong,' said Dr Owen. 'Years of being told she was psychologically young and naive. Too young to have a boyfriend. Too young to think of sex.'

'But not psychologically strong enough to walk away?' said Wheeler.

'That would have taken considerable psychological intervention and support. She will need years of psychotherapy to truly recover,' said Dr Owen. 'No, the primal response, the reptilian brain would have told her to kill the beast. And so, she had him killed so that she could live. And her anger she transferred to Nick's mother, Sarah, for having colluded with Michael for so long.'

'And Nick Price?'

'Nick had shown early indications of Attachment Disorder, but his mother, like so many parents, ignored the signs. They believe their child to be merely boisterous, or temporarily angry. The lack of remorse, they put down to immaturity. All the signs were there that there could be a disorder, but unfortunately, Sarah Price, like many parents, wilfully overlooked them and explained them away.'

'Then two misfits, Paula and Nick, reached out to each other on social media,' said Wheeler.

'What a nightmare,' said Ross.

'And the online dating site Nick created for Sarah was all false. It wouldn't have mattered which guy Sarah had chosen, they were all made up. Nick took various photographs off the internet and created a site. Logged on as various people. Sarah thought it was an actual site. All bogus. Didn't matter if she chose Rob or Charlie or whoever, there was no one else on the site. And Nick had access to all his mother's online data, plus her favourite foods, books, etc. He made a couple of profiles suit her specifically. Fascinating from a psychological perspective but awful from a human perspective.'

After another half-hour of talk, Wheeler ended the interview. She thanked Dr Owen for her insight.

An hour later, over a drink with Ross, Wheeler sighed, 'Paula was the victim, wasn't she?'

'Makes me never want to have kids,' said Ross again. 'Bloody minefield.'

'Well, Michael O'Donnell was abusive to Paula for all those years. And Nick's mother too, remember. Sarah colluded with Michael in keeping Paula in a childlike state. Paula tried to talk to her, to ask Sarah for help, but Sarah always sided with Michael. We found the online Lovers' Tryst. Paula called Sarah a colluding bitch.'

'How much do you reckon that Sarah actually knew? Maybe she just thought that Michael was a doting father?' Ross sipped his wine.

'No, I'm certain that she saw it all but chose not to intervene,' said Wheeler. 'She fancied Michael O'Donnell for herself and didn't really care what the cost was. Even if Paula was suffering.' She heard a text come through. Hawk. *Are you free for dinner tonight? I'm cooking right now. And we could talk about my book.*

She ignored it.

'Meanwhile Michael became paranoid that he was losing control of Paula. He lost it when he went to confront Dr Buckley. I think, since we know Dr Buckley was tenacious, that he wouldn't back down. Plus, he was going to publish his research, so it would go public.'

'Jayla's sister, Rivera, wants us to prosecute Michael, post death, for his wife's murder. Do you reckon he did it?' asked Ross. 'I mean, did he shoot her and then stage her suicide?'

Wheeler sat back in her chair. 'If I'm being honest, then yes, I do think that Michael O'Donnell killed Jayla. Can we prove it? That I'm not sure of.'

'It won't get priority,' said Ross. 'Or will it?'

'I don't know,' said Wheeler. 'What with the station

closing and our cases being shipped out to the other stations, it may get lost in the paperwork.'

'A shame,' said Ross.

'Carmyle Police Station closing, or the Jayla O'Donnell murder getting lost?' asked Wheeler.

'Both,' admitted Ross.

Wheeler studied the profiles. 'Nick Price created all these fake profiles. He and Paula wanted to lure Tala De Luca to her death just to appease Paula's ego. Nick had slept with Paula once on her birthday, at the cottage, and Paula had so much rage. She demanded revenge.'

'Christ, what a nightmare.'

'All through jealousy. Tala and Nick had spent just one night together. Tala didn't realise that Nick and Paula had been dating. Paula exacted her revenge.' She'd read over the profiles and the techs had confirmed the messages had all been sent from one account. Nick's.

MATTIO ROSSI: *Finché non è il mio turno* (until it's my turn).

FANTINE ALLARD: *Pour toujours* (for ever).

ANA SOFIA: *Nos vemos en el otro lado* (see you on the other side).

INES: *Eu vejo o quão bem você fez. Minha próxima vez* (I see how well you did. My turn next).

ALEXEI: Друг мой, я приветствую вас за вашу храбрость (My friend, I salute you for your bravery) Алексей

She sighed. 'How disturbed are these two young people? I mean, in one way, Nick Price and Paula O'Donnell were made for each other. Both nuts.'

'Crazy.'

'Craig Brennan has come forward, now that the dEADdOG shit is public,' said Wheeler. 'He knew that Nick thought that he was flirting with Paula. He wasn't. He was just trying to be nice. Nick wasn't so impressed. He thought he had to warn Craig off. But Paula helped him with the beating. Remember what Craig said, there was a girl's voice too?'

'Bastards.'

'Now Craig's in a relationship with Joanne Reilly, she lives in Cornwall. He goes down every weekend. They didn't go public because her father is a bit of a psychopath.'

'But are Craig and Joanne happy?' asked Ross.

'Yes, apparently so. That's the good news,' said Wheeler.

'Is there bad news?' asked Ross.

'It's a result. The DNA that was found on the missing beauty therapist's scarf?'

'Zoe Wishart? Disappeared over by Ian Price's house?' said Ross.

'The DNA is a full match for Nick Price. He was a killer even before this. He's confessed to where he buried her. Up by Balmaha. A team are out there now.'

'Jeez. Kids today.'

'I still think about the rest of the Missing Persons,' said Wheeler. 'I can't help but wonder about where they are.'

'It's upsetting, I know. But on the upside, you nailed two killers, Nick Price and Paula O'Donnell. Plus, we know that Michael O'Donnell killed Dr Buckley. You must be happy about that? Surely?'

'Of course,' said Wheeler. 'But it's not the whole story.'

'How did Nick Price get Dr Buckley's dog?' asked Ross.

'Paula knew that her father was going to see Dr Buckley.

Knew that Michael hated him. Next day she found a bag of bloody clothes at home. She called Nick to check it out. Nick found Dr Buckley's body, ignored it, instead took the dog.'

'Plus, Nick squealed on his father's gun stash up at Balmaha. So that's a result,' said Ross. 'You were right. Ian Price was a keeper of guns.'

'Gut instinct, plus the money he was spending didn't add up to the money he was earning. And his background was pretty specific.'

'You did well, Wheeler.'

'This whole case makes me long for my earlier days at the station. When things seemed less complicated.'

'Are you looking back with nostalgia, Wheeler?'

'I know, what the hell's wrong with me?'

'How long do you have?' Ross smiled.

She slapped his arm.

'So, what was with the LT salute that Nick and Paula shared when they were being put in the cars?'

'Lovers' Tryst. Their online communication. It was all about them. They had been dating ever since Paula sent Nick some erotic selfies online. But then he went and slept with Tala on her birthday up at Balmaha. And Paula was bloody furious. She wanted to exact revenge on Tala.'

'Geez,' said Ross.

'Paula hated Sarah for colluding with Michael,' said Wheeler.

'And Nick had never bonded with his mother,' said Ross.

'Yes. He had little or no attachment to her. And one of the symptoms of Attachment Disorder is a struggle to develop a conscience.'

'So, it was easy for him to torture his mother, a figure he felt no emotional connection to?'

'Yes,' said Wheeler quietly.

'So, what about Tala De Luca? ' said Ross. 'Tell me that's better news?'

'The CoVA hasn't been as damaged as feared. It should be workable again in six months. The fire crew were here extremely quickly, plus the snow kept the blaze at a minimum.'

'And Tala?' repeated Ross.

'She was the victim in this. She won't get the prize. But with her gran, Ruby's, money, she will be able to go to art school. Hopefully she'll succeed. Her father, Marc, has flown in from Geneva. Apparently, he's "utterly distraught".'

'You don't think he is?'

'I don't think he's been bloody paying attention to his daughter and her needs.'

'And the prize, who does it go to?' asked Ross.

'Hudson Lennox.'

'Bloody hell,' spluttered Ross, 'the satanist?'

'The tutors reckon that was an affectation. The guy just wants to get noticed. Apparently, he's a bit of an introvert. Seems he's had a troubled background. They reckon this prize is just what he needs to set him on the right path.'

'On the upside,' said Ross. 'What are you up to later?' He tried for a smile.

She heard the tension in his voice. 'Nothing as yet. You?'

'I'm young, free and single,' replied Ross.

'Well, free and single.' Wheeler paused. 'You've got that much.'

'I'm hurt,' said Ross.

'You'll get over it,' said Wheeler. 'What about Aubree?'

'There never was an "us". Plus, she's a psycho nutjob and tried to kill my dog. She needs professional help. I think she will get it. But as far as dates go, I think that's a "no", what do you think?'

'Wise choice,' said Wheeler. 'I'd say you got off easy.'

'What about the delightful Sebastian Hawk?' said Ross.

'Not so bloody delightful as he appeared,' said Wheeler. 'As I said, a bit of a control freak.'

'Go on.'

'He tried to tell me who to see and when.'

Ross laughed, 'And how did that go for him?'

'What do you think?'

'Fucking badly,' said Ross.

'Yep.'

'Will you two still be friends?'

'Friends don't dictate who you can and can't see, so that's a big fat no. He called earlier. I told him he needed to look elsewhere for a model for his paintings.' She paused. 'The dog?'

'She's going to be OK. The vet says she's become quite robust.'

'I'm not surprised, the amount you feed her.'

'She's a good weight, I don't want her too skinny.'

'I think you've definitely achieved that.'

'She's fine. Thank goodness.'

'I'm glad.'

'Me too, she means a lot to me.'

'I know.'

'Dinner?' said Ross. 'The posh place?'

'That would be lovely but you probably needed to make a reservation,' said Wheeler.

'I already have.'

'Presumptuous,' laughed Wheeler.

'There's no one I'd rather have dinner with,' said Ross.

'Your treat,' said Wheeler.

'It always is,' said Ross, smiling.

'Well, you'd better get used to it,' said Wheeler.

'Fair dos,' said Ross, standing. 'You coming?'

'Wouldn't miss it for the world,' said Wheeler. 'Let's go.'

Acknowledgements

Thank you to all the readers and bloggers who have responded so positively to the Wheeler and Ross series. I very much appreciate you all.

Thank you to my agent Jane Conway-Gordon, and to Krystyna Green, Amanda Keats and all at Constable who have contributed to *Deceived*.

Thank you, too, to Sandra Ferguson for her copy-editing skills.

Anne Randall
RIVEN

First he kills
Then he waits.

First he kills.
A psychologist is found brutally murdered, an addict jumps to his death and a student is found dead. These are the facts. And they are all that DIs Wheeler and Ross have.

He waits.
As Wheeler and Ross weave through the layers of Glasgow's underbelly they find a subculture where truth and lies are interchangeable commodities and violence is the favoured currency.

He watches.
The killer stays one step ahead of them as Wheeler uncovers a web of deceit in which her own nephew is entangled.

He leaves his legacy...
And as the case draws to a close, Wheeler has to confront her own integrity and face the dilemma: is justice always served by the truth?

Anne Randall

SILENCED

DYING is the easy part

He buried his victim alive. And now he's escaped from prison and is on the run in the city.

Fiona Henderson, the daughter of the victim who'd descended into a world of silence following her mother's murder, has gone missing. Her sister Annabelle scours the city in a desperate attempt to find her. And then the body of a homeless person if found among the rubbish in a deserted alleyway.

As DIs Wheeler and Ross investigate, more suspicious deaths occur and a pattern emerges: the victims are all homeless. And so the police are pitched against a killer who is hellbent on a mission to rid the streets of the vulnerable and dispossessed.

As Wheeler and Ross descend further into Glasgow's netherworld, their investigation reveals not only a flawed support system for the disaffected, but also a criminal class ruthlessly willing to exploit them. A city of double standards, where morality is bought and sold.

But it's when the killer begins stalking DI Wheeler, that she and Ross realise that the threat is now personal.

'Brilliant'
Sun

Anne
Randall

TORN

When obsession
ends in murder

A fast-paced, gripping thriller with a shocking twist.

2004

The court case had been harrowing. The fifteen jurors sat in silence while the prosecution produced evidence of how a man with obsessive sado-masochistic fantasies had turned into a killer. Fourteen of the jurors were repulsed. One man was secretly enthralled. A new world of possibility had opened up for him.

2014

When an actress is found dead, the ligature marks suggest that she had been involved in extreme sex games. When DIs Wheeler and Ross begin to investigate her death, they uncover not only an industry with varying degrees of regulation but also a sinister private club where some of Glasgow's elite pay handsomely to indulge their darkest fantasies. Club security is run by Paul Furlan, ex-army veteran and a former adversary of Wheeler. As Wheeler and Ross uncover the secrets and lies surrounding the club, they realise that their investigation is being blocked not just by Furlan but by some of Glasgow's most influential citizens.

Meanwhile Skye Cooper, Scotland's latest indie-rock sensation is playing the final gig of his sell-out tour but his dreams of stardom are on a collision course with the obsession threatening to consume him . . .